Raptor

BOOK SIX

Lindsay Buroker

Raptor

by Lindsay Buroker

Copyright @ Lindsay Buroker 2015

Cover and Formatting: Deranged Doctor Design

No part of this book may be reproduced, scanned, or distributed in any printed or electronic form without permission. Please do not participate in or encourage piracy of copyrighted materials in violation of the author's rights. Thank you for respecting the hard work of this author.

This is a work of fiction. Names, characters, places, and incidents either are the product of the author's imagination or are used fictitiously, and any resemblance to locales, events, business establishments, or actual persons—living or dead—is entirely coincidental.

Foreword

Greetings, good reader, and welcome back for another adventure with Tolemek, Cas, Ridge, Sardelle, and their comrades. If you read The Blade's Memory (Book 5) without picking up Under the Ice Blades (a novella set between Books 5 and 6), I highly recommend taking a peep at that story before jumping into this one. In addition to showing the world through Captain Kaika's eyes, it introduces a new bad guy, one that plays a big role in this story. It's also a fun adventure!

Raptor is the longest Dragon Blood novel yet, and I hope it will keep you entertained. As always, I would like to thank my beta readers, Cindy Wilkinson and Sarah Engelke, my editor, Shelley Holloway, and the cover designers at Deranged Doctor Design for sticking with me for this series. Now, I'll let you jump into the story!

Prologue

"HOPE WE GET HER DELIVERED before the rain starts." Jort clucked at the horse team, encouraging greater alacrity on the muddy street.

"That's why she's under a tarp." Jort's comrade, Ox, yawned and scratched himself, the wooden bench shivering as the big man adjusted his weight. "A few raindrops won't hurt her."

"I was thinking of us." Jort eyed the late spring clouds scowling down from the heavens. "Figured we'd be delivering this to base housing, not some dead-end out in the middle of nowhere."

"We're less than twenty minutes from the city walls."

"It *feels* like the middle of nowhere." Jort waved at the towering firs and hemlocks closing in on either side of the puddle-strewn road, the branches leaving only a strip of cloudy sky visible overhead. "Besides, twenty minutes is a powerful long time if you're getting poured on." He spotted an algae-covered pond up ahead, marking the end of the road. They had only passed three houses since the turnoff, and he had checked the addresses on all of them. No sign of 374 yet. "You wouldn't expect a general to live out so far."

"Bet his witch picked the place."

"Don't say things like that." To ward off evil magic, Jort circled his heart with two fingers, his movements so hasty that he dropped the reins. "There's no such thing as witches. Not *real* ones." He circled his heart again before picking up the reins, just in case. A man couldn't be too safe.

"If you believe that, you can knock on the door and be the one to talk to her."

"You don't think she'll be *there*, do you?" Jort licked lips that suddenly seemed drier than the white-sand deserts. He didn't believe in magic, but he'd heard plenty of stories about General

Zirkander's lady friend, stories that would make any man twitchy. She supposedly had all sorts of potions and kept the famous pilot under her spells. And she had a sword that could melt a man's balls off. No wonder the general had bought her such an expensive piece of furniture.

"Better be there," Ox said, not sounding concerned. "Someone's got to sign for the couch."

Jort's heart rate was up about five hundred percent by the time the horse team stopped in front of the last house on the road, a cozy two-story cottage with a tidy, green lawn out front and picnic tables and a horseshoe pit in the back. It looked innocent enough, but the tall trees along the borders hid it from its neighbors, and nothing but an overgrown blackberry patch occupied the lot across the street.

"It looks… private." Jort eyed the windows, wondering which room the witch used to brew her potions. A curtain upstairs stirred, and he froze. He couldn't see anyone, but he felt certain someone was watching them.

"Yup." Ox hopped out of the wagon and strode around back to untie the canvas tarp.

A raindrop spattered Jort's nose, and he tore his gaze from the cottage. He needed to help his partner so they could deliver the couch and escape back to the safety of the city.

"They probably like it private so they can get wild without anyone hearing," Ox added, dropping the gate on the back of the wagon. "Maybe on this very couch."

"Gross."

"Pilots got needs, same as anyone else. Now, go knock and ask the witch where she wants it."

"Don't *call* her that." Jort glanced at the curtain that had shivered. "Not when she might hear."

Ox gave him a dramatic sigh. Jort wiped his hands on his trousers and walked up the flagstone path to the door. He took a bracing breath and lifted his hand to knock.

The door opened before he touched it, and he jumped back. He almost found himself reaching for his hip, where he had carried a sword during his infantry days, but the barefoot, brown-haired girl standing there in a paint-stained sundress was not an imposing figure. She certainly didn't look old enough to be the witch Jort had expected. She didn't even seem old enough to be the girlfriend of anyone without pimples and a squeaky voice.

"It's here," she blurted and clapped her hands. "Sardelle will be *so* happy."

Sardelle. Yes, that was the name on the clipboard.

"I think she was secretly pleased that Ridge's last couch was blown up along with his house," the girl went on. "Did you ever see it? I never did, but I heard about it." She shuddered.

"Uhm, no, miss." As if the legendary General Zirkander would invite Jort to his house for dice and cocktails.

"That's it, isn't it?" The girl pointed to the wagon, where Ox had removed the tarp and levered the couch partway out. "It's so sleek. Is that suede?"

"Yes, miss. Where do we put it?" Jort allowed himself to relax slightly. Maybe the witch wasn't here, and this girl could sign for the couch. He and Ox could be back in the city before the rain grew serious.

"In the front room, here."

"Good, we'll bring it right in as soon as you sign this." Jort held out a clipboard.

The girl gave him a blank look. She pulled a wet paintbrush out of her pocket and raised her eyebrows.

Before Jort could explain that a pen would be better, a man walked into view and stopped behind her. He had silver hair that fell to his shoulders, a strange color for someone who appeared no older than twenty. His eyes were an eerie yellowish brown, reminiscent of a wolf, and he had a presence that made Jort want to take a step back. *Several* steps back. Fortunately, the intense gaze did not land on him. The man stepped past the girl and looked toward the sky. He rested a hand on the girl's shoulder, and they stared at each other. They didn't talk. They just stared, as if some kind of communication was happening that didn't require words.

"We'll, ah, get that couch now," Jort said, stumbling as he

backed away. He turned and strode toward his partner. Maybe there were *multiple* witches staying here. A coven. Wasn't that what a bevy of witches was called?

"You get the signature?" Ox asked.

"Not yet. Let's just hurry and get it in there. This place is creepy." Jort glanced back toward the house. The young man was standing in the yard now and waving for the girl to go back inside, while his gaze remained locked on the cloudy sky.

"Boss will throw our balls in an apple press if we don't get it signed for." Despite his protest, Ox shrugged and pulled the couch out further. Jort jumped into the bed to push from inside. He and Ox had never gotten such a heavy piece of furniture off the wagon so quickly. Ox did not appear worried—he had not seen the man's eerie eyes—but with his brawny arms, he had no trouble carrying his half of the couch and matching Jort's pace.

They were halfway up the walk when the girl shouted. "Look out!"

"Get in the house," the man ordered, raising a hand toward her. The girl staggered backward, and the door seemed to shut of its own accord.

Jort was so busy finding that unnerving that he was completely surprised when Ox dropped his end of the couch.

"What are you doing?" Jort blurted. "If it's damaged—"

"Run," the young man ordered. His voice was calm, but it cut through Jort's words like a sword through butter.

A huge gust of wind struck Jort in the back, and the horses screeched. Jort tumbled over the couch, and then was hurled through the air in the direction of the wagon—or where the wagon had been. It and the horses were taking off up the road.

As Jort scrambled to his feet, a hand gripped him from behind. He yelled in surprise. It might have been a shriek. What in all the hells was going on?

"Get down, you idiot." Ox pulled him through a mud puddle, water spattering in all directions.

An utterly alien cry thundered from the sky. Jort looked up and promptly wished he hadn't. He had only seen pictures of dragons in history books, but he recognized the massive flying creature for what it was. There was no doubt. The cry came again, the ear-splitting noise a cross between a roar and a scream as the golden-scaled creature descended, its wings pulled close to its huge muscular body as it plummeted toward the yard.

Jort and Ox backed across the road as quickly as they could. Jort expected the young man to get out of the way, too, but he stood, staring defiantly at the sky.

At first, it looked like the dragon would crash into the earth, but like an eagle diving for a fish, its wings unfurled from its body to slow it at the last moment. Those wings easily spanned forty feet, stretching from the house to the road. The dragon's giant fang-filled mouth opened, and a gout of fire streamed forth. Flame poured onto the grass, the couch, *and* the man standing in the yard.

Even from across the street, with the blackberry bushes clawing at the back of his shirt, Jort could feel the heat. He lifted his arm to protect his face, but he couldn't tear his gaze from the yard. Impossibly, the man wasn't burned from the fire, even though the grass had yellowed, then disintegrated, as flagstones cracked and smoke poured from the tormented earth.

The dragon's talons grasped at the air where his prey stood. At the last instant, the man rolled to the side, moving for the first time under the assault. Those talons bit into the ground where he had stood, tearing a gaping hole before the dragon's powerful wings flapped, taking it into the air again.

The draft batted at Jort, almost pushing him farther back into the brambles. The young man jumped to his feet. The door opened slightly, but he flung a hand, and it closed again. Then, as if Jort hadn't been shocked enough, the man leaped into the air. Before his feet came back down again, his clothes disappeared and his body transformed, silver scales replacing skin, and wings replacing arms. He also expanded in size, and while Jort stared, his mouth hanging down to the ground, the figure became a dragon.

Without hesitating, the former man flew over the house and into the trees behind it. Branches shivered as he passed, alternating between flapping his wings and tucking them in close to streak between the evergreens. Jort's first thought was that he meant to fly into the sky to confront the other dragon, but he stayed in the trees. The gold dragon didn't seem surprised at having its prey transform. It gave pursuit immediately, soaring above the treetops and breathing flame into the branches. The damp wood smoldered and did not catch fire, but it charred and fell limp under the fiery assault.

"Phelistoth," came the girl's voice from the house. She opened the door and ran outside.

Without glancing at Jort and Ox, she raced around the corner of the house and into the woods. She would never catch the dragons. Even with the impediment of the trees, they were too fast. Before long, they disappeared from view.

Jort's gaze lowered to the destroyed patch of yard where the young man had stood. And where the *couch* had stood. It had burned to the ground, only four charred stumps remaining where its legs had been. The cushions, the frame, the suede… gone. Completely gone.

"You should have got that signature," Ox said.

Chapter 1

CASLIN AHN STOOD UNDER THE portico in front of the double wooden doors, heedless of the rain as she stared at them. Should she knock? Or walk straight in?

She had grown up in this house, learned to hunt and shoot on the grass and tree-filled acres that stretched on all sides, and she had sat on the bed in the mini tower on the north side, gazing down the hill and toward the city, wondering what it would be like to go to school and have friends like a normal girl. Instead, she'd had tutors and a father who insisted she learn the skills needed to have a role in the family business. Such as it was. Considering her father had started it, and nobody else had ever worked in it, it wasn't as if they had some generations-long legacy to maintain. Still, he would finally get his wish. If he would have her.

After listening to the rain spilling off the red clay roof tiles into the gutters overhead for a few more seconds, Cas opted for knocking. It had been too many years to presume she could walk into the house, too many years since she had visited. Besides, the last time Cas had seen her father, she had tried to stop him from his mission while her commander shot him.

Several moments passed without an answer. Maybe the rain had drowned out her knock. She leaned to the side and tugged on the rope, and a bell gonged inside. She always hated that thing. It had made her feel like a monk living in a Temple of Tharon.

As the reverberations faded, she wondered if her father had gotten rid of the staff, deciding he didn't need help since he lived alone now. Or maybe he hadn't yet returned from Owanu Owanus. She felt a twinge of guilt that she hadn't come by the house to check on him. He'd been *shot*, after all. But he had chosen to be there, working for the enemy, damn it. It wasn't her fault.

And when had there been time to visit? She had been sucked into Colonel—*General*—Zirkander's self-appointed mission as soon as she had returned to the country, where she had been possessed by an ancient sword and killed Apex…

She closed her eyes. In the weeks since then, she could have come by, but she'd been too busy mourning. Sulking. Feeling utterly and completely lost.

Despite the long delay, when the door opened, Cas wasn't ready. She lifted her chin, doing her best to wipe the conflagration of feelings off her face, to be the logic-driven creature her father had always thought she should be, a calculating sniper who never let feelings factor into a mission. Or relationships.

He stood before her, wearing black trousers and a high-necked gray shirt, his sandy hair neatly combed to one side. He gazed blandly at her, his fine-boned features recently shaved, his blue eyes as cool and emotionless as ever. The several weeks that had passed since he had been shot probably had not been enough for a complete recovery, but she couldn't see any lingering signs of the injury, except perhaps a hint of stiffness in the way he held his left shoulder.

"Father," she said.

"Caslin," he said.

They stared at each other, each waiting for the other to continue the conversation. Cas did not have many childhood memories of long conversations, certainly none that had involved frivolous subjects. Reminding herself that she was the one who had come to him, she groped for something to say, a way to ask what she had come to ask. Perhaps she should just do that. But it seemed awkward to come right out and ask for a job when they had last met as enemies.

"Has your wound healed?" Cas asked.

"Sufficiently, yes."

Should she apologize for the part she had played in giving it to him? No, he had made his choice, just as she had made hers. Just because he had tried to warn her to stay out of that ancient pyramid, that didn't mean she owed him anything.

"Have you heard about…" Cas waved vaguely in the direction

of Harborgard Castle, the top towers of which were visible from their elevated vantage point above the city. As far as she knew, what had truly happened there had never come out in the newspapers or even in official military reports, but her father had a way of knowing things.

"You resigned your commission."

"Yeah."

Cas didn't know if that meant he knew everything or not. "I can't go back. Are you... At one time, you wanted me to work for you."

For some reason, she had a hard time asking the actual question, asking if he would hire her now. She had thought this was what she wanted—or rather, the life she deserved. Now, however, with the question on the tip of her tongue, she doubted her decision. Her father worked for money, assassinated people for the highest bidder, not questioning whether the target deserved that fate or not. Of course, she had never questioned if the Cofah soldiers she'd shot had deserved their fate, but somehow working for the military and the king made it all seem much nobler. She was always certain she was defending her country, her people. But that was an honor reserved for those who could be trusted to guard their comrades' backs.

"Father, I would be interested in working for you, if you're hiring." The words sounded odd, as if she were somewhere outside of her body and hearing someone else speak them.

"You've run out of money?" he asked coolly.

Cas clenched her jaw. He thought she was coming to him as a last resort? Because she would be living on the streets, if not for him? She wasn't *that* poor. She'd never spent lavishly, and she had money in the bank, plenty to cover the modest room she had rented. All right, maybe it *had* crossed her mind that she didn't know what else she could do for a living. She shot things. She was a pilot, too, but ninety percent of the fliers in the country belonged to the military, so civilian jobs were nonexistent. She didn't have the skills to get a *normal* job.

"No," she said. "I'm not out of money."

She had a few months before she had to worry about that.

Also, Tolemek had invited her to stay with him, even though she had been avoiding him of late. She didn't feel she deserved his company any more than she deserved the company of her Wolf Squadron comrades. Nor did she like the pitying look she caught on his face whenever they were together. Logically, she knew she should appreciate his support, and she did, but she didn't want to be pitied. She wanted to be blamed. Why wouldn't any of them do that? It didn't make sense. Even if the sword had held some magical influence over her, it had been her weak mind that had allowed it to gain a hold.

"I'm not hiring currently," her father said. "I can let you know if that changes."

The rejection did not surprise her, not fully, but it stung, nonetheless. She had always believed that no matter what happened between them, they were still blood and he would still take her back. Wasn't that what parents were supposed to do?

"Is this because I sided with my unit out there?" Cas asked, her cheeks heating. Her emotions must be all over her face, but she didn't care. "You always said that you can't let feelings or even relationships interfere with doing your duty. I was doing my duty."

"I understand," he said.

He did not add, *and I forgive you for it*. She wasn't sure why she had thought he might. She also did not know why she cared. They had barely spoken for years. If they didn't have any kind of relationship now, it was as much her fault as it was his. He had never come to her, but she had also never gone to him. She had been busy with her army training, and then with the flight training, and then working with Wolf Squadron. There hadn't been time to notice her lack of family or to miss it. But now…

It must make her emotionally weak, but a part of her felt like an eight-year-old girl again, standing in front of her father and hoping he would offer comfort over some wound she'd received while playing. When she'd been young, he'd occasionally relented and hugged her. Maybe her mother had insisted. She didn't know, but she remembered a few hugs here and there, even if it had been fifteen years.

"Caslin." Her father sighed, ever so faintly. "At this time, I can't trust you to join in with my business. I believe your loyalties would be to your unit and to those aligned with the king."

Those aligned with the king? She couldn't imagine going against King Angulus, nor could she imagine why her father would back his opposition. Surely, he must have suffered repercussions for choosing to take an assignment from the queen, especially when that queen had been responsible for having Angulus kidnapped. Or had her father bought his way out of legal trouble? Maybe nobody had been left alive who could prove that he'd been trying to kill Phelistoth because of the queen's wishes.

"No, I wouldn't agree to act against the king, but I fail to see why any loyalty I might feel toward my old comrades would matter." Unless, Cas realized as soon as the words came out of her mouth, he had been hired to *kill* one of them. Her heart gave a lurch, and she stared into his eyes, wishing she had Sardelle's knack for mind reading. Unfortunately, she had never been good at guessing her father's thoughts.

"It's possible that your loyalty would one day be a cause for conflict," he said without giving anything away.

One day? Or did he have an assassination assignment *now*?

The sound of clanks came from around the corner of the house, and a sleek black steam carriage with silver piping came into view. A driver she did not recognize rolled the vehicle around pond-sized puddles and stopped in front of the walkway.

Her father plucked a black jacket from the coat rack and stepped forward, closing the door behind him. "It's good to see that you are well, Caslin," he said. "I have an appointment I must attend."

He started past her, but paused, looking down at her.

She tensed slightly, aware that she hadn't brought any weapons. She had turned in her sniper rifle with the rest of her gear when she resigned from the army, and, despite being her father's daughter, she didn't keep a rack of guns under her bed. She didn't truly believe he would attack her, not here, when there wasn't a logical reason for them to be at odds, but she never felt at ease around him.

"Perhaps," he said slowly, "you could come back another time, on a less dreary day, and we could shoot at the range." He inclined his head toward the expansive backyard that had stationary targets as well as an automated machine that threw up clay disks.

A normal father would ask if she wanted to go out for a beer or come over for dinner. Hers asked her to go shooting with him. Still, it was an offering of a sort. It just wasn't the one she had come for.

"I'll think about," Cas said.

"Good."

She waited under the portico, thinking he might offer her a ride back into town, especially since it was raining. He did not. Was he late for his appointment? Or was he worried she might get a whiff of what that appointment involved? *Who* it involved?

She started walking toward the road as the steam carriage trundled away, spitting black smoke from its stack. But her pace slowed as it disappeared around the trees at the end of the drive. She waited a few minutes, ignoring the rain trickling down the back of her neck, making sure her father wouldn't forget something and return. Then she turned and went back to the house. She assumed he had more staff inside, so she didn't knock or ring the infernal bell again. Instead, she went into spy mode.

Ducking low to avoid windows, she sneaked along the front of the house and around the corner to the three-story tower that had once held her room. Whether it still did, she didn't know, but the place was a mansion, so it wasn't as if her father would have needed to convert her bedroom to a study after she moved out.

She skimmed up ivy on trellises, smiling slightly as she remembered the day when her ten-year-old self had oh-so-innocently asked the gardener to plant the foliage under her window. It had long since matured, providing a way into and out of her bedroom window. She hadn't been much for trysts in her teenage years, but she'd sneaked out a few times when she had been in trouble and confined to her room.

As the ivy spattered droplets onto her face, she climbed to the third story. She jiggled the window just so, thwarting the lock she'd made to be thwart-able, and landed on the thick carpet inside without a sound.

Cas had intended to rush straight out the door, down the stairs, and to her father's office, but the familiar smells and sights of her old room distracted her. Nothing had changed, from the medals hanging from bedknobs to the half-burned lemon verbena candles on the fireplace mantle. Those medals brought back memories of all the shooting competitions she'd won as a youth, where she had been one of the few girls out there among boys who had always been older and taller than she was, most of whom had glared sullenly when she had beaten them. She'd always been the oddity growing up and then in the army, too, until she'd come to join Wolf Squadron, where she'd finally worked with people as odd as she was, people who appreciated her skills.

Cas blinked away moisture forming in her eyes and growled at herself. She wasn't going to weep during the middle of an infiltration.

"Some soldier," she muttered and rested her ear against the door.

When she didn't hear anything, she eased out into the hallway. She ghosted down the stairs, the house familiar and yet no longer home, not after almost eight years without stepping foot inside. A few unfamiliar scents touched the air, including something tomato-based wafting up from the kitchen. That meant at least one person was here.

She made it to the first floor without seeing anyone and hurried when she saw the door to her father's office was open. She almost turned into the room without checking, but remembered at the last second that he always kept it locked. If it was open...

A faint creak reached her ear, and she reacted instantly. She couldn't run to the next room without crossing in front of the open door, and she might not make it back to the stairs in time, so she hopped onto a side table that held a vase. If someone heavier had tried this, the table might have wobbled more, sending the vase to the floor, but she barely stirred it as she used the elevation to vault up toward the arched ceiling. She softened her touch as much as possible, thanking the tumbling tutor her father had brought in to teach her as a girl as she landed above the door with her feet on one hallway wall and her hands pressed against the other.

She didn't have time to inch higher before a maid walked out, carrying a feather duster, a bucket, and a sponge. Jartya. She had been working here for years. Cas sucked in her belly, wishing she had found a perch higher on the wall. Jartya had been a friendly face once, one to sneak Cas cookies and milk at night, after her father had sent her to bed for being too picky about dinner. Jartya might not say anything about Cas's infiltration, but that wasn't a certainty after all this time.

Jartya paused, snapped her fingers, and walked back inside. She plucked a spray bottle of cleaning solution from the desk. Cas used that moment to raise herself a bit higher, out of sight, but as she did so, water dripped from the hem of her jacket and splatted to the floor. She cringed, certain Jartya would notice it. What kind of thief tried an infiltration when she was soaking wet?

Jartya walked out again, and Cas mentally urged her to hurry. But the maid noticed the water droplets.

Don't look up, Cas silently urged. *Don't look up...*

Jartya bent and swept the sponge across the water. She glanced at her bucket. *Yes,* Cas thought, *those drops came from your bucket, not from the woman with trembling forearms braced above the door.*

There was no way for Cas to stem the drops falling from her hem, not with both her hands occupied. As Jartya was cleaning up the mess, a new drop fell, plopping onto the back of her white uniform. She didn't seem to notice. For the moment. Another drop fell. Jartya stood up with a sigh. She had gained weight and a few gray hairs in the years since Cas had been here. She probably wouldn't appreciate a hundred-pound woman falling onto her head.

Sweat slicked Cas's palms, and one started to slip. She flexed her shoulders, pushing harder to keep herself in place. Finally, Jartya headed down the hall. She disappeared around the corner that led to the kitchen without looking back.

Cas dropped down, wincing when she couldn't make her landing silent. She hurried into the office, afraid someone would have heard her. Jartya might also return to lock the door again once she put away the cleaning supplies.

Her father's tidy office and clear desk made it easy to spot something out of the ordinary. A single envelope lay on a corner, the top sliced open. It was addressed to the Trim and Tight Landscaping Service, one of her father's businesses that covered up what he truly did. Cas wiped her damp palms and pulled out a single page inside the envelope. She skimmed the short letter inside, pausing on key terms. *His celestial highness... authorized me to hire you... the traitor Tolemek Targoson. Fifty thousand nucros or good imperial gold.*

Cas slumped against the chair. Tolemek.

* * *

Sardelle knocked on the door to Ridge's office on the second floor of the brigade headquarters building in the middle of the army fort. Thanks to King Angulus, she now had a fancy piece of paper that could get her past the guards without chicanery. Nonetheless, she had expected to have trouble this time, since she had Tylie with her. The guards *had* questioned Sardelle, but one look at Tylie's paint-stained dress and the grass-thong sandals she had grabbed after the attack, and they'd decided she wasn't a security threat. Fortunately, they did not know she had the potential to be a powerful sorceress someday and had already learned a few skills.

"Come in," Ridge said, then silently added, *You don't ever have to knock.*

Sardelle had already brushed his mind, letting him know they were coming, so she was monitoring him for comments.

I wouldn't want to catch you doing something embarrassing. She tried to make her tone light, though her mood was anything but light after the dragon incident. She hadn't yet told him about that, just that there was trouble and they needed to talk.

Generals don't do embarrassing things in their offices. They're proper and staid.

The man across the hall has his door locked and is vigorously looking at a calendar with naked women in it, Jaxi informed them both.

Well, Ridge replied, *he's only a colonel.*

How does one look 'vigorously'? Sardelle wondered before she could think better of it. She opened the door and waved Tylie inside, glancing at the closed door across the hallway.

"No need for details," Ridge blurted, frowning at Jaxi's spot on Sardelle's hip. How a soulblade could pulse mischievously, Sardelle did not know, but Jaxi managed it.

Sardelle walked over, hugged Ridge, and kissed him on the cheek. He looked quite handsome in his freshly pressed uniform—General Ort would be proud, since his boots were even mud-free at the moment. She would have enjoyed lingering for more than the perfunctory kiss, especially since he had been sleeping on base most nights of late, ever since Phelistoth showed up at the cottage. He was staying close and assisting with Tylie's teaching. Sardelle couldn't blame Ridge for being uncomfortable having a dragon wandering around the house at odd times of the day. It rattled her too. But it meant that *she* slept alone. She didn't feel that Tylie was old enough to stay out there by herself, and Tolemek was away on a mission for the king, so Sardelle had been taking care of her.

You did agree to teach her, Jaxi said.

That was before I knew I'd get a dragon with the deal.

Technically, Phelistoth is her *dragon. He just tolerates you because you came with the house. Much like Ridge's original couch.*

I doubt the dragon belongs to anybody.

Reluctantly, Sardelle released Ridge and stepped back. "We have trouble."

"So you said." He winced. "It's not the house again, is it? We've barely been there a month."

"The house is still standing."

"The couch was incinerated," Tylie said, waving her arms in an expansive gesture. "And Phel is missing. The other dragon chased him away."

"The *other* dragon?" Ridge braced himself against his desk.

"The thousands-of-years-old criminal one that escaped from his magical prison in that cavern." Sardelle had arrived only for the aftermath of the mission Ridge had gone on with Captain Kaika, General Ort, and King Angulus, but she had seen the big gold dragon flying into the sunrise, and she had felt the power of his aura from miles away.

"Angulus was worried he would be a nuisance." Ridge sighed. "I didn't think he would be a nuisance to my house. *Or* my brand new, paid for in installments that haven't been installed yet, couch."

Sardelle squeezed his arm, tempted to let him know that she felt the loss of the couch even more keenly than he. She had been delighted when he had agreed to take her and his mother shopping to replace his atrocious plaid sofa, and that he had allowed himself to be persuaded from dubious choices by the joint efforts of Sardelle and Fern. The dragon was, of course, a more pressing concern.

"I'm worried about him," Tylie said, gesturing and pacing. Somehow, her sandals had come off by the door, and she was walking barefoot across the polished wooden floor. "He's a silver. And a scholar! He's no match for a gold dragon."

"Phelistoth is a scholar?" Ridge's eyebrows rose.

"So he tells us." Sardelle hadn't been home when the incident had occurred, but Tylie had shared the events with her through a mind link. She thought about having Tylie do the same thing with Ridge, but he might object to telepathic sharing with Tolemek's little sister. Sardelle touched his arm and relayed the incident herself, including the way it had ended, with Phelistoth leading the other dragon away.

"Well, that's going to alarm the neighbors. Especially if they figure out that those dragons started out on our lawn." Ridge eyed Tylie, who had walked around his desk to stare out the window as she worried her lower lip with her teeth. "I've heard the gold dragon has been flying around the Ice Blades, terrorizing mountain communities. There have been deaths, of people as well as livestock. I'm sure the king is considering ways to deal with it, especially since—" He glanced at Tylie again and finished with a shoulder shrug.

Sardelle decided not to tell him there wasn't much point in leaving secrets unspoken around Tylie. She sensed what others were thinking without meaning to. Sardelle had been working on teaching her to wall off her mind so she wouldn't be bombarded by the thoughts and emotions of those around her, but since she spent so much time flying off with Phelistoth, her education was at a rudimentary level. Tylie already knew the king had been, however inadvertently, responsible for freeing the gold dragon. Phelistoth knew too. Sardelle hoped the silver dragon would know better than to react out of spite, especially now that he seemed to be a target.

Sardelle realized she didn't know *why* he was a target. "Tylie? Do you know why the gold dragon went after Phelistoth?"

"Morishtomaric," Tylie said, turning from the window. "That's his name." She frowned down at her bare feet, or perhaps the floor, then picked up a ladybug that had found its way inside. "Did you know ladybugs have very focused minds? They're always on the hunt for insect eggs, and that's always in their thoughts. Do you have any insect eggs in here, General Ridge?"

"Sorry, Private Domez cleaned in here last night. We're out."

"Morishtomaric told you his name, Tylie?" Sardelle had learned it from reading the plaque and doing research on the dragons imprisoned in that cavern, but she doubted Tylie had plucked the name from her thoughts. Unlike Ridge, Sardelle knew how to keep a barrier around her mind, both for protection from snooping telepaths and as a courtesy to those who were sensitive, such as Tylie, and were uncomfortable with the constant background noise of loose thoughts. In her time, it had been much more of a concern.

"He told Phel." Tylie looked around the room, studying the corners of the ceiling as the ladybug strolled across her hand. She opened the window and stuck her head outside, looking in either direction from their second-story perch. "You should have a garden out here, General Ridge. There's no good place for her."

Sardelle winced. She'd gotten used to Tylie's eccentricities and her young mind, at least somewhat, but she worried Ridge would see her as an oddity—and that she would sense that and be stung.

"Maybe you should take her to the house," Ridge said. "If the trees haven't been incinerated by itinerant dragons, there ought to be spider eggs all over the woods out back."

Tylie considered this, then nodded. "Yes." She tucked the ladybug into one of the loose pockets on her dress.

"Tylie," Sardelle said. Time to try again. "Did the dragon communicate with you?"

"Morishtomaric has been looking for Phel. He told him to be his... assistant." Tylie spread her arms. "That isn't the right term. They were speaking in dragon, and I don't understand all the words. Maybe slave? Servant?"

"Wait," Ridge said. "You understand *some* of the words? In dragon?"

"Yes. Phel speaks to me that way. It was a long time before I learned to understand him."

"He spoke to us in the king's tongue." Ridge rubbed his head. "Strongly."

"He prefers his own language," Tylie said. "Phel didn't want to serve the other dragon. He refused. Morishtomaric came to punish him and make him change his mind." She bit her lip and looked out the window again. "I can sense him, through our link, and I think he's in trouble. He's not responding to me." She looked back toward them, her brown eyes moist and imploring.

Sardelle almost walked over to offer her a hug, but thus far, Tylie had shied away from physical contact with anyone except Tolemek. She wished *he* were here and hoped he'd return from the king's mission soon.

"He didn't say what he wanted Phelistoth to do as a servant, did he?" Ridge asked.

Tylie shook her head.

"Finding a creature that can cross all of Iskandia in a few hours isn't going to be easy," Ridge said, nodding to Sardelle. "And figuring out how to kill it, or at least get it to leave the country and become someone else's problem, won't be fun."

Sardelle thought Tylie might object to the idea of killing a dragon—she certainly wouldn't have wanted Phelistoth harmed—but she merely firmed her chin and said, "Magic can kill a dragon."

"But do we have powerful enough magic for that?" Ridge raised his eyebrows.

"I certainly don't. Jaxi doesn't."

A small harumph noise sounded in Sardelle's mind, but even Jaxi wasn't cocky enough to think she could match a dragon.

"What about that other sorceress?" Ridge asked. "She was here in Iskandia a few weeks ago. We're pretty sure she wasn't trying to do anything that would *help* us, since last we heard, her goal was to rule over Iskandia as the Cofah emperor's agent, and since she annihilated two of our officers." His jaw tightened, but he took a breath and continued. "Is it possible that she could defeat a dragon, if we could make a deal with her?" From his expression and aura, Sardelle could tell making deals with enemy sorceresses was the last thing he wanted to do, but he would if it meant protecting his country.

"She's more powerful than I am," Sardelle said, "but she still wouldn't be a match for a gold dragon. Or even a silver or bronze. No single human can equal a dragon in power. There are old fables of sorcerers using craft and guile to defeat dragons, but one wonders how often that actually happened."

"It only takes once to become the stuff of legends."

"Exactly. And to be retold and embellished into hyperbole. Like the exploits of pilots."

Ridge's eyebrows flew up. "My exploits are perfectly factual."

"Oh? The last I heard, you single-handedly brought down a whole armada of flying fortresses sent by the vile Cofah Empire."

"An armada? Who's been saying such things?"

"It was in an article in a magazine from Provalian County. I saw it at the library when I was doing dragon research."

"Ah, Provalia." Ridge waved a dismissive hand. "They're very rural and quaint. They probably don't know the difference between an armada and a single floating fortress. Duck was raised in Provalia, you know. He didn't learn to read until he joined the military."

"I thought that was because he was raised by wolves."

"Yes. Rural wolves from Provalia."

"As opposed to urban wolves?"

"General Ridge?" Tylie asked—she hadn't quite gotten the hang of properly addressing someone in the army. "We need to help Phel."

Ridge lifted an apologetic hand. "Yes, I know. Sorry. I haven't seen much of your teacher lately, and I enjoy chatting with her about frivolous subjects." He smiled at Sardelle.

She enjoyed chatting about frivolous subjects with him, too, but Tylie's concerned eyes reminded them that this wasn't the time for it.

"I'm scared too," Tylie whispered, her voice so soft, Sardelle wondered if she had heard correctly.

"For Phelistoth?" she asked.

"Yes. And for me. Morishtomaric wanted to take me away with him."

"What?" Ridge asked. "How do you know?"

"He said a Receiver would be useful. And that he'd show me how to use my power. He said it would be an honor for me, but I was scared of him. I want to stay with Phel and Tolie."

And me, Jaxi added. *She doesn't know it yet, but she's growing attached to me.*

I didn't know you spoke to her that often.

I don't, but what I say is wise and fascinating.

Sardelle snorted inwardly. She wished Tylie *would* grow attached to Jaxi—and to her—since the only thing keeping her in Iskandia was her brother. It would be unfortunate to teach her, only to have her lured back to Cofahre to end up working for the emperor one day. Sardelle didn't like hearing about this other dragon wanting Tylie, either. She couldn't imagine why such a creature would find a human of any talent interesting.

Phelistoth had been a unique case, with Tylie being the only one he'd been able to communicate with, however subconsciously, while he had been sick and locked in that pyramid. Whatever this Morishtomaric wanted of her, Sardelle doubted it was anything good.

"All right, ladies," Ridge said, closing a logbook on his desk and grabbing his cap and flight jacket. "I'm convinced something needs to be done. We'll see if the king has time to talk to us. He needs to hear about his dragon cavorting about so close to the city."

"He wasn't cavorting," Tylie said sternly.

"Frolicking?"

Sardelle waved for Tylie to put on her sandals and slapped Ridge on the arm for teasing her. He wriggled his eyebrows and captured her arm, linking it with his as they walked out. Tylie jogged ahead, her sandals slapping on the bare floorboards.

"*We* should frolic later," Ridge suggested softly as they trailed after her.

"I'd be amenable to that. There hasn't been much time for a good frolic lately."

"I know. Despite Angulus's promise to give me an assistant to do the paperwork, I've been busy from dawn to dusk, if not midnight." He leaned closer to kiss her temple and breathe in the scent of her shampoo. Sardelle flushed, pleased with the attention. "You should have accepted his offer for a room at the castle," Ridge added. "It's just up the hill. I could have come over during my lunch breaks. To visit."

Yes, more than once, she had second-guessed her request for Ridge to rent a cottage beyond the city walls. She had thought it best to find a secluded place, since she would be teaching Tylie, and who knew when a dragon would show up on the lawn. But the idea of being closer to Ridge was appealing. He *had* come home to visit at lunch back when she'd been sharing his house on base.

"I suppose I could reconsider his offer, but I'm not sure it's appropriate for officers to pop into the castle for lunchtime dalliances."

"Why not? Kaika does."

"I think it's different if your dalliances are *with* the king. Rules probably don't apply."

"No? Too bad I don't want to dally with him."

Outside, the rain had stopped and humidity thickened the air. Ridge released Sardelle so he could return the salutes of the officers and soldiers walking down the busy thoroughfare between headquarters, administration buildings, the vehicle pool, and the front gate. Tylie dropped back to walk beside Sardelle, shyly avoiding the curious eyes that turned toward her.

"Phel said I should ask you about something," Tylie said as they approached the gate.

"Oh?" Sardelle tilted her head. As far as she knew, the dragon hadn't suggested she could be of any use at all to Tylie. He wasn't rude, but he was dismissive.

And arrogant, Jaxi said.

Less so than this new dragon, I'm beginning to sense.

I don't know about that. All dragons think themselves superior to everyone and everything else on the planet.

You're awfully worldly on this matter, considering dragons didn't exist in your era any more than they did in mine, Sardelle observed.

I'm very well read on the matter. And not, Jaxi was quick to add before Sardelle could interrupt, *all from romance novels. Trust me: all dragons are arrogant.*

I see. At least Phelistoth hasn't lit any of Ridge's furniture on fire.

A moot argument, since bronze and silver dragons can't breathe fire.

"He said you might be able to help me find a soulblade," Tylie said.

Sardelle blinked a few times. She recalled that Tolemek had come to Iskandia hoping to find one for his sister, but it hadn't occurred to her to try and find one for her new student.

Because soulblades aren't for new students, Jaxi said, sounding a touch arrogant herself. *They're for accomplished sorcerers who have proven themselves worthy of a powerful companion. They're certainly not for children.*

I wasn't that much older than Tylie when we were bonded.

You'd been studying for more than fifteen years. And *you'd saved the life of High Inquisitor Valdon. You heal the right people, you get a sword. It's a rule.*

Sardelle snorted, and Tylie glanced at her.

"Sorry," Sardelle said. "I'm discussing it with Jaxi."

"She doesn't think I should have a soulblade?"

"She didn't say that." Not exactly. "We're talking about where other ones might be located."

You shouldn't lie to the girl if you want her to trust us and stick around.

I'm not lying. We're now going to discuss locations. A dozen of them should be buried in the rubble of Galmok Mountain, along with the remains of the Referatu headquarters. You never mentioned if you'd been chatting with any of your brethren during my three-hundred-year nap.

That's because I wasn't. The other blades all went dormant shortly after their handlers were killed. That's what happens if the link isn't continually remade and reaffirmed through contact between two magical beings.

Sardelle hadn't known that.

Could a dormant blade be woken? She couldn't believe that a soul could be lost simply because a soulblade wasn't used for a while.

Possibly. Three hundred years is a long time. We were never meant to be gifted with immortality. Just a chance to continue on for a time as advisers.

Kasandral seems to have been alive and throbbing with magic for a few millennia, Sardelle said, naming the dragon-slaying blade that had been in Colonel Therrik's family for centuries.

Kasandral is a tool, not a former real person, and besides, he's been taken out and handled now and then.

Sardelle grimaced, remembering the blade in Cas's hands, how it had tried to kill her, how it *had* killed Apex.

"Do *you* think I should have a soulblade?" Tylie asked, plucking at the material of her dress. It was hard to wait patiently while someone else had a telepathic conversation.

A major had fallen in at Ridge's side and was talking to him about something. The officer glanced at Tylie after she made her comment.

I'm considering it, Sardelle responded, speaking telepathically. Even though the king had made it clear that Sardelle was to be allowed in the city and on the base, she couldn't let herself forget that the average Iskandian subject found magic to be something despicable and evil, if he believed in it at all. *It could make sense,* she added to Tylie. *In my time, soulblades were only given to mature sorcerers who had proven themselves, either in battle or in their field. Healing, in my case. But there are so few people who remain who are trained at all. We must consider that the times have changed.*

Good luck getting a soulblade to believe that and consider her, Jaxi stuck in, the words clearly only for Sardelle.

If we could find a soulblade willing to bond with you, Tylie, Sardelle went on, *the soul inside could become a mentor and help with your training.*

I already have Phel to train me, Tylie said, her voice musical and pleasing in Sardelle's mind.

Tylie had learned telepathy from Phelistoth long before Sardelle had met her, but beyond the rudimentary skill, there was an appeal, almost an allure to her mind that came through the link. Receivers, people gifted with extreme telepathic range, had been rare even in her own time, and she had only worked with one, but she remembered the woman having a similarly pleasing aura that drew a person, almost like a moth to a flame. Sardelle wondered if the dragons felt some of that, too, and if it had to do with why Phelistoth—and now Morishtomaric—wanted to stay close to her. She would have to do some more research. Unfortunately, the records the Iskandians had kept spoke very little of magic, sorcery, and dragons. So much had been lost over the centuries, if not willfully destroyed. Sardelle wouldn't mind a visit back to Galmok Mountain for more reasons than to hunt for soulblades. She remembered all of the books that those miners had extracted and wondered if they had been kept after Ridge had left as the fort commander. She hoped so.

There's no reason why you can't have two mentors, Tylie. Or even three. Sardelle touched her chest.

Except a soulblade would get grumpy at having his or her tutelage countermanded by a dragon, Jaxi interrupted.

Is it just me, or are dragons not the only ones who have arrogance problems?

I don't know what you're talking about.

Hm. Addressing Tylie again, Sardelle said, *When I studied at the Referatu Youth Institution, I had instructors for each subject. You can learn much by having multiple tutors.*

Tylie smiled agreeably. "Good. Phelistoth said that having a soulblade would help me protect myself when he's not around."

"That's true."

Sardelle did not mention the other reason the idea of a Referatu soulblade for Tylie was growing on her. Any sword they found buried in Galmok Mountain would be of Iskandian make and would have an Iskandian soul nestled within it. It wouldn't take kindly to being taken to the empire. She had been looking for a way to tie Tylie to this continent. This might be it.

CHAPTER 2

TOLEMEK DROPPED HIS PACK BESIDE the door of his lab, inhaling the familiar chemical-scented air, mingled with the faint earthy odors from the reptile cages. He lit a few lanterns to drive back the encroaching twilight and hurried past cabinets and worktables to check on his creatures. The lab assistant he shared with the biologist across the hallway had promised to feed and water them. He needed to head out to Zirkander's place to see Tylie and thank Sardelle for watching her, but the lab was on the way, and he wanted to return the equipment he had taken.

Before he reached the cages and terrariums, he paused, an uneasy feeling coming over him, a sense of something wrong. Someone had been in his lab while he had been gone. He looked around, trying to remember how he had left everything. He couldn't put a finger on what was amiss, but some subconscious memory promised him something was.

"The lab assistant," he muttered. Who else could it have been?

Walking slowly and peering into all of the alcoves and corners, he continued to the reptiles and arachnids. He couldn't shake the feeling that someone had been here, someone not authorized to be here.

Against the back wall, a cabinet door stood ajar. That was odd. After his years aboard airships, airships that often saw battles that shook their frameworks, he had a habit of closing doors and drawers securely. Would the lab assistant have been snooping in a cabinet of chemicals? He doubted it. Those chemicals could be found in labs all over the building. Also, the people here left him alone, and they left his work alone. Having had the moniker of Deathmaker as a pirate kept the curious away.

Tolemek detoured to look in the cabinet. He didn't see anything missing, and the jars had not been pushed about.

"Tolemek?" came a soft voice from the doorway.

He spun, almost knocking a spider terrarium to the floor. He hadn't heard her approach, but he recognized that voice, and all thoughts of snooping and intruders fled from his mind.

"Cas!"

He had only been gone for a week, helping the king's team move its secret weapons facility to a new home, and given how seldom she had been about even before he left, he hadn't expected her to be waiting to greet him. Delight filled his heart when he spotted her face peeking around the doorjamb. He almost laughed at his reaction. He had been trying to steel his heart to what had seemed inevitable of late, that the distance she'd been constructing between them meant she didn't want to be with him anymore, and that she would eventually tell him.

"I just got back." Tolemek lifted an arm, offering a hug, though he feared she wouldn't accept it. She'd been shunning hugs of late, shunning any display of sympathy or tenderness. Even if she hadn't physically pushed him away, ever since Apex's death, she hadn't returned any of his gestures of affection.

To his surprise, Cas raced across the lab. She spread her arms and engulfed him in an embrace, a surprisingly strong one given her slender arms. This was more than a hug of affection. Something had happened. Something bad.

"What's wrong?" His certainty of a problem didn't keep him from returning the embrace. He pulled her close, lowering his face to the soft, short hair on the top of her head. His own long ropes of hair fell about her face, creating a curtain of privacy, not that they needed it. This late in the day, there had been few lanterns on in the other labs as he had walked through the building. Still, he liked this sense that he had her here, alone and to himself.

"The Cofah want you dead," Cas said, her voice muffled, her face pressed to his chest.

"That's not a revelation." Tolemek waited for a further explanation.

"I went to see my father."

Tolemek took a deep breath. That wasn't exactly a revelation, either. She hadn't told him she was going, but she'd made a few offhand comments about how she might as well be working for him now that she had cold-heartedly killed a good man. He had tried listening, arguing, and sympathizing with her self-recriminations, but nothing had seemed to be what she needed. He'd known she wouldn't be happy as an assassin, but had kept the words to himself, thinking she was just talking, that nothing would come of it.

"He had a job offer on his desk," Cas said, tilting her head back to look up at his face. "From someone with the authority to sign on behalf of your emperor."

"He's not *my* emperor. He hasn't been for a long time." As he had recently promised to King Angulus.

"That's good, because he wants you dead. He's offering my father a lot of money to be the one to kill you."

Tolemek looked toward the cabinet door that was still ajar. Was it possible that Ahnsung had been the one to come snooping in his absence? His shoulder blades itched at the idea of someone with Cas's sniping skills—along with a host of other life-stealing talents—hunting him. "And he took it?"

"I can't know for certain from the letter, but I know…" She bit her lip, her hesitancy rare. She didn't usually mince words. "He doesn't like you. For me. I know he's never even talked to you, but that came out in a conversation he had with General Zirkander." Her mouth twisted. Yes, apparently, her father had an easier time talking to her C.O.—her *former* C.O.—than his daughter.

"Would he like anyone for you?"

"Probably not, but he never accepted assassination assignments for the others."

Cas had never spoken much of "others," and he'd had the impression that there hadn't been many. He didn't particularly want details on them now, so all he said was, "Perhaps they had more savory reputations than I have."

"Not really. More savory hair, perhaps." She wriggled an arm free and pushed a few clumps behind his shoulder.

Her humor had been so rare of late that he didn't know how to respond to her teasing. He almost forgot to respond at all since her touch sent a shiver through him, making him aware of how close they were. Teasing wasn't the only thing she—*they*—hadn't done since Apex's death. Would news of his impending assassination kindle passionate thoughts within her? This probably wasn't the time to ask, but he lifted a hand to her face, wondering if she would respond to his touch as she once had.

"You said you liked my hair long the last time we were horizontal together." He rested his hand on the side of her head and brushed her cheek with his thumb. Her hair was slightly damp, and she smelled good, of flowers and spring rain. Thoughts of times they had spent together—too damned few—came to mind.

"I said it tickled," Cas said dryly.

"And that you liked it." He lowered his gaze briefly to her chest, reminding her of *where* it had tickled.

An appealing rosy flush warmed her cheeks. The temptation to kiss her swelled inside of him. He leaned down, his gaze snagged on her lips.

Cas drew back, releasing him. "We should be serious."

"Aren't we serious most of the time, already?" Reluctantly, he lowered his arms to let her go. He would have liked an excuse to be playful for a while.

"My father is a dangerous man." She turned sideways, frowning toward a dark window. "He hasn't failed many missions. I came to tell you—Tolemek, maybe you should go."

"Go?"

"Leave the city. If anybody else was after you, I would volunteer to help you hunt the bastard down, but—" Cas turned back toward him, a rare helpless expression softening her eyes, "—how am I supposed to do that when the bastard is my own father?"

"Maybe we should go talk to him and convince him not to accept the assignment." Tolemek had no idea how he would do that, unless he could make a better offer. How much had the emperor agreed to pay? Tolemek wasn't swimming in riches, but he had made money quickly before when he'd needed it. A number of his formulas had commercial value. Still, the notion of outbidding an emperor's coffers was daunting.

Judging by the face Cas made, she didn't think much of the idea.

"Wouldn't he just follow me if I left town?" He didn't want to leave anyway. He had a fabulous lab here. And he'd started to make friends, of a sort. Sardelle, anyway. And some of the other researchers working in the building had stopped skittering away at his approach. And then there was Cas... if she would allow herself to remain a part of his life. "He went all the way to Owanu Owanus to find Tylie's dragon."

"That is true." Cas pushed a hand through her hair, ruffling it.

He wanted to smooth it, to touch her in any way that she would allow. He snorted to himself. And here he'd thought he had been convincing himself to stop caring so much in preparation for the inevitable breakup. All she had to do was hug him, and he couldn't stop thinking bedroom thoughts.

"Cas. I—"

She lifted a hand and spun toward the door. An instant later, he heard the footsteps too. Heavy footsteps, at least two sets of them. Tolemek didn't know who it was, but it wouldn't be Ahnsung, not with that noisy tread.

Cas slipped a throwing knife out of a thigh sheath that held two more—he hadn't noticed she was carrying the weapons, only that she hadn't been carrying around her sniper rifle lately. Tolemek didn't have any of his own chemical weapons at hand, but he grabbed a bottle of acid from a shelf and stepped up beside her.

The footsteps stopped outside of his lab, and a man cleared his throat. A hand snaked around the jamb to knock on the already open door.

"Sergeant Arnost on the king's business," the owner said.

"The king's business?" Cas mouthed to Tolemek.

He shrugged, but since he'd just returned from some of the king's business, he wasn't that surprised. Had he forgotten to do something before leaving the dirigible? He hadn't thought that he needed to report back to the castle, since he had only been along to help. He hadn't been in charge of the mission.

"Come in," Tolemek said.

The two soldiers were wearing the black of the king's staff, men who guarded the castle. They were big, strong, and intimidating, until they crept uncertainly into the lab, glancing in all directions, as if they were heading into a witch's cave and some mutant guard creature might leap out and eat them.

"The king needs something from me tonight?" Tolemek asked.

"Ah." The one who had introduced himself as Sergeant Arnost tore his gaze from a shelf of organs in formaldehyde. "Yes. I mean, no. We're here to get Lieuten—I mean, Ms. Caslin Ahn."

"Me?" Cas glanced at Tolemek, as if he would have a clue what this was about.

He could only shrug again.

"Yes, ma'am." The sergeant looked at her throwing knife—she hadn't slid it back into its sheath yet. "Will you come willingly? We're authorized to use force, but we'd rather not."

"Because you know she'll shave the hair off your balls if you try?" Tolemek asked. Cas wasn't truly a master at unarmed combat, but he'd seen her fight often enough to know she could often find a way out of the grasps of bigger opponents, even when she didn't have a firearm at hand.

The sergeant's lips flattened. "Because she's Raptor from Wolf Squadron. She's a hero."

Tolemek nudged Cas with his elbow. "Notice that wasn't a denial."

She put away her knife, not noticeably charmed by his humor. Her mouth had tightened at the word *hero*. He chose to believe she was irked at the reminder of her past, not at him.

"Mind if I come along?" he asked.

"No," Cas said at the same time as the sergeant said, "Yes."

"Then it's settled," Tolemek said, walking toward the door with her. He hadn't ever tried to receive preferential treatment based on Cas's position on the legendary squadron—he hadn't even thought it might be possible to do so—but maybe it would work.

The sergeant opened his mouth, but took in the grim expression on Cas's face, then shrugged and told his comrade, "The king's secretary will kick him out if he doesn't want to see him."

"You're in charge, Sergeant."

"Lucky me."

* * *

General Ort was waiting inside the castle courtyard when Ridge walked in, accompanied by Sardelle and Tylie. The guards had waved the three of them through without question, as if they had been expected. General Ort's presence reminded him—uncomfortably—of the times his C.O. had accompanied him to the castle to make sure Ridge didn't do something inappropriate in the presence of the king.

He didn't stop you from climbing up that frozen vine, Jaxi said into his mind. She'd been keeping up a running commentary on his thoughts for most of the trip to the castle. If he didn't know better, he would assume she had been missing him.

I miss monitoring your unpredictable antics. It's a touch boring out in the woods with so few people around. Tylie's so innocent, I barely know what to say to her.

Does she not appreciate it when you inform her that the neighbors are looking vigorously at pictures of nudes?

She gives me blank looks. She's led a very sheltered life. I can't imagine what Phelistoth finds to discuss with her.

Ridge couldn't imagine, either, so he merely nodded. Jaxi seemed pleased by his agreement.

"General," Ridge greeted Ort with a thump to the shoulder, hoping to distract him from looking down and making disparaging comments about the state of his boots. It wasn't his fault it had rained on the way over here, or that a steam wagon driver with an appalling lack of respect for a military uniform had charged through a puddle, spattering mud on his trousers.

"Before you say anything, it wasn't my fault."

He expected a lecture—Ort was so good at them, he could spit them out without thought. Instead, Ort nodded gravely at Ridge and gripped his shoulder.

"I was sorry to hear the news," he said solemnly.

Ridge stared at him, his stomach sinking. What had happened? A loss of one of his men? Some accident he hadn't heard about yet?

"News?" Ridge glanced at Sardelle, wondering if she knew anything.

Surprisingly, a faint smirk curved her lips.

"I heard about the couch," Ort said.

"What? How? *I* just heard about it." And was that truly what Ort was offering condolences about? A piece of furniture?

"We've *all* been looking forward to seeing that beastly green couch replaced." Ort lowered his hand and nodded toward the double doors leading to the castle interior. "You know you can call me Vilhem now, right, Ridge?"

"Yes, sir, but General Ort is what comes out. And what do you mean *all*? Who's *all*?"

"I can't tell you how relieved I was when I heard you were letting Sardelle pick out the new one." Ort shook his head sadly. "I heard it was handsome—and all one color—an *appealing* color. I'm sad I never got a chance to see it."

"If I thought you had a sense of humor, I'd laugh, but I'm afraid you're deadly serious."

Sardelle, walking behind Ort in their little procession, gave Ridge a slight nod.

"We're all hoping Sardelle will be a good influence on you, Ridge." Ort nodded to the guards and walked in. Once again, nobody questioned their group. "It's time for you to grow up."

"Of that, I have no doubt, but I didn't realize sofas were a reflection of one's maturity level."

"They can be." Ort headed up the stairs toward the king's office. "Angulus is waiting for us."

"He was expecting us?" Ridge glanced at Sardelle again—*she* hadn't been communicating with him, had she? Or maybe Jaxi had. She'd spoken to Angulus at the end of that last mission, he recalled.

"A dragon almost burned down your house, which is located less than two miles from the city walls, Ridge," Ort said. "What we've been trying to figure out is why it took you so long to come here to report it."

"*I* just learned about it."

"No excuses." Ort propelled Ridge up the stairs with a push. "The king's waiting."

"He's grumpy," came a whisper from behind them. Tylie.

Ridge started to smile, but Sardelle responded with, "I've noticed that many of Ridge's superiors are when they deal with him."

Ridge paused at the top of the stairs to shoot her a dirty look. She smiled innocently at him.

Ort cleared his throat, and Ridge resumed his trek past priceless models of ancient ships and urns depicting flat-nosed dancing dragons. They might have been lizards. The artwork made it difficult to tell. Fortunately, or perhaps unfortunately, this part of the castle had not been damaged by Kaika's explosives. The art could certainly use updating. Even more so than his much-maligned couch.

The door stood open, and the guard—one of the king's alert bodyguards this time—nodded them in. Angulus stood in front of his desk, his arms folded over his chest, and he scowled at Ridge.

Why do I have a feeling this meeting isn't going to go well? He asked the question silently, not expecting an answer, but both Jaxi and Sardelle turned out to be monitoring his thoughts.

Because he looks even grumpier than Ort? Jaxi asked.

You'd think his dalliances with Kaika would have helped alleviate some of that, he thought.

Maybe she didn't come for lunch today.

Sardelle snorted—not aloud but into his mind, and probably into Jaxi's too. *He's upset about the dragon, not you. Even without prying, I can feel his emotions rolling off him. He feels responsible.*

For the loss of my couch?

For the loss of lives *this dragon has caused in the last couple of weeks.*

Ah.

"Sire," Ridge said respectfully, making his salute crisp and precise. This wasn't the time to irk Angulus with irreverence. "I understand you've been waiting for us?"

Angulus opened his mouth, but Tylie padded in after Ort and Sardelle, and he hesitated. Ridge didn't know if it was because he was surprised to see her or if her presence made him want to curb an outpouring of profanity. If the latter, Ridge would have to remember to bring her to future meetings with the king.

"I need a dragon-hunting team, Zirkander," Angulus said. "You're in charge of it."

"Because I have a couch vendetta to pursue?"

Angulus scowled at him.

So much for holding back on that irreverence.

"Because dragons fly. And nobody's done more crazy flying than you."

That was possibly true. As long as the adjective *crazy* was attached.

"General Ort will be your co-commander on this mission. Also, I'm hoping Sardelle will agree to help." Angulus's tone was civil and his scowl much lighter for her. "And then anyone else you want, I'll arrange it. This problem is my fault. I'd appreciate it if you fixed it."

You should ask him to buy you a new couch if you succeed, Jaxi suggested.

I'm trying to keep my irreverence to a minimum.

Jaxi made a skeptical noise in his mind.

I also don't think I should ask for favors when he's clearly cranky.

"How *much* of a problem has he become, Sire?" Sardelle asked, her face and tone concerned. She couldn't have been inappropriately irreverent if she had tried.

Not to a king, no. Sardelle twitched an eyebrow in his direction. *They taught us not to do that in my century.*

Angulus turned toward his desk, reaching for a rolled-up map.

He's just a man. You know the saying—he puts his hand-tailored, calfskin breeches on one leg at a time, the same as the rest of us. Though I'm expecting he spends less time in them now. While Angulus's back was still turned, Ridge flashed her a wicked grin.

You're tickled by that relationship, aren't you?

I am. Angulus needs someone fun.

Ridge wondered what Angulus would think if he requested Captain Kaika for this dragon-hunting team. Would he feel protective toward her now and want to keep her safe? Ridge doubted *Kaika* would appreciate being kept safe. At least, he hoped not. She was the best demolitions person Ridge knew, and it was a forgone conclusion that pistols weren't going to take out dragons.

"A lot of the attacks have been in the Ice Blades," Angulus said, stepping aside so they could see the spread map. He had circled several towns and placed Xs next to others. They ranged throughout the foothills on the western side of the mountains, running about three hundred miles north and south along the bottom half of the range. "The Xs are sightings, and the circles are villages that he attacked. He swoops in and takes sheep and cows to eat, but he likes to burn buildings while he's there, not worrying about whether anyone is inside. In Loon's Lake, the villagers shot at him, and he killed them all." Angulus clenched his teeth and stared hard at the map.

A soft knock sounded on the door, and Kaika walked in. She wore her usual uniform, with weapons and a sack of gear slung over her shoulder, and she saluted professionally when Angulus looked up. Only her lips expressed anything suggestive, quirking at the corners when their eyes met.

"Reporting for dragon-slaying duty, Sire," she said.

"I thought I was picking my own team," Ridge said dryly.

Kaika winked at him. "We knew you'd want me."

Ridge resisted the urge to make a joke, especially since Angulus's eyes narrowed slightly as he followed that wink. Ridge got that look from boyfriends and husbands often, so he recognized it well, though he wouldn't have expected Angulus to feel threatened by Ridge's reputation. Kings were greater prizes than pilots. Any girl would say so.

"Loon's Lake isn't far from your facility," Sardelle said. "Your former facility."

Angulus nodded, shifting his attention to her. "Yes, the dragon has been sighted near there a couple of times. I'm wondering if he's making plans to free the rest of the dragons in that cavern. I've got people watching the mountain right now. You were there when I had Kaika set off those controlled explosives to bury the entrances, and we've since brought down the old research facility, too, in an attempt to make that cavern inaccessible, or at least not easily accessible. I didn't want to try to destroy the statues outright, not until you'd finished your research. If some of them could be talked into alliances with Iskandia, it might be worth the risk of dealing with criminals. By all accounts, dragons are more deadly than an armored dirigible filled with soldiers and guns."

"Very likely," Sardelle said neutrally. She had told Ridge she didn't think any of the dragons should be trusted or set free, but he didn't know if she had expressed that sentiment to Angulus.

He knows, Jaxi said. *But he's worried about the empire, right now, and is willing to take risks to gain big advantages. Apparently, he was recently trying to negotiate a peace treaty with the emperor when the Cofah army blew up the dirigible carrying the envoy he'd sent.*

Are you supposed to be cavorting in his thoughts and sharing them with me?

Yes.

Ridge snorted, drawing a couple of glances. He needed to learn not to respond aloud to Jaxi. "A couple of those towns are within seventy-five miles of the Magroth crystal mines too." He pointed at spots farther north.

"I noticed that," Angulus said, "but my understanding is that the crystals wouldn't be of any interest to a dragon, that he could make anything magical that a human sorcerer could have made."

"Technically, we made things that dragons never did, more because they didn't have a need to, rather than because they didn't have the power to," Sardelle said. "You're right, though, in that our lamps wouldn't be of any interest. There are other tools up there, though, and books full of information." She glanced at Ridge. "Some of those were taken out in the time I was there."

"So it's possible something there might interest a dragon?" Angulus asked.

"Possible. I'd have to think about what that might be, and of course, I wasn't aware of all of the contents of the vaults and libraries, as I didn't have a full-time teaching or government position there. Regardless, I agree that it seems likely that he might want his brethren back, to create a full squadron of dragons that would answer to him."

A full squadron of dragons. Ridge hadn't even seen the destructive capability of one firsthand yet, but he shuddered at the idea of encountering such an entity in the skies. The sorceress had incinerated fliers with a wave of her hand, and she was just a human.

Technically, she's one-eighth dragon, Jaxi said. *She claimed to be the great granddaughter of one. Of course, she could have been lying.*

You didn't cavort in her thoughts to check?

You can't cavort with people who know how to shield their minds from intrusion. She could be a hermaphrodite with scales instead of body hair, and I'd never be able to pry the secret from her.

I'd like to think I'd be able to detect that secret.

"Perhaps..." Sardelle looked at Tylie, to whom Ridge hadn't been paying any attention—she was kneeling in a corner and stroking the strings on a lute resting against the wall. "If we could get permission, Sire, we'd thought to return to the crystal mines to try and find a soulblade for Tylie."

Angulus frowned. "Can't that wait?"

"It would be a second weapon that would be useful in an attack against a dragon, and it would be useful for Tylie to have another *Iskandian* mentor." She raised her eyebrows at Angulus.

Angulus nodded slightly, apparently understanding why she gave that word emphasis.

"Would Tylie fight against the dragon though?" he asked. "I don't like the idea of sending a girl into battle."

"Girls can do a lot of damage in battle." Kaika had been standing quietly by the door, but she set her bag on the floor and ambled over to a chair and flopped down.

"Mature women can, I'll agree."

"I don't know that they have to be *that* mature," Kaika said, smirking.

Tylie was currently peering into the hollow behind the lute strings, seemingly unaware that everyone in the room was looking at her. She smiled brightly over her shoulder at Ridge. "There are spider eggs in here."

"Pardon?" Angulus asked.

"You might want to ask the king before you release the ladybug into his lute," Ridge said.

Angulus curled a lip, more at the thought of an infestation in his instrument than because of strong feelings about ladybugs, Ridge guessed.

"May I?" Tylie dipped into her pocket, then spread her hand, palm up. The ladybug hadn't escaped on the walk over—or maybe it hadn't *wanted* to escape. It strutted around on her palm.

"I suppose," Angulus said, then grabbed a pen and scribbled on a notepad on the desk. "I'm going to have a talk with the cleaning staff about nooks and crannies."

After the ladybug had been set on the rim of the lute, Tylie faced everyone. She curtsied for the king and smiled shyly at him. "I can fight if it's to protect Phel."

"Phel?"

"Phelistoth, Sire," Ridge said. "The silver dragon."

"I see." Angulus rubbed his jaw. "Very well. Maybe I'll send you two over to get the sword, while—"

Another knock sounded at the door.

"Send her in," Angulus said without waiting for an announcement. "We've been expecting her."

We? Ridge wasn't expecting anyone, so he turned curiously toward the door.

His jaw dropped when Caslin Ahn walked in.

CHAPTER 3

WHEN CAS SLIPPED PAST HER escort and into the king's office, she tensed as soon as she saw the collection of people waiting for her. Seeing General Zirkander flooded her with guilt, and at the same time, wariness crept in, causing her shoulders to bunch. Zirkander had tried hard not to let her resign, and her first thought was that this was some scheme to get her to come back. A part of her wanted to come back—she missed her job and her comrades more than she'd ever thought she would—but she couldn't. Not after what she'd done. Couldn't he understand that?

As soon as the king set down a map and turned to face her, she realized her thought had likely been wrong—and self-absorbed. Whatever was going on here, with Tylie, Sardelle, Zirkander, General Ort, Captain Kaika, *and* the king in the room, it had to be about more than her old job. Besides, she doubted Zirkander could have talked King Angulus into intervening in regard to her resignation.

"Tolie!" Tylie blurted and scampered across the room.

Cas stepped aside, lest she be bowled over. Tylie was only a few inches taller than she and lacked Tolemek's sturdy, muscled build, but she wore a determined smile as she flung herself into her brother's arms.

Tolemek returned the hug, but he wore a stern expression as he gazed around the room, a what-is-going-on-and-why-was-my-little-sister-involved expression.

"Ms. Ahn," the king said, ignoring Tolemek's sternness and the family reunion. His gaze locked onto Cas.

Ms. Ahn. That sounded strange after being Lieutenant Ahn for almost two years. But she did not have time to lament the loss, as she was soon busy worrying that she was in trouble. Had he decided to punish her for Apex's death? Or her role in his wife's death? Or something else? Even though she hadn't gone, she had been invited to the dinner and awards ceremony for those pilots who had been pivotal in destroying the flying Cofah fortress, so she had assumed her sins had been forgiven—even if they shouldn't have been. Maybe something had changed.

"Yes, Sire?" Since she wasn't in uniform, she genuflected, the movement awkward since she'd rarely been in the king's company and had the opportunity to practice it.

"We have a dragon problem."

Startled, Cas spun toward Tolemek. Phelistoth?

"She's not in the loop anymore, Sire," Zirkander said. "She doesn't know about the new one."

A *new* dragon? How had they gone from dragons being extinct a couple of months ago to having two of them in the world?

"Oh? Tolemek knows." Angulus looked toward Tolemek, frowning slightly.

"We haven't… spoken of it, Sire," Tolemek said. "I was given to understand the dragons were as secret as other matters."

Cas caught that hesitation. They hadn't spoken of it—or anything—because she had been avoiding him. A fresh wave of guilt washed over her for that. Tolemek did not deserve to be avoided, not without an explanation, but she was so poor at articulating her feelings. She just felt so uncomfortable around him now—around *all* of them. She couldn't see them without thinking of her old life and of Apex—of the horrified and pained expression on his face as she had cut into him with that vile sword. She'd been crying out with rage inside, unable to control her own body, but she remembered everything she'd seen and done. And heard. His scream had been almost as bad as the horror of her betrayal in his eyes.

"Cofah agents infiltrated a secret research facility at the southern end of the Ice Blades," Angulus explained. "When we went out to hunt for them, we found a nearby ancient cavern with ten dragon statues in it. Or so they first appeared. One of the statues had been half melted away, revealing the golden scales of a real dragon. We believe the same sorceress that we faced in the flying fortress found them and released this one partway in order to speak to it and try to recruit it to her cause—taking over Iskandia for the empire and for herself." Angulus made a face, looking like he wanted to spit. "The evidence pointed to that, and the dragon corroborated that story, but the dragon also proved himself a liar in communicating with me."

With *him*? Had the king gone out there personally? That seemed insanely dangerous, especially if that sorceress had been there. Nobody else in the room seemed surprised by this information. They'd all known, she realized. Maybe some of them had even been there.

Even though her resignation had been her choice, she felt stung that everyone knew about this except for her.

"The dragon convinced me to release him," King Angulus said. "He promised to help Kaika and me escape from the cavern. Foolishly, I believed him."

"Sire, he had a powerful mind," Kaika said. "I was sympathetic to him, too, and that's not normal for me. Not when dealing with giant monsters with fangs bigger and sharper than swords."

From the way Angulus's lips thinned and he shook his head, he didn't forgive himself, powerful mind notwithstanding. Cas understood all too well how hard it was to forgive oneself when one had committed an unforgivable error.

"Regardless of the circumstances," Angulus said, "the dragon is free now, and it's wreaking havoc in rural areas. It's been close to the capital as well." He extended a hand toward Zirkander.

"Apparently, it feels particularly venomous toward furnishings," Zirkander said, earning a flat look from Angulus.

"He attacked the silver dragon you helped free," Angulus said, "a dragon we're hoping might be an ally to Iskandia one day." He glanced at Tylie, being more honest with her in the room than Cas would have expected. "At the least, Phelistoth hasn't proven himself an enemy, and we hope that will continue."

"He doesn't attack people," Tylie said. She had released Tolemek from the hug, but still clasped his hand. "He's a scholar. He's interested in finding out what happened to his kind, that's all." A troubled line creased her brow. "He doesn't want to fight for anyone."

Angulus spread his hand in an accepting gesture, though he had to secretly be hoping for some dragon allies. That could tip the scales against the empire. Or at least cause the empire to think twice about attacking Iskandia, and as far as Cas knew, that was all her country wanted, to be left alone.

"We're planning a dragon hunt," Angulus told Cas. "General Zirkander and General Ort will spearhead it."

General Ort had not said anything since Cas had arrived. He stood to one side of the room, hands clasped behind his back in a crisp parade-rest stance. Cas hadn't spoken to the man very often, but thought he would be a good commander. But why was the king telling her about this, when she wasn't on the army's payroll anymore? Did he want her to go? That was all she could imagine, but why? She doubted bullets would harm a dragon. They hadn't even done anything in fights against human magic users.

Cas rocked back on her heels with the realization of what the king must be thinking—and why he had called her here. Colonel Therrik had been reassigned to the crystal mines, so he wasn't around to consult. Too bad. He would be much more knowledgeable when it came to Kasandral, the dragon-slaying sword. The sword that was happy to slay *anyone*, dragon or sorcerer or not.

"I intend to get the dragon sword out of its locked vault," Angulus said.

For the first time, the other people in the room stirred. Sardelle didn't look surprised, but she was the only one. Zirkander, Ort, and Kaika all looked at *Cas*. Heat flushed her cheeks, and she wanted to crawl into the corner and disappear. Zirkander looked away quickly, perhaps not wanting to remind her of her bad memories. Too late.

"I don't think that's a good idea, Sire," Cas whispered. "It can't be trusted. Its wielder can't be trusted, either, not when Kasandral is in hand."

"I'm aware of the details of Apex's death," Angulus said.

Even though hearing Apex's name came as a stab to the heart, Cas appreciated the king's bluntness versus the way Tolemek and Zirkander talked around it. They were trying to spare her feelings, and she understood that, but it didn't help.

"That's why I've brought you here," Angulus said. "I want to stack the odds in our favor. We'll take explosives, at least one soulblade, and fliers and an airship so we can reach the dragon, but if I understand my history, that sword was designed to *kill* dragons." He looked toward Sardelle, who nodded once. "It's the ideal weapon to use, and I've also been told that if it's kept in that box, a dragon or sorceress shouldn't be able to sense it." Another nod from Sardelle. "If Zirkander flies up to meet the dragon and takes a wielder with him, someone who would keep the sword boxed until the last moment, perhaps that person could get close enough to strike a mortal blow."

"Oh, so that's my part in this," Zirkander said. "You don't want a mission co-commander, you want a sacrifice to the dragon gods. And the dragon."

Cas ignored him—as did Angulus. Zirkander might grouse, but he would also complain if someone else was given the suicidal task. Cas was more concerned about this talk of an unnamed wielder, especially since Angulus was looking steadily at her. Seven gods, he couldn't be thinking of asking *her* to do this, could he? Out of some notion that she had experience with the blade and was thus the logical choice? Her experience had been *tragic*. She should be the last choice for anything that dealt with it.

"I need to choose someone to wield the sword," Angulus said. "It would help if you could give me any information that might be pertinent. Are your thoughts your own when you hold it? At least most of the time? Could someone who had been trained as a sorceress wield it, or would it reject that?"

"I can answer that, Sire," Sardelle said. "Kasandral zapped me when I touched the scabbard. I'm not sure what would happen if I tried to grab the hilt, but I'd like to keep both hands, so I would decline the opportunity. Kasandral hates magic, and he hates those who wield it."

"That's unfortunate, because I thought someone who'd had the mental training that sorceresses get might be better at deflecting its manipulation attempts."

"The manipulation is a danger," Sardelle said, "but it wasn't until the queen uttered a certain phrase that Cas lost control. I think Kasandral was designed to have the ability to take over, so that even someone without sword skills could be effective at wielding him."

"When it's in control," Cas said, refusing to give the sword a gender, "you're aware of what it's doing. You just can't stop it. You're locked up, a prisoner in your own body. The rest of the time, it affects you more subtly. Such as, you start feeling irritated at your friends, and you don't know why. Your friends who have dragon blood in their veins, that is."

Tolemek rested a hand on her shoulder. A part of her wanted to reject the support—the sympathy that it included—but a part of her was glad for it. She hadn't ever wanted to talk about this again. As much as she wanted to do nothing more than clinically state the facts, the facts were tangled up with memories and emotions.

"Does anyone recall the words that Nia—the queen—spoke?" Angulus asked.

Cas closed her eyes, trying to remember. She'd been caught so unaware, and everything had happened so quickly. She knew they hadn't been in the modern tongue, but all she could do was shake her head.

"Unfortunately, I don't remember the words, either," Sardelle said. "With the pre-Occupation versions of our language, I've only seen the words written, not heard them spoken. I'm also not positive Kasandral originated in Iskandia, so the words could have been in another language altogether."

"Nia must have learned them somewhere here. I wonder if Therrik has them. Maybe they were handed down through the family."

"We can ask him if we go up there." Sardelle tapped her fingers on Jaxi's hilt. "It's also possible some of the books that were excavated from Galmok Mountain would have the information we need. My people had a library full of history texts related to dragons and magic. All of the modern books I've seen that deal even peripherally with such topics seem to have been edited or destroyed."

Angulus grunted, not denying that the city's libraries—probably the entire continent's libraries—had been so manipulated in the past centuries.

"Do we *want* to know those words?" Zirkander asked. "If they're what made Ahn go, ah, AWOL?"

"I wouldn't mind never hearing them again," Cas said.

"It's likely the command is what caused the sword to flare to full power," Sardelle said. "Kasandral has some power when he's quiescent—perhaps enough to cut through dragon scale—but he definitely grew stronger once he had been fully awoken. Perhaps if the words could be learned, the wielder could be the one to use them at his or her discretion."

"Another reason to detour to the crystal mines then," Zirkander said.

Another reason? What was the *first* reason? Cas felt that she had come into the middle of a conversation.

Angulus frowned. "Perhaps."

"Would I be safe piloting someone carrying the sword?" Zirkander asked. "I'm open to taking a flier up to catch a dragon, even if that sounds extremely unwise, but I wouldn't want to be concentrating on flying, only to get brained from behind."

"You don't have any dragon blood," Sardelle said. "The sword shouldn't object to you."

"*Shouldn't.*"

"Cas," Sardelle said, "you mentioned feeling irritated toward Tolemek and me when you were carrying the sword. Did your feelings toward Ridge or anyone else in our group change?"

"Not that I remember, but—" She spread her arms helplessly, not able to voice that Apex hadn't had dragon blood, either. He'd just... gotten in the way.

From the bleak expressions in the room, she did not need to say the rest out loud.

"Kasandral was made to protect humans from dragons

and, to a lesser extent, sorcerers," Sardelle said, breaking the uncomfortable silence. "You shouldn't need to worry about being brained. Unless you irritate your passenger with your flying."

Zirkander snorted. "So long as you don't stick Colonel Therrik behind me. He doesn't appreciate my maneuvers."

"That's actually who I had in mind," Angulus said.

Cas stared at him. He wasn't serious, was he? She'd assumed... well, she had believed the king might be leading up to assigning *her* to go along on the mission. She had intended to object, of course, since she couldn't trust herself to touch that sword again. But the idea of having someone like that hot-headed Colonel Therrik holding it was even more appalling.

"Is that a joke, Sire?" Zirkander asked. "Because it's hard to tell when you're telling jokes. Your tone is so dry all the time."

"It's not a joke. It's his family's sword. And I'm positive that somewhere in his military career, he's found time to train at swordsmanship."

"Oh, I'm sure he's trained with every pointy, bladed, or blunt weapon in existence, including his own head."

Tolemek snorted. He'd lowered his hand from Cas's shoulder, but remained close behind her. She'd forgotten what it was like to have him there. She'd forgotten how much she liked it. What she didn't like was imagining Therrik with Kasandral. He didn't like Zirkander, and he didn't like sorcerers. What if he used it as an excuse to attack Sardelle? With Jaxi's help, Sardelle had fended off Cas when the sword had taken over, but with Therrik's strength and combat expertise, he would be a more dangerous opponent.

"You have another candidate in mind?" Angulus asked.

Zirkander only hesitated a second before looking at Kaika. She had her hands clasped behind her head as she lounged in the chair, but she sat upright now.

"Uhm?" She did not appear enthused about the idea. And why would she? She had been there for Apex's death and had seen what had happened firsthand.

"No," Angulus said, his tone cold.

"Why not? She's got the same kind of training as he has, and

I don't think she has any secret fantasies about braining me—or Sardelle." Zirkander must have been having the same thoughts as Cas. Someone who already loathed magic shouldn't be allowed around that blade. The idea of someone using it as an excuse to get rid of what he considered unsavory people appalled her.

"She'll be busy launching explosives at the dragon," Angulus said, though he sounded a little uncertain.

"She can set up some bombs and hand them to someone else to launch," Zirkander said. "Like Tolemek. Is he coming? We could use some of his concoctions too. Maybe he can fling a nice acid in the dragon's eyes so it can't fly. Or hand it a pill to swallow that will make it pass out. We could stick it in a piece of steak. That works with dogs, so why not dragons?"

"Why can't I be in the same room as that man for more than ten minutes without him turning me into a walking pharmacy?" Tolemek muttered too quietly for anyone but Cas and Tylie to hear.

Tylie grinned up at him. "You're good at making things, Tolie."

Angulus sighed, ignoring Zirkander and facing Kaika. "Do you want to do it?"

"Not really, but I will if that's what the mission calls for. I haven't used swords often though. I've gone to all the knife classes, but that's not really the same."

"Perhaps we could recruit someone new from the elite forces," Angulus said. "Someone who shares Therrik's passion for old weapons but who doesn't share his attitudes."

"And someone who doesn't get airsick," Zirkander added. "That's another reason Therrik couldn't do it. He'd end up puking all over the dragon. Or more likely, his pilot."

As the conversation continued around her, Cas's thoughts turned inward. Earlier, she had cringed to think that she might be asked to wield Kasandral again, but as no superior candidates were nominated, she started to realize that she might be the logical choice, even if her soul quivered at the idea of volunteering. She was familiar with the sword and would know what to expect. This time, she might do better at controlling the feelings of annoyance it would inflict upon her in regard to Sardelle and Tolemek. And if they kept it in the box until the last moment, its effects might be minimal. Maybe. She remembered Sardelle theorizing that some of Therrik's belligerence toward her and Tolemek might have been a result, at least in part, from sleeping with the sword under his bed.

Even if Cas couldn't control her responses, wouldn't she still be a logical choice? She might not be a blade master, but she already had a stain on her soul. If the sword forced its wielder to kill another ally, and that wielder was she… well, wouldn't that be better than someone else having to carry that burden?

It took her a moment to answer that question and to accept the answer, but she finally took a breath and said, "I'll do it."

The arguing had continued while she'd been thinking, and at first, nobody heard her. She cleared her throat and raised her voice.

"I'll do it," she repeated.

This time, everyone stared at her.

Tolemek gripped her shoulder. "What are you doing?" he whispered harshly.

"If you're taking the sword in the box, and General Zirkander is flying, you'll need someone light," Cas said. "And I have experience with the sword. Maybe that would help avoid further atrocities." She closed her eyes, inhaling another deep breath, afraid—terrified—that she would regret this. "I'm the logical choice."

Since Tolemek was behind her, Cas couldn't see his face, but she could feel the tension in his fingers. And she could see the expressions of the others. Zirkander's face crumpled with distress. Sardelle and Kaika looked shocked. Ort barely knew Cas, except by reputation, but he also appeared stunned. Angulus was frowning, though Cas couldn't tell if it was a frown of rejection or just a continuation of the frown he had worn for most of this meeting. Tylie had left Tolemek's side to peer into a lute in a corner. At least *she* wasn't distressed.

"All right." Angulus nodded to Ort and then Zirkander. "You two have another team member."

"Yes, Sire," Ort said.

Zirkander merely shook his head, his expression still bleak.

"Ort, see to getting a dirigible ready. No, make that one of the airships, so fliers can come and go from the deck. Take two with you and leave room for others. Sardelle and Zirkander will try to get a soulblade and those command words, and then meet up with you for the hunt. Everyone else who's going—" Angulus looked at Tolemek as well as Kaika, "—will go on the airship and start out scouting the skies around the cavern. Scouting *only*. You will not engage until Zirkander and Sardelle are there to help. Do you understand?"

"Yes, Sire," Ort said, with others echoing him this time. Cas felt too numb to say anything.

"And you two—" Angulus waved at Sardelle and Zirkander, "—don't take too long on this sword hunt. Get the command words. That's the important thing. If you don't find a soulblade, go back later, after the dragon has been dealt with."

"Yes, Sire."

"Dismissed."

Cas almost bumped into Tolemek when she turned to walk out the door. He raised a hand, as if to stop her, as if to stop all of this, but when she looked sadly up into his eyes, his shoulders slumped, and he lowered his arm. He didn't want to fight—she saw that. She didn't know if it was a good or a bad thing. She hoped she hadn't just condemned herself to a deeper hell.

Chapter 4

Clouds drifted past, leaving moisture on Sardelle's cheeks as they passed through them. The flier occasionally wobbled or dipped, responding to some air current, but Ridge quickly compensated. The Ice Blades loomed ahead of them, wreathed in thick clouds, the top half of the mountains still blanketed in snow, despite spring's progression in the lowlands.

It's very noisy, Tylie informed her. *Not like riding on Phelistoth.*

Tylie rode in the back of Lieutenant Duck's flier. Ridge had picked him for this detour to the mines, though grudgingly so. He hadn't wanted to bring Tylie at all. Given the rough nature of the mines, Sardelle couldn't blame him, but she needed to come to pick out a soulblade, to see if they could find one that would waken and accept her.

Phelistoth doesn't have propellers, Sardelle replied.

I prefer flying on his back.

Sardelle couldn't imagine how Tylie even stayed on the dragon's back when they flew. If not for her harness, there were countless times when she would have been thrown out of Ridge's flier. Dragons must swoop and dive just as crazily when they battled each other.

Do you know where he is? Sardelle asked. If anyone could find a dragon, it ought to be another dragon.

General Ort and the airship team had left at the same time as Ridge and Duck had hopped into their cockpits, but they had soon left them far behind. Given the languid pace of that craft, Sardelle couldn't imagine it catching up with a dragon. Perhaps that was a good thing, at least for now. She and Ridge could finish their errand and join the others before they found

Morishtomaric.

Phel is in the mountains. I think he's hiding. He's not answering me when I call to him. I hope he's not injured. What if Morishtomaric is hunting him? He's mean. Why would he want to fight when there are only two dragons in the entire world?

I don't know, but Morishtomaric sounds like a stoat's hind teat.

Such foul language, Jaxi said. *Should you be teaching a young woman such profanity?*

Aren't you busy monitoring the ground down there, Jaxi? Ridge asked for a warning if the sorceress shows up and starts flinging fireballs.

I can watch for her and monitor your profanity at the same time. I have an expansive mind.

You have a nosy mind.

Many words can be used to describe the cornucopia of wealth that is a soulblade.

I'm not going to argue with that.

"Sardelle?" Ridge called over his shoulder. "Any sign of trouble?"

Jaxi?

I don't sense any dragons or evil sorceresses.

Sardelle leaned forward and rested her hand on Ridge's shoulder as a warning that she would answer telepathically. He rarely seemed surprised by that anymore, but she did not like to presume too much.

We don't sense anything, she told him.

You're sure? Because this didn't happen that long ago. Ridge stuck an arm out of the cockpit and pointed toward the ground ahead of them.

Sardelle had to fight with her harness to lean far enough to the side to see what he was pointing at. As soon as she did, a knot of worry tightened in her stomach. Several columns of black smoke rose from a farm village surrounded by a patchwork of fields. From this height, she couldn't see any flames, but the destruction must have been recent if the destroyed buildings were still smoldering.

"General?" came Duck's voice over the communication

crystal in the cockpit.

"We see it, Duck. Looks like Prinvale had an incendiary visitor."

"Is the visitor around?"

"Sardelle doesn't think so, but keep an eye out," Ridge said. "This is farther out from the mountains than any of the towns that were circled on the king's map." He lowered his voice to add, "Of course, *our* house wasn't circled, either. The king's map seems to be out of date."

Sardelle appreciated that he'd called it their house. He'd been out there so seldom since they signed the rental agreement that she'd wondered if he'd been thinking of it as the out-of-the-way place where he stashed his strange magical friends rather than his home.

She squeezed his shoulder, letting her hand linger. Given the dire circumstances, she shouldn't find this outing with him appealing, but it felt good to be heading off together again.

Should we go down and see if they need help? Sardelle asked.

Ridge hesitated. "We're still within communication range of the city. I'll send word back, so the army can get some people out here to check on the village. We better not deviate from the mission. I already got the feeling Angulus wasn't pleased that we wanted to detour to the crystal mines before joining the dragon hunt."

Sardelle waited for him to send his message before responding. *If we can learn more about Kasandral while we're here, he won't be displeased. My people's library had a great deal of information. It seems likely there would be a record of that cavern of criminal dragons too.*

You don't have to justify the trip to me. *I'm always pleased at the chance to go off alone with you.* Ridge turned and gave her a quick leer, though it didn't last long. The clouds were thickening, and he had to pay attention to the air ahead.

Not quite *alone.* Sardelle glanced toward Duck's flier, though she shifted her hand to stroke the side of Ridge's neck, sliding her fingers under his scarf.

A general ought to warrant a private room there. We'll arrive late enough that I think we can justify spending at least one night. Keep playing with my ear, and we might not make it to nightfall, though.

Sardelle suspected work would pounce on Ridge as soon as they arrived, and he would be more likely to end up cloistered in a room with Colonel Therrik than with her, but she allowed herself to hope otherwise.

He's here, Tylie spoke into her mind.

Phelistoth? Sardelle asked, but Tylie's tone had lacked the exuberance it always held when she spoke of her companion.

The other one. Over in the other flier, Tylie shrank low in her seat.

Sardelle understood the feeling. If they encountered a gold dragon, what could they do? The fliers' guns would be useless. It would be up to her and Jaxi, and they wouldn't have a chance if it picked a fight.

We'll try to avoid it, Sardelle told Tylie. *Jaxi? Do you sense it yet?*

I'm looking. She has amazing range for someone from this time period.

Ridge? Sardelle asked.

You've stopped fondling my ear. Should I be concerned?

Yes.

Damn. Sorceress?

Dragon.

How far? Ridge's head swiveled, scanning the horizons. The clouds limited visibility.

Forty miles, Jaxi said. *I can sense him now.*

Which direction? Ridge must have also heard her comment. *Maybe we can avoid him.*

He's to the east. Which way are we going?

East.

Ah.

Will he be looking for us for any reason? Ridge asked. *Or will he see us as insignificant?*

He won't see me *as insignificant.* Jaxi sniffed.

Sardelle? Ridge asked, apparently wanting a second opinion.

I'm not sure, Sardelle said. *He'll definitely sense that we have a soulblade, and he may be able to tell that Tylie and I have dragon blood, at least when he gets close. He may also be attracted to her.*

What? Why?

I'm not sure exactly, other than it would have to do with her gift, but he spoke to her earlier, when he came for Phelistoth. Tylie said he wanted her to come with him.

Wonderful. Well, let's do our best to avoid him. If we can get to the crystal mines first, we'll at least have artillery weapons to shoot at him. I don't have a lot of faith that bullets will damage a dragon, but maybe cannonballs.

Sardelle didn't have faith that either weapon would bother Morishtomaric, but she kept the thought to herself. If they had to face him, she also would prefer to do it with the assistance of a couple hundred soldiers and their weapons. If nothing else, cannonballs might distract the dragon so that she and Jaxi could come up with something else.

Like what? Jaxi asked.

I'll let you know when I figure it out.

"Duck," Ridge said over the crystal. "Drop down in elevation. We may have a dragon up ahead. We're going to hug the ground and hope the contours of the land keep us out of sight as much as possible."

"I thought the *other* team was supposed to be hunting the dragon," Duck said.

"It is. Little did they know they should have stayed with us. That reminds me…" Ridge switched to broadcast mode with the crystal as the flier dipped in elevation. They were passing the last of the cleared farmland and would be cruising over a forest of deciduous trees. "General Zirkander to base. Lieutenant Salvant, are you still in range?"

From the back seat, with the wind whipping past and the propeller buzzing, Sardelle always had to listen closely to hear the responses over the crystals, but this time, the response was so broken up that she could barely make it out. Someone had responded to Ridge, but only every third word came out, and they were softer than usual.

"Can you repeat that, L.T.?" Ridge asked.

Even fewer of the words came through.

"Sardelle?" Ridge called back. "Is that because we're at the edge of the range, or is something else going on? I haven't heard the crystals do that before."

Sardelle hadn't, either, and even though she had designed them, she wasn't positive what was going on.

I think the dragon is getting closer to us and that his aura might be strong enough to affect lesser magic, Jaxi suggested.

Jaxi thinks it might be something to do with the dragon, Sardelle told Ridge, *but I don't remember having trouble before when Phelistoth was nearby, so I'm not sure. It is true that Morishtomaric is more powerful and might exude even more of a magical field of energy. But we're just guessing.*

All right. Thanks. "To Lieutenant Salvant or whomever might hear me," Ridge said, "Wolf Squadron has encountered the gold dragon between Prinvale and Triumph Mountain. Please relay this message to the king's airship team." *The king said something about setting up Tolemek with a lab on that airship,* Ridge added silently. *I hope he's busy creating dragon-destroying potions.*

So do I. Sardelle did not know whether Tolemek could come up with something that would be useful against a dragon, but if anyone could, he could.

She lifted her gaze toward the sky ahead of them. A faint pressure was building in her head, the same type of pressure she had experienced when they had first come near Phelistoth in that jungle. He could dampen his aura when he did not wish to be noticed—she could barely sense him when he was in human form—but the gold dragon had no reason to bother. He clearly wasn't worried about being noticed.

He's heading toward us, Jaxi said. *Toward Tylie, I think.*

"Duck," Ridge said. "Can you still hear me?"

"Yes, sir." Duck's voice sounded fainter than usual, but it came over the crystal clearly.

"The dragon might take special interest in you and your passenger."

"Uh?"

"Mostly your passenger. We're going to do our best to make it to the mines. You've never been out there, right? Stay on my tail."

One of Ridge's shoulders hitched as he dug into his pocket. He fished something out. From behind him, Sardelle could not see it, but she knew what it was, his lucky dragon charm. He slid his thumb over it, then glanced back and reached his hand over his shoulder.

"Want to rub my dragon?" he asked.

Sardelle smiled. She felt silly participating in his superstition, but she gave the wooden figurine a pat. "Always."

Ridge returned her smile as he tucked it back into his pocket.

The dragon came into sight, his huge winged figure appearing more brown than gold in the drab daylight, dulled by the thick clouds. His presence pressed against Sardelle like wind blowing at her from all directions. She couldn't believe the dragon had flown so many miles so quickly.

They're faster than the mechanical fliers, Jaxi said.

That's not good for us.

No.

Rain spattered the windshield in front of Ridge. Even nature was against them today.

"The coordinates you gave me are still fifty miles away, sir." Duck glanced back at Tylie.

"Then you'll have a good long time to admire my backside."

"I think that's more of an interest to Sardelle, sir."

"What are you saying, Duck? My allure doesn't have universal appeal?" Ridge dropped lower to skim across a lake. A flock of ducks protested and flapped out of the shallows.

"Yes, sir. No, sir. Should we be flying this *low*, sir?"

"Just follow." Ridge guided them up a river heading roughly east. The clouds had lowered, a thick mist coming in, and Sardelle couldn't see the mountains anymore, but she knew they were there. They had gotten closer, but as Duck had pointed out, the mining outpost was still nearly an hour away.

"Yes, sir."

The two fliers soared up the river, scaring more birds as they buzzed through, following the winding waterway. Maples and oaks lined the banks, their ancient limbs stretching outward, fresh young leaves offering camouflage, but only against opponents that relied upon eyesight. The dragon had disappeared from their view, but Sardelle doubted Morishtomaric would have any trouble finding them, despite Ridge's attempts to hide. Just in case it would help, she used her magic to muffle the sound of the propellers.

He's coasting around up there, Jaxi observed. *I think he's here for us, but he doesn't seem to be in a hurry to engage.*

Good. Why don't you tell him about the delicious elk that live in this forest?

It's been a long time since I've sampled the elk from this forest. I'd hate to promise him something that might not be true.

I think lying to the enemy is allowed as a legitimate war tactic.

Not when the enemy can melt you with his mind.

The river narrowed to a stream as the miles passed, though Sardelle barely noticed when Ridge left it to travel through a valley. Her gaze was riveted to the sky. She couldn't see the dragon, but sensed that he was closer than ever. Perhaps three miles away. He could cover that distance in seconds if he wanted to.

Wind gusted through the valley, and the flier wings shuddered. Heavy droplets of rain splashed Sardelle's face. The wings provided some protection from the weather, but not much. Before long, their clothes would be soaked.

Don't worry. You'll be warm soon enough. Jaxi finished her words with an image of a stream of flames shooting toward them.

Thanks for your— The dragon cruised into view, much closer than he had been before, and Sardelle forgot her words.

The flier had reached the end of the valley, and Ridge took them up, climbing into tree-covered foothills. They were getting closer to the Ice Blades, but not close enough. They must still have thirty or forty miles to the mines.

Massive, golden wings flapped lazily as the dragon turned to follow them. It kept up easily, then gained ground. Sardelle considered the terrain around them, searching for inspiration in the trees. Here and there lay a road or a hunting cabin with a moss-covered roof, but she didn't see anything that could be useful to them. She imagined throwing a gust of wind at the dragon, the way she had at the giant owl familiar that had attacked Ridge the last time she had been in these mountains, and laughed without humor. What would that do against a dragon?

She was going to have to try *something*, but she feared nothing she could do would matter.

Speak for yourself. I'm warming up for some pyrotechnics.

Good.

"Do we have a plan, sir?" Duck craned his neck to peer backward.

"Swoop through the trees." Ridge led by example. "We're smaller than he is. Should be able to maneuver in tighter spaces."

The dragon was less than a mile behind them. Tylie had sunk down deeper in her seat, so that only the top of her head was visible. It wouldn't matter. If the dragon wanted her, he knew exactly where she was. Still, Sardelle couldn't give her up without a fight.

As they swung through the treetops, branches skimming by inches above them, she sensed some of the wildlife she had mentioned earlier. Not elk, but deer. Maybe the dragon was hungry. Using her mind, she broke off a dead branch near the animals. Startled, they scattered, racing through a meadow where the dragon was sure to notice them.

Laughter filled Sardelle's mind, rattling around in her skull like a marble in a tin can. *Do you think you're dealing with a dumb animal, human?*

The voice carried such power that Sardelle's already existing headache elevated to throbbing pain. The dragon soared just above the forest, tracking them easily as the fliers weaved through the treetops. Ridge cut his route so close that Sardelle ended up with broken branches in her lap and leaves beating her face.

I know what I'm dealing with, Morishtomaric, Sardelle responded, even if it was a lie. Her only experience with dragon battles came from reading history books. When humans had won in those ancient battles, they'd had dragons on their side to help.

You know my name. The dragon sounded pleased, and like he expected nothing else.

Sardelle wished Phelistoth would show up to help them, but she assumed Morishtomaric would sense it if the other dragon got close. He didn't seem worried.

Actually, I think he might be out there, Jaxi said. *It's hard to sense anything with Behemoth Breath hogging up so much aura space out there, but I thought I caught another powerful entity at the edge of my range.*

There aren't that many dragons left. Sardelle directed her thoughts toward their pursuer. *It's easy to know the names of them.*

Is your strategy to make him angry? Jaxi asked.

I'm hoping he'll pine with loneliness so intense that he forgets about us.

Yes, that's definitely going to happen.

The dragon pumped his wings a few times and overtook the fliers. He sailed past Duck's craft and matched Ridge's speed. Sardelle braced herself to make a shield around them, even as she hoped her defenses could withstand the brunt of his attack.

Morishtomaric opened his jaws, and flames roiled out, an inferno of orange that shot straight toward the flier. Sardelle threw up her barrier as Ridge veered sharply to the right. She was flung sideways, the craft twisting onto its side to fit between two thick oaks.

Startled, she almost lost her concentration—and their shield. With Jaxi's help, she kept the barrier up. Ridge's wild flying took them away from the core of the attack, but flames still hammered into the back of her shield. Her invisible wall of energy deflected them, but more than fire lay behind the assault. Sheer power accompanied the flames, and it drained her strength far more than simple heat would. If the attack continued unabated, Sardelle wouldn't be able to keep the barrier up for long.

Fortunately, Ridge continued weaving and darting through the forest, and they escaped the attack. Behind them, trees burst into flame. Wood snapped and charred, and leaves went up in smoke.

"You going somewhere, Duck?" Ridge asked, his voice stern.

"To shoot that ugly—" The crystal cut out.

"Duck, just fly to evade. Unless Jaxi has something special up her sheath, I don't think we can do any damage."

Either Duck did not hear the order, or he chose to disobey it. Sardelle twisted in time to see his flier shoot out of the trees and veer toward the tail of the dragon.

What do you want with us? Sardelle asked, hoping Morishtomaric would focus on her instead of noticing the other flier.

I'm taking the girl. The voice sounded smug. He knew they had no way to harm him.

Why?

Ridge left the trees, looked toward the mountains, then grumbled something and turned back toward Duck.

She pleases me.

Tell Tylie to stop being so pleasing, Jaxi advised.

Machine guns opened up in the distance. Duck had found a spot he liked, sailing right toward the dragon's backside. Bullets pinged into the giant creature's scales and bounced off, as if they had struck a metal wall.

Why? Sardelle asked, speaking quickly. Morishtomaric was banking, turning to address the other flier. *She's just a human, like the rest of us. She can't be of any use to you.*

Duck stuck to the dragon, staying behind that tail. He knew better than to let that smoking snout point at him, but that hardly mattered. The dragon could attack with his mind as easily as he could with his maw. Duck kept firing, but Morishtomaric gave no indication that the bullets hurt him, or that he even felt them.

Sardelle? Tylie whispered into her mind. *What do I do? I tried to make him go away, but it won't work.*

I'm having the same problem. Wall off your mind, the way I showed you, so he doesn't know your thoughts. We're coming to help.

As Ridge took them closer, Duck stuck to the dragon. He kept firing, but he was like a mosquito buzzing around a wolf, unable to bother the creature through its defenses.

At first, Sardelle was pleased that the dragon didn't seem to be able to turn quickly enough to face Duck and Tylie, but then the tail lashed out. It had been streaming behind the creature, but it snapped toward Duck's flier so quickly, Sardelle barely had time to react. More on instinct than conscious thought, she threw up a barrier around the other flier. At this distance, it wouldn't be as strong as one she could craft around herself, but she held her breath, hoping it would keep the blow from landing.

Duck dipped below the tail, but he would have been too late. The sinewy appendage snapped toward his head. At the last second, it thumped off Sardelle's barrier. The physical blow wasn't as energy-draining as the magic-fueled flames, and her shield held. Duck flew away, the craft undamaged.

Before Sardelle could exhale with relief, an invisible force struck Duck's flier. The craft was thrown sideways, rolling several times as it spun out of control toward the treetops. The propeller sputtered. Had the crystal been damaged?

Ridge was close enough to fire at the dragon now. "Look at us, you bastard," he growled as he unleashed bullets.

Sardelle wrapped her shield around Duck's flier, cushioning it, this time from the treetops instead of the attacks. Duck's face was twisted in a rictus of concentration as he struggled with the flight stick. The rolls slowed, but Sardelle did not know if he would be able to regain control of the craft. What if it had been too badly damaged?

As Ridge flew closer to the dragon, aiming for its eyes with his bullets, Sardelle found Jaxi in her hand, though she did not remember drawing the blade. Jaxi flared to life, glowing red, then shooting out a crimson beam of energy. She, too, aimed for Morishtomaric's face. For good or ill, the attacks got his attention.

"Duck?" Ridge asked. "Can you hear me? Can you get out of here? Head for the mountain."

"Yes, sir, but I can't leave you." Duck had righted his flier, but it flew with a hitch, like a fishing bobber being tugged at from below.

"You can't do any good. Get out of here. Get to the mountains. See if Tylie can look for a cave, a small cave." *Can she do that?* Ridge added to Sardelle.

Maybe. She didn't have time to explain Tylie's current list of capabilities.

Sardelle let her shield around Duck's flier fade as it limped away—she and Ridge would soon need that protection for themselves.

Jaxi's beam should have burned into the dragon's eyes, but Morishtomaric had shields of his own. Unlike the bullets, Jaxi's power must have been more of a threat, since he addressed it instead of ignoring it. His shield, an invisible barrier similar to Sardelle's, deflected the attack. The beam shot back toward them. Sardelle gasped, and she felt Ridge's alarm, too, as he flew abruptly upward. Jaxi stopped the attack before the beam reached them.

Silly humans, the dragon said, sounding bored. *You amuse me. But I will have the girl now.*

Sweat dripped down the sides of Sardelle's face, her head felt like someone had been beating her skull with a cast-iron pot, and their adversary was bored. Not comforting.

There's nothing in the terrain to help, Jaxi said, firing another beam at the dragon as Ridge took them past it at an angle. *Maybe in the mountains we can do more. Drop some giant boulders on his head.*

I like Ridge's idea of hiding in a cave, Sardelle replied as the flier circled to follow the dragon, who was taking off after Duck and Tylie again, not bothering to respond to another attack from Jaxi. Why bother? Once again her beam glanced off the creature's shield. This time, Jaxi angled it so that it couldn't streak back toward them, or maybe that was a result of Ridge's flying.

That's because you're still trying to find a way to get cloistered alone with him.

Ignoring the bullets and the beams of energy, Morishtomaric continued after the other flier, picking up speed as his great wings beat at the air. Cursing, Ridge gave chase, but they soon fell behind.

I can't believe he doesn't feel that, Jaxi grumbled. *I've melted through vaults and pyramids with that energy.*

Sardelle sighed. *Our magic is no match for his. We have to outsmart him.*

How?

I haven't figured that out yet.

Sardelle? Tylie's fear came through the telepathic link, and even without seeing her, Sardelle knew that tears leaked from her eyes. *I don't know what to do. I— Never mind.*

When the contact broke, Sardelle straightened in her seat, trying to see past Ridge, past the dragon, and through the wings of Duck's flier. In the end, she needed to use her senses to tell what was going on. Tylie had unfastened her harness and was rising in her seat. She peered over the side, toward the trees blurring past below.

Don't, Sardelle warned. As far as she knew, Tylie had no way to shield herself from a fall or soften her landing. These trees were tall, forcing them to fly more than two hundred feet above the ground. She would never survive the drop. *Tylie, stop.*

He wants me, not you or Duck. Tylie lifted her leg over the side, though she struggled to find the balance to do so, with the flier hiccuping along.

"Duck," Ridge said, "don't you dare let her jump out."

Duck glanced back, his eyes widening, as he saw Tylie and how close the dragon was to their tail.

Stop! This time, the cry was not Sardelle's. It boomed into her mind—into everyone's mind, judging by the way Ridge winced. Tylie halted, straddling the side of the flier, one leg in the seat and one dangling over the side.

Morishtomaric looked to the side, and Sardelle couldn't help but look too. The voice had come from that direction.

Phelistoth, a gray arrow as he streaked down from the clouds, aimed straight at the gold dragon.

No, Tylie cried with her mind, *he'll kill you.*

Stay, Phelistoth ordered. Neither was bothering to pinpoint their communications to each other.

Morishtomaric did not appear worried by the silver dragon plummeting toward him, gravity and momentum adding speed. He blew fire at Duck's flier again. Sardelle threw up her hand, creating her barrier once again, though she worried the distance and her growing fatigue would make it ineffective.

Ridge fired his machine guns. He had to be careful of the angle—anything that bounced off could hit them. Sardelle didn't know why he bothered when the bullets did nothing. Because there was nothing else to do and he felt helpless, she supposed. As flames slammed into her barrier, she groaned in pain, understanding perfectly that helplessness. The fire chewed into her barrier like an incinerator melting an ice cube.

Duck dipped down toward the trees, clearly aware of the inferno trying to swallow them from behind. Tylie looked back at the dragons, one of her legs still dangling over the side.

Get back in, Sardelle warned her, tempted to nudge her mentally to force her to do so, but she was too busy keeping that barrier up. She could feel Jaxi channeling her energy into it, as well, making the ice cube last a little longer.

Phelistoth, the silver arrow from the gray skies, slammed into Morishtomaric's side. Claws sank into scale, and the two dragons rolled side over side, raking and biting like alley cats in a fray. A fray two hundred feet above the ground.

The stream of flames disappeared, but Duck continued whipping evasively through the treetops. He hadn't seen the dragons engage behind him. Ridge lifted the nose of his flier, taking them over the battle, where the dragons were starting to fall as they clawed and bit, their tails thrashing at each other. For a few seconds, Sardelle didn't have Duck's flier within view.

Phel! Tylie's anguished cry sounded in everyone's minds.

Ridge cursed again, tilting his flier toward the trees. Tylie was falling. He would never make it in time.

Almost dropping Jaxi, Sardelle gripped the edge of her seat with both hands, closed her eyes, and found Tylie with her mind. With her waning energy, she gathered air beneath her flailing target, forcing herself to remain calm, to take her time and do it right. That was easier thought than done as Tylie plummeted toward the ground, smacking leaves and being clawed by branches on the way down. Sardelle thickened the air under her into a dense column. Tylie slowed, then stopped five feet from the ground. Carefully, Sardelle set her down.

When she released her magic, she slumped back in her seat. She was panting, her breaths sounding loud and hoarse in her own ears. Her collar and shirt stuck to her skin, as wet from her own sweat as from the rain.

Ridge might not want to cloister himself with you tonight, Jaxi observed.

Sardelle was too exhausted to do more than glare at her.

Sorry. You did well. It's hard keeping teenagers alive, I hear.

"Sardelle?" Ridge asked. They were still flying, and Sardelle tried to rouse herself enough to pay attention to the situation. "Is there any chance…" He looked back at her, his face grim. "I can't see anything or get down there. Too tight. Did she—"

"She's alive," Sardelle said. Her head hurt too much for telepathy.

I'll tell her to run to a clearing where we can get her. The dragon fight isn't going to last for long. Phelistoth is getting clawed to pieces.

Sardelle relayed Jaxi's message to Ridge, both of them. For a moment, he'd worn an expression of relief, at hearing that Tylie lived, but the grimness soon returned.

"Understood," was all he said.

Chapter 5

Tolemek left a couple of dragon-blood experiments running in the laboratory that he had set up on the airship and walked out onto the deck to get some air. In truth, it wasn't the *air* that interested him. He hadn't seen much of Cas since they left, and he hoped to find her. To ask her what in all the levels of hell she had been thinking in volunteering to carry that cursed sword again. She hadn't yet recovered from what it had made her do the *last* time she had held it. Maybe she never would. Yes, it was nestled in its special box, the box he and Zirkander had found under Colonel Therrik's bed the night they had been spying, but Tolemek did not trust that to dull its influence completely.

He must have been grumbling his thoughts aloud as he walked, because several of the soldiers—artillery and airship crew—glanced at him when they passed by. He forced himself to wipe away his glower. Few of them knew him as anything other than Deathmaker, the ex-Cofah soldier and ex-pirate who had been responsible for far more deaths than Cas would ever claim. Even though everyone knew he now researched for King Angulus, he'd run into quite a few Iskandians who would happily help him accidentally fall over the railing of the airship.

Tolemek slowed his pace as he neared the open section of deck that held two fliers, the bronze dragon-inspired craft with their painted fang-filled "snouts" quite laughable now that he'd seen a real dragon. He hoped he might find Cas working near them, loading the machine guns or helping with some bit of maintenance. He had glimpsed her in the area earlier, back in her military uniform, albeit with the rank removed. Her hair had been freshly cut, and she had carried her Mark 500 sniper rifle on her back. It had seemed right for her, reminding him of when they had first met. Oh, she hadn't been wearing her uniform or weapons then, not as a prisoner of war in a Cofah dungeon, but she had been every bit the confident and competent soldier, the woman with whom he had, against all wisdom, fallen in love.

Unfortunately, he didn't see her by the fliers now. A pimple-faced young man was doing maintenance there instead, painting scratches near the nose of one of the craft. Tolemek did not know him, but he wore the Wolf Squadron wolf-head pin on his uniform, along with flier wings and a lieutenant's rank on his collar. Tolemek frowned slightly at the man's youth, imagining him flying Cas up to fight the dragon if Zirkander did not return in time. How much experience could this pup have? As much as Zirkander rubbed Tolemek's fur the wrong way at times, he couldn't deny the general's skill. If Cas had to go out for an air battle with a dragon, Tolemek wanted Zirkander to be the one flying her.

He walked up behind the young officer, about to ask if he knew where Cas was, but two mechanics strolled past the front of the fliers, and one of them addressed him first.

"You missed a few spots, Pimples." A sergeant carrying a toolbox pointed a wrench at a scratch on the nose. "The flier's not supposed to look like your face."

The young man flushed red. "That's *Lieutenant* Pimples, Sergeant."

The sergeant had at least ten years on the lieutenant and waved the wrench dismissively as he and his comrade continued past. The lieutenant's shoulders slumped. He must have been in his early twenties, but he seemed barely older than Tylie. Tolemek wondered why he had been chosen for the mission.

The lieutenant walked toward the railing. Tolemek followed him, but paused when he saw him approaching General Ort. Unless visiting his kitchen in the middle of the night counted, Tolemek had not interacted with the officer, and he hesitated to walk up unannounced. For all he knew, Ort shared some of Colonel Therrik's prejudices about magic—and those who could wield it.

"Sir," Lieutenant Pimples asked, "should I *do* something when they disrespect... an officer?"

General Ort had been staring pensively over the railing at the farmlands plodding past below and might not have heard the "disrespect," but he faced the younger man now. "You have to earn their respect."

"But they don't even know me. The dirigibles have their own hangars, and I've barely seen them before. It's one thing when Wolf Squadron harasses me—I'm used to that—but..." He shrugged his shoulders helplessly.

Tolemek supposed he should back up. He shouldn't be eavesdropping on the conversation, and he didn't care that much about the lieutenant's problems. He just wanted to find Cas.

"I don't know why we have to get such embarrassing nicknames," Pimples said. "Not everybody does. Ahn gets to be Raptor. And what about Blazer? And Crash? Well, Crash probably isn't that flattering, but I don't get why we all can't get respectful names when we're up there risking our lives."

Tolemek's resolve to back away faded at the mention of Cas's name, his curiosity roused as he wondered if they would speak about her and what they might say.

"It's part of being accepted into the squadron," Ort said. "You should know that. There are more embarrassing nicknames than not, I believe. I don't think anyone dared peg Raptor with anything too unflattering, given who her father is. Also, she was one of the rare ones who performed admirably—more than admirably—on her first mission. She utterly destroyed four gunners on a pirate airship by herself, as I recall. Most people flub things early on, when their nerves get the best of them. Takes a while to grow out of that. Just be pleased you survived your early missions. Not everybody does."

"I suppose. I've always wondered... how come General Zirkander doesn't have a nickname, sir? Was he like Raptor? Too good to mock?"

General Ort snorted.

Tolemek leaned his shoulder against the flier. It might have been Cas's name that had kept him here eavesdropping, but he wouldn't mind some ammo to use against Zirkander at an appropriate moment.

"Let's just say," Ort said, "that he's relieved that everyone who knew it has retired, passed away, or transferred out of a flight unit."

"Oh, let's say more than that, sir. Please? *You* know it."

"Yes, and it's a shame he doesn't go by it anymore." General Ort had struck Tolemek as a serious officer, not someone who made jokes or found much amusing in life, but he sounded like his eyes were gleaming now.

"What is it?"

"Don't you have some paint left to apply, Lieutenant?"

Tolemek frowned, almost as disappointed as Pimples, no doubt. Sardelle had tried to teach him a few techniques for telepathic communication and sensing other people's thoughts, but he didn't know enough to try and read whatever Ort was thinking about yet. The king kept him too busy with his other research, the work where his talents flowed out naturally without conscious thought.

"Aw, sir. If you tell me, I won't tell anyone else. And I'll paint the scratches on your flier too. And oil the seat. And wipe down the control panel. And I'll bring you lunch."

"Weren't you going to do that anyway?" Ort asked.

"Uhm. Maybe not the lunch part."

"I see. Since you've made such a magnanimous offer, it would be rude of me not to accept it." Ort lowered his voice and leaned close to Pimples.

Tolemek leaned around the nose of the plane, afraid he wouldn't hear. He needn't have worried. Pimples repeated the whispered word loudly and incredulously.

"*Puddles?*"

"Yes. I wasn't stationed anywhere near the capital back then, but it's in his records. Apparently, he was more scared than a dog in a thunderstorm when he took off on his first real assignment, and it was a killer. Cofah military disguising themselves as a ragtag band of pirates harassing the northern coast. They had four times the numbers and weapons than intel had led our men to believe.

Half the squadron didn't make it back. Ridge was probably hoping nobody would notice that he'd had a small accident at some point during the sheer terror of that battle, but we had khaki uniforms back then. Dark spots were quite noticeable."

"He *peed* on himself?" Pimple asked.

"Puddles stuck for a long time afterward. It wasn't until he took command of Wolf Squadron that he managed to stamp it out."

"Sir, that is the most wonderful thing I've heard."

"Good. I'll expect extra pickles on my sandwich. And coffee. Black."

"Yes, sir."

A finger poked Tolemek in the back, and he jumped, whirling.

"Looking for someone?" Cas asked, lowering her arm.

Even though she was a foot shorter than he and looked more curious than stern, he couldn't help but feel guilty. He was fairly certain that fearsome ex-pirates and research scientists appointed by the crown were supposed to be above eavesdropping.

"Yes." He leaned a hand casually against the flier. "You."

Lieutenant Pimples jogged past on his lunch-acquisition errand, pausing to look at them. And to wonder how long Tolemek had been standing there? No, he barely glanced at Tolemek. Instead, he gave Cas a quick, shy smile.

"Pimples," Cas said by way of greeting, her tone neutral.

"Good to have you back, Raptor." Pimples saluted her, his smile broadening, then he ran off.

An admirer, was he? Tolemek hoped he had nothing to worry about from a gangly insecure kid named after the pockmarks on his face.

"I was hoping to talk to you today," Tolemek said. About the sword, he almost said, but there was a tenseness about her eyes, an expression that had grown familiar of late, and he doubted she wanted to be questioned on her decision. "About coming up with a weapon that might work against dragons," he said instead. He would be happy to talk to her about his experiments, thus making the statement not quite a lie. And maybe he would bring up the sword at the end.

"Oh. All right."

Aware of the general standing by the railing, Tolemek asked, "Do you want to see my new lab?" He believed he would get more honesty from her if they spoke in private. Then he doubted the decision, wondering if she would think he wanted to get her back there for sex. The lab *did* have a bunk in the corner, but he'd gotten the message from their recent encounters that she didn't want anything to do with anyone, physically or emotionally. "The king must expect miracles, because he gave me some fancy new equipment." There, that addition should make the request seem innocent.

And it was. He didn't want to trick her into anything, except explaining her reasoning with the sword. It was probably too late to change her mind about being the one to wield it, but it might not be. Captain Kaika was on the airship, too, and she'd said she would accept the responsibility if the king wished it. Tolemek didn't want anyone to wield that monster, but he hated the idea of Cas doing it again. What if she *did* lose control, magical phrases notwithstanding, and the sword made her kill Sardelle? Or slice Zirkander's head off while he was flying her? That would destroy her even more surely than killing Apex had.

Cas smiled faintly. "Have you been making ice cream again?"

"Not yet, but I could."

She waved toward the nearest hatchway that led below decks, and he took the lead. They passed soldiers lugging up shells for the big artillery weapons mounted at intervals around the deck. Tolemek doubted they would bring down a dragon. He had more hope for his own work. If he came up with something—and he was trying to, based on the same acid he had created to destroy the dragon blood powering the Cofah fortress—Cas wouldn't need to risk herself with the sword. Besides, he found the idea of fighting a dragon with a sword ludicrous. Even with a flier, how would a person ever get close enough to hit it?

Tolemek ducked through the low hatchway and invited Cas inside. She wrinkled her nose at the chemical scent, or maybe she was noticing that there weren't any chairs. He usually stood up when he worked, so he had barely noticed that the bed was the only place to sit. Maybe if he moved some of the gels he had running, they could sit on the counters. He eyed the low ceiling. If he hunched.

Cas did not comment on the lack of seating. She walked past the counters to the inner bulkhead that held the built-in bed and sat on it. She leaned her elbows on her thighs, clasped her hands together, and looked up at him. Her expression made his heart ache. Usually, she seemed older than her twenty-three years, serious rather than playful, confident rather than uncertain. For the first time, she appeared younger than her age, small and lost.

"What is it?" he asked quietly, sitting and mirroring her position on the opposite end of the bed.

"I thought I wanted to be alone, that it would be torment being on the airship and surrounded by so many people again, but with that sword here… I'm afraid of being alone. It's like I can feel it, the way Sardelle says she can feel magic. It makes my skin crawl, and I can't stop thinking about everything, reliving that day. Over and over. If I close my eyes, I see it, the queen, the explosion, the floor falling away. Apex's death."

"Cas." Tolemek wanted to reach out and pull her into his arms, but she still had her hands clasped, her shoulders hunched, as she stared at the floor between her boots. "Why did you volunteer to deal with it again?"

"If something happens…" She flexed her hands, her gaze shifting to her palms. "I didn't want anyone else to have to have anyone's blood on their hands. Not a friend's blood."

"So you're going to sacrifice yourself?" he asked, feeling incredulous. *That* was what had prompted her decision?

"You can't sacrifice someone who's already dead."

"You're *not* dead."

"Part of me is," she whispered. "And the rest… it's not fair, is it? When fate spares one life and takes another without any weight given to who might deserve life more?"

Tolemek scowled, both at the idea that she believed she was condemning herself to more blood on her hands and at the idea that Apex's life might have been worth more than hers. "It's *not* fair, but you can't blame yourself for being the one who survived."

"No? Not even when the person who died did so by my hand?"

"Not when a magical blade guided that hand, no."

"I picked that sword up. I knew it was… strange, but I didn't hurl it into the sea, like I should have."

"You didn't know. You should blame the asshole who made such an idiotic weapon in the first place. Some thousand-year-old version of me who didn't think through what he was creating and ended up making something that could kill friends as well as enemies."

For the first time, Cas looked over at him. Yes, she wasn't the only one who'd had innocent people die because of choices she had made. She should blame him for his past every bit as much as she blamed herself for hers, but she never had.

"Why can you accept faults in others that you can't accept in yourself?" he asked softly, barely aware that he had spoken the words aloud.

"I don't know," she whispered back, her green eyes glistening with moisture. "It's a flaw."

He scooted closer. This time, he spread his arms to hug her without hesitating. She squinted her eyes shut and leaned into him, burying her face in his shoulder.

"It's a strength." He kissed her neck, then rested his face against her hair. "If you don't let it kill you."

"I'm afraid," she said into his shoulder. "I'm afraid it'll happen again. I'm afraid I made a mistake. But I can't take it back. I don't want anyone else to have to live with this."

He stroked the back of her head. "How about I come up with some mighty dragon-slaying concoction that doesn't kill friends and that will make it so you don't have to take that sword out of its box?"

"I'd appreciate that." For the first time, her voice held a hint of hope.

He closed his eyes, praying he could do what he was promising. He did *not* want to disappoint her, or see her hurt again.

"Good," he whispered. "I've missed being appreciated by you."

"I know. I'm sorry."

"Don't be. Just come by and murmur approvingly at my

formulas now and then."

She snorted and leaned back enough to look at his face. Some of those tears had made their way to her cheeks, leaving wet lines. Seeing that made his throat constrict with emotion, made him wish he could fix everything for her, but at least she wore a slight smile now.

"Even the strange glowing goos?" she asked.

"Especially them."

"All right."

He told himself to release her, that he needed to get back to work, so that he would *have* a dragon-slaying concoction by the time they found the dragon. But it had been weeks since she had smiled up at him like this.

"Cas, I—"

She slid her hand around to the back of his neck and leaned closer to kiss him. At first, he was so surprised that he merely sat there with his lips hanging open. But his body reacted even if his mind had forgotten what to do. He kissed her back, pulling her into his lap before he thought better of it. Having her arms around him, the warmth of her body against his, filled him with heat and desire. For the first time in a long time, she kissed him ardently, with passion he'd forgotten she had.

He might have happily pulled her back onto the bed with him, but his mind started working again, and he realized that her passion was because he had promised her a way to avoid the horrible fate she'd been expecting out here. If he came up with something and she didn't have to touch that sword, then he would deserve this, but not before then, not when he wasn't sure there was time to make anything. Maybe he had been foolish to speak so quickly, to get her hopes up. He hadn't expected it to lead to this, to something he'd forgotten just how much he wanted.

A timer dinged on the other side of the lab. If it hadn't, he might have found it impossible to pull himself away. But he had to check the results. For her.

"Cas," he whispered, forcing himself to remove his lips from hers.

"Mm?" Her fingers had drifted higher, and they curled into his scalp, sending shivers of delight through him.

"I want this—you—but I have to get back to work. Otherwise..."

She lowered her hands to his shoulders and leaned back. "I understand. Do you need any help?"

"I don't think so." Belatedly, he remembered that he had originally lured her back to his lab under the pretext of wanting advice.

One of her eyebrows twitched. "So you just wanted to check up on me?"

"I've been worried about you."

"Thanks."

His own brows did some twitching. He hadn't expected her to actually appreciate it, or that she would admit it if she did. She so rarely shared her feelings.

"You're welcome." He slid a hand through her soft hair again, then eased her aside and stood to check on his experiments.

"Tolemek?" Cas asked softly.

"Yes?"

"Do you mind if I stay here? The sword is in my cabin." Her lips twisted with displeasure.

"If you don't have any work you have to do, I *expect* you to stay here. How else would you murmur approvingly at my goos?"

She smiled again, and his heart soared. He had wondered if she would ever be able to do that again.

"Good," she said.

***

Ridge couldn't see the dragons anymore, but he did not allow himself to feel any relief, lest it be premature. Tylie, back in Duck's flier after quick apologies and an even quicker stop to pick her up, had promised him she would look for caves where they might hide. They were following the rocky cliffs and steep slopes of the Blades now, heading north and further east as he led them in the direction of the mines. Had the visibility been better, he might have seen Galmok Mountain in the distance, but they were still a couple of peaks away and flying slowly. Duck's battered craft could barely manage enough speed to keep them aloft. Ridge hoped the engineer he had worked with at the outpost was still stationed there.

There are a few caves on the southern face of that mountain up ahead, General Ridge. Tylie spoke quietly and tentatively into his mind.

He had never communicated with anyone except Jaxi and Sardelle this way, but he might as well get used to random voices in his head if he was going to spend so much time with budding magic users. Sooner or later, Tolemek would probably butt in too.

He looked back at Sardelle. Her eyes were closed, and he couldn't tell if she was sleeping—or unconscious.

She's not drooling, Jaxi informed him. *Just a light doze.*

Jaxi sounded tired enough to doze—and drool—herself.

Possibly so, but that would take creating condensation from the air, and that sounds like too much work right now. I suggest this cave. Jaxi flashed an image into his mind of a steep, scree-littered slope up ahead.

Ridge recognized the spot. He didn't know these mountains as well as the coast back home, but he had still flown through them on his way into and out of the mining outpost.

Are you sure it's necessary? Ridge asked. *We're less than twenty miles to the outpost.*

It's necessary, Jaxi said.

The dragon?

He beat up Phelistoth, left him for dead, and he's gaining ground on us again. I can sense him at the edge of my range.

"Follow me, Duck," Ridge said. "We're going to investigate a cave."

A long moment passed before Duck responded with a subdued, "Oh."

I guess he figured out why, Ridge thought. He hadn't wanted to say too much over the crystal, where Tylie could hear. Maybe she already knew Phelistoth had lost the battle, but if not, Ridge didn't want to be the one to tell her.

I think he'll recover eventually, Jaxi said. *If the gold doesn't go back for him. Dragons are good at healing themselves. Even if they don't use their magic, their wounds regenerate quickly. It's another reason why they're so tough to kill.*

As if Ridge and Duck had even been able to pierce the gold dragon's scales. He'd felt utterly useless out there, and he'd been cursing himself since the dragon first appeared in the sky. Why hadn't he demanded better weapons to take along? There had to be a weapon out there that would do *something*. After all, Angulus had a secret facility making bombs or rockets or whatever it was. But no, Ridge and everyone else had assumed that the ship that had a dragon-slaying sword and was actually looking for the dragon would be the one to find it. Why had he not suspected that he and Duck might chance across it? He hoped his message had gotten through to someone who had been able to relay it to General Ort.

The cave came into view, a slit in the rock-covered mountainside. Ridge would have to fly sideways to enter it. *Does it open up inside?* he asked, hoping either Jaxi or Tylie was still monitoring him. So long as they didn't monitor his mind at other, less mission-oriented times.

Such as when you and Sardelle are cloistered in your private room together? Jaxi asked.

Yes.

You're noisy enough in there that it doesn't take a telepath to figure out what you're doing.

We are not *noisy. Now, can you show me the cave interior, please?*

Whatever the general wants.

Jaxi shared a picture of the inside. The floor wasn't level, but with the thrusters, he thought they could land two fliers. Probably. It would be tricky.

"We're going in there, Duck. It won't be an easy landing. Let me go in first."

"Yes, sir, but you should know... I can see the dragon."

Ridge grimaced and glanced back. The mountainside was coming up quickly, so he couldn't take the time for a long look, but it was enough. The rain had stopped, and the sun was dropping toward the horizon below the clouds. Its red rays gleamed on the dragon's golden scales. The creature did not appear injured, at least not in any way that Ridge could see from here. There weren't any hitches in his powerful wing beats.

"Understood," he said, and tilted sideways for the approach.

Sardelle groaned.

"Headache?" he asked as they arrowed for the narrow cave entrance.

"Yes," she said, her voice croaking.

If she was talking instead of speaking telepathically, Ridge guessed it was because her head hurt too much to contemplate magic.

Good guess, Jaxi informed him.

"We'll land soon, and you can rest." Maybe. Ridge glanced back at the dragon again—it was flying fast and gaining on them quickly. "I'm heading in, Duck. Keep me updated on the dragon."

"Yes, sir."

His flier glided between the walls of the entrance. He cut the power to the propeller, though that was risky before the thrusters had been activated. He couldn't do that until they were upright again.

The inner chamber—and the back wall—came up quickly. He tilted the craft as he pulled the nose up, flicking the switches that ignited the thrusters. The energy crystal glowed as the power demand increased, and white light pulsed, illuminating the cave. Their forward momentum stopped a few feet from the back wall. There wasn't room to turn around or be choosy about landing spots. He just hoped Duck would be able to avoid him. The cave wasn't much wider than the wingspan of his flier.

"I'm in, Duck," Ridge said, "but I'm taking up a lot of space."

"Yes, sir. That's what generals do."

"Hope you're not implying that I've gained weight since my promotion." Ridge unbuckled his harness and stood in the cockpit. "I don't spend *that* many hours at a desk."

"Actually, I was thinking that you've been forgetting some meals," Sardelle said. "You need to let your mother fatten you up a bit."

"If Mom had her way, I'd be as round as that gray cat of hers."

"Which one?"

"All of them."

"Coming in, sir," Duck said, his voice tense.

Ridge hopped down from the cockpit, hoping he wasn't about to witness a crash. "Where's the dragon, Jaxi?"

The cave darkened as Duck's flier streaked into it. He was coming too fast. Ridge didn't need to see Duck's and Tylie's bulging eyes to know that.

"Sardelle," he blurted, wanting to tell her to jump down—or to do something magical to stop the crash—but there wasn't time for either.

Duck yanked up on his flight stick so hard that the tail of his flier scraped the floor of the cave. The wheels and thrusters filled Ridge's vision as the belly of the craft lifted toward him. Flames scorched the air in front of the cave entrance, but he was too busy skittering backward and lifting an arm to shield his face from the heat pouring out of the thrusters to notice.

The heat vanished abruptly, though the light remained. Ridge moved his arm so he could open an eye. The thruster jets were striking an invisible barrier, light and flame bending in midair. Then the thrusters went out, and the craft clunked to the ground. It was only inches from Ridge's flier.

He rubbed his face, aware of how close they had come to destroying both fliers and having to find a way to walk to the outpost, which might not be possible. These mountains were about as hospitable as that dragon, especially at this elevation.

"Thank you, Sardelle, Jaxi, or whoever stopped that crash," Ridge said. They would have to physically lift the fliers and rotate them around in order to fly out, but that was better than walking.

You're welcome, Jaxi thought.

The flames that had been blocking the view beyond the cave disappeared. Ridge imagined the dragon swinging around to make an attempt at flying inside or perhaps Morishtomaric might stand on the perch and roast them with flames. Ridge grimaced, feeling very trapped. Maybe he shouldn't have gone along with Jaxi's suggestion. Maybe they should have kept going and tried to reach the outpost before the dragon caught them.

He hopped up and pulled his rifle out of the cockpit. It wouldn't do a thing against Morishtomaric, but he felt better with it in his hands. Sardelle slid down beside him, her face grave as she turned toward the entrance. Duck was helping Tylie down while also staring at the entrance. She gasped in pain.

Remembering her fall, Ridge ran over to help. She'd been clubbed by a multitude of branches before Sardelle had managed to stop her descent.

To his surprise, she lurched toward him as soon as Duck lowered her from the cockpit. Her arms went around his shoulders, her legs curling up to her stomach, and Ridge nearly pitched over, surprised by her weight. After a moment, she dropped her legs to the ground, but did not otherwise release him. She cried into his shoulder, whether because she was in pain or because she thought her dragon had just died, he didn't know.

"Uhm." He struggled to get an arm free and hand his rifle to Duck, who seemed as surprised as he was. Then he attempted to pat her back consolingly, all too aware that he didn't have any experience with kids or how to comfort them. True, she was a little old for weeping inconsolably in a father's arms, and this wasn't exactly a good time for it, but he didn't know what else to do.

"Are there any women that you *don't* get, sir?" Duck smiled as he accepted the rifle, but it was a quick gesture. He focused on the cave entrance.

"Nobody's getting anybody." Ridge knew it had been a joke, but he scowled anyway at the idea that anyone would "get" Tylie. She was too young for that, in mind if not in body. "Is our crotchety friend still out there, Sardelle?"

"Yes." She came up behind him and rested a hand on his back.

Ridge wondered if he could foist Tylie on her. Women were good at comforting people, weren't they? "Tylie, Jaxi said Phelistoth was still alive and could probably heal himself."

She sobbed. "He didn't want to fight," she said, the words

barely distinguishable. "He came for me. Why'd he do that? And why won't he leave me alone?"

Ridge assumed the second he was the gold dragon, but it was hard to decipher anything Tylie said.

"What's he doing?" Duck fingered the trigger on Ridge's rifle as he watched the cave entrance. "He can't fit in here, right?"

Ridge wasn't so sure about that. It would be a tight fit, but unlike a flier, a dragon could fold its wings into its body. He eyed the sides of the cave, gauging whether there was any place for them to hide if Morishtomaric decided to pour in flames and turn this place into an oven.

"If he can't, he could shape-shift into human form," Sardelle said.

Ridge groaned. He had forgotten about that. "I don't suppose dragons are any easier to kill if they've changed into humans?"

I actually don't know the answer to that. Jaxi sounded shocked that there was a hole in her knowledge base.

Not shocked. Just surprised.

Surprised it wasn't covered in your dragon romance novels?

Jaxi glowered amazingly well, considering she had neither eyes nor a face.

"I don't know, either," Sardelle said. "I'm sure he would still be formidable."

The entrance darkened, something outside blocking out the daylight. Ridge pried Tylie's arms from around his neck and set her down, though it wasn't easy to get her to let go. Bruises and bloody scrapes marked her face, and he grimaced, feeling like a poor mission leader for letting her get hurt.

"Go hide behind the flier, please," he told her. He wished he had somewhere better to tell her to hide. That dragon fire could probably melt the fliers if Sardelle couldn't shield them, and he didn't know if she had the strength left to do so.

Tylie hid behind *him*.

Ridge grimaced again, wondering how he'd been designated the protector. He felt far too inept to take that role, but he put himself between her and the cave entrance.

You liked her ladybug, Jaxi suggested.

Is that *why? I didn't like it. I just told her to take it to the woods.*

I'm just guessing. I can't read her at all. She took quickly to guarding her thoughts.

A rumble came from somewhere above them. The ground shook.

"What now?" Ridge groaned, remembering the earthquakes in the king's secret facility. According to Angulus, those had been caused by Morishtomaric's pain. Ridge doubted the dragon was in any kind of pain this time.

Above them, deep within the rock, snaps sounded.

"Get back," Sardelle whispered. Her hand shifted to his arm, and she tugged him toward the back wall.

Trusting her, Ridge said, "You heard her, Duck."

He swooped Tylie over his shoulder and ran to the deepest part of the cave. Duck and Sardelle crowded into an alcove with them. The ground pitched, and Duck almost fell onto him. More rocks snapped, and a roar came from above them, or maybe from outside. The noise filled the cave, and it was too hard to tell.

Stay close, Sardelle ordered. *Everyone. Jaxi and I are making a shield to protect us.*

Can you protect the fliers too? Ridge hoped he wasn't asking too much, but he didn't know if they could get off this mountain without them.

And he thinks Tylie *is needy*, Jaxi thought.

I didn't think that. Ridge did his best to cover Tylie's and Sardelle's heads as rocks started falling. Barrier or not, he wasn't positive they wouldn't be in danger.

That was you *thinking that, Jaxi*, Sardelle thought. *Ridge was being fatherly.*

Fatherly. Hardly. He'd been thinking that a father might know what in the hells to do.

Ah, was that it? I knew someone *thought it—and wondered why Tolemek wasn't here to take care of his sister.*

Boulders tumbled past the cave entrance. One stuck, halving the light inside. Smaller rocks tumbled past, some falling inside, others bouncing away. The light grew dimmer and dimmer as the entrance filled with rubble. Despite the quaking, their roof wasn't falling, at least not yet. Dust and a few pebbles bounced off Sardelle's barrier, but nothing more substantial.

Are you doing that? Jaxi asked.

Thinking the question was for him, Ridge started to respond, but Sardelle said, *No. I thought you were.*

Not me.

What? Ridge asked.

Ssh. Jaxi said. *Don't talk for a minute. Or think. Any of you. And don't move. Don't make any noise.*

Ridge had no idea what they were talking about, but did as ordered. He tried to still his mind and think nothing of the rocks pounding down the slope outside, of the entrance filling the entire way and leaving them in darkness. The flier crystals had powered down, so not even they glowed to break up the blackness.

The sounds of the rockfall dwindled and stopped. The entrance remained blocked, but nothing had fallen within the cave itself. Ridge's back ached from the position he had crammed himself into, his arms over Sardelle and Tylie. Sardelle knelt, also with an arm around Tylie, who was huddled in a ball, with her hands over her ears. Duck was pressed against Ridge's side, standing utterly still, barely breathing. Jaxi's order must have been for all of them.

"He's leaving," Sardelle said.

"He just wanted to trap us?" Ridge asked. "I was expecting him to roast us to a crisp."

He wasn't trying to trap *us.* Jaxi's pommel started glowing, giving them some light. *He was trying to bury us and smash us into a thousand pieces. Tylie is muting our auras somehow. I believe the dragon thinks we're dead, and that's why he's leaving.*

"*Tylie?*" Ridge stared down at the girl balled up at his feet. He knew she could speak telepathically with Phelistoth and had been learning things from Sardelle and the dragon, but he wouldn't have expected her to be the one to save them. "What do you mean *somehow?*"

None of us taught her how to do it, Jaxi said. *She came up with the idea on her own too.*

"Thank you, Tylie," Sardelle murmured, resting a hand on her head.

Tylie looked up, her battered face streaked with tears. "I have to keep doing it until he flies out of range. He sensed me before from a long ways away."

Sardelle nodded. "Keep doing it as long as you have the strength. If he thinks you're dead, all the better. He won't come back for you again."

"I wish I'd figured out how to do it before. Then Phel wouldn't have been hurt."

"I don't suppose any of you can tell which direction the dragon went," Ridge said.

To the northeast, Jaxi said.

Ridge frowned.

"That's the direction of the mines, isn't it?" Sardelle asked.

"Maybe it's a coincidence," Duck said. "What's there that a dragon could want?"

"I don't know," Ridge said, "but I hope my message got back to base and that our dragon-hunting airship has been informed that their prey isn't where they think it is." He also hoped Therrik was alert up at the fort, not drinking himself unconscious, the way the officer who had commanded the fort before Ridge had been. Magroth wasn't friendly to soldiers or officers. "We better assume it didn't and make all possible haste to the mines."

Duck looked to the dark, rubble-filled entrance. "Sir, I find it hard to make haste through tons of rock."

"Jaxi?" Ridge gave a pat to Sardelle's sword scabbard, wondered if Jaxi liked pats, and asked, "Would you be able to melt those boulders or fling them away?"

I prefer having my blade oiled to being patted. By handsome young men with a nice touch.

"So if Duck rubs your blade, you'd melt those rocks for us? Because I can order him to do that."

Duck gave him a funny look. "I feel like I'm only hearing half of this conversation, but I'm not sure I want to hear the other half."

"Jaxi likes young men with good hands," Ridge said.

Young, handsome men, Jaxi thought. *Duck has big ears.*

"I promise I'll find someone suitable to your tastes." Ridge extended a hand toward the rubble. "Colonel Therrik likes swords."

Now you're just trying to annoy me.

"Did she reject me?" Duck asked. "I feel like the omega wolf that just had his pee covered by the alpha's pee."

Ridge should have known better than to speak aloud in a conversation with Jaxi. "Nah." He thumped Duck on the shoulder. "She just wasn't sure about your hands after witnessing that landing. Come on. Let's see how much rubble we're dealing with."

Approximately twenty feet, Jaxi said. *It's going to take me a while. Especially if you want to be able to get your fliers out of here.*

That would be ideal.

You might as well take a nap.

Sardelle slipped out of the alcove and found a place to lay Jaxi so she could aim a beam of energy at the rubble. Ridge did not like the idea of napping or standing uselessly around. If that dragon was heading toward Magroth, his team needed to get out of here as quickly as possible to help. Nobody else could get there in time. Magroth hadn't had a telegraph station when he'd been there, probably because nobody was supposed to know the remote outpost existed, and he doubted that had changed in the last few months.

After placing her sword, Sardelle stopped beside Ridge and clasped his hand. "Might as well rest. This will take a while. Jaxi was almost as depleted by the dragon as I was, and that's a lot of rock. Also, her energy beam uses oxygen, and she's concerned about burning up all of our air."

"I appreciate her concern. I'll have to find her *two* handsome young men to oil her." Ridge spread his arm, and Sardelle leaned against his chest. He pulled her into a hug and rested his chin on her head.

"I need to check on Tylie, heal her when I gather some energy."

From the way she was slumping against him, he wasn't sure if she should try. They had thrown everything they had at that dragon and hadn't even given it a hangnail. It didn't seem like Phelistoth had bothered it much, either, and that was alarming. Would Kasandral, a human-made sword, have the power to do more than another dragon?

When Sardelle didn't move and seemed on the verge of dozing off, Ridge looked over at Tylie. "I can get my first-aid kit out and patch her up until you're ready."

Tylie had been walking—and clinging to his shoulders—with minimal difficulty, so she couldn't have been too grievously injured, but she was clearly scared and might appreciate some attention. She was sitting with her back to the cave wall, her knees drawn up to her chest and her arms wrapped around her legs as she watched Jaxi. The sole lighting came from the soulblade, which now glowed an orangish-red. Jaxi had started to melt a hole in a large boulder, and the scent reminded him of the geysers outside of the Cofah volcano.

"I'll do it," Sardelle murmured, her head resting on his shoulder. "Just give me a minute."

He tried to exude energy for her to use, though he doubted it worked that way. He stroked her hair. She had it back in a braid. He liked it when she wore it down, but that wasn't practical for flying—or dragon fighting, he supposed. "This isn't quite the private room I had in mind for us for tonight."

"I knew that wouldn't happen."

"Oh?"

"I was fairly certain you would end up in a private room talking work with Therrik."

"Well, this might be an improvement over *that*, then."

She chuckled softly, kissed him, and walked over to sit next to Tylie and take her hand. Ridge thought wistfully of the last time he and Sardelle had been trapped in a cave together. That time, his men had been considerate enough to get trapped in their own caves. He supposed this was just as well. Sardelle would be too tired to roll around on a bumpy stone floor this time.

"I can stand guard, sir," Duck said. "If you want to get some sleep."

Ridge snorted to himself. Duck must have caught his longing

gaze toward the floor. No, sleep wasn't what was on his mind. It wasn't even dark out, as far as Ridge knew. More than anything, even floor-rolling, he wanted to get to the outpost.

"Thanks, but I think Jaxi will fry the nuts off anyone who tries to get in through the hole she's making. I'm going to check the fliers."

Chapter 6

Cas watched the snow-covered peaks of the Ice Blades growing on the dark horizon, the clouds and rain clearing as the night deepened. She doubted she would see a dragon out there amid the stars before Tolemek sensed it nearby, but one never knew. He was so busy with his experiments that he hadn't even noticed her slipping out of his lab. She couldn't resent that, not when he was working on a weapon to use against the dragon, a weapon that might keep her from having to take Kasandral out of the box. Her stomach twisted in knots at the thought of even unlatching the lid.

"This thing is slower than a slug at a slime-slicking race, isn't it?" Captain Kaika asked, ambling up to join her at the railing. She flicked a finger toward the dark ground, where fields and farmhouses had given way to forest. She wore a pistol and dagger on a utility belt full of pouches, and also carried a rifle slung across her back. A woman ready to face some trouble.

Knowing what that trouble entailed, Cas would prefer it waited until Tolemek came up with his weapon.

"A slime-slicking race?" she asked. "Did you get that expression from Lieutenant Duck?"

"Nope, but the fellow who used to say it all the time *was* from the backwoods. Don't think he was raised by wolves. Though he did *howl* like a wolf in bed." Kaika scratched her jaw. "I never could decide if that was flattering or off-putting. I don't mind the man having a good time, but I better be getting some joy too. Know what I mean?"

Cas decided it was a rhetorical question and that she didn't need to answer. She had no interest in discussing her joy, or sharing details of past partners' habits. Not that there had been that many. She did not lament that. She only cared about finding one person with whom to share… joy. She hoped that there would be time to make things right with Tolemek, to let him know that she cared. He made her laugh, and he understood, even when she wasn't sure she wanted to be understood.

"Is it true you're having joy with the king, ma'am?" a new voice asked from behind them. Cas hadn't heard Pimples' approach. He was also wearing all of his gear, and Cas wondered if she had missed a meeting about preparing for something.

"'Course not," Kaika told Pimples, then winked at Cas. "What'd the general say, Lieutenant?"

"He said no." Pimples flopped against the railing next to Cas.

She watched him warily. They had been in Wolf Squadron about the same length of time and had endured hazing from the veterans together, so she considered him a friend, but she hadn't been sure how to act around him since he had kissed her after she'd returned from being a prisoner in Cofahre. She hadn't thought she had ever flirted with him—she didn't even know *how* to flirt—or encouraged anything romantic, so that had surprised her as much as it had surprised the rest of the squadron, all of whom had been witnesses to the kiss.

"I even offered to take Raptor and her sword," Pimples said.

"What?" Cas faced him, a jolt of unease darting through her belly and all concerns about kisses fleeing her mind.

"The captain and I thought we could take a flier out and have a look around, try to locate our dragon. General Ort said not to go looking for dragons until we're ready to deal with them, specifically until Sardelle is with us." Pimples wrinkled his nose. He was close to twenty-five but could still have passed for fifteen, especially when he made silly faces.

Cas slumped against the railing, relieved Ort had turned him down. She did not want to go anywhere with that sword, and she agreed that it would be wiser to wait until Sardelle and Zirkander caught up with them.

"Are we just going to go hover over the old weapons facility and wait for them to join us then?" Kaika drummed her fingers on her holster.

"Guess so," Pimples said. "I don't see why we couldn't try to find where that dragon is hiding."

"If you find him, you could end up dead," Cas said.

"We wouldn't fight him by ourselves. Just find him, then turn around and come back."

"What if he gave chase and you couldn't *make* it back?"

"Our fliers can go eighty miles an hour. There's no way a dragon can outfly us."

"You don't think so? I wouldn't take that bet." Cas had never seen Phelistoth fly at full speed, but she remembered him soaring away from Owanu Owanus with Tylie on his back. His speed had been comparable to a flier, and he hadn't appeared to be trying that hard.

"Oh really?" Pimples asked. "How fast can they go?"

"Phelistoth has never run sprints for me so I can clock him."

"You call him by name? Have you *talked* to him? What's he like?"

Kaika turned a curious eye toward her at the question. Cas hadn't interacted with the dragon since he had returned, so she didn't truly know. She also hadn't spoken to Sardelle or General Zirkander much lately. They would be the ones who could answer this question. Her only impression of Phelistoth came from the pyramid. He had seemed big, scary, and powerful, even when sick. And he hadn't been pleased to have Iskandians crawling all around him.

"I don't—"

A boom sounded in the distance, somewhere ahead of the airship. Kaika gripped the railing and stared toward the mountains.

"Was that a gun?" Pimples peered over the railing toward the forest instead of outward.

Cas shook her head. That had definitely come from the mountains and from an elevated position.

"No," Kaika said. "Explosive. Shh." She held up a finger and listened intently.

Cas and Pimples stopped talking, but there was other activity on the deck, a soldier scrubbing the barrel of one of the big guns, someone below shouting for more coal for the furnaces, the creak and groan of the thick steel cables that tethered the craft to the oblong balloon overhead. When the second distant boom came, Cas couldn't pinpoint the source any better than she had with the first. It *was* an explosion, though. She agreed with that assessment.

"Did you hear that second lesser echo?" Kaika asked, still staring ahead, toward the mountains. "That's a Tiger-10, I'm sure of it."

She thumped her fists on the railing, spun, and raced in the direction Pimples had come from.

"What's a Tiger-10?" Pimples asked.

"Tigers are a line of Cofah explosives." Cas only knew because she'd had some thrown at her. "Were we expecting any Cofah out here?" She had only been told about the dragon, but she'd arrived late to that meeting in the king's office.

Pimples shrugged. "Nobody's told me anything. I'm not even sure why I'm here, instead of one of the more experienced pilots. Probably because I'm expendable."

Cas frowned at him. "I'm sure that's not it. Did someone say that?" Her hackles bristled at the thought of someone picking on him. Hazing was tradition in the flier squadrons, but calling someone expendable would be going too far.

"Nah, I just know I don't get that many kills. I'm not anyone who gets picked for special missions usually. Not like you." Pimples smiled sadly at her. The gesture did not seem to hold bitterness or envy. No, his words usually didn't. Just self-deprecation.

"You've never crashed, either, nor been hit by anything but a glancing shot off a wing here and there," Cas said, reasoning aloud as she considered why he might have been chosen. Had Zirkander picked him? Or Ort? "You're squirrelly up there. And you can do calculations in your head. Most of us carry a pen and notebook jammed in our flight suit pocket."

"I do too. That's part of the uniform."

"Yeah, but you're not plotting vectors to solve wind correction problems like the rest of us. You use yours to draw house plans."

"True." He smiled wistfully. "Want to see my latest? It's two stories. With a tower!"

"How're you going to pick one design when you actually save enough money to build a house?"

"Aw, I'll never have enough. Not unless I put my house way out in the country and build it all by myself."

"I think that's what General Zirkander did with his cabin. A place to get away from his legions of fans."

"I don't have fans. Or that many friends. Nothing to escape from."

Cas waffled between telling him to quit being morose and giving him a sympathetic nod—it wasn't as if she was good at making friends, either. Before she had decided which to do, Kaika came thudding across the deck toward them, a bag slung over her shoulder. Other soldiers were spilling out of a hatchway behind her, heading toward the big shell guns. A corporal with a spyglass raced for the crow's nest attached to the front of the ship between the deck and balloon.

"We're going out," Kaika announced with a grin. "Pimples, you're flying me. General Ort himself is taking you out, Ahn."

"Taking me out?" Cas mouthed the words, sure she had heard incorrectly. "I don't need anyone to take me. Those are Wolf Squadron fliers."

Her first thought was that this had to do with her resignation, that Ort didn't trust her to fly a military craft anymore. But the king himself had sent her along to help, and it hadn't been that long since she'd been in the air. She was still qualified, even if she wasn't officially an officer anymore. Just a month before, she had performed well in the battle with the flying fortress. She'd even tried to save Zirkander from falling to his death. It wasn't her fault that he'd decided to wait and jump into the cockpit with some Cofah pilot instead.

"Yeah, but you're taking the sword. The general must have figured you'd have a hard time waving that around while piloting."

"The sword? To deal with someone tossing explosives?" Cas took a step toward the hatchway. She needed to talk to General

Ort, to see what he was thinking. This didn't make any sense.

"To deal with a *sorceress* tossing explosives," Kaika said.

Cas halted. "What?"

"We don't know she's out there, but she was the source of the trouble when I was here two weeks ago. Same area. She was making fliers invisible, fliers that we later learned had been sent to pick up Cofah operatives tunneling around in the hills down there. They were stealing electricity from the king's secret facility and trying to blow up a bunch of dragons like the one that got out and has been burning the countryside." Kaika laid a hand on Cas's arm, her face bleak. "She was doing more than hiding fliers. She threw a big ball of fire, the same kind we dealt with at the fortress battle, and it incinerated my C.O. and one of your pilots. Colonel Troskar."

Cas stared at her, then toward the dark mountains looming closer. Colonel Troskar had died? She had missed so much in the last month.

Kaika released her arm. "I've been to far too many funerals in the last few weeks. We're all hoping, the king included, that you and that sword can kill the sorceress as well as the dragon."

Cas winced at the mention of funerals. She hadn't gone to Apex's. She had been too afraid, too horrified to face his friends and family—to see him waiting to be buried. She had wanted to wish him well in the afterlife, but she'd been his murderer. How could she have gone?

"I thought it just slew dragons," Pimples said.

Cas shook her head slowly, remembering how it had compelled her to swing at Sardelle and how it had made her resent Tolemek too. She thought of the kiss they had shared just a few hours ago. She didn't *want* to resent him, especially not now. She had just gotten comfortable with the idea of caring about something—*someone*—again.

"It loathes anyone with dragon blood in their veins," Cas said.

"Ahn, Pimples, Kaika," came General Ort's call from across the deck. He stood next to Major Cildark, the airship commander. "Get your gear. We're going in two minutes."

Feeling numb, Cas forced herself into a jog, a jog that would take her below decks to her cabin, to where that box waited. "I hope General Ort doesn't have any dragon blood in his veins," she muttered.

* * *

Cas sat in the back of the flier with her cap and goggles on, feeling useless as she alternated between searching the sky ahead and staring at the back of General Ort's head. His cap and scarf hid his gray hair, but she couldn't help but feel odd at having a general flying her around. Her rifle rested in her lap, and she had her legs squeezed around the heavy sword case, both weapons reminding her why she was in the back instead of piloting. She wasn't here to fly; she was here to kill. Her stomach soured at the thought, but wasn't that exactly what she had been planning for her new career? Better to take out an enemy sorceress in service to her country than some target her father assigned her for pay.

She thought of Tolemek. He ought to be safe up here on the military airship, but what would happen once they returned to the capital? How could he avoid her father? And what was the solution? To kill her father? Why was death the solution to every equation she ran lately?

"Nothing in sight yet, sir," Pimples reported over the communication crystal.

He was flying to the side of Ort, and Kaika was anything but a still passenger behind him. She kept leaning over the sides and rising up to peer over his head.

"No, and I can't hear any explosions over the noise of my propeller," General Ort said.

Cas had nothing to add, but once again, she noted how strange it was being a passenger and not having access to the crystal. She would have to lean over Ort's shoulder if she wanted to be heard, and that would be uncomfortable. One didn't *lean* on generals.

"I still hear them here," Major Cildark said. "They're right over that southern peak."

Cas hadn't realized the airship had a crystal, too, but it made sense.

"Deathmaker's with me," Cildark added. "He says that's where the secret facility was. He thinks the Cofah might not realize it's been moved and that they're late sneaking forces over here to destroy it."

Cas hadn't had a chance to say goodbye to Tolemek—there had only been time to grab her weapons and flight jacket. She regretted that and hoped nothing happened that would make her regret it more.

"They could also be there to destroy the chamber of imprisoned dragons," General Ort said.

"To what end?" Cildark asked.

"To ensure Iskandia isn't able to free the dragons and turn them into allies."

"I suppose it's possible, sir, but the one that got out hasn't proven itself much of an ally. We wouldn't be hunting it otherwise."

"I would wager they were sent to destroy the research facility," Tolemek said, and Cas leaned in so she wouldn't miss hearing his voice. For a silly second, she thought of leaning forward and telling him to be careful or that she loved him, but this was hardly the place for that, not when everyone could hear this channel, and she would have to yell the words past General Ort's ear. "Now that I've seen some of what Angulus's people were constructing in there," Tolemek continued, "I can assure you that my—that the Cofah would want the weapons destroyed. Desperately."

Once again, Cas felt as if she had missed much by skulking in the shadows this last month.

A red flash appeared in the distance, about halfway up the side of a dark mountain. They were close enough now that they could hear the rumble of falling rock even over the propellers.

Ort veered in that direction while maintaining a high elevation. Yes, that was what Cas would do. Try to attack from above. But she couldn't see anything in the air over where that flash had been.

"I have no knowledge of this facility, sir," Cildark said dryly.

"I know," Ort said. "It's top secret. Deathmaker should be keeping his lips tied."

Cas frowned at the back of Ort's head.

"It's been *moved*," Tolemek said. "It hardly matters if people know where it *was*. I shall say nothing of where it is now."

"Should I be upset that a former pirate knows top secret things that I don't know, sir?" Cildark asked.

"Not now," Ort said. "Just keep up with us the best you can. If the sorceress is involved, know that she likes to keep her people invisible, so we could be fighting with blindfolds on out here. We'll need all the help we can get."

"Yes, sir."

"I think it's a certainty that magic is involved, sirs," Pimples said. "Otherwise, we would see fliers or an airship by now. Captain Kaika says those explosives are definitely being dropped from above."

Another flash lit up the mountainside. In the darkness, Cas couldn't tell if there was a cave opening—or if the rocks were burying a cave opening—but she assumed the Cofah hadn't achieved their goal yet. Her finger found the trigger of the Mark 500. They were a good two miles out and not close enough to fire, not that she had a target. She could make an estimate about the vertical plane the bomber was on based on those flashes, but whatever was dropping them could be fifty feet above the detonations or five hundred feet.

"Sir, does Kaika know if those bombs have a set fuse length?" Cas asked loudly. "Like how many seconds pass between when they're lit and when they blow up?"

"You hear that, Captain?" Ort asked.

"Yes. Maybe." Kaika's voice also sounded distant, since she was yelling from the back seat. "They can be adjusted, but if the artilleryman is uncreative, three seconds is the factory setting."

Cas's mind boggled slightly at the idea of there being such a thing as a bomb-creation factory, but she accepted the information with a nod. "Pimples, do some math for me, will you? How high above are the men dropping the bombs likely to be? General, can you fly parallel to the mountainside? Get us within five hundred meters."

She felt presumptuous making requests of a general, but it

wasn't as if she could control their route.

"Roughly 44.1 meters, Raptor," Pimples said.

Ort obliged by paralleling the mountainside. "Fly above us, Pimples," he ordered. "See if Kaika can find something to drop a bomb on."

"Yes, sir."

Ort had a steady hand on the stick. Cas could already tell he wouldn't have Zirkander's flash in a battle, but he might be perfect for a backseat sniper. She settled low, aware that someone could be targeting *her* from behind that barrier of invisibility. She wished she knew if they were dealing with a couple of fliers or an airship or both. The sound of their own propellers was echoing off the rocky mountainside, bouncing back to them. She didn't hear any other noise out there, but it was so difficult to tell with the constant buzz in her ears.

The flashes had stopped. The Cofah must be staring straight at the Iskandian forces, waiting for them to go away. Or they could be preparing an attack. Cas wished they would drop one more explosive. Gauging Pimples' forty-four meters would have been easier if she was certain of where the last bomb had gone off. She searched the mountainside below, trying to spot freshly scarred earth. The area was full of scree and boulders, with no trees until a valley that ran north to south below their flier. The ground had been chewed up, but the darkness made it difficult to guess the precise place where the bombs had landed.

As soon as she believed they were within range, Cas fired her first shot. She wouldn't get that many chances to try before the flier carried them too far. Her first bullet banged off a boulder on the mountainside.

"Flying straight is making my shoulder blades itch, Ahn," Ort said. "I'm going to vary it up."

"Yes, sir. Understood." Cas wouldn't be surprised if someone was aiming at them right then. It was quiet out there. Too quiet.

Orange flared, not a bomb striking the mountainside, but a fireball blooming in midair. It raced straight toward them.

Ort dipped as Cas ducked low, leaving only her eyes above the rim of her seat well. Her eyes and her rifle. Before the fiery inferno streaked above their heads, she was returning fire. The heat scorched her scalp through her cap, the crackling of flame filled her ears, and the intense light nearly blinded her, but she did not hesitate. She aimed for the source of that fireball and fired to either side of it, as well, imagining the sorceress in the back of a flier, the same as she was. If she couldn't hit the magic user, maybe she could take out the pilot.

A male scream followed the third shot, and she allowed herself a grim nod of satisfaction. One of her other bullets seemed to thud off wood.

"Shouldn't be much wood on a flier," she muttered.

Ort accelerated away from the area, and Cas was soon out of rifle range. "We were lucky I was already dipping," Ort said. "Those fireballs are almost as fast as bullets."

"Stay out of range, sir," Pimples said. "We're dropping a—"

A boom rang out, drowning his words.

"Understood," Ort said.

Cas craned her neck, trying to see behind them. The night had been lit up by the explosive, but she still couldn't see the enemy craft. For a few instants, she *could* see a blurry gray blob that mimicked the terrain of the hillside. From a different plane, it would blend in, but from her viewpoint, she could see that the blob stuck out a good thirty meters from the slope. That blob was far too big to belong to a flier.

"Airship, sir," Cas warned. "Take us back."

Whoever she had hit must have been on the deck with the sorceress, not piloting her in a flier.

"No, don't go back in," Kaika yelled. "We dropped a Jag-4 on it, and it bounced off without doing any damage. I think that witch has them shielded now."

"We have to do something," Ort said. "Having them invading our nation and dropping bombs on our mountains is unacceptable." He sounded so stiff and affronted that under other circumstances, Cas might have laughed.

"I could try the sword." Cas had no idea if Kasandral could cut through a sorceress's shield, but if there was a chance, they had to try.

"If that could work," Kaika said, "cut a hole…"

"Maybe you could drop a bomb through," Pimples blurted.

"You'd have to jump out," Ort said. "There's no way you can cut anything from back there. But where are you going to jump? It's dark, and I can't see a thing." He was bringing the flier around, climbing up toward the top of the mountain, where Kaika and Pimples were buzzing around. "She shouldn't be able to hit us with a fireball up here, if their big balloon is in the way, right? Zirkander had you all flying under the fortress to avoid her, yes?"

He sounded nervous about dodging more fireballs. Cas couldn't blame him. It had been more luck than skill that had allowed them to evade the first one.

"I could try climbing up on the wings." Cas pointed toward the top wing that stretched above the cockpit.

Ort glanced back but only long enough to shake his head. "That would be suicidal. You fall, and you're dead."

"I'm going to try dropping some more bombs on them," Kaika said. "Sardelle gets tired after a while when she has to use a lot of magic. Maybe this witch will get tired if we bombard her."

Sardelle had also said this other sorceress was much more powerful than she was. Cas wouldn't bet on her getting worn out, though it did seem like she must be doing a lot. Maintaining an illusion of invisibility, maintaining a shield, and she'd sent out that fireball. So far, she had only sent one fireball. Maybe that meant that the culmination of everything she was doing was taxing her?

"Or maybe it means I'm being wishful," she said.

Shots rang out. They didn't come from Pimples' flier. Their own airship was visible on the horizon, the lights on its deck making it stand out against the dark sky, but it was still at least three miles back—too far for bullets.

"We're being fired at from below," Ort said. "I'm circling. Trying to keep us above where I *think* their envelope is."

"Sending another Jag down," Kaika announced.

"Wait," Cas yelled over Ort's shoulder. "Let me try to hit it with the sword first. Maybe I can cut a hole in the shield. Then you can drop the bomb into it." She had no idea if one could cut a hole in a sorceress's shield, but they wouldn't know what, if anything, Kasandral could do to the woman's magic until they tried.

"How can you cut a hole in something you can't see?"

"It's a big something. I'm hoping to get lucky."

"We could use some luck," Pimples said, turning to stay above the area where they thought the airship was. If it was anything like Iskandian dirigibles, it wouldn't be able to go anywhere quickly.

"How do you plan to hit it with the sword, Ahn?" Ort asked, his tone cool, a warning of you-better-not-be-thinking-of-unbuckling-yourself-and-climbing-on-the-wings easy to hear in it.

"I haven't quite figured that out yet, sir, but I'm going to try." Not exactly the truth. Cas had a fledgling idea, but she would only have one shot. It wasn't an idea General Ort would like, so she decided not to explain it further. Afterward, he could yell at her. She unlatched the ancient box and tried to ignore the way the sword hummed with contentment when she gripped the hilt. "Go ahead and throw that bomb, Captain. I want to verify that the airship is still under us. Then get another one ready to go immediately after."

"Whatever you say, Ahn." Kaika's tone sounded wry. Not used to taking orders from retired lieutenants, was she?

If Ort had offered up an idea that was less insane, Cas would have gone with it, but he was simply flying around and glancing toward their incoming airship. Hoping the cannons and shell guns might do something? Maybe they would, but their large and very visible craft would also be an easy target for the sorceress.

"Dropping it," Kaika said.

A couple of seconds passed, then a new explosion lit up the mountainside. Their own fliers, almost directly above where it hit, shuddered, the wings wobbling as the shockwave washed over them. Once again, Cas detected a disturbance in the air, a place where the illusion blurred and didn't quite match its surroundings.

"There, sir," she blurted.

"I see it." He turned them slightly, angling toward the blurry spot that was already disappearing as the light from the explosion faded.

Cas lifted the sword with both hands, but not in a typical grip. She held the hilt with one and the blade with the other, careful not to cut herself. All she wanted was to guide it towards its target. A sickly green glow oozed from the sword, and an uncomfortable hunger stirred in her mind. She had a fierce desire to find and kill the dragon-tainted sorceress below.

Before they could fly past the Cofah ship, Cas rose up in her seat and hurled the sword downward like a spear.

"What're you doing, Raptor?" Pimples blurted. From his position, flying parallel to Ort, he saw what she had done sooner than the general did.

Ort soon saw and responded. "Did you *drop* it?" he roared.

The sword hit something, landing point first a hundred feet below their flier. Cas craned her neck to keep track of it as Ort curved to turn around, as if he might fly down and catch the sword before it landed in the valley far below. But the blade hung in the air where it struck, the green glow spreading across the invisible barrier that it was stuck in. That barrier flashed, shimmering in the night air. For a moment, a giant oblong bubble was visible, a bubble large enough to protect an airship. Then it vanished, and Kasandral started falling again. It bumped something invisible, was knocked to the side, then plunged toward the dark valley below.

Cas held her breath, afraid the sorceress would see it and use some magic to levitate it onto the Cofah ship. But she was either too distracted to do anything, or she didn't want anything to do with the magic-hating blade. It tumbled through the air until it landed in a meadow. The green glow winked out. Cas did not know if it had been damaged, but they could get it later. Her only worry had been that she would miss or that it would fall onto the ship and become a gift for the Cofah.

"Bombing the stuffing out of them," Kaika said, and Cas glanced in her direction in time to see two small packages dropping toward the location where Kasandral had struck. A match flared as Kaika lit another one.

Good. Cas hadn't expected the entire shield to go down, and she couldn't be positive that was what had happened, but if it *had*, they needed to act quickly. It probably wouldn't take long for the sorceress to rebuild her barrier.

The first bomb exploded a few meters from the spot where Kasandral had struck. This time, more than a blur came into view. The dark brown of a Cofah airship balloon appeared in the air, and even more delightful, the explosion tore a giant hole into it. Kaika's second bomb struck ten meters farther along the envelope, tearing another massive hole in the fabric. Even better, the invisibility field disappeared, and the entire ship grew visible. From up above, Cas couldn't see the deck or the crew, but she heard alarmed shouts.

She closed the box between her knees and took up her rifle again.

"Sir," she said, "now would be the time to attack."

"You're as crazy as your C.O.," Ort growled, apparently forgetting she wasn't Zirkander's officer anymore. Regardless, it didn't sound like a compliment. Nonetheless, the nose of their flier dipped, and they dove.

The deck came into view, and Cas started firing, her eyes locking onto a target immediately. Even as she shot, she used her peripheral vision to look for more targets, hoping to find the sorceress. A bullet probably wouldn't take her down, but maybe she would be discombobulated, and Cas would get lucky.

Ort raced toward the deck, flying under the balloon to strafe the crew. Return fire came, and artillery weapons swung toward them. The shaven-headed Cofah soldiers kept their equanimity, and bullets cut through the wings of Ort's flier. Cas kept firing, though she would have created more of a zigzagging path if she had been at the stick. Then she saw the sorceress, the long-haired woman holding a glowing sword aloft, its light gleaming off the golden armor she wore. No wonder Ort was flying straight. He was going straight toward her, his intent clear.

Cas kept firing, knowing they might only get one chance at this. She couldn't shoot at the sorceress from her position, not without risking hitting Ort or their own propeller, but she picked out men on the deck who looked like they might be officers.

The sorceress's eyes narrowed as they approached, and she flung up a hand without fear.

"Dodge!" Cas yelled, certain what would come next. From this close, they would never be able to get out of the way in time.

Ort's bullets clipped the deck at the woman's boots, and Cas thought he might not listen, that he wouldn't turn away, but he pulled them to the side. The fireball leaped from the sorceress's fingers. Ort had turned soon enough to evade it, but her sword added its own attack. A streak of lightning flew from the blade and branched to follow them. It struck the side of the flier, right behind Cas's seat. She should have ducked—a sane woman would have—but she fired, trying to strike the woman in the chest.

Her aim felt true, but the sword pulsed, and a tiny flame burst to life in front of the sorceress's chest. Her bullet, Cas realized. Incinerated.

More rifles fired, and holes pierced the tail of their flier. Cas had no idea where Pimples and Kaika were, but she and Ort were taking the brunt of the Cofah attack. As Ort sped away from the airship, flames licked the side of the flier where the lightning had struck.

Reluctantly, Cas jammed her rifle between her legs along with the box and twisted in her seat. She unfastened the top half of her harness and, with nothing else to use, yanked her uniform jacket over her head. She leaned back and batted at the flames, afraid they would spread if they weren't put out.

As she beat at the fire, she saw the airship receding behind them. The deck was at an odd tilt, and flames leaped from one side of the balloon. Cas hoped that the sorceress couldn't put those out. She spotted Pimples' flier near the rear of the craft. Kaika drew back her arm and hurled another explosive. This one headed toward an empty area on the deck, on the opposite end from where Cas and Ort had battled the sorceress. Someone had run up to the woman, but she was waving him away. She looked like she wanted to hurl more fireballs.

"Did you get it?" Pimples asked.

"Boiler and furnace should be right under there," Kaika said. "We'll see. We'll see…"

The explosion flashed, the boom ringing out. It ripped another hole in the envelope, this time from below, but even better, wood from the deck and the side of the ship splintered and flew in all directions. A moment later, a second boom rang out. The sky lit up in an orange ball as Pimples and Kaika streaked away from the airship. At the front, men and women toppled to the deck, even the sorceress.

"Was that the boiler?" General Ort asked.

"I think so, sir." Cas hefted her rifle again. "Will you take us back in? While they're distracted?"

"Cool your blood lust, Ahn. That craft isn't going anywhere except into the mountainside. In the meantime, we're finding the priceless sword you so casually hurled to the earth."

Hurled? Cas's gamble had allowed them to take down the airship. She frowned at the back of Ort's head as he took them downward, toward the dark valley below. Maybe this was why General Zirkander always butted heads with Ort, a lack of appreciation for calculated risks that paid off.

"Surely, attacking the sorceress while she's distracted and maybe wounded should be the priority, sir."

Ort leveled a cool glare over his shoulder. "That sword is our *only* weapon to use against the dragon."

"Can *we* go back in?" Pimples asked. "Kaika has two more bombs."

"Go on. Just don't get hit by a fireball. Fliers are expensive."

"Your concern for our *craft* is noted, sir," Kaika yelled, managing to sound dry even from the back seat.

"We'll clean up whatever is left," Major Cildark said. "We're close enough to fire now."

Ort might have been right, that there was no need to finish off the airship. Above them, the sky was alight with flame, and the craft was descending toward a copse of trees at the north end of the valley. Down in the grass, Kasandral had lost its glow. Tall stalks of grass waved in the breeze. She grimaced. It might be harder than she realized to find the blade in all that.

"Did you see exactly where it hit?" Ort asked.

"Not… exactly." She studied the mountainside and the terrain of the valley, wishing she had taken note of nearby landmarks when the sword had struck. She had been too worried about the sorceress and bringing down the airship.

Ort might have snapped something sarcastic, but all he said was, "Let me know if you see it. I've heard your vision is legendary, so I'm relying on you."

Cas leaned over the edge, deciding not to point out that it wasn't her vision that was good but her aim. And aim wasn't terribly helpful if a person couldn't see the target.

The grass did not part for her eyes, but she did feel an uncomfortable itch along her spine, and the hairs on her arms seemed to rise. A strange sensation called to her from across the valley. Was that Kasandral?

Trusting her instincts—or the damned blade's pull on her—Cas said, "Two o'clock, sir. I think it might be over by those stumps."

Without questioning her, Ort veered in that direction. He activated the thrusters before they reached the stumps. "I think this is going to be an on-foot quest."

"Yes, sir." Cas waited for the craft to stop, then hopped out. As she followed the strange pull she felt, she looked toward the sky again. She didn't see the other flier, but she was in time to watch the Cofah airship crash, flames leaping from the half-burned balloon and smoke pouring from the destroyed rear of the craft.

The pull of the sword led her inevitably to it, and she was bending down to pluck it out of the grass before she saw it. As soon as her hand clasped around the hilt, a surge of alien feelings charged through her veins. Irritation at having been dropped, a fierce desire to slay that sorceress, and a craving for blood.

Shuddering, Cas pulled her sleeve down, so her skin wouldn't be in direct contact with the sword. She hurried back to the flier and was glad when she heard General Ort speaking on the crystal, if only for a distraction. Even if she agreed with the desire to end the troublesome sorceress's life, she couldn't wait to lock Kasandral back in its box.

"…need help," came a voice over the crystal. That wasn't Pimples, and it wasn't Major Cildark, either. Cas didn't recognize the speaker.

Ort was beckoning to her as he listened. "Hurry, Ahn. More trouble." He pointed toward the sky behind her.

As she ran, nearly tripping in holes hidden by the tall grass, she stared back at flames visible above the trees. They weren't coming from the already-crashed Cofah ship. *Their* ship was on fire.

Chapter 7

SARDELLE WOKE TO THE SMELL of lava and the soft glow of an orange beam eating into boulders. Her head felt stuffy, and she did not know if it was because the enclosed cave was low on breathable air or because the effort of defending everyone from the dragon had bruised her brain.

Your brain is fine. I'm less certain about the air, but I'm not far from the exit. Less than an hour. Rocks shifted, clunked, and thudded into new places. Jaxi pulsed in irritation. *Maybe two hours.*

We appreciate your efforts.

Now I remember why I never tried to burn my way out from under Galmok Mountain.

I'm surprised you didn't try. You certainly had the time. Sardelle noticed she wasn't lying entirely on the uneven and very hard rock floor as she had been when she first dozed off. Earlier, Ridge and Duck had been coercing Jaxi into helping them get the fliers turned around, so they would be ready to take off as soon they could escape. At some point, he had settled on the ground beside her. She didn't remember moving, but she was leaning against his chest and using his shoulder as a pillow. He had wrapped an arm around her, and she much preferred that cushion to the rock. She might have snuggled closer for a kiss, since she sensed that he wasn't sleeping, but Tylie had passed out on her other side and was using *her* for a pillow. Only Duck remained on his own, whittling a clump of wood while he sat in the cockpit of his flier.

What would I have done once I got out? Jaxi asked. *Lain on the mountainside and rusted in the elements until some shepherd picked me up and hung me above the door in his yurt for decoration? Besides, I did try. The rock just kept collapsing into whatever hole I made. It was rubble that buried me, not a solid slab of stone.*

Well, I would have been terribly disappointed if I'd woken up and you weren't there.

That's the real reason I didn't escape on my own. I was thinking of your needs.

Of course you were.

Another boulder shifted, and pebbles tinkled to the ground. Ridge stirred at Sardelle's side.

Jaxi said another hour or two and we'll be out, she told him silently, not wanting to wake Tylie.

Tylie hadn't been able to sleep earlier. While Sardelle had been healing her cuts, she had seemed more agitated than the wounds had explained, so it was good that she had finally found some rest. Her distress might be linked to Phelistoth's pain, and Sardelle had no idea how to heal that. She had to trust that the dragon would fix his own wounds and put an end to the problem. She shuddered to think how Tylie might react, however, if Phelistoth died.

No hurry, Ridge thought back, leaning his chin on her head. *This is cozy.*

She smiled at the words, even if they weren't entirely sincere. *I thought you knew better than to lie to me. Sitting in here, not knowing if the outpost has been attacked, is eating at you like a flesh-eating bacteria. And you have a pointy rock jabbing into your left cheek.*

Maybe I like *having pointy things jabbing me in my butt, Miss Smarty Sorceress.*

She arched her eyebrows. *That begs for a joke about sexual preferences and whether it was truly an accident that you ended up under Colonel Therrik's bed.*

True, but you're too polite and well socialized to make it, so I'm safe. Now that he knew she was awake, he squirmed a bit, trying to find a better position.

I could make such a joke, Jaxi said.

Aren't you too busy over there? Ridge asked. *I can feel your heat from here.*

That's because I'm magnificently radiant. Like a star.

Sardelle thought Ridge might get up and stretch his legs

—and rub his butt—but he wrapped his other arm around her and snuggled closer.

You can go back to sleep if you want, he thought. *Nothing more exciting than pointy rocks here. And Tylie muttering in her sleep. You think she'll be all right?*

Probably when Phelistoth heals himself and she knows he's safe.

Ridge made a sour face—she didn't have to see it to know it was there.

Sardelle?

She hesitated, already sensing the gist of his question. She'd been expecting it, especially since Phelistoth had started walking around in human form when he visited them, and she wasn't sure how to answer it. The truth was, she didn't know the answer to it. On the surface, Tylie was as open and honest as a spring flower, but since Sardelle couldn't get a sense of her thoughts, only of what she displayed on the outside, she did not know anything about her for certain.

You're about to ask what exactly is going on between them, Sardelle thought.

Yeah. And if I should be threatening to beat him up if he has any... intentions *toward her. Because she seems way too young for that, even if it were with a kid her age. I know she's seventeen, but she acts like she's about ten.*

I really don't know. I'm sorry I don't, because it's been a concern of mine, too, but as I've told you before, dragons were long gone in my era. All we have are historical texts. And fictionalized accountings. Sardelle decided not to point out that pairings had to have happened fairly often back then, given all the sorcerers that had been roaming around in the old days. She also didn't mention that the dragons seemed to find something appealing in Tylie's mind or talents. She would look up Receivers while they were at the outpost too. Another item for the research list.

Since Ridge was still frowning down at her, she knew she would have to give him something more—or maybe distract him.

Would you truly try to beat up a dragon that came courting? I don't think that would go well.

He snorted. *No, I don't think so, either. But if Tolemek didn't, I would.*

Maybe if the two of you worked together, you could give him a black... toenail.

Ha ha.

She brushed his jaw with her fingers. *Have I mentioned that it's sweet that you want to protect her?*

How can you not want to protect someone who wanders around looking lost all the time?

She's probably conversing with Phelistoth when she looks like that.

Is that supposed to be comforting?

No, and she shouldn't have mentioned it. Hadn't her goal been distracting him? *Have you ever given thought to having children, Ridge? I know your mother harps on you about it, and that probably makes you not want to do it, but I think you'd be a good father.* And maybe she had Fern Zirkander to blame, but she had started to wonder herself what it would be like to be a mother.

Seven gods, why?

That wasn't quite the response she'd expected, and she felt stung, until she realized what he was questioning. Not the act itself but her suggestion that he'd be good at it. *You don't think you could help raise little baby Zirkanders?*

Not well.

Why not?

I'd be a horrible role model.

The statement surprised her, and she thought it might be false modesty, but he honestly seemed to believe that. *That national hero of Iskandia? A bad role model?*

He slumped lower against the rock wall and gazed toward Jaxi. *Sardelle, do you know that I've often been relieved that I met you—that you met me—this year? And not when I was younger? I'm still not entirely sure why you don't think I'm a reckless twit, but I assure you that I was much more of one when I was in my twenties. You never would have put up with Young Ridge.*

Curious, Sardelle made an encouraging noise. He'd told her about many of the air battles he'd been engaged in over the years, and he shared humorous stories about his squadron mates to entertain her, but he hadn't spoken much of his own history, aside from a few childhood anecdotes.

It's a miracle I didn't get myself killed. I got myself pegged with an embarrassing nickname after my first battle, and I spent the next five years doing my damnedest to prove I was better than that. Add to that that I came from a poor family, and most of the officers were still drawn out of the nobility back then, and I felt I had a lot to prove. So I was reckless, sometimes to the detriment of my teammates, but I got what I wanted, what I thought I wanted, the attention of the reporters and a degree of fame. Though back then, I suppose it was more notoriety than fame. There were times I should have been kicked out of the service, but I was taking down Cofah airships and making pirates fear harassing our ships and coastlines. They needed me, and I knew it. Most of my swagger was about flying, but I was inordinately pleased that the attention from the newspapers turned me into someone that women wanted to sleep with too. And that happened. A lot. He shifted, glancing uncomfortably at her. It wouldn't have taken telepathy to sense his embarrassment, at least when relaying these things to *her. I was careful not to create any baby Zirkanders, as you call them, but you would have thought I was an idiot. I* was *an idiot. I never even tried to have a grownup relationship until I was in my thirties, and then I found I was lousy at it. I thought I was so amazing, and the girl was so lucky to be with me. That wasn't a real solid place to start from.*

She snorted softly to herself. She doubted he had been *that* arrogant. Still, maybe part of the reason they worked together was that she had a power he couldn't touch and had to respect, something that could humble even a famous pilot. Though she would be the first to admit that literal power didn't always matter in a relationship. She'd felt helpless once, trying to keep something together with a man who hadn't been nearly as invested in their pairing as she had been. She might have been the stronger magic user, but his indifference had, as counterintuitive as it seemed, given him the greater power.

What changed? she asked, more interested in his past than in hers. His story wasn't completely surprising, but Sardelle had often thought he was actually well grounded and even humble for someone who received as much attention as he did.

I got my best friend killed.

Sensing the sudden grimness in his thoughts, she waited patiently for him to continue.

He was the Wolf Squadron commander, Colonel Abagon "Squirrel" Mox. I was a major at the time. He was a few years older, but we'd been in the squadron together since it had formed ten years earlier, and I was—still am—the godfather of his children. She saw the flash of a memory, of birthdays and picnics and the realization that he needed to check in on the family, even though that had been uncomfortable and difficult since Mox's death. *He always put up with my cockiness and was good at placing me in positions where I wouldn't endanger others. Usually. But five years ago, we had a thorny mission, a big battle over our shipping lanes, which the Cofah were trying to usurp. Again. We had to fight imperial dirigibles and also deal with naval artillery. It was an ugly battle, all at night, so many fires on our ships and theirs, so much death. I thought I could do something brilliant and get rid of two airships at once. We didn't expect them to have cargo holds full of explosives. I signaled and convinced Mox to follow me in, that it would be fine, that we'd come out as heroes, as we always did. And then I left him, when I knew he'd been hit and didn't have full control. Just for a second, I told myself, because there was the Cofah armada commander in my sights, and if we could kill him—* Ridge shook his head, the words stopping, but the images came through, and Sardelle received a clearer vision of the battle—the deaths—than she would have liked. The downside of being a telepath and linked closely with another person.

So Mox was dead, and the way it happened, not many people knew it was my fault, if any. But I knew. And I couldn't bring myself to fudge my report, though you better believe I considered it. I knew that might be the end of my career, if not cause for further punishment. So I told the truth to Mox's commander, a man who also considered him a friend.

General Ort? Sardelle guessed. She had occasionally wondered why Ort gave his star squadron commander a hard time.

General Ort, Ridge agreed. *He hadn't been commander of the flier battalion for more than four months. And I'm sure he hadn't heard anything good about me.*

He obviously didn't kick you out of the military.

No, he promoted me. To Mox's position. Ridge grunted. *I'm sure he would have demoted me swiftly enough if it hadn't worked out, but I think he wanted to see if giving me some responsibility would teach me something. I'm not sure if it was that or just Mox's death, but it worked, to a certain degree. I'm still reckless. I know it. But it's more calculated now. And I watch out for my people.*

Yes, she had seen that. He was almost obsessive about it. She smiled down at Tylie, once again imagining him showing up with fists bared to threaten Phelistoth with pummeling if he didn't have her home before midnight.

Sardelle laid her hand on his, brushing her thumbs across his knuckles. *While I find it interesting to hear about your past, in a heart-wrenching kind of way, I don't see why all this makes you feel you'd be a poor father.*

You don't? Of all people, how could I ever discipline a kid with a straight face? Tell him to do the right thing? What kind of role model would I be, having been a self-absorbed ass for most of my life?

I'll admit I'm not an expert in this area any more than you are, but I think it matters more who you are and what you do after *your children are born, rather than before.*

Ridge was quiet for a moment before grudgingly saying, *I suppose there's something to that.*

What children know or care what their parents did in their lives before they were born? Have you ever asked your mother or your father about their school days? Their early careers? What they did?

I don't even know what my father does now, *most of the time.*

See?

Hm.

Sardelle squeezed his hand. *I just wanted to share my thoughts with you. I don't want to pressure you into anything.* All seven gods, even Moltsoth the Blind, knew his mother did enough of that already.

I didn't think you were. I— Ridge paused, dumbfounded. *Were you asking because you* want *to have children?*

It's been in my thoughts a few times of late. I would be open to a discussion.

She grinned as the realization dawned over him that he'd been self-absorbed again, thinking of himself and his own perceived deficiencies, instead of realizing why she was talking to him about fatherhood. He had the good grace to flush and feel embarrassed. She shifted her weight so she could kiss him. Maybe he was right and that it was a good thing she had met him at forty instead of at twenty or thirty. She was rather fond of *this* Ridgewalker Zirkander.

Though he still seemed chagrined, he returned the kiss. *It's too bad we're not alone in this cave or you could seduce me again, and we could discuss it right now.*

After the mission perhaps? Sardelle broke the kiss, too aware of Tylie leaning against her other side. Even if she was sleeping, Duck was up in his cockpit, whittling very assiduously and doing his best not to look in their direction.

I'd like that.

Also, you keep trying to rewrite the history in that cave. You were clearly the one who seduced me.

Ridge smirked at the old argument. *You were the one caressing my chest.*

I was healing your wounds.

While caressing my chest. Seductively.

Am I the only one in the cave listening to this and wishing you were making babies now *instead of engaging in all of this mushy talk?* Jaxi sounded tired and grouchy, probably more from the continuing demands on her energy than from mushy talk. She loved to mock that, after all.

We thought you were too busy being radiant to eavesdrop on us, Sardelle said.

Please. I'm never too busy to eavesdrop.

A crack and a bang sounded, followed by a delightfully refreshing draft that whispered into the cave.

Jaxi's beam disappeared, and the lighting diminished, only the glow from her pommel remaining. Night must have fallen outside, because no light entered from the hole Jaxi had created.

Hours ago. It will be midnight by the time you get your flying crates to the mines.

"*Crates?*" Ridge asked.

How about you strong men come finish this off? Jaxi pulsed, shining a beam of light toward the rubble. *I'm tired.*

Duck dropped his knife and stared toward the naked blade.

"She's talking to *you* now, eh?" Ridge asked.

"I... yes, sir."

"She probably wants you to oil her blade later." Ridge gave Sardelle a parting kiss, then extricated himself and rolled up his sleeves.

Though Sardelle wouldn't have minded resting for another ten or twelve hours, she eased Tylie off her and rose to help. The sooner they cleared the way, the sooner they could get to the outpost. She just hoped it hadn't been attacked. Most of the miners and soldiers hadn't treated her well when she had been there, but she wouldn't wish them death by dragon fire.

Especially when they can help us dig out another soulblade.

Yes, that was my first concern too, Sardelle gave Jaxi a sideways look as she joined the men in the cave mouth.

What can I say? I've missed my own kind. Besides, I want to see your soul snozzle ordering Colonel Therrik around. He had many unkind words about us.

I don't think Ridge is going to order him *to do the digging.*

No? That's disappointing.

* * *

Tolemek gazed toward the dark valley from the railing of the airship, trying to see Cas's flier down there. He had left the helm when she and the others had engaged with the Cofah, and he'd watched helplessly as that sorceress hurled that fireball at her. He had a rifle with him, but it was useless at such a range. Fortunately, Cas and the others hadn't needed his help. The Cofah airship was flaming where it had crashed at the other end of the valley, and he was about to let himself relax when an unwelcome sensation crawled up his spine.

His first thought was that he felt the sorceress using her magic from somewhere below, but he hadn't sensed anything earlier, when she had flung that fireball. Had he been too far away then? He searched the sky to either side of their airship, hoping he did not sense a dragon's approach. This sensation *did* remind him of how he felt in Phelistoth's powerful presence, but this presence wasn't familiar to him the way Phelistoth's aura would be. Could the other dragon be nearby? Hidden by the night?

A thunderous boom shook the airship, and the deck tilted. Tolemek lurched, his stomach thrust into the railing, and he almost dropped his rifle.

"Water," came a yell from behind him. "Fire suppression team, get up here."

Tolemek spun toward the voice and gaped at the side of the ship, where a long section of the railing had been destroyed, along with part of the hull. Flames licked at the broken decking, and smoke roiled inward. The balloon hadn't been damaged, but if someone was out there throwing grenades at them, it could be the next target. But *who* was throwing grenades? He could see both sides of the ship from his position, and there was nothing in the sky around them. Nothing *visible*.

He glanced down at the valley, at the bonfire that was the Cofah airship. The sorceress was *on* that ship. She couldn't be up here, turning other aircraft invisible, could she?

One of the ship's artillery weapons fired with a more controlled boom. The gunner couldn't have seen anything, either, but he was aiming toward the air beyond their port side. Whoever had hurled that grenade must have done so from over there.

Tolemek ran to a section of the railing that still stood and hunted for something to aim at with his rifle. The other guns on that side of the ship joined in with the attack, and the roar was deafening. Smoke filled the air, both from the fire and from the firing weapons, and he doubted he could have seen a craft even if it hadn't been invisible.

Kneeling behind the railing for cover, he fired a couple of shots randomly into the night, but that was pointless. He tried to gather his thoughts and use the senses that Sardelle kept promising him he possessed. Maybe he could *feel* the presence of an invisible craft. He'd thought he had sensed something before the attack, hadn't he?

The shouts and booms made it hard to concentrate, but he *did* start to get the sense of something out there and where it might be. It felt large, like another airship, maybe a smaller one than theirs, but it was definitely bigger than a flier.

"Fire high," Tolemek yelled. "I think they're above our own balloon."

The closest artillery officer frowned at him, probably wondering who he thought he was giving orders, but he did adjust his aim. Tolemek shot a couple of times, but it was pointless. He couldn't do anything useful with a rifle. He had some of his knockout and smoke grenades in his lab.

"I'll be back," he announced to nobody in particular and ran to the hatchway that led below decks.

He almost tripped over a team tugging a giant hose across the deck. He had to stop to let them pass and cursed at the delay. But that extra few seconds gave him a moment to look around, and he saw something he would have heard if there had been less noise. A grappling hook latched onto the railing on the starboard side of the ship.

"Attack from the starboard side," Tolemek yelled.

Most of the crew was focused on the port side, and he winced, knowing he had been the one to promise their enemy was over there. Were they dealing with two ships, or had that one flown up and over them to the other side? Airships weren't the most maneuverable craft, but it was possible.

Even as his thoughts whirred through his head, he found cover behind one of the artillery stations and fired into the night, guessing as to the exact origin of the hook. All he could see was a taut rope disappearing into the night sky. Others ran over and joined him in firing to that side, but four more grappling hooks latched onto the railing.

Two shaven-headed Cofah soldiers in uniforms leaped out of the darkness and landed atop the railing less than five feet from Tolemek. There wasn't a grappling hook there, so he hadn't expected them. He jumped back and fired, clipping one of the men in the shoulder. But they were already leaping onto the deck, swords and pistols pointed in his direction. The soldier he'd injured slashed down at the corporal manning the artillery station. The second one leaped straight for Tolemek.

There wasn't time to fire again, so he dropped back, whipping his rifle across to block a sword strike meant to cut his skull open. A second slash followed the first. The Cofah soldier was a veteran, with a scar on his jaw and lines creasing his forehead. He must have survived countless battles. He pressed Tolemek back with his speed, the swift movements of his blade difficult to track. The damned rifle was a poor weapon for a sword fight, but Tolemek couldn't put enough space between himself and the soldier to fire it again. Why had he come up on deck without any of his grenades in his pockets?

"Idiot," he growled at himself, already panting from the exertion of the fight.

Another slash cut for his face, and he barely managed to duck. He almost missed seeing the soldier aiming with his pistol hand before the sword finished its attack. Tolemek dropped to the deck, but not before the weapon fired. Pain seared the side of his head, and utter fear almost froze him, terror that he had a bullet lodged in his skull, in his *brain*. But the soldier wasn't done with him, and there was no time to freeze. The man charged in, slashing toward Tolemek's face with the sword.

From his side down on the deck, Tolemek twisted to avoid the blade while kicking out. The soldier was almost too fast for him, but his boot clipped the inside of the man's knee. He faltered slightly, and his sword clunked into the bulkhead behind Tolemek.

Tolemek found the room to jab upward with the muzzle of his rifle. If he'd had a bayonet on the end, he would have eviscerated the man, but as it was, he struck his target in the belly with enough force to bend him over. Tolemek scrambled to his knees, using his upward momentum to launch a punch at the man's exposed jaw. It wasn't a good punch, and it stung his hand, but it was nothing compared to the fiery pain blazing at the side of his skull. He channeled his pain into rage and shoved the soldier back. The man was quick to recover, and Tolemek almost received a sword cut to his chest. But a soldier from another battle had fallen behind the Cofah, and his heel caught. The tiny distraction gave Tolemek enough time to finally jump back and bring his rifle to bear. He fired, the bullet slamming into his foe's chest.

The man tumbled to the deck, opening up the view around Tolemek. Dozens of men, Iskandians and Cofah, were battling near the railing now. The artillery man who had been attacked at the same time as Tolemek lay dead below the weapon, his throat cut. The airship that had to be out there was still invisible, but more men were running out of the darkness, balancing on ropes, risking a deadly fall to reach the battle.

Tolemek fired at one, knocking him from the tenuous perch, but he did not want to stay where he was, not when the Cofah ship would have artillery weapons of its own, and he was in plain sight. A boom somewhere off to his left confirmed that the airship was firing. What he needed to do was make that ship visible, so the Iskandian gunners could see their target.

With that thought in mind, Tolemek backed away from the battle and sprinted for the hatchway that would take him to his lab.

"Coward," an injured soldier growled as he ran by.

The condemnation hurt, but there was no time to argue with it. Tolemek raced through the hatchway, jumping to the deck below instead of bothering with the ladder. His head throbbed with each step, and blood trickled down the side of his face. A problem for later.

He swung into his lab and went straight to a cupboard full of chemicals and minerals. He yanked out a bag of talc and almost returned with just that, but he looked around, muttering, "Dispersal method. Dispersal method."

He grabbed a couple of his shrapnel grenades. Not ideal, but they ought to blow the powder around sufficiently. He tied them to the bag, making an ugly bomb that Captain Kaika would be sure to mock, then crafted a quick sling. Booms and shouts continued to sound outside of his walls—his lab was right under the fighting.

Tolemek sprinted back up to the deck, almost crashing into a fight that had devolved into swords and hatchets. He dodged around the men, hoping nobody shot him. Several of the boarding ropes had been cut, but one still stretched into the darkness. He pulled the fuses on his grenades, then hurried to swing his sling before they detonated. He released it, and the talc bag and the grenades strapped to it hurled into the air. He lacked Cas's aim, and he was guessing as to where the gap between the deck and the envelope would be. As his clumsy weapon sailed away, all he could do was crouch down behind cover and watch.

His explosives were meant for use in infiltrations and hand-to-hand combat, not to take down entire buildings—or ships—so their booms sounded anemic compared to the ones going off all around him, but they were enough to blow open that bag. A cloud of white powder formed instantly, coating everything around it. The outline of an airship came into view, the craft about half the size of the Iskandian one. The talc also stuck to the men manning their weapons.

"Fire at those people!" someone nearby yelled.

Machine gun blasts joined the louder bangs of the ship's weapons. A flier? He caught sight of one racing toward the Cofah airship and hoped it would be Cas, but he recognized Pimples' young face in the cockpit. Captain Kaika was standing up in the seat behind him, and she hurled something as the flier cruised past the powder-outlined airship. Tolemek glimpsed a tiny dot of orange—fire burning on a fuse—before it disappeared into the invisibility field.

The bomb exploded, and flames and white powder flew everywhere. The Cofah soldiers who had boarded the Iskandian craft glanced back toward their ship, and their eyes grew round. The men kept fighting, but when Major Cildark yelled for a surrender, some of them hesitated, looking toward their leaders for advice.

A second flier appeared out of the night, this one with General Ort in the cockpit. Cas rode in the back, her sniper rifle aimed at the deck of the Iskandian craft. Shaven-headed soldiers started dropping before they knew what was happening. With her deadly aim, she dropped five men before the flier had passed out of range. Clearly, she hadn't thought twice about shooting onto a deck filled with allies as well as enemies, but Tolemek wasn't surprised. He hadn't seen her miss often.

Cildark shouted again for surrender. This time, nobody hesitated. The soldiers dropped their weapons. Cildark ordered a couple of squads of men to round up their new captives and lock them below.

Tolemek should have gone to his lab—or maybe sickbay—but he was reluctant to leave the deck before Cas landed and he had seen that she was, indeed, safe. He wanted to know if she had used that sword, too, and if so, how it had affected her. He grimaced at the idea that she might return and be giving him the frosty treatment again, especially when she had been appreciating his company earlier in the day.

"Traitor," one of the Cofah soldiers growled as he was marched past. He spat at Tolemek's feet.

The other Cofah men must have known who he was, too, because they also glared or spat. Tolemek stood straight, accepting the criticism, though a part of him wanted to lash out, to tell them they were wrong, that their own people had wanted nothing to do with "Deathmaker" after the Camp Eveningson incident. He hadn't even been able to sell them healing salves that could have helped thousands of people. Only the Iskandians had been desperate enough to take him in, despite his sins. But what would it matter to these men? Tolemek was Cofah, and here he was, standing beside Iskandians. That was all they saw.

There were times when that was what *he* saw too. He hated fighting his own people and wished the gods would let him hide in his laboratory and not think overmuch about the work he was doing and how it was being used. Sardelle had once suggested he use his skills to create formulas and inventions that could help people, healing sicknesses and injuries. Unfortunately, nobody wanted to give him time to do that. Weapons were all anyone seemed to want.

"Deathmaker," Major Cildark said, walking up, soot smearing the side of his face, the hem of his uniform jacket charred. "Good work with the white gunk."

In the wake of his dark thoughts, Tolemek couldn't manage to thank the man. He nodded once in acknowledgment and stared out to starboard. Smoke still muddled the air, but the airship had started its inexorable descent, and was no longer visible.

"Are we going down to check on the first ship? The sorceress? If she's wounded, now would be the time to deal with her."

"Yes, as soon as we get these prisoners all stowed away." Major Cildark continued past, saying, "Your head is bleeding," over his shoulder. "Might want to see to that."

"He was waiting for me, sir," came Cas's voice from the side.

Tolemek spun toward her, his curtain of gloom lifting. She sounded like herself. Did that mean she hadn't used the sword?

She strode toward him, her jacket even more ripped and soot-stained than the major's, and she carried her rifle on a sling and the oblong sword box over her shoulder. She didn't appear tall enough to wield *either* weapon, but everyone here knew the truth.

"Are you here to appreciate my goos?" he asked, lifting his right arm. His knuckles still smarted from that punch, but that wouldn't keep him from hugging her—if she would allow it. He glanced at the box again.

"The healing goo looks like it needs to be taken out." She stopped a few feet away, nodded toward his head and toward injured men being helped below decks. "I better put this away first, though." She twitched her shoulder, shifting the box. A difficult-to-read expression crossed her face, and he wasn't sure what it meant, but it spoke of discomfort.

"Of course." He lowered his arm and told himself not to feel disappointed. Hugging her when she held a sword that wanted to kill him wouldn't be that much of a reward, right? "Will you come to my lab afterward? You look as battered as I feel." He wiped away of droplet of blood before it dripped from his jaw. "We can share Healing Salve Number Seven."

"Number Seven? An improvement over Six?"

"Yes. I occasionally steal a free moment to work on things that don't kill people." He couldn't quite keep the bitterness out of his voice. As much as he wanted to brush aside that accusation of being a traitor, it was hard.

"I know that," Cas said quietly.

He sighed. "I know *you* do."

"Any chance of a bathtub in your lab?" she asked, smiling slightly as she brushed soot off her sleeve.

She was trying to change the subject, to make him think lighter thoughts. He wasn't sure he wanted to think lighter thoughts, but he appreciated her effort. Nobody else here would bother. He also appreciated that she was smiling instead of glaring. Maybe as long as the sword stayed in its box, it couldn't affect her.

"No bathtubs," he said with genuine regret. They had never shared a tub before, and he could see finding that even more invigorating than a generous dose of Healing Salve Number Seven. "I do have a nice basin and some sponges."

"Sponges?" A single eyebrow rose dubiously.

He was debating whether he wanted to say something suggestive when Captain Kaika ambled up, giving Cas a slap on the back.

"Sponges?" She grinned, her teeth flashing white against soot-darkened skin. Her entire *face* was bathed in the stuff. "Sounds erotic. Have fun."

"Erotic?" Cas's other eyebrow climbed to join the first.

"I'm sure Tolemek can demonstrate." Kaika continued past, thankfully not sharing the details of her own experiences with sponges, and headed for the hatchway.

Pimples and Ort were heading their way, too, so Tolemek stepped back, making room for them to pass.

"If General Ort doesn't send us back out right away to search—" Cas waved toward the valley far below, "—I'll come by soon to tend your wound."

She didn't make any promises about sponges, but the offer of tending sounded promising. He would make sure not to clean his wounds too much before she arrived, so she would have plenty to do, standing close, skin touching skin...

Tolemek snorted at himself as the other pilots passed. Kaika had a way of putting notions in a man's mind.

"Good fighting out there, Raptor," one of the airship crewmen said as she passed. "You too, Pimples."

Several others joined in with the praise, and Cas received a few more pats on the back before she managed to escape below decks. From the hunch to her shoulders, he knew she would have preferred not to be acknowledged, that she didn't think she deserved any praise.

He understood, but a part of him couldn't help but feel envious that she still had her people's respect. He supposed Major Cildark had acknowledged that he had done something useful, but he couldn't get the traitor comment out of his mind, nor could he forget the Iskandian soldier who had been so quick to judge him a coward. He wondered if he would ever find a place where he could feel at home again.

Chapter 8

The light from the flames came into view before the fliers crested the ridge, and Ridge could see into the small valley that lay behind Galmok Mountain and was fenced in on all sides by peaks. Up here, above twelve thousand feet, snow still covered the rocks, as it likely would well into the summer. Right now, that snow was orange, reflecting fire. Trails of smoke drifted up from charred and broken buildings within the stone walls of the outpost, the black haze making the stars fade in and out. As Jaxi had predicted, it was nearing midnight, but Ridge could see people moving around in the courtyard where he had rebuilt a wrecked flier the winter before. He had no idea how many might have died in the dragon attack, but he was relieved that at least some people had survived.

His relief faded as his flier drew closer and lower, and he realized that the people he had assumed would be putting out the fires were fighting each other.

"Damn it," Ridge growled, memories of his brief but stressful command of the outpost pouring into his mind. He remembered all too well the precarious situation, where criminals condemned to work the mines outnumbered the soldiers guarding them seven to one. Those soldiers constantly lived in fear of an uprising.

"Sir?" Duck asked over the communication crystal. "Should we land? Or…"

The idea of raining bullets into the courtyard flashed through Ridge's mind, but uniforms mingled with the coarse wool and fur garb of the miners.

"We're landing. Let's try to make an impression that might stop the fighting." Ridge was well aware that once they were on the ground, he and Duck would only be two more soldiers with guns. "Sardelle?" Her eyes were closed, but she sat upright in the seat behind him. "Are you awake?" He wasn't sure how much of her energy she had recovered, but hoped she could do something to help.

Yes, she spoke into his mind, her eyes remaining closed, her lips unmoving, the wind tugging at some of the raven locks that had escaped her braid. *Go ahead and land. I'll make it memorable.*

Light burst from beneath his flier, and orange flames licked the air all around his cockpit. Though alarmed for a second, Ridge soon realized they weren't giving off any heat and weren't burning anything. Behind him, Duck's flier received the same treatment. An illusion he trusted, but to those below, they must look like comets approaching.

He hoped the trick did not backfire. The miners had been particularly superstitious and scared when it had come to magic—the soldiers too. Even though he was approaching in a military flier, he could envision a situation where everyone in the courtyard, friend and foe, turned as one to shoot at the evil magic.

I'll protect you if they do, Jaxi proclaimed. *Bullets are easy compared to dragon fire.*

I thought you were too tired to protect anyone else tonight.

I'll draw on my reserves to save the future father of my handler's children.

Ridge was glad to have the excuse of concentrating on the landing, a tricky one on the roof of the stone headquarters building. He did not know how to respond to the jab, even if that was all it was. He'd dismissed the idea of children years earlier, so it would definitely take some consideration. He found it flattering that Sardelle would consider *having* children with him, but could he see himself as a father?

Shaking his head, Ridge engaged the thrusters and cut off the propeller as he headed for the rooftop, leaving room for Duck to land next to him. Their fiery approach had paused the fighting in the courtyard, but the combatants still held weapons—rifles and swords for the soldiers and pickaxes and improvised clubs for the miners. Flames leaped from the wooden buildings, the men's and women's barracks, the mess hall, storage warehouses, and several smaller structures. Only the stone headquarters building and the machine shop with the library on the top floor remained in good shape, and even their walls had been charred, with wooden shutters seared off.

As soon as the flier settled, Ridge grabbed his rifle and hopped through the flames still ringing the craft. He landed and strode to the edge of the rooftop, hoping that his representation of authority would convince the miners to drop their weapons and that they wouldn't think to count how few "authority" figures had actually shown up.

If they shoot at me, I'll take that protection, Jaxi, he thought, hoping she was monitoring.

All of the eyes in the courtyard focused on him as he propped his leg up on the lip of the roof and looked down. He spotted Colonel Therrik right away, standing with a hatchet and a sword in hand and with his back to a wall. At least a dozen dead miners lay around him. Hells, they weren't going to want to have anything to do with authority figures, also known as their masters. But he had to try.

"Why are you all fighting each other?" Ridge yelled, aware that the courtyard had fallen silent, except for the crackling of burning wood. "When there's a dragon to kill?" He thrust his rifle toward the sky, hoping he looked like some famous general of old rallying his troops, rather than some out-of-touch cloud-kisser from the capital.

"Colonel Zirkander," someone yelled.

Well, at least someone remembered him. He squinted in the direction of the speaker and was surprised to see that it was one of the miners. The man looked familiar, one of the ones he had encountered during his inspection of the tunnels several months earlier.

"He's back!" another miner shouted.

"He's a general now," someone else shouted. That was a soldier, though not anybody Ridge recognized.

On both sides of the courtyard, men charged toward the

headquarters building, shouting and waving their weapons. His first instinct was to step back, and perhaps hide behind Sardelle, but he slowly realized the people weren't shouting so much as they were cheering. Soldiers and miners crowded into the mud and gravel under the roof and waved up to him.

Over in the corner, Therrik, who had been deprived of his opponents as they ran to see Ridge, lowered his weapons and glowered fiercely. He opened his mouth, but if he said anything, Ridge couldn't hear it. People below were still cheering, and they were yelling up toward him now too. The cries mingled together, and he couldn't understand much, but he heard his name, along with promises that he would "fix everything" and give them "days off."

He rubbed his face, feeling the weight of expectations settling on his shoulders. This was almost worse than gunfire.

That will teach you for being a liberal overseer, Jaxi said. *Having Therrik show up to take your place probably made them cranky.*

"Of that I have no doubt," Ridge muttered. Therrik was stalking in his direction now.

Ridge made a cutting motion to Sardelle, telling her to turn off the flames. Even if these people saw him as some kind of benevolent commander who might improve things, they were bound to remember they were afraid of magic eventually. He kept his rifle in hand as he headed for the steps.

Do you want me to stay close to you? Sardelle had climbed down from the flier and had her palm on Jaxi's pommel. *Or would it be better if I remained out of sight?* She glanced at Tylie. *Both of us.*

I'd love you close to me, but you're probably right about staying out of sight, at least until we get the miners settled down. They might remember you.

Less fondly than they remember you, yes.

Her tone was wry and without malice, but Ridge winced, anyway. These people's rejection had to hurt, especially when she had saved them all from that shaman and the Cofah soldiers. What had he done? He'd gotten in an air skirmish with the shaman's pet owl. Gee.

Don't stay too far out of sight, please. There are probably injured people. Ridge knew she would want to heal them, even if they were stoats' teats to her. He doubted he would have that kind of generosity if he had her power.

You're right, she thought after a moment. *There are.*

I'll check on it, get things organized. That was the last thought Ridge had time for. He had reached the bottom of the stairs.

A few soldiers pushed their way to the front and tried vainly to hold back the miners. Ridge's instincts were to respond similarly, but he wanted to appear confident. He waved the soldiers aside, giving them pats on the back, then clasped some of the grasping hands of the miners, ignoring how grubby and dirt-smeared they were. After squabbling with a dragon, he was probably grubby too.

"You came back, Colonel," another said. "They told me I couldn't have my days off. But I read those books!"

"We heard about the fortress," someone blurted. "That's cracking. Death to the Cofah!"

"Death to the Cofah! Death to the Cofah!" At least fifty voices took up the cry, with more men streaming out of the mines and the burning buildings to join the crowd.

Therrik had reached the back of the massive gathering and started pushing his way through, nearly flattening men in his way.

"We'll get it all straightened out," Ridge said, hoping to placate everyone before Therrik riled them up again. "But first, I need to know everything about the dragon, what happened, and where the injured people are. If you'll just—"

He hadn't been inviting the entire crowd to tell him—he'd been hoping to let them know he needed to talk to Therrik—but they all started speaking with great enthusiasm.

"Wait, wait, please," he called, patting the air with his hands.

"All of you idiots, shut your holes," Therrik roared, his belligerent voice cutting over the clamor.

I can't imagine why they're revolting, Ridge thought.

I'm not sure if King Angulus thought this through, Sardelle responded. *This might have been a bigger punishment for the miners and soldiers than for Therrik.*

I'm not arguing.

"Go back to your posts," Therrik continued. "Sergeants Mandor, Fixston. Take their tools. Get everybody on fire suppression duty. Nobody's going to eat if we don't get the fires in those warehouses out. Now!"

The miners shrank within themselves at his tirade, and the soldiers did too. They all looked to Ridge before acting. Even though he outranked Therrik now, he didn't want to stir the pot too much. He was just passing through, after all.

"I know I'd like some griddle cakes and bacon in the morning," Ridge said, waving at the two sergeants Therrik had singled out. "If those fires all get put out in the next hour, we'll all have an extra big breakfast."

The cheers erupted again, and men ran across the courtyard toward piles of snow that had already been brought in, most likely for that purpose. Ridge didn't know how efficient the miners would be at firefighting, but as long as they weren't trying to kill the soldiers, that was a good thing.

"You bring extra rations with you in those two fliers, Zirkander?" Therrik growled. "Because the fixings for bacon and griddle cakes don't come in that often."

Ridge thought about reminding the grumpy colonel that it was *General* Zirkander now, and he expected to be sirred, but Therrik was probably irked enough from having Ridge end the rebel takeover simply by showing up.

"If we succeed in killing the dragon, we can roast it on a spit," Ridge said.

"Killing it? Our cannonballs bounced *off* it. It's not coming back, is it?" Therrik stared at the sky in alarm.

It was the first time Ridge could remember seeing him daunted. He didn't enjoy the expression nearly as much as he would have expected.

"I'm not sure. We don't know what he wants." If Morishtomaric wanted Tylie, and he had believed that Tylie was dead, why would he have come to attack the fort? Had he been in the mood to wreak havoc and it had been the closest spot?

Therrik's gaze shifted past his shoulder and up the stairs.

Ridge tensed, worried that Sardelle had come down, which might spur Therrik to greater irritation.

Sorry, no. She slipped away when I was trying to gauge how many wounded there were. Be right there.

Tylie was padding down the stone steps in her grass sandals. Ridge grimaced. He specifically remembered handing her boots and a parka before they left. She was wearing the fur-trimmed garment, but her toes had to be freezing on the cold stairs. Even if it wasn't as cold here as it had been in the winter, it still wasn't warm.

"Did you lose something, Zirkander?" Therrik asked.

Sardelle hustled down, catching Tylie before she could descend all the way.

"We're going to help," Tylie announced brightly.

Does that cheerfulness mean Phelistoth is better? Ridge wondered.

I think it might. I can't sense either dragon at the moment.

Good. The outpost has had enough winged company today.

Will he let us pass? Sardelle glanced at Therrik. *There are a lot of people who were burned and hurt in the fighting. Tylie is going to help me with them. I've taught her a few things, and I believe she can be useful.*

After giving Sardelle a frosty stare, Therrik jerked a thumb toward Tylie. "What is this?"

"Those are females, Therrik," Ridge said. "I didn't think you'd been out here long enough to forget what one was." Technically, the outpost housed a small contingent of female criminals, but they were as tough and grubby as the men, and didn't tend to stir the male imagination.

Therrik's frosty glare turned toward Ridge. He smiled affably and clapped the colonel on the shoulder—a move he wouldn't have tried when they had been the same rank. "Tell me what's been going on, and I'll tell you why I'm here. If you're curious."

"Not really."

"Good. Then it'll be a brief meeting. We have a lot to get done. Also, Sardelle and her new apprentice would like to be shown to your injured people to help with healing." Ridge looked up the stairs to see if Duck had followed them down. He wanted someone he trusted watching over Sardelle and Tylie while they worked. He well remembered how the locals felt about magic.

"Healing." Therrik clenched his teeth, the tendons in his throat springing out. He looked even leaner and more muscular than the last time they had met. He had probably been throwing weights—and soldiers—around instead of drinking.

"Yes, healing," Ridge said. "They're going to wriggle their fingers and wave powerful magics all over your injured people."

Should you be antagonizing him? Sardelle rested a protective hand on Tylie's shoulder, her gaze on Therrik.

Being a general wouldn't be much fun if I didn't *get to antagonize lower-ranking officers. Besides, you said I didn't have to be a good role model until after we have children.*

I'm not sure those were my precise *words.*

Therrik kept grinding his teeth and glowering. Sardelle was waiting on the steps, but she couldn't get by unless Therrik moved. Or unless she magicked up a powerful gust of wind to hurl him across the courtyard and onto his ass. Ridge wouldn't mind seeing that, but it shouldn't be necessary.

"You've got injured people, Colonel," he said, dropping the sarcasm from his tone. "Let her do something about them."

"We have a medic."

"You have one beleaguered man, who's recruited three soldiers who barely know what they're doing," Sardelle said. "Let me help."

Therrik's dark eyes grew a touch wild at this proof that she knew more than she could by mundane means.

"Come on, Therrik." This time, when Ridge reached for Therrik's shoulder, he kept his hand there. "We need to talk." He jerked his chin to the entrance of the headquarters building. He was well aware of the way Therrik tensed, as if to repel an attack, but Ridge trusted—hopefully not naively—that the man wouldn't strike a superior officer. His indoctrination to the military should supersede his hatred—his *fear*—of all things magical.

Therrik growled and stalked off the stairs, jerking his shoulder from Ridge's grip. So long as he let Sardelle and Tylie pass.

"Duck?" Ridge called up before following Therrik into the building. Duck had trotted down the stairs and stopped behind Sardelle. He was looking around the outpost with curiosity. "Watch them while I'm getting my report and telling him what we want."

"Yes, sir."

"And be especially careful of the miners. They're all criminals who chose this over an executioner's axe."

Duck's eyes widened, but then he nodded, glancing around the courtyard again. Numerous unconscious and dead men lay in the mud, people who had been taken down in the uprising before Ridge arrived. "I get it now, sir."

"We'll be fine." Sardelle touched Ridge's arm as she and Tylie passed, heading straight toward the machine shop. As one of the few stone buildings that hadn't been damaged by the fire, it must have been turned into an infirmary. There was a real infirmary inside of headquarters, but it was a small room with a single bed. Even without Sardelle's senses, Ridge was sure there were a lot more injured than such a space would accommodate.

"Is there anything you want me to ask specifically about?" Ridge called after her. *Aside from asking about soulblades?* he added silently, not wanting to yell that across the courtyard.

To anyone watching, all she did was shake her head and wave. Mentally, she said, *Do ask if any swords have been recovered, please. Jaxi will start the research while I'm healing people. She can peruse the books here without being in close proximity to them.*

Yes, I recall how she helped you win days off from me. He smirked after her as she opened the door to the machine shop.

The look she sent back across the courtyard was a touch embarrassed. He gave her a lazy two-fingered salute, made sure Duck was staying close to her and Tylie, then pushed open the door to the headquarters building. Not surprisingly, Therrik wasn't standing there waiting for him with a cup of coffee. He must have already stomped up to his office.

Despite his earlier antagonizing, Ridge decided he should be professional, not sarcastic, and certainly not smugly superior. If Morishtomaric came back, Ridge and Therrik would have to defend the outpost together. They didn't need internal hostilities when they already had a dragon that wanted to kill them and hundreds of criminals who would gladly help with that. Besides, Therrik had been the one who had broken him out of jail so that he could find King Angulus. As much as Ridge wanted to pretend it wasn't true, he owed the man something. If not a favor, then perhaps a bit of civility.

Aw, you are *practicing to be a role model. That's sweet.*

Aren't you supposed to be researching something, Jaxi?

I'm looking for those books that were dug out the last time we were here. I thought they might be in that building. I'm hoping they're not in one of the smoldering ones.

Try the library over your head.

That implies a degree of organization I wasn't expecting from this place. Also, an openness to let anyone on the compound access books written by witches, as you people call us.

You people? Ridge made it to the second floor and the office that had once been his without encountering Therrik.

Not you *specifically. Sardelle has trained you well.*

You're the one who's more likely to incinerate one of my favorite body parts if I don't address you properly.

That's possibly true. Sardelle is a tolerant soul.

Ridge found Therrik inside, standing behind the desk in a rigid parade rest, with two logbooks open. He stared past Ridge's shoulder toward an uninteresting spot on the doorframe without blinking very often. His jaw was still clenched. A hard man to be civil with and an even harder one to want to do favors for.

"Relax," Ridge said, though he doubted Therrik knew how. "I'm just here to look for a sword and do some research on the way to hunt down that dragon."

Therrik's gaze flicked toward him. "You should have brought the dragon-slaying sword."

"Lieutenant—Ms. Ahn has it." Something Ridge wasn't excited about—he still couldn't believe she had volunteered to wield it again. He couldn't help but wonder if she was hoping she would get herself killed doing this. That thought made him want to cry inside. Maybe on the outside too. He hated the idea of losing another of his people to a mistake. That dragon shouldn't even exist. It wouldn't be roaming Iskandia now if humans hadn't set it free.

"A pilot." Therrik's lip curled. "The king should have commanded me to carry it. It's *my* family's weapon, and I would gladly fight a dragon, especially now." He glowered toward the night sky beyond the window. Yes, he would probably welcome a chance to redeem himself in the king's eyes.

"Your name came up, but we're assuming it's going to be an air battle. You'd have to fly up to meet the dragon. Probably with lots of loops and rolls." Ridge made squiggly motions in the air with his finger.

"You were afraid I'd puke on you?"

"The thought crossed my mind."

"I'd still kill that dragon."

"I'll let the king know that you're interested," Ridge said. *After he and Ahn and the others had already defeated the dragon.* At least that was how he hoped it turned out.

Therrik shot him a suspicious look, then his face softened, ever so slightly. "Good."

"About that sword, you don't by chance know any magical words that can control it, do you?"

"No."

"The queen knew them."

"The queen had an organization doing research for her." Therrik shrugged. "There was nothing in the box it came in."

Of course not. That would have been too easy.

"All right," Ridge said. "Have you pulled any other swords out of the ground here? The king would like a few more blades with the power to hurt a dragon around in case we need them."

"Magical swords." The hard expression returned.

"Yeah, magical swords, and guess what? Kasandral is magical too. You've been sleeping with a loused up magical sword under your bed."

"It's anti-magic, not magic, you fool. It *kills* those with magic in their veins."

"There's no ore in these mountains that can give a sword power and tell it to take swings at dragons. It's magical." Ridge wasn't sure that was an accurate statement, but he assumed *some* kind of magic had been used to craft it. "And that's General Fool to you."

"Are you officially inviting me to call you that?" Therrik's eyes glinted. Amused, was he? That was better than belligerent. Possibly.

"I'm officially inviting you to show me any swords or other interesting artifacts you've pulled out of the mines, aside from the crystals." Ridge stepped away from the doorway and extended a hand toward the hallway in invitation. He had no idea if artifacts had been found, but it would make things easier if Tylie's special sword could simply be plucked from a pile in an office somewhere.

Therrik headed for the door, and Ridge allowed his hopes to rise. Maybe this would be easy, after all. Maybe he and his team could depart at dawn to join the others, leaving Therrik to the inmates.

He almost bumped into Therrik's back when his guide stopped after only two steps into the hallway. After unlocking a door to the right, Therrik stepped into a room beside the office. He scraped a match on the wall and lit a lantern.

Ridge looked out over neatly stacked crates and shelves lined with what appeared to be a lot of mundane junk. A bookcase held a bunch of old tomes—might those be what Jaxi sought? But as far as magical swords went, the silverware sets, pans, bookends, fans, ink pots, quill holders, and something that looked to be a racket for a sport were not promising. There were a few weapons leaning in a rack in the corner, but none of them had the intricate blade work or sheer splendor of Jaxi.

You think I'm splendorous? Thank you.

Compared to this stuff? Ridge picked up a fork with a missing tine. *Yes.*

Compared to all things, I should think. Jaxi sniffed. *Since you're wondering, yes, those are all Referatu items, but there are only two things in that room that are imbued with magic, a dented piece from an automatic clothes washing machine and a self-turning pottery wheel. Many of the books, which I am already reading, also have magically treated pages and ink-preserving dyes. The swords are practice blades from the training hall I was buried near.*

No soulblades, huh?

Alas, no. I, too, would have preferred not to take a journey back into the mines. I spent far too much time down there already.

"You saving that one for the griddle cakes?" Therrik asked. He'd taken up a position by the window, looking toward the sky, aside from occasional glances at Ridge.

The fork Ridge still held had string tied to it, along with a label that proclaimed it a silver fork found on Level 13 North, Kitchen, #3732. Every item in the room was tagged similarly. Ridge walked to a table with a logbook open on it and found all of the items cataloged there. It was the kind of thorough job Apex would have done, if he'd been given such a task. And he'd still been alive.

Ridge returned the fork to its shelf. Even though he was sure Therrik had assigned someone this chore, the fact that he'd bothered spoke to more of a commitment to organization than Ridge would have guessed he had. He supposed it was childish that he would have preferred to find Therrik up here drunk. That more closely fit his notions of the man being little more than an overly muscled combat thug.

"Good work here, Colonel," he forced himself to say, waving to the room. "Unfortunately, all it did was make it easy to see that what we're looking for isn't here. Sardelle will have to search for that herself. Let's talk about the attack and making the outpost fit to stand another one, shall we?"

"What's your plan for doing that? You don't know a damned thing about fortifying installations."

Nothing like offering a compliment and getting an insult in return. Ridge forced himself to smile. "I know what makes installations weak against aerial attacks."

The dragon is back, Jaxi announced.

Ridge's smile vanished. *What? Why?*

Oddly, he didn't tell me. He's up on a mountaintop about twenty miles from here. He seems to be perching up there, rather than coming closer, but I don't know how long that will last. There's nothing else up here that could be interesting him.

"What are you doing, Zirkander?"

They had been on their way out of the room when Ridge had stopped to talk to Jaxi.

"Admiring the whorls on this wood paneling. Also receiving information that you're not going to like."

Therrik mouthed the word, "Receiving," before scowling and saying, "I don't like anything you say. Ever. Spit it out."

"Not ever? I had nice things to say about your fork-organization skills."

His eyes narrowed further. "If I throttled you, would you whine to my superiors about it?"

"Depends on how *hard* you throttle me. Do I get to walk away? Would there be marks?"

Therrik grunted. "Are you afraid of anything, Zirkander?"

"I'm moderately concerned about the dragon sitting on a peak and keeping an eye on us from twenty miles away."

"You saw that?"

Not personally, but... "He's there."

Therrik pushed Ridge toward the door. "Next time you come to visit me, leave your witch and bring me my sword."

Ridge wanted to punch him until he stopped calling Sardelle a witch. He hoped she had the opportunity to save him from dragon fire and that he would have to live to a ripe old age, knowing he was completely in her debt. In lieu of that, he would still enjoy seeing her hurl him across the courtyard on his ass.

He gritted his teeth and said only, "I'll keep that request in mind."

He allowed Therrik to push him into the hallway. He was going to have to deprive Sardelle of her guard. Someone needed to fly south and get within communication range of the airship team. Duck was the only logical choice, since if Ridge left, the miners would be back at the soldiers' throats. Of course, even if he stayed, there was no guarantee that such a thing wouldn't happen.

* * *

Cas walked the passageway toward Tolemek's door later than she had anticipated. General Ort hadn't sent the fliers back out to check on the downed Cofah craft, but the airship itself had descended far enough to lower infantry soldiers to the ground to round up injured prisoners. Ort had asked Cas—and the sword—to go with them in case they had to deal with the sorceress. She had stood nearby, dread curdling in her stomach. Logically, she knew they needed to find the sorceress and deal with her, but she hadn't wanted to face her with just Kasandral. Even though the sword could hurt the woman, she would have felt far more comfortable dodging fireballs and attacking from within her flier. In the end, it hadn't mattered because the sorceress hadn't been among those that the troops had rounded up. Cas wasn't surprised. The sorceress had been one of the few Cofah to escape from the flying fortress. Ort was questioning the prisoners as to where she had gone, but Cas doubted he would learn anything useful.

She knocked lightly on Tolemek's door, half expecting him to have tended his own wounds and gone to sleep already. Still, as soon as she had returned, she had washed, donned a clean uniform, and grabbed a first-aid kit.

Tolemek answered the door instead of hollering for her to come in. It was just as well, since she might not have heard him. A lot of shouts and banging noises came from above decks. The crew, along with many of the gunners and infantrymen, had been pressed into starting repairs right away. She wasn't sure how she had avoiding being included on a work crew, as other officers had been pulled into duty, but nobody had pointed at her, Pimples, or Kaika. Maybe they had appeared too battered for extra work. Or maybe they were being rewarded for taking down the first airship. Cas grimaced at that idea. She didn't want to be rewarded for anything, especially when all she had done was drop a sword. She would have preferred extra duties, or perhaps to be assigned to the team General Ort had ordered to sweep through the ship and make sure there weren't any Cofah stowing away.

"I see you've come wearing smiles," Tolemek said, standing in front of her bare-chested and with a towel slung over his shoulder. He glanced down. "And sexy attire."

Cas snorted, since the formless military fatigues were anything but. "I didn't know you were supposed to bring sexy attire along on dragon-slaying missions." Even back home, the only thing she had that possibly qualified as sexy was a nightgown with some lace on the hem. "I couldn't imagine needing it to hurl swords at sorceresses."

"Hurling swords? I don't think that's the proper use for such a weapon."

"We're living in unique times." Cas could have stood there and admired his chest for a while, especially since she hadn't seen much of it of late, but she remembered her mission and peered up at the side of his head. It didn't look like he had treated his wound yet, though he had washed the blood off his face. Knowing him, he had gotten caught up in some experiment and forgotten that a bullet had sliced through his locks and left a furrow in his scalp. "Want to sit down and let me rub goo on that?"

"Yes." Tolemek took a few steps into the room, then paused. "Just to clarify, you're talking about my *wound*, right?"

"Yes."

She followed him inside and waved for him to sit on the bed. As she set down the first-aid kit, she realized that had been a joke. Some kind of innuendo. She should have responded with a wink or a flirty statement that would let him know she'd gotten it. Except that she hadn't. Why did these things always go over her head?

"It was good of *you* to dress in something sexy," she said.

That did not come out as flirty as she had intended, so she rested a hand on his shoulder, hoping it would get the point across. She really ought to be less awkward with him by now, but after she had barely spoken to him for the last month, she felt less certain of his feelings. And she had *never* been good at flirting, not with anyone. For most of her life, it had never occurred to her to try.

Tolemek touched his palm to his bare chest, his chin tilted down as he looked up at her through his lashes, his ropes of hair hanging down to frame his face. "I didn't think you noticed."

"I always notice." And she did. She liked looking at him with his shirt off—with other things off too. How he remained so fit when he worked in a lab all day, she didn't know. She'd caught him doing chin-ups from a bar in the corner a couple of times, but didn't know if he truly exercised with any intent these days. As a pirate, he had, so he could look fierce and use his body and reputation to intimidate people, so he rarely had to fight. Maybe he still felt he needed to do that here in Iskandia.

"Do you? I rarely notice you noticing."

"Your eyesight isn't as quick and agile as mine." Cas pushed his hair back so she could get a better look at the gouge, letting her hand linger on his shoulder.

"I don't think I can argue with that."

"Good. Where's your healing gunk?"

"Gunk? Healing Salve Number Seven is on that counter." He shifted to get up, but she pressed down on his shoulder to stop him.

"I'll get it."

"I thought you were going to spend more time admiring my formulas, calling them by appealing names, perhaps."

Cas returned with the jar. "Perhaps if you came *up* with an appealing name, I would use it."

"Hm."

She found a basin he had filled, gave the sponge a wary look, then brought it over to dab his wound clean. She tended it carefully, certain it must be painful, given the depth. It started bleeding anew as she worked, so she hurried to dab some of the goo on. As she recalled from personal experience, it caused wounds to close up and heal much more quickly than a mundane concoction would.

Though she worried his pain might be making him

uncomfortable, Tolemek gazed at her contentedly as she worked, a rare smile curving his lips upward. Though he was more playful with her than he was in general, he often managed to look somber, even when he was trying to be mischievous. It was as if he could never quite forget his past, never allow himself to relax completely and enjoy life. But then, who was she to think such thoughts? When was the last time *she* had enjoyed anything? Wasn't it a crime to contemplate enjoyment, after what she had done? It seemed like it would be more of a crime to let herself forget. It bothered her that the others were willing to do just that. Oh, Pimples didn't know, and she wasn't sure if even General Ort knew exactly what had happened in the castle, but Kaika did. Zirkander did. Sardelle did. Nobody had frowned at her in condemnation, not then, and not at the king's meeting. She had a hard time understanding why not. Especially with Zirkander. He'd been Apex's commanding officer for years, longer than Cas had even been in the squadron.

"Such a serious nurse," Tolemek murmured, watching her eyes. "Did anything happen out there? Any sign of the sorceress? Did you have to use the sword?"

The sword. She did not want to think about the sword. Kasandral had seemed grouchy with her when she put it back in its box, but how could a blade convey such a thing? Surely, it had been her own mind making that up.

"She got away. I used the sword briefly to break through her barrier around the airship." She nodded at him, wanting to avoid talking about Kasandral. "You seem far more contented, especially for a man with a hole in his head. What are you thinking about? Sponges?"

Tolemek startled her by laughing. "No. Not yet, anyway. I was thinking of our kiss from earlier."

She had thought of that kiss a few times, too, remembering how much she had enjoyed it, especially after so long with just her own company. She wasn't sure she *should* be enjoying such things, but she had.

"Good," she murmured.

"Good?" He looked hopeful.

Cas screwed the lid back on the salve and picked up a roll of bandages. "I'm not sure I'd know what to do with sponges. Sexily, anyway."

"Oh." He chuckled again. "Just washing, I think. Slowly and enticingly. Though I suppose Captain Kaika could have had more in mind. She's more worldly than I am."

"Me too." By far. Cas considered his head. "I'm not sure how I'm going to wrap this bandage. Around your hair? It's going to be awfully lumpy if I try." She prodded one of the ropes of hair on the other side of his head. "Maybe we could do something with these."

"It'll stop bleeding soon, now that the salve is on it. No need to shave my head."

"I was envisioning tying it back, not shaving it. I like to be able to tell you apart from the Cofah soldiers."

She'd meant it as a joke, but his smile faltered. It was easy to forget he had been exactly that, a Cofah soldier.

"I don't think anyone will mistake me for one of them again," he said. "*They* certainly won't. I seem to be quite recognizably a traitor."

"Sorry. I didn't mean to—"

"It's fine." The smile didn't quite return, but he tugged at the hem of her uniform jacket. "Do you have any wounds you'd like me to apply salve to? You looked a little rough when..." He trailed off, his hand lowering, and his head turning toward the door.

It was still closed. The noises on the deck above had died down, and she hadn't heard anything in the passageway. Tolemek stood up, his head brushing the low ceiling of the lab. He reached over and cut out the closest lantern, then headed for another one beside a stack of beakers and test tubes that had survived the air battle.

"Did you bring a pistol?" he asked softly.

"I didn't think I'd need one against the sponges." Trusting his instincts, Cas pulled a folding knife out of the first-aid kit.

Tolemek extinguished the second lantern. Darkness fell across the cabin.

Before Cas could decide if she wanted to question him,

someone knocked on the door. It was a light knock, as if the owner didn't want to be heard. Tolemek did not answer it. Cas thought he had moved away from the lantern and closer to the door, but the darkness was absolute, and she could not be certain.

The latch clunked softly, and the door opened. Cas had a glimpse of a bearded man with short, tousled hair, but he darted inside so quickly, closing the door behind him, that she couldn't make out more. All she knew was that with the beard, he was not part of the Iskandian, all-military crew.

She opened the knife and lowered to a crouch, breathing shallowly so she wouldn't make a noise. The creaking of the cables and an occasional shout filtered down from the deck above. Someone walked through the passageway outside, boots clomping on the polished wood. Whoever had come inside did not make a noise. She did not think he had come far into the cabin, but if he was an expert on moving about stealthily, he might have done so without her noticing.

A faint click came from the middle of the lab, then the sound of something rolling across the floor. Cas took a deep breath, expecting one of Tolemek's knockout grenades. Indeed, she caught a whiff of a familiar sickly smoky scent at the end of her inhalation. She wouldn't have much time to act before she had to draw in air. Tolemek must mean to do something quickly. She was tempted to try and detain the intruder herself, but if he was doing the same thing, they could get in each other's way.

A thump sounded, and the door opened. The man was trying to escape. Cas took a step forward, but Tolemek acted more quickly. He threw himself onto the man's back. Their combined weight made the door slam shut again. Thumps and grunts followed as the men crashed to the deck and wrestled. Someone kicked a cabinet, and glass rattled.

Not about to jump into a knife fight in the dark, Cas eased across the room toward the lantern. Still holding her breath, the smoke in the air tickling her nose, she found it by feel. Tolemek had fully extinguished it, so she couldn't simply turn it back up again.

More thumps came from near the door, followed by

something that sounded like a head cracking against a bulkhead. Neither man cried out, and she didn't know who had been hit. She fumbled at the base of the lantern for the match compartment. Wishing she had a pistol in hand, she drew out a match and scraped it across the striker. A small flame burst to life.

She held it aloft before lighting the wick, wanting to make sure Tolemek wasn't about to be slain. He was on his knees, holding a knife to the throat of the man who'd come in, a man whose eyes were crossing. A few feet away, the knockout grenade sent tendrils of smoke into the air. Tolemek looked at it and jerked his head. Toward the door? He was holding his breath too.

With her lungs starting to call out for air, Cas hurried to light the lantern and grab the grenade. The metal was warm against her palm, and whatever was in the formula for the smoke made her hand itch. She looked around for somewhere to stuff it. Should she throw it into the passageway? No, other people were out there. With her breath running out, she jammed it into a drawer, smothered it with a towel, and slammed the drawer shut and latched it.

She stepped back and sucked in a big breath. Maybe she shouldn't have, not so early. Right away, her head felt thick, her thoughts foggy.

Tolemek dragged his captive over to a switch on the wall. He threw it, and a noisy ventilation system kicked in, grinding and clanking like a dying steam carriage. "Cas. There's a truth serum in that vial in the rack on the far counter there. Will you get it, please?"

Cas's heart lurched, memories flooding back to her at the mention of his truth drugs. She'd confessed her entire life to him and that awful pirate captain when she had been their prisoner. She had also spoken openly of Zirkander, of adoring feelings she'd had for him in her younger days. Even months later, the memory made her cheeks heat with embarrassment.

Telling herself the drug was not for *her* this time, Cas headed to the rack he had indicated with the jerk of his chin.

"Is he Cofah?" she asked, returning with the vial.

The man's chin slumped to his chest, and his body fell limp in Tolemek's arms.

"We can ask him when he wakes up. Would you mind opening the door?" His voice sounded slow, but Cas didn't know if it was the way he was speaking or if she was simply drug-addled. Tolemek blinked a few times, his eyes glassy. "The ventilation fans are not up to modern standards." He let his unconscious captive slide down to the deck and started searching him.

Cas stumbled a couple of times, which made her feel pathetic, because there wasn't anything on the floor or in her way. She nearly fell into the passageway as she opened the door. She sucked in the relatively fresh air out there—in truth, it smelled like unwashed laundry and smoke, but anything was better than the tainted lab air.

"Raptor?" came a concerned inquiry from down the hall. "Are you all right?"

Pimples stood a few doors down in his undershirt, with a damp towel slung over his shoulder. From his frown, Cas judged she looked even more unwell than she felt.

"Fine." She braced herself against the doorframe. "Air quality issue."

Pimples strode forward, the concern on his face turning into something else. Anger?

With her thoughts still muzzy, she struggled to figure out why he would be mad.

He touched her arm and scowled into the lab. "Have you been *fighting?*"

"No. He toppled over before anything escalated to a fight."

Belatedly, it occurred to her that Pimples must have thought she and *Tolemek* had been fighting. That might have been preferable to breathing one of his concoctions.

She shook her head and pointed at the figure slumped at Tolemek's feet. "We have a visitor."

Some of the righteous fury on Pimples' face faded, but he still looked suspiciously at Tolemek, his long hair falling wildly about his bare chest. Finally, he focused his frown on the more appropriate figure.

"We missed one of the Cofah?" he asked.

"It would seem so."

"We can handle it." Tolemek had dumped a dagger, throwing stars, a pistol, a bone-handled garrote, and a couple of tiny ceramic jars onto the deck, the contents of the man's belt and pockets.

Pimples walked inside. Cas was reluctant to leave the doorway—she much preferred the air out there. Tolemek hadn't passed out, but she felt queasy and logy. She remembered the time she'd shared wine with her comrades after a successful mission. It had muddled her thoughts, and she had been ready to collapse into her bunk after one glass. She had stayed away from alcohol since then. As she stumbled back into the cabin with heavy feet, she made a note to herself to avoid Tolemek's concoctions in the future too.

"You don't look good, Cas." Pimples gripped her elbow, like he worried she would topple over if he didn't support her.

Tolemek caught the touch, and his lips thinned, but he did not say anything. He continued removing weapons—their visitor had been carrying a small armory on his person.

Cas extracted her arm. "I'm fine. Thanks. Let's worry about that fellow, eh?"

"Sure, Raptor." Pimples nudged the downed man with the toe of his boot. The figure groaned, stirring slightly.

Tolemek jumped to his feet and dug through a nearby drawer. He definitely had not been as affected by the gas. Cas picked up the pistol to aim at their captive, feeling much better with a projectile weapon in hand. No matter how much gas she had inhaled, she trusted her aim better than her ability to grapple with the man.

"You want me to hold him down?" Pimples asked.

"No." Tolemek didn't seem to be interested in accepting help, at least not from him.

Now that Pimples realized Tolemek hadn't been pummeling her, he seemed quite curious about the intruder. "Think he's here for Raptor? Or for you, Deathmaker?"

"It's Tolemek, and I've already been informed there's a bounty on my head." He withdrew a coil of rope from the drawer and stepped over the man to tie him up.

Cas had been leaning against a counter for support, but she stood straight at his words. She had assumed this was some soldier from the Cofah airship, even if he lacked the typical shaven head, but as her head slowly cleared, she realized Tolemek must be right. This man had all of the gear of an assassin, even if he hadn't turned out to be a very good one.

"I thought we'd be safe from that out here," she murmured. A foolish assumption, perhaps. Her father had traveled all the way to Owanu Owanus for a mission.

Tolemek smiled bleakly at her. The man's head jerked up, and he flexed his shoulders, trying to lash out. Tolemek had already tied his hands behind his back, and he kept him on his knees, so he couldn't use his legs.

"You have the vial, Cas?" he asked.

"The truth serum?" She dug it out of his pocket and held it out.

"Open it and wave it under his nose."

"It doesn't need to go in a sandwich?" She couldn't hold back a dark look as she approached. Even if she and Tolemek had become close since then, she'd confessed things that day that she never would have told another.

"No." Tolemek kept his face and his tone neutral. "It actually works more quickly if it's inhaled."

Keeping the pistol in her left hand and aimed at the assassin's chest, Cas thumbed the cork out of the vial with her other hand.

"Don't inhale it yourself," Tolemek said.

"Sure, *now* I get that warning." She glanced toward the drawer where she had stuffed the grenade.

The man flexed his shoulders again, trying to twist away from Tolemek.

"Want me to hold the pistol on him?" Pimples asked.

Tolemek gave him a flat look.

"Or I could stand over here and look threatening," Pimples said.

Cas snorted. Even in his cockpit with his machine guns firing, Pimples couldn't manage to look threatening.

The assassin tried to twist his head away, to avoid the

approaching vial. Cas jammed the muzzle of the pistol under his chin and kept her face cold and indifferent, lest he think the threat was not serious.

"I don't care that much if we kill you before you can tell us what you know," she said. Since this man had come to Tolemek's lab, intending to kill him, she would have no qualms about doing just that.

"You'll kill me, anyway." Surprisingly, he did not have a Cofah accent. That made Cas pause. He sounded Iskandian.

"Not necessarily." Tolemek shifted his grip so he could hold the assassin by the back of the neck and keep his head still.

"We might just throw you over the railing," Cas added.

"How far up are we?"

"I'm not sure, but if you count how many seconds it takes for you to hit the ground, Pimples over there can probably tell you how far you fell."

Pimples grinned, probably pleased at being included.

Cas waved the vial under the man's nose. He held his breath. Cas settled into a crouch to wait.

"Did the Cofah emperor hire you?" she asked.

The man stared mulishly at her. He had not taken a whiff of the vial yet, and his face had turned red.

"I wonder why he wants me now," Tolemek said.

"The emperor?" Cas asked.

He nodded. "He never seemed to care about me when I was a pirate. I was concerned, back then, that my actions might cause someone to take retribution on my parents or on Tylie. Tylie's out of their reach now—" he glanced down at his captive, "—or at least I hope she is." He looked like he might say more, but he glanced down again and kept his mouth closed.

Cas had never gotten the sense that Tolemek was that close with his parents, especially his father, but that didn't mean he wanted them killed, or that he wanted to see the home he had grown up in destroyed. She understood all too well.

A frustrated gasp came from their captive, and he inhaled deeply. His lungs had won the battle over his mind. He tried to twist his head again, but Tolemek had an iron grip on the back of his neck.

"It'll take a couple minutes," Tolemek said. "He'll lose the will to fight and start answering honestly."

"Yes, I recall."

Pimples stirred, frowning over at her. She closed her mouth. She didn't want to explain what had happened back then to anyone else. She needed to stop bringing up the past. Though, as she had been proving to herself of late, she had a hard time letting things go.

The tenseness disappeared from the assassin's body. He lifted his head, no longer seeming aware of the vial held under his nose. He gave her a flirty smile.

"Who sent you?" Cas asked again.

"Let's go to your room, and we can chat about it."

Tolemek's eyes narrowed. Cas wondered if the assassin was aware of the drug and doing something to keep from answering questions. When she'd been under the influence of a similar serum, she hadn't been aware of it. Tolemek's captain had sneaked it into a sandwich that she had been too ravenous to reject. But the assassin had watched her holding the vial. Greater awareness might make him warier.

"We'll discuss it here," Cas said, and changed the question in case that helped. "Who did you come to kill? You're an assassin, right?"

"I am. A good one."

Not very good. "Who are you here for?"

The man leaned forward as far as he could with Tolemek gripping him from behind. He whispered conspiratorially. "Deathmaker. They want him dead, you know. Deathmaker dead." He giggled.

"Yes, I've heard that. Who did you say wanted him dead?"

"I'll earn fifty thousand drakkons if I bring his head back."

"To whom?"

"The emperor's agent. At the docks in the capital."

"The *Cofah* emperor, right? But you're Iskandian, aren't you?"

The assassin nodded. "They want our people to do it. So they won't get blamed. I'll gladly do it." The serum should have left him feeling happy and contented—Cas remembered how silly and open she had been—but he managed a sneer. "Tanglewood. He killed everybody at Tanglewood. What's the king *thinking*?"

"You're an assassin, and you're judging Tol—Deathmaker for Tanglewood?" She had judged Tolemek for Tanglewood, too, and she would never be able to take those hundreds of innocent deaths lightly, but she was surprised someone like this would be bothered.

The man shrugged easily. "I kill people who deserve it. Those people didn't deserve it. There were women. Children."

Cas glanced at Tolemek and caught him looking away, his face hard, but his eyes haunted, as they always were when this subject came up. Years had passed since that incident. She imagined that she, too, would always be haunted by the memory of Apex's death. Everyone had regrets, mistakes they had made, but not everybody's mistakes resulted in people's deaths.

"Why are the Cofah worried about being blamed?" Pimples wondered. "We already have lots of things to blame them for, and it's not as if they care. They sure don't stop trying to invade Iskandia."

For the first time, Cas was glad he had inserted himself into the interrogation. Her own dark thoughts had distracted her, and she might not have thought to ask that question.

"Yes," she said, making sure the assassin knew the question was for him. "Why do the Cofah care if they're blamed for Deathmaker's death?"

"Deathmaker's death." The man giggled again.

Cas shook her head at Tolemek. "It's possible your serum could use further refinement."

"He's expressing his honest amusement."

"I'm not sure people should be amused when they're betraying their countries." Of course, Cas admitted, if he was Iskandian, he might not see this as a betrayal. She tapped his jaw with the pistol to pull his attention back. "Why do the Cofah care?"

"The emperor cares. That's what the agent implied. He doesn't want to be a target."

"A target for whom? And doesn't he have a thousand bodyguards?"

The man leaned forward again and lowered his voice. "Deathmaker's witch sister. They say..." He glanced to either side and licked his lips. "They say she has a dragon. A real dragon."

"Hm." Cas could not know if the Cofah emperor truly feared the dragon—this fellow might just be guessing, based on rumors he had heard—but she supposed it would make sense. A thousand bodyguards could keep an army of humans back, but would they be enough against a dragon?

"Guess the emperor doesn't have a glowy green sword," Pimples said.

They couldn't know that for sure, but Cas did find the idea comforting.

"If he's Iskandian," Tolemek said, "how did he get onto a Cofah airship? And damn it, how did he and the Cofah even know we were—I was—coming out here? Does the king have a leak in his security?"

"Ahnsung told me," the man said cheerfully. "I think he's starting to like me. He gave me the job and set me up with a Cofah contact in the city."

Ahnsung. Her father. Cas wanted to crawl under the bed and disappear.

All she could do was hope that she hadn't inadvertently given her father information. She hadn't told him of her departure, of the king's summons, or of anything. She hadn't even seen him since sneaking into the house. Still, he could have had her followed, knowing she would lead him to Tolemek. She frowned at the floor. Except that Tolemek's lab in the city wasn't a secret. Her father could have gone there on his own if he had wanted to kill him.

"Who's the Cofah contact?" Pimples grabbed a pencil and a small pad of paper. "The general will want to know that," he added to Cas.

Cas nodded. Though she felt numbed by her father's involvement, Pimples was right. The names and locations of spies in the city were important information.

Since she seemed to be the official interrogator, she repeated the question.

"Martus Finch at the Petals and Pearls Florist."

A florist? Well, why not? Her father used a landscaping company as a cover for some of his business.

"Anyone have any other questions?" Cas asked as Pimples wrote down the spy's information.

"I've heard enough," Tolemek said. "Lieutenant... Pimples—do you actually go by that?"

"You can call me Farris," Pimples said brightly. Almost eagerly. "Or Lieutenant Averstash. There's no *rule* that people have to use that horrible nickname." He glanced at Cas. "There isn't, right?"

"No."

"Lieutenant Averstash, help me take this man up to see your boss, will you?"

"Absolutely." Pimples stepped forward, then paused and looked at the pile of weapons and vials that Tolemek had removed from the assassin's pockets. "Do we need to take all that?"

"Leave the vials. I'll take a look at them. See what young assassins these days are bringing on missions to kill me."

Cas handed the pistol to Pimples and sat on the bed. She could have offered to help them drag the man off to the brig, but she doubted they needed it. Also, she felt drained and tired. More tired than she had been after the battle. She couldn't believe she had gone to her father and asked for a job. What had she been thinking? An act of desperation. She ought to be relieved that he hadn't accepted her offer, but all she could feel toward him now was frustration. Why couldn't he leave the affairs in the capital alone? Why couldn't he leave *Tolemek* alone?

She was still brooding when Tolemek returned. He sat on the bed and draped an arm around her shoulder.

"*You* look like the one with assassins after you," he said dryly.

"I'm tired of running into my father. And I'm tired of him *meddling*." Cas leaned into his embrace, afraid for him all over again. She'd thought he would be safe out here, away from the city, at least from assassins.

"Did he?" Tolemek asked after a thoughtful silence. "It sounds like he gave that man the job instead of accepting it himself."

Cas tapped her fist on her knee. *Had* he? "I thought he might have delegated it and that he would simply do it himself once he finds out that this man failed."

"You think your father would delegate anything he cared about to that toadstool?"

"Hm. He wasn't very good, was he?"

"I probably could have stood there in the dark and waited until he bumbled into something potent and knocked *himself* out."

Cas snorted.

"It crossed my mind that Ahnsung might have sent him to get rid of him. Or because he just didn't care. I'll wager he was positive the man wouldn't get past you and to me."

Cas snorted again, this time at the silly notion that she was some kind of guard dog. "Assuming you're right, what does that mean? That my father doesn't want you dead? That can't be right."

"You're so certain he loathes me? We've never sat down and chatted."

As if her father "chatted" with anyone. "Apparently, he's chatted with Zirkander *about* you. He never comes to see me, but he has no trouble visiting my commanding officers to check in on me." Visiting and threatening her commanding officers. Well, perhaps just Zirkander, since he had been the one who had gotten her into the flight academy and then invited her into Wolf Squadron. Her father had always made it clear that he thought pilots were suicidal fools. "I gathered that he didn't approve of you as a suitable match for me."

Tolemek tilted his head. "Does he actually care about you enough to care with whom you match yourself?"

"I don't know. He never gives the impression that he does." She lifted a shoulder.

"Maybe he does, and maybe he decided you'd had enough strife in your life and that losing me would distress you terribly."

Cas snorted. She really needed to stop doing that. It wasn't very feminine.

"Are you making those noises because you wouldn't be distressed at my loss or because you can't believe your father cares that much?"

She shoved him with her shoulder. "Let's not assume anything. Stay alert for the rest of this trip—and when we're back in the city too. We should probably share a cabin, so that if there's another assassin, he'll be less likely to catch you when you're sleeping."

"I am incredibly amenable to that." He pulled her closer and kissed the top of her head.

Cas tilted her face up, hoping he would kiss something more sensitive.

His eyelids lowered halfway. "You didn't answer my other question. About whether my passing would distress you terribly."

"I—"

A knock sounded at the door.

"That better not be your lieutenant friend," Tolemek said. "I'm quite positive I did nothing to suggest that I wanted to share my cabin with *him* tonight."

General Ort stuck his head in the door.

Cas jumped to her feet. Even if her relationship with Tolemek wasn't a secret, seeing the general made her feel guilty, like she should be working somewhere instead of sitting on a bed with Tolemek and getting her head kissed.

"Fifteen minute recall," Ort said without commenting on beds or head kissing. "Keep your gear close at hand and be ready. We're heading to the Magroth Crystal Mines."

"Did something happen, sir?" Her stomach, which had finally recovered from the knockout smoke, gave a nervous little flop.

"We got word from Lieutenant Duck. The dragon attacked there, and it might be returning."

Chapter 9

Sardelle leaned back, her shoulders aching and her eyes gritty, the hard, cold cement floor pressing into her knees. Dozing in the cave earlier hadn't been that refreshing, and after hours of knitting wounds back together and sealing blistered flesh, she felt like she had been awake for days. She couldn't see a window from her position amid the rows of injured men laid out on blankets in the half of the machine shop that wasn't filled with tram cars and battered ore carts. Still, she suspected dawn had come a while ago.

"Looks like he's sleeping peacefully," a man spoke from the wall behind her.

Sardelle lurched around. Duck had been back there the last time she had been aware of anyone in here except for herself, Tylie, and the injured soldiers and miners. She recognized the man, a broad-shouldered fellow with tattoos covering his burly forearms. He had helped Ridge fix the flier here last winter.

"Hello, Captain Bosmont." Sardelle hadn't spoken to him often—as she recalled, he was a man of few words—but Ridge had liked him well enough. "Yes, just a burn for this miner. His body will finish the healing process while he rests. Do you need… a healer's services?" Remembering how much the common man feared magic, she kept her question vague. She hadn't seen much of Bosmont after it had come out that she was a sorceress. He had a cut on his forehead and blisters on the back of his knuckles, but he also carried a rifle and a sword, so he looked more like an officer on duty than a patient.

"No, ma'am. Just here to keep an eye out. The general asked me to when your other feller took off."

Other feller? Duck? Sardelle realized that he was, indeed, gone.

How long had it been just her and Tylie? She had checked on Tylie numerous times over the course of the night, to see if she needed help and if she was effectively assisting the patients Sardelle had given her. Currently, she sat cross-legged three people down, with a rough-looking woman's hand clasped between her palms. She wasn't doing the bandaging or minor burn healing that Sardelle had tasked her with, though the pieces of sticky bandages attached to her parka and feet suggested she had been wrestling with that earlier. Instead, she seemed to be doing something telepathically—soothing the woman? It was hard to tell. Her patient was barely awake, and Sardelle would have had to take a few minutes to look closer. She trusted that Tylie wasn't doing anything harmful, as that seemed against her nature.

"How long ago was that, Captain?" Sardelle asked.

"'Bout three hours ago, ma'am."

"Ah." She'd told Ridge she didn't need a protector, but maybe that wasn't true if she hadn't even noticed Duck leaving.

"You're doing real good work." The captain nodded. "Even if not all of 'em appreciate the magic, I reckon they're happy to get touched by a beautiful woman. That doesn't happen much up here."

"Thank you. Yes, I remember the populace is largely male."

A bang came from the doorway, followed by a thump and a stream of cursing.

"You can't make me go to no witch," a man growled, gasping every other word. Sweat bathed his forehead and blood dripped to the floor as two soldiers carried him inside. Even from across the cavernous room, Sardelle could feel the pain radiating from him. The man wore a wrinkled, blood-saturated uniform, his rank proclaiming him a corporal.

Sardelle stood and took a deep breath. He wouldn't be the first person that night who had fought her, and she'd had to promise more than one man that she would only use mundane bandages and sutures and burn creams on them. Of course, that had usually been followed by sedating them with her talent and healing the wounds surreptitiously. Lying made her uncomfortable, but she *had* left their wounds bandaged, even if they'd no longer needed such measures then. They could curse her later.

"Bring him down here, please." Sardelle pointed to an empty blanket.

"No!" The man twisted, then gasped, grabbing at a broken metal bar embedded in his abdomen.

Sardelle rushed to help the soldiers carrying him. A wound like that would kill him. Why hadn't he been brought in earlier?

Though she did not voice the words aloud, the soldiers must have read the question on her face. One winced and said, "Found him hiding, ma'am. Doesn't want to be treated by a wit—by, uhm, magic."

"I wouldn't, either," the second soldier muttered, his eyes wide, like those of a spooked horse as he glanced from her to the patients and back to her.

"Quiet," his comrade hissed to him. "She's the general's wit—thing. Woman."

Had Sardelle not been guiding the wounded man to the ground and worrying about his injury, she might have laughed at the soldiers. Or maybe not. They were both tense and nervous, and she reminded herself once again that Ridge's pilots weren't indicative of the common soldier. Just because she had earned a place with them did not mean every other soldier would give her a chance to prove herself an ally.

The injured man seemed to have passed out, but he roused as soon as his back was on the blanket and she touched his chest. All she wanted to do was examine the wound to see if she should extricate the jagged bar before starting the healing process, but he jerked away from even her light touch.

"No witches," he cried, pain and terror contorting his face. "Don't wanna… be possessed. Evil." He panted, knocking her hand aside.

"The only thing possessing you is that piece of metal," Sardelle said, keeping her tone calm and smiling at him. "All I'm going to do is remove it. Then we'll bandage it up."

"Don't touch me. I'll kill you if you touch me."

"Don't say that, Drok," one soldier hissed. "She's the general's woman."

"Possessed him too! That's what they say. Witches are evil." Blood trickled from his mouth as he gasped and writhed. Why couldn't he pass out naturally? This would be much easier.

"Hold him down, please," Sardelle told the soldiers. She was too tired to do it herself. She needed to save her energy for healing, especially since others were still waiting.

The more helpful of the two soldiers came forward and squatted by his head, pressing his shoulders down. Sardelle touched her patient's chest again, this time reaching out with her mind to manipulate the part of his brain that would cause him to lose consciousness. Once he slept, this would be a much simpler matter.

Be careful, Jaxi warned. She sounded tired too. She had been quiet the last few hours, busy researching. *He's thinking about his pistol.*

Of using it on me?

The man's eyes widened as he seemed to sense what she was trying to do. He fought her, both with body and mind. In his agitated state, she couldn't soothe him enough to make him pass out.

"There's no need for all this," she said quietly. "I want to help."

He grasped his pistol. Sardelle pulled back and raised a shield in front of herself. It only took her a split second to realize she'd made a mistake, that she wasn't his target. Before she could change tactics, he jerked the pistol up to his head and jammed it to his skull. She lunged for it, but he pulled the trigger first.

This close, the bullet firing sounded like a bomb going off. She drew back, her limbs shaking as she looked away. It was too late to unsee the sight of the man's skull being blown open.

"Seven gods, Drok," the soldier who had been holding him said. "What were you thinking?"

The dead man did not answer.

It took a moment before Sardelle could still her shaking hands and find words. The two soldiers were staring at her. She didn't know if they were shocked that the man had taken his life or if they wondered if she had caused it. She didn't know what to tell them.

"I'm sorry," she said. It seemed so inadequate.

Her limbs wobbly, she pushed herself to her feet. There were others who needed help, others who would accept it. She had to keep working, to stay in professional mode, even if she wanted nothing more than to run across the compound and find Ridge for a hug.

"You two," Bosmont said, walking over. "Help me move the body over there with the others. We'll do a group funeral tomorrow."

"Yes, sir," they mumbled.

Sardelle was relieved Bosmont was there to do something, as her mind kept hiccuping. There had already been blood on her sleeves and her trousers, but the fresh splatters seemed a condemnation. Why hadn't she focused on knocking him out sooner? As soon as they brought him into the room?

Because people aren't supposed to kill themselves, Jaxi said. *It wasn't your fault.*

"Sardelle?" came a whisper from behind her. Tylie touched her arm. "What happened? Why did he do that?"

Somehow, having her there gave Sardelle more strength than she would have had alone. She was the teacher, the mentor. She needed to hold it together so she could advise someone who had seen far less death than she had.

"Sometimes fear overrides common sense." Sardelle offered her arm for a hug, since Tylie appeared just as shocked as the soldiers had been, as well as lost and confused. "People are afraid of magic, especially these days."

Tylie leaned against her, staring down at the bloodstained blanket where the man had died. Better than looking toward the bodies of those who had been beyond saving. Before she had arrived, the medic had started setting them in a dark corner of the machine shop.

"But you were trying to help," Tylie said.

"Yes." Sardelle groped for something more useful to say, an explanation that would make sense, but in her century, when magic had been more commonplace, this kind of irrational fear had not been typical. People had feared sorcerers, yes, but they'd known healers could help, and she had never encountered anything like this.

"They were afraid of me at home," Tylie whispered. "I didn't have much magic, not like you do, but when I started hearing Phel… sometimes, I said things that didn't make sense. Father was embarrassed, and Mother was afraid of me. She had to know I wouldn't do anything to hurt her, but I could see her thoughts. I knew she was afraid of me and afraid for me. The girls I used to play with stopped talking to me. I miss them. We played fairies and mushroom rings, and we even pretended to have magic when we were little. But then when I did some things by accident, they thought I was a freak. Booksy Betta called me a harbinger of death. The others said I was possessed, like that man said. Can you do that? Possess someone?"

"No sorceress with any scruples would try to control another's mind." Sardelle had seen degrees of that between enemies, especially when mind magic was involved, but she didn't want to get into that now. She just wanted to finish up, so she could wash the man's blood off her hands. "I'm sorry your childhood wasn't a comfortable one."

"Tolemek was the only one who didn't think I was a freak. I wish he'd been there more, but he was at the soldier school, learning to fight and command. And then he was a soldier. But he played with me when he came home. I pretended I had a ranch. He was the horse."

Sardelle managed a wan smile. "I'm sure he loved that."

"Not really, but he neighed and carried me on his shoulders. He—" Tylie blinked and looked toward the door in the back, where Bosmont was directing the others to carry the bodies outside. "Phelistoth is coming."

"Coming to the mountains?" Sardelle stretched out with her senses, though it was hard to feel much beyond the outpost, since the other dragon was still out there, his aura dampening how far afield she could search. "Or here?"

"I hope he comes here."

"Uh." Sardelle hoped he did not. How would they explain to a fortress full of people who had just been attacked by a dragon that the silver one was on their side—or at least wasn't going to burn the place down?

When she sensed Phelistoth's approach, he was closer than she would have liked and traveling closer quickly. She released Tylie and reached out, trying to find Ridge in the outpost. She needed to warn him that they would have company.

She had no sooner than found him than a white owl glided through the open door and toward them. Even though Sardelle knew that dragons could change shapes, she wouldn't have guessed it was Phelistoth if she hadn't had her senses stretched outward. His aura wasn't anywhere near as overpowering as it was when he was in dragon form.

"When he shape changes, other dragons can't find him as easily," Tylie whispered, waving cheerfully at the owl as it settled onto a giant wheel leaning against the wall.

The "owl" transformed, feathers melting away as the figure grew and turned into the human form Sardelle had seen several times. With straight silver hair that fell to his shoulders and a handsome clean-shaven face, he might have passed for a human, but his eyes were not quite right, having an amber hue that always reminded her of a wolf rather than a man.

Most of the people on the blankets were sleeping, but one who was awake and recovering gasped. He grabbed his shoes and ran toward the back door. He glanced back as he turned the knob and tried to run outside before he had it open. His head thudded into the wood, but that didn't slow him down. He sprinted into the daylight, slamming the door behind him.

Sardelle sighed. Having shape-shifting going on in her presence would do nothing to improve her reputation here.

Oblivious to the terrified man's departure, Tylie ran over and hugged Phelistoth. "You're better!"

He did not return the hug, but he also did not push her away.

Iskandian, his voice rumbled in Sardelle's head with all of the subtlety of a foghorn. *Why are you not seeking a soulblade for Tylie?*

My name is Sardelle, she reminded him for the fifth or sixth time. He had come by the house several times, eaten their food, and observed her lessons with Tylie, but he couldn't be bothered to use it. She did not know if he used Tylie's name because of the bond they shared, or because in his eyes, Cofah humans deserved names. *We have people to heal first. You wouldn't care to help us, would you?*

You wish me to heal Iskandians? Even though his expressions weren't quite human, when he gazed at her with those cool amber eyes, she had no trouble reading his distaste.

Yes, they're the ones who can help us get the soulblade. They've already dug miles and miles of mines through the mountain, so it will be easier to find the ruins.

Phelistoth surveyed the blankets. *They will dig after they are healed?*

Sardelle hesitated. She did not know what Ridge's plans were or how much help she could expect, so she did not want to promise that these specific people would assist in the sword hunt. *Once people are healed, the outpost can focus on building up its defenses again, and we should be able to get some of the miners to guide us through the tunnels.*

Defenses. Phelistoth sniffed in a derisive manner that reminded her of Jaxi, even if Jaxi lacked nostrils to give it the additional nasal flare.

Please, Jaxi thought. *He's far more derisive than I am. I'm only mildly disdainful. And I don't leave owl pellets on things.*

Because you haven't figured out how to shape-shift yet.

I'm working on it.

Maybe if we find an older soulblade, he or she will share the secret with you.

Sardelle thought Jaxi might issue a derisive—or disdainful—snort, but she sounded intrigued when she responded. *That could be interesting.*

There is no magic to guard this settlement, Phelistoth continued. *It will fall if my rival wishes it to fall. Iskandians have grown weak.*

The Cofah have turned their backs on the ways of magic as well, Sardelle said. *And in case nobody told you, a Cofah sorceress is the one who freed your rival. He was a prisoner for millennia until she released him. Now it seems he wants you dead as much as he wants us dead.*

Phelistoth gazed at her, his arrogance the only thing readable in his aura. *You tell me nothing I do not know, Iskandian.*

Tylie squeezed Phelistoth's arm. "Please help her. She wants to help us."

Phelistoth's lip curled. *She wants you to feel indebted to her people so you'll stay with them and fight against the empire.*

Sardelle held her breath. She hadn't been trying to hide her intentions from Tylie, but she also hadn't been that blunt about them. She would have helped her no matter what, since she had promised to do so to Tolemek months ago, but would she have helped a Cofah girl under other circumstances? Knowing she might be creating an enemy for her people?

"But I like her." Tylie smiled.

You like too easily.

"You don't like easily enough. And you're grouchy."

Sardelle almost coughed at Tylie's fearless criticism of the dragon. She wasn't one to fawn herself, but everything she'd read about dragons suggested that tact and diplomacy were wise when dealing with them.

Phelistoth glared down at Tylie. Most people would have wilted under that glare, but Tylie pointed at Sardelle and kept talking.

"Please heal the people, so we can go look for a soulblade. Then I won't be defenseless when we fly together. And Jaxi can have someone to play with!" Tylie seemed delighted at that last idea.

Soulblades do not play, Jaxi said, possibly speaking to all of them, because Tylie grinned.

"Everybody should play and have fun," she said.

"Good advice," Sardelle said. She wished she could think of playing and having fun, but the soldier's suicide was too fresh in her mind. "I'm going to finish here. If you decide to help, Phelistoth, I can tell you what to do."

His nostrils flared. *I do not need to be told what to do.*

You know, he's not any more charming than the gold dragon, Jaxi said.

He hasn't burned anything down or incinerated any of our furniture, Sardelle responded. *I find a degree of charm in that.*

You're almost as easy to please as Tylie.

I will heal these humans, and then I will lead the search for a soulblade, Phelistoth announced. *A Cofah soulblade.*

"Ah, this was a Referatu stronghold," Sardelle said. "Only Iskandians lived and worked here."

That does not mean your people never stole soulblades from the Cofah. You even have stolen dragon artifacts down there, among all of your buried junk.

"We—what?" Now that she thought about it, Sardelle could believe her people might have brought captured Cofah soulblades home from missions, but his certainty that there were dragon artifacts startled her. She had never heard anything about that.

You heard me. Come. I will show you, and we will find Tylie a worthy blade. His amber eyes narrowed. *A Cofah blade.*

Though intrigued to learn there might be artifacts related to dragons in the rubble down there, Sardelle grimaced at this new twist. An Iskandian blade with a loyal Iskandian soul inside might have helped convince Tylie to become a permanent resident of the country. A *Cofah* soul might work very hard to convince her to do the opposite.

Phelistoth never smiled, but he was smiling slightly now as he met her eyes, like the fox that had just outsmarted its prey.

"The healing?" she asked, thinking she might delay him. Not that a delay would help much. Unless the other dragon came back to attack the outpost, she couldn't justify not going down into the tunnels to look for soulblades, not when that had been their main reason for coming here.

Yes. Phelistoth held out a hand, palm down, fingers spread. Yellow light gathered around it, growing so intense that Sardelle had to look away.

The presence of powerful magic filled the building, muffling her senses, so she couldn't tell what was happening. The light surged, growing and filling every nook of the machine shop. Someone gasped. Someone else groaned. Several of her patients sighed with what sounded like relief.

After less than a minute, the light faded. Phelistoth lowered his hand.

Sardelle looked out over the patients. Most remained sleeping, but a few eyes had opened. She could feel the absence of pain in those who were awake. Though she still struggled to use her mental senses with Phelistoth's overpowering presence so close, she saw that some people had been affected by an energy that had changed their auras, at least temporarily. To her mind's eye, they glowed the same way those with dragon blood did, and those auras were regenerating their wounds. In most cases, it had already been done.

They are healed, Phelistoth informed her. *They will have an increased energy to regenerate wounds for the rest of their lives.* Phelistoth tilted his head, regarding her in that dismissive and arrogant way. *You are welcome, Iskandian.*

Sardelle. She felt stunned—and also regretful that he hadn't come twenty minutes earlier, so he might have healed the soldier who had killed himself. His method had been so quick that there wouldn't have been time for an objection. Though his arrogance was off-putting, she managed a sincere, *Thank you.*

Come. Phelistoth nodded toward the door. *We will hunt.*

* * *

He healed everyone? Ridge asked. *By just waving his hand?*

Yes. Sardelle shared the memory with him as the tram cage bumped and clanked its way into the lowest levels of the mine. She wasn't sure her range would allow her to communicate with Ridge once they were all the way down in the mountain, so she was filling him in on the way. *You can tell Therrik that a dragon healed his people instead of a dirty witch.*

Ah, I was thinking that Therrik and Phelistoth should never meet. The king would probably blame me if his outpost commander ended up incinerated while I was in the room.

I don't think silver dragons breathe fire. Phelistoth would just stop his heart with a wave of his hand.

There's a way I could get blamed for that too. I'm sure of it. Also, you're not a dirty witch. You're always very clean and tidy, even when we're fleeing from lava-spewing, ash-spitting volcanoes.

Sardelle grimaced, all too aware of the blood on her clothes right now. *Jaxi is keeping an eye on the other dragon*, she said, not wanting to share her failure with Ridge now, especially not when she had just told him about Phelistoth's far superior ability. *If I'm not able to talk to you from down here, she'll let you know if he's coming close again.*

All right. Duck just got back—the airship is on its way. With luck, it will arrive before the dragon does. Or better yet, the dragon will get bored and go somewhere else. There aren't any sheep for him to eat here.

You did mention griddle cakes.

Not sheep-flavored griddle cakes.

I believe dragons can eat other things. I saw Phelistoth eating cheese last week.

Is that *what happened to my block of Premja Paneer? I thought you* ate it all.

Tylie shared it with him.

Today my cheese, tomorrow my beer.

Sardelle held back a snort, remembering that she had company. *Have you even had any beer since getting promoted? The same three bottles have been in the icebox all month.*

After she asked the question, she wished she hadn't. If he had been drinking beer elsewhere to avoid his uncomfortable new roommates, she wasn't sure she wanted to know about it. If Tylie was going to continue having dragon visitors, she and Ridge were going to have to find another living arrangement once they got back.

But Ridge's mournful, *No*, assured her he hadn't been out drinking and carousing with the boys—or any other girls, either. *I don't drink when I'm on duty. And I'm always on duty now.* He did the mental equivalent of laying his head on her shoulder. *After this, we need to find time alone somewhere. Perhaps in a cave, where you can stroke my chest.*

Or we could spend our leisure time in a more enhanced locale.

Like a cavern?

Maybe your cabin by the lake. Especially if she could convince him to have an indoor toilet installed.

That sounds agreeable. He smiled—she could tell even from fifteen levels down into the mountain—but then it faded, and his words grew serious again. *I am concerned about the other dragon. Why would he be lurking nearby? That's odd, don't you think? Is it Tylie again? Has he realized she's still alive? I can't understand why a human girl would mean so much to such a powerful creature.*

Sardelle started to answer, but then Phelistoth's earlier statement came back to mind, slamming her with a realization.

"Phelistoth," she said before a question fully formed in her mind. He and Tylie were standing next to her in the dark cage as they descended, neither speaking, at least not out loud. For the moment, their group was alone, though Captain Bosmont had arranged for several soldiers stationed down in the mines to accompany them. She wished Bosmont himself had come, but he'd been pulled away because of his engineering expertise. The soldiers were trying to rebuild the fortress, as much as possible, in case Morishtomaric returned. Ridge and Therrik had been outside, arguing over some wall fortification when she had passed through the courtyard. "The dragon artifacts you mentioned—what are they? Something you would value?"

I do not know what they are. I can sense my kind's signature on them. They shine like suns down there, with the human artifacts like distant stars.

I never sensed anything of such power, Sardelle said, switching to telepathy, since she could see light now at the end of the tram shaft, *and I spent years coming in and out of Referatu Headquarters.*

Your senses are as impressive as those of a goat.

Jaxi snickered in her mind.

Aren't you busy doing research? Sardelle asked.

Very busy. That's why I didn't comment on the cheese or chest stroking.

They are all located in one place, Phelistoth said.

The tram came to a stop. The door opened into a hollow chamber crisscrossed with ore cart rails. A couple of those carts rested next to the tram cage, filled to the brim with dirt and ready to be hauled out. Four soldiers stood in a line, rifles in hand as they shuffled with unease. Sardelle could feel their discomfort before she saw their faces. Though she wished it had to do with the dragon attack, the way the men shared significant looks with each other and stole surreptitious glances at Sardelle, Tylie, and Phelistoth implied otherwise.

"Good morning." Sardelle smiled and tried to appear as friendly and unthreatening as possible.

Phelistoth did the opposite, his stare cold and his demeanor haughty. They gave him even more glances than Sardelle received. She wondered if Bosmont had mentioned him. Phelistoth had drawn looks up in the courtyard, too, even though Sardelle had hustled him through quickly. Nobody had questioned her. She did not know if that was because Ridge had given orders that she was to be permitted to go wherever she wanted to go, or if everybody remembered who and what she was, and they were simply afraid to question her.

Seemingly oblivious to the men's unease, Tylie waved cheerfully and immediately started wandering around the chamber, peering into the tunnels. The layout was familiar to Sardelle, but she thought they might be a level or two lower than had existed the last time she had come. The water she had flooded the lower part of the mine with had been pumped out.

"I'm Sergeant Jenneth," the man who had opened the cage door said. "Captain Bosmont said to take you wherever you want to go." His forehead wrinkled as he considered the tunnels, some well lit and with clanks drifting from them and others dark and silent.

Sardelle doubted these soldiers were asked for tours often.

"Excellent. Thank you." She smiled again, not that the gesture put them at ease. She might as well have been displaying a mouth full of fangs. That thought made her glance at Phelistoth, to make sure *he* wasn't doing such a thing, but aside from the not-quite-right eyes, he appeared fully human. No fangs. "Which tunnel?" she asked him.

She had intended to take the lead, but since she would be guessing based on where she had been found, where she had found Jaxi, and what she remembered of the complex, she wasn't confident that she could find a soulblade in a timely manner. Many Referatu sorcerers and sorceresses had been in the compound the day of the explosion, so she estimated there would be ten or fifteen soulblades, assuming nobody had moved them. But she hadn't been keeping track of where the handlers had been in the hours before the explosions detonated.

"I will lead." Phelistoth walked past the soldiers without acknowledging them and strode down one of the lit tunnels.

Sardelle hurried after him, glad he hadn't chosen a dark one, because he might have lit it by magical means. Unless dragons saw in the dark. She had no idea. The history books hadn't covered that.

Tylie chose to walk at Sardelle's side instead of catching up with Phelistoth. The soldiers trailed behind them, not closely.

"Are you *sure* General Zirkander said they're supposed to be down here?" one muttered to the other.

"That's what the captain said," his buddy muttered back.

"Civilians aren't allowed down here. Unless they're mining."

"I know, but she's with the general. You know, *with* the general."

Sardelle glanced at Tylie and wished the men would mutter more quietly. They hadn't said anything lewd yet, but she wouldn't be surprised if it escalated to that. Tylie might not understand innuendo, but even so, Sardelle had a notion that she shouldn't allow herself to be denigrated in front of her student. Her natural inclination was not to cause trouble, but would Tylie think her weak? Would a *Cofah* sorceress stand for being spoken about behind her back?

Are you having insecurity issues again? You usually save those for Ridge. Like when you're worried he's been drinking beer with other women.

That was not *what I was worried about.*

Yeah, it was. Subconsciously. You seem to forget that you're attractive and that he finds you quite witty and appealing. Probably because of me.

What do you have to do with my wit and appeal, Jaxi?

I'm part of the package. I suspect the inside of Ridge's head was very boring before he had my insights in there.

Are you sharing insights with him right now? Sardelle couldn't imagine that he would appreciate that when he was trying to fix his fortress walls.

Possibly. Mostly I'm reading a book about swords and other tools crafted to fight dragons and sorcerers. Mostly dragons, since they did so much damage in battle, but sorcerers could be harmed by them as a byproduct.

So I've seen. Sardelle still had a scar from the cut she had taken in her fight with Kasandral-ruled-Cas.

I also wanted to warn you about your escorts.

If it's that they're not one hundred percent on our side, I've gathered that.

One of them is thinking that it would be better for Ridge and the world if you disappeared down here. Another is fantasizing about your ass and wondering if witches are any different for rutting purposes.

Lovely. Sardelle lamented anew that Captain Bosmont hadn't been their escort.

He had thoughts about your ass, too, albeit he felt guilty about having them. Remember, these are men who don't get to see comely women very often.

I know. I'll be careful. I still remember how to give rashes.

I was going to offer to melt the lusty one's gonads for you, but a rash would be acceptable.

"It's lifeless down here," Tylie whispered, brushing Sardelle's arm.

The tunnel wasn't so narrow that they needed to walk that closely, but Tylie eyed the roughhewn walls and ceiling as if they might collapse at any moment. The air *did* feel thick and oppressive, even though Sardelle could hear a fan working in the distance, bringing in fresh air.

"There are miners working," she said quietly.

Some solace. The criminals-turned-miners would probably be even less enthused about roaming "witches" than the soldiers. She distinctly remembered how she had entered this new world, with the two hardened men who had helped pull her out of her stasis chamber radiating thoughts of lust and sadism. They would have acted on those thoughts, had she not deployed her rashes.

Even though much had happened in the last few months, now that she was back here, she remembered the incident vividly, as if it had taken place yesterday. She might not have reacted to the soldiers' mutterings, but she would not let Tylie experience anything close to what she had endured.

"No plants, no insects, no animals," Tylie said, then lowered her voice to a whisper. "The people are scary. Afraid. Hate. Anger. So much anger. All of them."

"The people? The miners? Are you shielding yourself, the way we've been working on?"

"Yes, but I can still feel them."

Sardelle wrapped her arm around Tylie's shoulders. "We won't stay long. Most sorcerers I knew who had soulblades had to go through a trial before being given the opportunity to bond with them. You can think of this as *your* trial."

Sardelle had no idea if the Cofah had possessed similar rituals. She was trying not to think about the fact that Phelistoth wanted to lead them to a *Cofah* soulblade. She hoped they would come across an Iskandian one first, one that would be a good fit for Tylie, and that there wouldn't be time to keep searching for others.

Up ahead, Phelistoth gave her a long look over his shoulder.

Sardelle kept her chin up and did not look away, though the idea that he was reading her thoughts made her uncomfortable. She had her mental shields up, as she always did around him. They would have been sufficient against most sorcerers, but perhaps he had some mind-reading power that was different, that could breech her defenses without her knowing it. He had been certain about her hopes of keeping Tylie here, in this country. She didn't know how he could feel loyal to the Cofah, not when they had been the ones drawing his blood for their own purposes and keeping him weak in that pyramid. She stared at the back of his head, willing him to hear *those* thoughts.

This time, he did not look back.

A group of miners had come into view. They were in an area that appeared to have been recently hollowed out with explosives. Several half-filled carts sat on freshly laid iron rails. The men held pickaxes and shovels, but they had all stopped working. They watched Phelistoth, Sardelle, and Tylie approach.

Several whispered conversations passed between the rough men. Dirt coated their hands, and their clothes were worn, ripped, and equally dirty, though it wasn't their appearances that made Sardelle tag them as rough. As Tylie had mentioned, most of their minds were full of anger and discontent. Sardelle did not want to open herself to it, but she was aware of Jaxi's warning and wanted to be ready if someone tried something.

"You men have work," Sergeant Jenneth said. "Get to it."

Several miners in the group of ten sneered at him. A few went back to shoveling, though they did not put much effort into it. Others simply stared at Sardelle and Tylie. Because they were women? Or because they remembered her and knew she was a sorceress?

"How much farther, Phel?" Tylie whispered as they passed the group, the men's gazes following them.

Sardelle pressed her fingers together, readying a defense if they needed it. The soldiers crowded close, and none of the miners stepped toward them. Only their eyes moved, watching.

She started to breathe out a sigh of relief once they'd passed out of sight, but distant shuffling reached her ears. Sounds from the tunnel behind them? Were those miners following them? She reached with her senses. Yes, they were.

"Wonderful," she murmured.

"What?" Tylie asked.

Sardelle flicked her hand in dismissal. Tylie probably already knew. If she didn't, Sardelle did not want to worry her, though she might have to bring it up eventually. The men seemed to be up to something. Given the animosity that shrouded the miners, she suspected that more than curiosity motivated their interest. It was amazing that Ridge had managed to gain some respect from these people when he had been the commander here, far more than the previous commander had managed. And, from the brief scene she had witnessed as they landed, also far more than Therrik had managed.

Therrik isn't a national hero. And he doesn't wear that dashing cap and goggles.

I'll let Ridge know you find his headwear appealing.
He already knows. I told you I share my insights with him.
Ah, yes.

Phelistoth turned off the main tunnel and into a dark one. The soldiers shared more mutters with each other. Sergeant Jenneth grabbed the last lantern near the intersection. Two other men jogged back to get more.

Phelistoth took more turns, entering a spider web of narrow passages. In spots, uneven alcoves and divots had been chiseled out of the rock. Had some of her people's belongings been found here? The walls were not the homogeneous stone of the mountain itself, but rubble that had been compacted over the centuries, with dirt smashed between the boulders like mortar.

The tunnel widened, then ended in a larger chamber with piles of dirt and rock mounded against the walls. Ore cart tracks had not been laid this far back, and there were no timber supports as there had been in the main passages.

The two remaining soldiers lingered farther back, the light from their lanterns barely illuminating the low-ceilinged chamber. Sardelle could scarcely see Phelistoth's outline in the deep shadows. She could have conjured light, but she was aware of the nervous glances the soldiers kept trading—and the fact that the other two hadn't rejoined them. When she reached out with her mind, she found them still back in the main passage, leaning against a wall and rolling cigarettes. At least the group of miners had disappeared.

Probably to get more shovels and pickaxes to swing at us, Jaxi thought. *We may have to fight our way out.*

I'm sure we can get past a few men armed with digging tools.

Shall I warn Ridge that his soldiers aren't being assiduous with their tour guide and protection services?

Sardelle nibbled on her lip. She could no longer reach Ridge herself, and she worried that Jaxi's phrasing might cause him to worry. Even if Jaxi was circumspect, he might worry. Sardelle did not want him to feel obligated to send more troops down, not when he needed all of the men up there to fortify the installation.

No, she decided. *We'll be fine.*

You say that, but you haven't seen what Phelistoth is planning yet. You can't read his thoughts, can you?

That would have been useful.

No, Jaxi said, *but I can guess based on the way he's studying that chamber and staring up into the rock above it. I doubt he's looking with his puny human eyes.*

"Stand back," Phelistoth instructed. He looked toward Tylie, and Sardelle had the impression the warning was for her and that he didn't care if she or anyone else heeded it. But then his gaze locked onto hers. "And shield yourselves." His gaze flicked to Tylie, then back to Sardelle.

A warning to protect his… whatever she was to him? Pupil?

Rider, Jaxi said as Sardelle backed out of the chamber, waving for Tylie to follow. *That's what the sorceresses who rode dragons into battle were called.*

I know that, but I don't think those people were necessarily Receivers or that they had the same relationship.

They might have been. There must have been some reason for the cranky, arrogant dragons to put up with having humans clambering all over their backs.

Should you be calling him cranky and arrogant when he's close enough to hear you? Sardelle asked. *I don't want him to melt you into a pile of scrap. Especially when you're attached to my waist.*

Ha ha.

Sardelle did wonder what relationship the sorcerers of old had shared with the dragons to convince them to fight with them. Or maybe it had been the dragons convincing the humans to fight with *them*. Though why they would need humans, she didn't know. Cannon fodder in the ancient wars? Had dragons been as territorial as humans? Maybe Phelistoth felt loyal to Cofahre because his ancestors had claimed that land when humans had been little more than hunter-gatherers roaming the hills.

"Where are we going?" Sergeant Jenneth asked, glancing in the direction of the main passage.

"Just a ways back there," Sardelle said, nodding for them to continue backing up.

"What's he going to do in there?"

"Search for something."

"Alone in the dark?"

"It's his way."

"Is he a witch too?" the second soldier, a private asked. He licked his lips, scurrying back to make sure Sardelle didn't come within touching distance of him.

"The term would be sorcerer, and not exactly."

Rumbles, snaps, and cracks came from the chamber and saved Sardelle from having to explain further. The ground trembled, and she raised a shield to protect herself, Tylie, and the two soldiers. The other two soldiers were too far away for her to include, so she hoped Phelistoth didn't do anything that might collapse the entire level. Her shield wouldn't be enough to protect them if that happened, and even Jaxi wouldn't be able to melt through the half mile of rock that would stand between them and the tram.

A nervous flutter taunted her stomach at the idea of being trapped down here. This time, there would be no stasis chamber to protect her.

I'm sure he doesn't want to trap himself, Jaxi said.

The cracks escalated and were accompanied by the sound of rocks pounding down, and Sardelle barely "heard" the words in her mind. It reminded her of the cave they had been trapped in on the way here, except the noise seemed even louder and larger in scope.

The tunnel between them and Phelistoth was dark, so she couldn't see what was happening in his chamber, but particles of dust and fine rock swirled on the other side of her barrier.

"Cave-in," Sergeant Jenneth barked.

He spun and tried to run toward the main passage. He only made it two steps before crashing into Sardelle's invisible barrier. Rebounding, he stumbled, almost falling to the quaking floor.

"What in all the hells?" he blurted.

The private jumped past him and tried to find a way through the barrier. He patted all along it, then spun toward Sardelle.

"You're doing this," he yelled.

"To keep the ceiling from falling on us, yes," Sardelle said calmly. She rested her hand on Jaxi's hilt. Performing two kinds of magic at once wasn't easy, so she would have a hard time defending herself while maintaining the shield.

You may want to let them go. I'll happily defend you from them, but I might cut off something they're fond of in my enthusiasm to protect you.

"The witch has us trapped," Sergeant Jenneth yelled, jumping to his feet. "Is anybody out there?"

Sardelle was about to lower her shield and let them run, but a boulder slammed to the ground, half blocking the route back to the main passage. She grumbled to herself. They wouldn't like it, but she had to keep them here until Phelistoth finished.

A flash of orange came from his chamber, the light cutting through the dust in the air. No, it *burned* through the dust, heat battering at her shield. The battering reminded her of the air battle with the other dragon, and for a bewildered moment, she thought he was attacking them. Then the light and heat disappeared, and she noticed the air was clear of dust. Had he incinerated it?

"He's melting a tunnel in the rock," Tylie said, her hands pressed to Sardelle's barrier as she gazed toward the chamber. "And getting rid of the molten stone as he goes."

Getting rid of? If her shields hadn't been up, Phelistoth would have gotten *rid* of the four of them.

He did warn you, Jaxi said. *By dragon standards, he was quite polite.* More urgently, she added, *Watch out.*

Sardelle spun back toward the soldiers as they drew their swords and stepped toward her. She started to draw her own blade, but Jaxi flicked the men back with a wave of her power. They stumbled into her barrier again, their eyes wider and more full of fear than ever.

"We'll let you go as soon as the shaking stops," Sardelle said, the words vibrating as they came out, her shield doing nothing to stop the earth from trembling under their feet. "You go out there, and you may die." Especially if Phelistoth's new hobby was heating the air by thousands of degrees to melt solid stone.

"*You're* doing this," one man said.

"Actually, our comrade is doing it. To get something valuable out of the rock." She doubted she could reason with them, but if she could keep them distracted from trying to fight her, that would be worthwhile. Worrying about them divided her attention and made it harder to keep the barrier up. She was concerned that the other soldiers and miners on their level would be affected by the heat. She hoped they had run to the tram as soon as the quaking started. Why hadn't Phelistoth warned them of what he planned?

Because he doesn't care if people get flattened. Or if we get flattened. Don't worry about these two. I'll keep them in line. As Jaxi finished speaking, the men gasped, dropping their swords. The grips of their weapons glowed cherry red. They hadn't reached for their pistols, but the butts of those were smoking.

One of the soldiers shrieked, startling Sardelle. She reinforced her shield before turning to look at what had alarmed him.

The end of a silver-scaled tail lay in the tunnel, the tip almost reaching her barrier. The rest of it disappeared into darkness and dust that had filled the air again, and she couldn't glimpse the body, though Sardelle had a sense that the chamber was much larger now—it had to be if Phelistoth had changed into his normal form. The tip of the tail swished back and forth, reminding her of a cat perched on a fence and watching a bird feeder. Then it froze.

"Phel?" Tylie called, her voice concerned. "The sword?"

An explosion of energy coursed through the mountain, and the ground heaved. Sardelle was hurled through the air. Her shield faltered, but even as she fell, she flung her arm upward and reinforced it with a shudder of power that Jaxi matched. Rocks hammered into their invisible barrier from the top, and boulders tumbled down all around them. Their lanterns fell and went out. Jaxi glowed, a silvery light that illuminated the rockfall that was in the process of burying them.

From her knees, Sardelle was scarcely aware of the soldiers huddling, their arms cupping their heads. Only Tylie had somehow remained on her feet, her hands splayed and stretched toward Phelistoth. The tail had disappeared under rubble. She screamed, but Sardelle could barely hear it over the cacophony of the boulders slamming down.

What seemed like hours passed before the roar of the mountain softened, individual clunks growing audible instead of the constant barrage of noise. By Jaxi's light, Sardelle stared at the wall of rocks all around them, of boulders lying atop her barrier, waiting to crush them if her concentration faltered again. The tip of Phelistoth's tail poked out from under the rubble wall, touching the edge of her shield. It wasn't moving.

"Phel?" Tylie called, a quaver in her voice.

Sardelle rubbed her face, her hand damp and gritty against her skin. She still felt the dragon's presence and didn't think he was dead, but how were they going to get out of here?

The tunnel is collapsed all the way back to the tram, Jaxi said. *And it looks like... yes, two levels above collapsed, too. Buckling down on top of us.*

Sardelle breathed deeply and slowly, struggling to stave off the panic that wanted to descend. This had been her fear, but she hadn't truly expected it to come to pass. They were trapped, and she had no idea how they would excavate their way to the tram—or if the tram shaft was clear. What if it had collapsed, too, and they were utterly buried down here, almost twenty levels below the surface?

The lower levels of the tram shaft filled with rubble, Jaxi said. *Someone will have to dig us out. Or that oversized lout will have to wake up and melt through about a billion tons of rock.*

Lout? Sardelle asked, not because she disagreed, but because she hoped the conversation would take her mind off the fact that they were buried alive. Also the fact that she should stop taking such deep breaths. They would have limited air down here now.

He had the soulblade in his sight—his mental sight—and then he took off after something else like a squirrel with too many nuts to choose from.

Something else? You can't tell what?

A collapsed room with a vault in it. There are some magical objects inside the vault, but I can't sense what through the sides. The vault seems to have a dampening effect. Maybe they're the dragon artifacts he mentioned. Weren't emergency rations and equipment kept down around this level? Who knows what all was stored in the basement?

The basement? Sardelle knew what level the miners had called this, but she did not know exactly where in the old Referatu compound they were. She and Jaxi had been on one of the lower levels when they had initially been trapped, but having the mountain fall in and smother everything had left her disoriented. *I don't remember anyone mentioning a vault of artifacts.*

Well, you were just a healer who worked with the military. It's not like you were stationed here full-time.

Sardelle had taught here a couple of summers, but she conceded the point. Most of the Referatu leaders had been older. If her people had survived, she might have been a part of the government and come to live here full-time someday, but there was no point in considering that now.

Sergeant Jenneth lifted his head, and he stared at her. "How—how do we get out?"

Sardelle looked at the inert dragon tail, only two inches of its silvery tip visible under, as Jaxi had put it, a billion tons of rocks.

"I don't know," she said.

Chapter 10

Ridge was hammering nails into screw holes to secure the fire-warped base of one of the outpost's big viper guns when the ground started shaking. His first thought was that Captain Bosmont had miscalculated in reopening the tower for personnel, or that one of the timbers supporting the charred structure had fallen away. The half-burned split logs under his knees trembled so fiercely, he expected the entire tower to break away from the fortress wall and tip over. That would make his repairs to the base of the gun irrelevant.

"Zirkander," Therrik bellowed from the courtyard. "What is your witch doing?"

Ridge climbed to his feet, bracing himself on the low wall surrounding the weapons platform. The tower continued to shake, but it wasn't the only thing doing so. Down in the courtyard, numerous soldiers wobbled as the earth trembled. Timbers erected as braces to support damaged buildings toppled over. A straw roof over the small stables collapsed. Bricks flew out of the crumbling walls of the mess hall.

Therrik stood in the middle of the chaos, his arms crossed over his chest as he glared up at Ridge.

"She's not powerful enough to make an earthquake," Ridge said, though he didn't care to discuss magic, especially not *her* magic, with so many people around who might overhear.

Someone ran up to Therrik, waving a clipboard and pointing to one of the oversized double-doored entrances to the mine system. Ridge ran down the steps, thoughts spinning through his mind. While he doubted Sardelle or even Jaxi could make an earthquake, he knew from recent and firsthand experience that a dragon could, simply with the power of its mind. Was

Phelistoth responsible? Sardelle had said that he had reappeared and had healed the injured men, but she hadn't mentioned if he had gone into the tunnels with her and Tylie. Ridge couldn't imagine where else he would be lurking, especially since that other dragon seemed to want him dead, but this shaking of the earth could also signal another attack by Morishtomaric.

Jaxi? Ridge asked silently. *I don't suppose you can hear me?*

He was not surprised when he did not receive an answer. He had no power to transmit his thoughts; if he wanted to communicate with Jaxi or Sardelle, he had to hope one of them was listening to his mind, however that worked. They were probably busy, maybe worrying about the exact same thing he was. The earthquake. As alarming as it was above the ground, it had to be doubly so down there.

By the time Ridge reached Therrik, the tremors were subsiding. He might have felt relieved about that, but as the shakes and the shouts of men died down, he could hear the report the young soldier was issuing.

"...been a cave-in. Down in the tram shaft. We're not sure how far back it goes, but we had nearly forty miners down on the bottom level, and some of our men too." The soldier looked at Ridge, opened his mouth, then closed it. He looked away.

Ridge gripped his arm, fear burrowing into his heart. "Which tram shaft?"

"B shaft, sir."

That was the one that led to the tunnels where all of the old books had been found and where *Sardelle* had originally been found. Ridge closed his eyes, trying to find control. It was too soon to worry. Besides, if anyone could take care of herself and survive a cave-in, it would be Sardelle. Sardelle and Jaxi.

"Sardelle went down that one, didn't she?" he asked, though he couldn't imagine that she would have chosen another one. Already his throat tightened at the thought that he might have lost her.

No. He wouldn't allow himself to think that. Not yet.

"Stay calm, you fool," he whispered. "Just like skirmishes in the air. Falling apart doesn't win battles."

"Sir?" the young soldier asked.

Ridge shook his head.

"The general is talking to himself, Corporal," Therrik said. "Ignore it. It's a sign of senility. That's all."

The corporal did not smile at the weak joke. Good man.

"As soon as we're sure the tremors are over," Ridge said, "I want some men and equipment down in that shaft. I want it cleared."

"Yes, sir."

Ridge stared at Therrik, half-expecting him to object to the use of men for anything other than rebuilding the defenses. But Therrik wasn't looking at him. His gaze had turned toward the northern sky behind Ridge's shoulder. The sun was out today, reflecting off the snow and glaciers on the surrounding mountains. The clear azure sky made it easy to see the large golden figure soaring toward them.

"Your witch is going to have to wait," Therrik said, then raised his voice to bellow. "Dragon incoming! Everyone to their duty stations. Sergeant Briner, close those tram doors. This time, none of those damned miners are going to sneak up here to make trouble while we're fighting."

"Yes, sir!" came a dozen calls from around the courtyard.

Ridge wanted to countermand Therrik, to demand that the doors remain open, but it hardly mattered. If the bottom of the tram shaft was blocked with rubble, nobody would be coming up from those lower levels until they cleared it. And as much as he wanted to order everyone to work on that, he couldn't, not with that dragon flying straight toward them. If Morishtomaric had decided to finish off the outpost, and his people weren't able to fight him off, there would be nobody left to dig out those trapped by the cave-in.

Sardelle, I'm sorry, Ridge whispered in his mind and raced to the wall.

***

The glowing blade swept through the hordes of shaven-headed warriors, moving impossibly fast, leaving a green blur in the twilight air as it cut through rifles, swords, and flesh. Cas charged forward, dodging attacks without effort as she pressed into her foes. Firearms cracked, and she whipped the blade up, somehow deflecting the bullets streaking toward her head. They clanged off the blade and disappeared into the swarm of Cofah soldiers surrounding her.

She was alone, her allies distant and indistinct shapes in the background. With so many men trying to kill her, she should have been terrified, should have run, but the familiar stones of Harborgard Castle rose up behind her. She couldn't let the Cofah soldiers have this road, the cobblestone drive leading straight to the gates.

Spinning and jumping with flair that her practical father would have chastised her for, she avoided all of those men. Satisfaction welled in her, pride over her skills and pleasure that the sword enhanced them. She lopped off heads and cut down soldiers, barely seeing faces, only knowing that she was protecting Iskandia from its enemies. Soon, her attackers all lay dead at her feet. All except one.

The sorceress in the golden armor strode toward her, a helmet pulled down over her face, a soulblade glowing in her hand. Cas screamed, remembering the men she had killed with her fireballs. She ran down the sloping road straight toward her.

Her foe raised a hand and flung one of those fireballs at her, but Kasandral came up, shielding Cas from the heat even as it cut through the flaming sphere. Sliced in half as if it had been a melon, the fireball parted, then dissipated. Cas barely slowed down. She leaped at the sorceress. Their blades met in a screech, metal clashing against metal. Sparks, flames, and glowing motes flew into the air all around them as they fought.

Cas was the shorter warrior, and the other woman had the advantage of reach, but Kasandral filled Cas with power, her entire body tingling and thrumming, making her feel like a god rather than a mere mortal. She pressed the sorceress back until the woman's heel caught on a loose cobblestone. For a split second, the sorceress lost her balance. It was all Cas needed. She batted aside the other glowing blade, then plunged Kasandral into the golden armor. The incredibly hard material dented but did not give all the way. Still, her blow knocked the woman onto her back. Her sword flew from her hand, and her helmet fell away. Cas leaped in, angling Kasandral down to pierce the one unarmored part of the sorceress's body—her face.

But as the green glow of her blade highlighted that face, it revealed not an evil Cofah sorceress but Sardelle, her blue eyes full of sympathy, of forgiveness.

Cas tried to jerk the blade away before it struck, but Kasandral had a mind of its own, and slammed downward, the blow inevitable. Cas screamed, dropping the sword and stumbling back. It was too late. She had killed another friend.

Cas woke with a jolt, clunking her head on the cabinets above the bed. She clenched the blankets with both hands, confusion racing through her thoughts, and she groped to remember where she was and what was going on.

"Cas?" came a soft voice from across the room.

She peered blearily toward it, reality slowly coming together for her. Tolemek. She was in his lab, the daylight beyond the porthole promising it was close to noon. After being up so late, she hadn't woken earlier. Probably because she had been busy dreaming that awful dream.

She rubbed her face with a shaking hand and inhaled a deep breath. Her jaw ached from being clenched in her sleep. Dampened with sweat, her nightgown stuck to her body, and it was rucked up, twisted all about her hips.

The bed creaked as Tolemek sat on the other end. "Bad dream?"

He touched her shoulder. Cas flinched away before she could catch herself. She saw the hurt in his eyes, but he didn't say anything. For a moment, she couldn't say anything, either. In part because her mouth was so dry, but also because looking at him filled her with a sense of anxiety, almost of irritation. He was the enemy, came a thought from the back of her mind.

She closed her eyes and clenched her fist. *No.* Not again.

"Yes," she made herself say. "Nightmare."

Tolemek was a friend—more than a friend. He wasn't an enemy, no matter what ancient blood flowed through his veins. In her mind, she glowered at Kasandral. She had left the sword in the box and tucked beneath her bunk on the other side of the ship, but it hadn't mattered. It had still touched her. Maybe not as powerfully as it had when she had been carrying it in a sheath on her back, but keeping it in that box, no matter how shielded it supposedly was, couldn't entirely extinguish its power, its reach.

"I'm sorry," Cas whispered.

Tolemek lifted his hand again, as if to reach out and touch her face, but he lowered it to his lap. "Can I get you anything?"

Cas's heart crumpled. She didn't want to be untouchable. She loved Tolemek, damn it. Why couldn't the sword get over that? Blood didn't make a man.

Even though her mind knew that, she couldn't get rid of the uncomfortable feeling she experienced from being so close to him. The day before, the sword hadn't seemed to be bothered by Tolemek—she had barely been aware of its presence. Maybe the battle with the sorceress's magic had wakened it. Or maybe her own treacherous dreams had called out to it somehow, rousing it from its rest.

"No. But thank you." Cas pushed herself free of the blankets and out of bed, tugging her rumpled nightshirt into place.

Tolemek looked at her for a moment—the damp garment hugged her modest curves—but quickly looked away. Cas winced. She wanted him to be able to look. They were both supposed to be able to look, to touch, to enjoy each other's company. She rested her hand on the side of his head and leaned forward to kiss him, but she kept it brief. Her senses crawled, newly aware of what he was, that he wasn't entirely human.

She backed away, almost feeling nauseated. "I need some fresh air."

She grabbed her pack with her clothes and belongings in it and hurried for the door.

"Cas?" Tolemek still sat on the bed, gazing after her, his eyes sad. "Are you sure there's not anything I can do?"

Throw the sword over the side of the airship and into some forgotten ravine, she thought. But that would be a betrayal to her country and to her king.

"Finish creating a weapon that can kill dragons and sorceresses, please." She forced a smile, though she was sure it was wan, then fled.

She washed up, changed into her uniform, and headed up to the deck. She hadn't been lying about needing fresh air, and she inhaled the mountain scents, damp grasses, fir trees, and moss, willing them to clear her mind of the lingering images of the dream. No matter how hard she had scrubbed in the modest washroom, she hadn't been able to scrub away the memory of the sword cutting down Sardelle.

Cas walked toward the railing by the fliers, in part to avoid the carpentry noises coming from the other side of the ship, repairs still underway, and in part because seeing the craft offered some comfort. Even if neither of these was her flier, the one she had always used while out on Wolf Squadron missions, they felt familiar, more a home than her barracks room ever had been. She ran a hand along one of the bronze hulls. With a pang, she realized she had missed them, missed being with the squadron. Years ago, she might have only entered the academy and the air school at Zirkander's suggestion, but somewhere along the way, being a pilot had become something she enjoyed, a part of her identity.

Clanks came from one of the cockpits. Judging by the bands of machine gun ammunition lying on the deck next to the flier, someone was doing a maintenance check and reloading the weapons.

Pimples sat up, his head coming into view. He leaned over the edge, about to climb out, but he paused. "Oh, hullo, Raptor. Can you hand those up to me?"

Cas lifted the bands so he could reach them. "Need any help?"

She should have also been up on deck, attending to one of the craft instead of sleeping so late. Even if General Ort had flown yesterday, it was expected that the lower-ranking officer would take care of maintenance. If she had been out here doing that, she might have been saved from that nightmare.

"Nah." Pimples bent, securing the bands. "This is my last task. These girls are ready for another battle, though I'm hoping our next foes won't be invisible."

Cas thought an invisible airship sounded more appealing than a dragon, but she kept the thought to herself. She would have preferred a straightforward battle against enemies that did not have any magic. Who would have thought she would miss the days of skirmishes with pirates?

Pimples clambered down, landing on the deck in front of her. "Thanks." He frowned at her. "You doing all right?"

Cas sighed. How poorly did she look that everyone was asking her that? "Fine."

"Is it Tolemek?"

"No."

"The sword?"

She hesitated. What had he heard about the sword? Had the truth finally come out about Apex? Did everybody know now? Surely not, or there would be accusing stares, not concerned ones.

"Sort of."

"Are you worried about the dragon?"

She didn't have to hesitate before giving that answer. "Yes."

"Me too."

"You'll be fine," she said. *He* didn't have to worry about piloting someone carrying a sword that seemed as content to kill allies as enemies. Cas waved a hand toward the railing. "I'm going to walk around the ship a bit." She hoped he would realize that she did not want company.

Pimples stuck his hands in his pockets. "Sure."

As she headed away, he stared after her. Then he took a step. "Wait, Raptor? Cas?"

"Yes?" she asked, afraid he was going to ask if she was happy with Tolemek and offer himself as an alternative. She hated feeling wary around someone she had considered a friend—and still wanted to consider a friend—but she couldn't help it. She didn't want to deal with relationship confusion, but she cringed at the idea of having to turn him down again. Of course, she hadn't exactly made her feelings clear back then, when he had kissed her in front of everyone. Zirkander had stepped in and waved him away. Maybe she shouldn't have brushed it off; maybe she should have talked to him about it. But she did not know what to say—she never had when it came to admirers. Right now, she couldn't even imagine why she would *have* an admirer.

Because he didn't know what she'd done.

Pimples stepped closer and glanced around. With most of the activity on the other side of the ship, they had the area to themselves, with only the craggy mountains drifting past as witnesses.

"I never got a chance to say… well, to apologize. We haven't really been alone since I, ah, well, since you came back from Cofahre."

"It's all right."

"I don't know what I was thinking. I mean I *do* know, but I shouldn't have been so, uhm, impetuous. I was just relieved to see that you were alive and that you'd made it home with all of your limbs and fingernails attached."

Cas relaxed an iota. He hadn't come any closer, and he didn't look like he would try to touch her. All he seemed to want was to clear the air.

"I was relieved about that too," she said.

"I imagine so. Anyway, I just wanted say I was sorry for surprising you and assuming, ah, you know. I was hoping things could be normal again and that you wouldn't be—well, things seemed awkward. And when you left the squadron, I was afraid—I mean, I wasn't sure if it had something to do with that. I didn't want—*don't* want—you to be uncomfortable."

Cas stared at him. He thought that her leaving might have had something to do with *him*? Because he'd kissed her last winter? Seven gods, how could he have thought such a thing?

Pimples was looking back at her, his lip caught between his teeth and the most earnest expression on his face.

"I didn't leave because of that." She almost laughed, but she didn't want to hurt his feelings. He probably didn't want to hear about just how little she had been thinking of him in the last month. She had hardly been thinking of anyone except herself. Did that make her selfish? Probably. "It was because of Apex."

"Oh." He nodded. "I miss him too."

"I'm the reason…" If nobody knew, aside from the core group of Zirkander's people who had been on the mission with them, maybe she shouldn't say anything. But if other people did know, maybe they would be less understanding than Sardelle, Tolemek, and Zirkander had been. Maybe they would blame her, as they should. She took a breath and finished with, "I'm the reason he died."

She couldn't make herself be utterly blunt, to say that she had killed him by her own hand. It wasn't evasion so much as she didn't want to explain the sword. Everything still hurt too much. She didn't want to talk about it. Already, she wished she hadn't said anything.

"Oh," Pimples repeated. "I'd heard—well, some people thought it might be something like that, that you blamed yourself. The general wouldn't say anything about it when people asked."

No, Zirkander always protected his people, whether they deserved it or not.

"I'm sorry." Pimples stepped forward and hugged her before she knew what was happening. "It must have been horrible for you."

Cas stiffened. "It was horrible for *Apex*."

"I know. But for you too. We all make mistakes, but for us, it's always possible one could cause someone's death. I worry about that, too, for me. About screwing up in a way that…" He shrugged and stepped back, releasing her. "Sorry. I guess I make everything about me, don't I? I'll work on that."

"I…" Cas didn't know what to say. She hadn't wanted him to give her sympathy. She'd thought someone might finally speak the truth, that Apex had deserved to live, that someone who could cut him down didn't.

She looked away, blinking aside tears of frustration.

"I'm sorry, Cas," Pimples said, holding up a hand. "I shouldn't have asked. Shouldn't have brought any of it up."

"No." She managed to pull her thoughts away from her own misery. Hadn't she just been acknowledging how self-absorbed she had been lately? "It's good that you asked, because I don't want you thinking any of this—any of my problems—are your fault."

"Good. I don't now." He stepped back, nodding and giving her more space. "But if you want to talk about anything, or want any math help, let me know, all right?"

She nodded. "Yes."

"And look... about Tolemek?"

Some of her wariness returned. "What?"

"Do you think you'll *marry* him?" His face screwed in an expression somewhere between good humor and disbelief.

Cas smiled slightly, glad to switch to a different topic, even if that one also wasn't that comfortable at the moment, with memories of the sword's influence fresh in her mind. "I haven't thought about marriage yet."

"Will you let me know if you do? And the month would be good also, or at least the year and the season."

She narrowed her eyes at him. "There's not some kind of gambling pool going on, is there?"

"No, no, of course not."

She narrowed her eyes further.

"Well, just a *small* one. Wolf and Tiger Squadrons only. And some of the boys on the maintenance crew. And General Ort."

"General *Ort?*"

"Sure, he's old and has money to throw around. He gets in on all the pools. He put in nearly fifty nucros on the baby pool."

"The baby pool?"

"For General Zirkander and Sardelle. For them, marriage seems a foregone conclusion, so we're betting on when babies will pop out."

Cas coughed, or maybe it was a laugh, at the notion of babies popping out like corks in wine bottles. She might have been disappointed that Pimples had so easily brushed aside her confession, but at least he had lightened her mood.

Major Cildark walked around the fliers, a coil of rope over one shoulder, and a bucket of sealant in his hand. He frowned at them. "If you two cloud-kissers don't have anything better to do, we could use some more help. We're less than four hours out from our destination, and we might be looking at an even bigger battle this time."

"Yes, sir," Cas and Pimples said together.

As they trailed after him, Cas tried to keep the light thoughts in her mind, such as did Zirkander *know* about the baby pool, but she couldn't entirely ignore the nervous twinges in her gut, the acknowledgment that in four hours, she might have to pull that sword out of its case again. She hoped Tolemek and Sardelle weren't anywhere around when she did so.

Chapter 11

Sardelle couldn't reach Ridge. Had he heard the cave-in up there? Did anybody know she and the others had been buried? Would help be coming, or would they be on their own? Even if Ridge had people clearing the cave-in right now, it would take days for them to reach all the way back here, if not weeks. Mundane mining methods weren't speedy, and she and the others did not have food or water to last that long. Not that supplies mattered when her shield would give out long before they starved to death. Their air might run out even before that.

You're full of cheery thoughts, Jaxi said.

I know. Can you tell Ridge what happened? I'd feel cheerier if I knew Captain Bosmont was working on a way to dig us out.

I can't reach Ridge, either. Phelistoth is exuding pain and doesn't have his mental shields up. His aura is trampling all over everything, making it hard for me to get past the noise. Why couldn't he have gotten himself squashed in human form?

He must have thought he'd be more likely to survive in his natural form.

Maybe it would be better if he hadn't *survived.*

Don't be uncharitable. Besides, I think we're going to need his help to get out of here. Sardelle pushed herself to her feet, grimacing at bloody scrapes on her palms. Dirt and grit stuck to the fresh wounds, and she gingerly brushed them off.

The two soldiers watched her, but not with hostility or fear, not anymore. They seemed to have realized their predicament and that she would be the only one who might get them out of it. If only she could.

"He's hurting," Tylie whispered. She crouched on the other

side of the bubble of protection, her arms wrapped around her knees as she stared at Phelistoth's unmoving tail, the two inches of it that they could see sticking out from under all the rubble.

Good, Jaxi thought.

Ssh. "He should be able to heal himself, so long as he's conscious. He *is* still breathing, isn't he?" Sardelle eyed the wall of boulders that hid the rest of Phelistoth from them. From everything she had read and seen herself thus far, it took a lot to kill a dragon, but even they weren't immortal.

"Barely."

Tylie stood up, padding barefoot to Sardelle's side. Where she had lost her sandals, Sardelle didn't know, but she was no longer surprised to find her without footwear. Tylie rested her hand on Sardelle's dirty sleeve, looking up with large, imploring eyes.

"Can you teach me to heal him?" she asked. "To perform *shurako*?"

"Did he ask for that?" Sardelle had never shared the term with Tylie before. "Healing through a mind link? Transferring your life's energy to him?"

"No, he didn't ask for it. He's not answering me. I don't think he's awake. But he told me about it once before. He said I wasn't ready to learn it, but he needs it now, Sardelle. He didn't get his defenses up in time—he was too focused on something up there." Tylie waved toward the ceiling. "The mountain is crushing him. What if he doesn't ever wake up?"

Sardelle rubbed the back of her neck, certain Tylie didn't know the ramifications of what she was asking. "Can you try to heal him normally, with what I've shown you? I can't while I'm focusing on this." She nodded toward the barrier above them, with the boulders and dirt pressing against it, ready to crush them if she released it for an instant. "His own body is strong. He probably doesn't need too much of your energy to heal."

Tylie looked dubiously at the visible nub of tail.

"If you're not practiced at *shurako*, you could hurt yourself." *Kill* yourself, Sardelle almost said, but most people passed out before that happened, at least when healing other humans. She had no idea how much more demanding it might be to transfer energy into a dragon. It would be like trying to fill a well with an eyedropper. She did know the term arose from those ancient times when dragons and human riders had shared links.

"I'll try." Tylie returned to crouching, as close to Phelistoth's tail as she could get without touching the barrier. Whether she meant to try healing or the transfer of energy was not clear, and Sardelle almost reached out with her mind to watch.

Go ahead, Jaxi said. *I'll keep the barrier up. You know I don't know* shurako *from a* shako. *Swords are indifferent to healing.*

You were indifferent to healing even before you became a sword.

True. I always found the healing arts to be... oh, what's the word?

Too challenging to be mastered by someone with an impatient mind? Sardelle suggested.

I was going to say boring. Jaxi spread a protective barrier, the field overlapping with Sardelle's.

Ah, I can see why such an uncommon vocabulary word would have eluded you.

Hush. I was trying to find a more tactful word, since healing is your career and passion.

A more tactful word that still means boring?

Essentially, yes.

Sardelle decided not to dwell on the fact that Jaxi being tactful usually meant she believed the end was near. With her now holding back the rocks, Sardelle knelt beside Tylie, who had her eyes closed, her chin to her chest.

"We'll do it together," Sardelle whispered, not sure if Tylie would hear or if she was already focused on her link with Phelistoth.

For the first time, Sardelle stretched out with her senses and examined the dragon. His pain washed over her, and she understood what Jaxi had meant, about his presence being so overpowering that it was hard to reach out to another. She cataloged his injuries, including broken ribs and a cracked skull. His scales and muscles protected him, but they weren't as massive and thick as she had expected. A dragon's magic must protect it more than its natural armor, which made her realize that if they could ever come upon their golden enemy sleeping, it would be a lot easier to kill him. Too bad they had to figure out how to escape this crypt before they could test that hypothesis.

Under the scales and muscle, Phelistoth's bones were hollow, like a bird's. Almost fragile.

You see the cracked ribs? Sardelle asked Tylie.

Yes. But his head...

I'll work on that. The swelling in his brain would take a delicate touch, but he would likely regain consciousness once that was relieved. *I showed you how to enhance the body's own regenerative abilities. Focus on the bones, please. I'll teach you about the complexities of organs another time.*

All right.

Though Sardelle had told Tylie to avoid the *shurako* technique, she used it herself. Most healing involved channeling and enhancing the patient's own energy, but with two people working on different parts of the same body, that could dangerously drain the patient's system. Trusting Tylie to use the standard technique, since that was all she knew, Sardelle dribbled her own life's force into knitting the bone of the dragon's skull, then on soothing the inflamed tissue in his brain. This most delicate of organs was always a challenge to work on, and though she had healed animals before, as well as humans, the dragon's brain was different from both and alien to her. Still, her techniques worked eventually, and the swelling gradually receded. When she sensed more blood flowing to his brain, she guessed he would rouse soon. She backed away, believing he could finish healing his own injuries once he woke.

Before she could withdraw completely, something grasped onto her incorporeal being, like someone gripping her arm and keeping her from stepping back. Fear flooded into her, fear that he would think she had been attacking him and react before he was fully awake and understood the truth. She started to raise her mental shields, trying to break the contact and protect her mind.

No, Phelistoth rumbled in her thoughts.

Sardelle froze, not certain if the *no* was a warning not to raise her defenses or a promise that he wouldn't attack. His aura draped over her, and for a confusing moment, she sensed the world through him, and she found herself looking down at Tylie from another perspective, watching as she worked hard to heal his ribs. She needed a lot more practice before she would be fast and proficient, but her sheer determination and focus helped her make progress. Phelistoth brushed her aura, the part of her touching him, healing him, and Sardelle sensed his appreciation and even something that might be called love, though there was an alienness to him and his thoughts, just as there was to his anatomy. Still, Sardelle was pleased that he seemed to genuinely care for Tylie. Pleased, but also a little uncomfortable, since she felt like she was intruding upon them now.

I was foolish, human, Phelistoth said into her mind, the power of his words more muted than usual.

She did not know if that was because the injuries had weakened him, or because he was being considerate, so his words wouldn't ring painfully in her head. His entire demeanor was muted, chagrined. She'd never sensed such an emotion from him.

I know you need my help, but I see that you would have healed me, regardless. Phelistoth stared into her naked soul, reading her as if she were broadcasting her every thought. *Pull her back and stand ready to protect yourself from the rocks again*, he said.

I will. Sardelle backed away—this time he allowed it—and grew aware of their small chamber again.

Tylie's tongue was tucked into the corner of her mouth, the concentration that had been visible in her aura just as visible on her face.

Sardelle touched her shoulder. *He can handle it from here.*

Tylie muttered something indistinguishable, but did not stop. She was determined to finish healing those ribs. Sardelle still had a sense of Phelistoth's thoughts, whether because he wasn't keeping his shields up right now or because they had been so close when she'd been healing him. Amusement touched him, in addition to the contentedness and appreciation he felt for Tylie's ministrations. If he cared that his body was still smothered under tons of rock, it did not come through in his thoughts.

After a few more minutes, Tylie finished. Sweat beaded on her brow, but she smiled in triumph.

Stand back, Phelistoth instructed.

One of the soldiers gasped, so Sardelle assumed everyone had heard the order.

Might want to reinforce that barrier, Jaxi. I have a feeling he's going to melt rocks again, and woe to anything unshielded that's nearby.

Yes, I haven't noticed that dragons have a lot of subtly in their attacks—or meltings.

Busy reinforcing the barrier, Sardelle refrained from commenting that Jaxi also tended to be on the zealous side when she attacked or melted something.

Please. I can fry the butt hair off a flea, if I so choose.

Before Sardelle could contemplate a response, a reddish-orange light surrounded them, the power so intense that closing her eyes and shielding them with her hand wasn't enough. She dropped to her knees, with her arms around her head and her face buried against the ground. She kept the shield up, but so much power railed against it that she was left breathless. Worse, the display of power was not brief. It went on and on, battering at her barrier. Sweat dampened the back of her shirt and dripped down the sides of her face to spatter onto the rocks. No heat made its way past her shield, but the drain of keeping the barrier up was akin to that of sprinting up the side of a mountain.

The roar of another rockfall pummeled her ears. Even without looking, she sensed fresh boulders pummeling the barrier. The light disappeared, but several moments passed before the barrage of rocks stopped.

As the bangs slowed to a trickle, Sardelle lifted her head. As far as she could tell, little had changed. Rocks still pressed in on them from all sides.

One thing changed, Jaxi said. *Look to your right.*

The tail was gone, and Phelistoth stood next to Tylie in his human form, *inside* of the barrier. When had he slipped through, and how? She hadn't felt the intrusion.

He melted lots and lots of rocks, then dove in here with us before the next layer fell and crushed him again.

How many layers are there? Sardelle stood up, fighting back a groan. The muscles in her shoulders and upper back ached, as if she had taken a few of those boulders herself. Her whole body was stiff and drained from the magic use. On all sides of her barrier, molten rock glowed red in the cracks between the boulders that had just fallen.

Layers may not have been the best word to describe the jumble that exists above us. It suggests organization that isn't there.

Phelistoth slumped against the wall, his human form appearing far more weary than Sardelle had ever seen it. Tylie clasped his hand and leaned next to him.

"Anyone want to explain what's going on?" Sergeant Jenneth asked, his voice squeakier than usual.

"No," the private said.

"Anyone else just pee down his leg?" Jenneth looked back and forth from the tunnel where Phelistoth's tail had been to the human version of Phelistoth standing next to Tylie. Had he seen the dragon-turned-human walk inside?

"No."

"Oh. Me neither."

The good news is that his aura isn't smothering me like an elephant lying on a mouse anymore, Jaxi said, sharing this image, as well as the words. *I can see what's going on up there now.*

Is it bad? Maybe Sardelle shouldn't ask.

Yes.

Naturally.

First off, Ridge can't do anything to help us in a timely matter.

And second?

The other dragon is up there, and I think he's figured out that Phelistoth is alive and down here.

* * *

When the door to Tolemek's lab opened, he grabbed a pistol and spun toward the intruder. Having that assassin sneak in had left him twitchy. He did not aim it at the person in the doorway, which turned out to be a good choice since it was General Ort.

Ort raised his eyebrows, and Tolemek laid the weapon aside.

"We're done with this." Ort walked in and held out the capped vial of the truth serum. "Thank you."

Tolemek accepted the vial, the contents significantly lowered, and returned it to the rack. "Did you find out anything else?"

He did not know if Ort would tell him if he had, or if the general considered the confessions of prisoners to be military secrets. Still, Tolemek had a reason to be interested in the assassin and whether they had extracted more information from him. He was curious about the questioning of the Cofah soldiers too. He had worked through most of the night on his experiments, and wouldn't have wanted to leave them in order to attend interrogations even if he had been invited, but he couldn't help but wonder what had come out.

"Not from your new friend, but we focused on questioning the Cofah soldiers we captured." Ort stepped back, as if that was all he meant to reveal, but he paused to consider Tolemek. "Maybe this will make more sense to you. As a whole, they're confused as to how they came to be in the middle of Iskandian territory. They were happy enough to engage us once our airship showed up, but unless your serum is faulty, none of them remember why or how they came to be here, and none of them had any recollection of bombing the mountain. They also didn't know what I was talking about when I questioned them in regard to how their craft came to be invisible. Only one of the men remembers the sorceress being with them on the ship."

"My serum isn't faulty," Tolemek said. "We used it on the assassin just a few hours ago."

Ort nodded. "I believe you. We questioned a lot of them, and their stories were too similar for me to suspect they were a part of some coordinated mass lie." His gaze flicked toward the rack of vials. "As someone who apparently has some experience with magic, what do you think? Could the sorceress have been controlling their minds? All of them? Between the two ships, there were fifty people. We captured twenty-five and questioned fifteen. It's extraordinary to imagine one person not only controlling that many people but then making it so they remembered nothing of the experience. The last any of these men knew, they were aboard routine patrol ships that keep an eye on Iskandia from out over the sea."

"I'm afraid my experience is only with creating formulas," Tolemek said. "I don't think Sardelle could fiddle with the minds of fifty men, at least not all at once, but I don't have a strong grasp of her capabilities."

"Not all at *once?*" Ort grimaced.

Yes, the idea of someone being able to manipulate another's mind, even one-on-one was alarming. Perhaps Tolemek shouldn't have implied that Sardelle could do that at all, especially since he wasn't positive she could.

"I always dismissed the sensationalist articles that claimed a witch was controlling Zirkander," Ort said. "I'm sure Sardelle isn't, but it's alarming to think that it could even be a possibility."

"I imagine that if she controlled Zirkander, he would be more polite, like she is."

Ort grunted. "Yes, I guess we'll know his mind isn't his own when he stops strolling into my office, flopping down on my leather chairs, and slinging his dirty boots over the armrests."

"You would need to ask Sardelle about what this sorceress might be able to do. She's a healer, and I know that required very specialized training. I wouldn't be surprised if there were other paths the sorcerers of old could take that would lead to different careers. Perhaps there were those who specialized in mind manipulation. Although..." Tolemek rubbed his jaw.

"What?"

"From what I've seen of this one, she seems more like the magical version of Captain Kaika. It's hard to imagine her sitting down to patiently learn how to do a more subtle form of magic."

"I don't know that Captain Kaika would find your comparison flattering."

"Perhaps not, but they both like to make things burst into flame. Wouldn't you think that would appeal to one particular personality? The personality of someone who would be bored pursuing a more sedate field?"

"I don't know. I'm completely ignorant on this subject." Ort shook his head and started for the door. He paused before leaving and looked back. "Would you be able to tell if that sorceress was nearby?"

"I did have a strange feeling of something—perhaps a presence—nearby before we were attacked. I may have been sensing the magic used to form that invisibility field on the closer airship." Except that Tolemek distinctly remembered feeling the same way he did when Phelistoth came close to him. On the other hand, he *didn't* usually feel anything when Sardelle stood next to him performing magic. It might be that the sorceress's magic was simply stronger, strong enough for someone with ill-honed senses to discern. "I don't know. It might have been nothing. I'm sure I couldn't track her, if that's what you're hoping."

"I would just like to know if she's stowing away on our ship somewhere."

"I wouldn't think so. We never actually landed to let the infantrymen down. She would have had to fly to make it up here."

"Are we sure witches can't do that?" Ort asked.

Tolemek opened his mouth to say yes, but he paused. Did he truly know? "She had to be flown off the fortress when it started to fall apart. In a flier. That should mean she can't turn into a bird or sprout wings at will."

"I'll try to take some solace in that. While I walk around with flour in my pocket."

"It was talc, and there might be some left in that cupboard there. General?" he asked before Ort could leave. "You didn't mention what the man who remembered her had to say." Maybe Ort hadn't intended to. "If I had more information, I might be able to come up with some idea as to what motivates the sorceress." In truth, he mostly wanted the information for his own curiosity. And so he could be better prepared in case she showed up again, especially if she showed up to hurl fireballs at Cas.

"This man was the captain of the first airship, and he seemed fiercely loyal to her. He was certain he was supposed to be there, but he couldn't remember when he'd received orders assigning him and his airship to her command. He did know that she only returned to the empire briefly after the defeat of the sky fortress and was sent—or chose to come of her own accord—back here. The emperor supposedly told her Iskandia is hers if she can secure it, and that she'll rule as his governor, reporting to him, but able to do whatever she wants with our country."

Tolemek nodded. Some of that had come out when he and Sardelle—mostly Sardelle—had battled the woman.

"Despite the emperor's generosity in offering her our country—" Ort paused to make an expression of distaste, "—he wouldn't give her any troops, aircraft, or naval vessels to assist her in her quest to conquer us."

"Which explains why she was here with two airships fully staffed by soldiers," Tolemek said dryly. He raised his eyebrows, expecting more of an explanation.

"For the second time," Ort said. "She had several soldiers and a couple of fliers when we encountered her out here a few weeks ago. One wonders if she's borrowing people from the emperor unbeknownst to him. I'm still flabbergasted at the idea that someone might be able to wave a hand and take possession—body and mind—of an entire military unit."

"We'll definitely have something to discuss with Sardelle. I do know she said the woman is extremely powerful, so she can do things that nobody else left alive in the world can do."

Ort grimaced. "Comforting."

"She must have some limitations, or she could simply walk into the king's castle with her sword, kill Angulus, and take over the government."

"Eh, taking over or destroying an entire government wouldn't be easy. Or at least I would hope it wouldn't be. King Angulus is important to us, but the system carries on, whether he's there or not, so a simple assassination wouldn't work. The rest of the ruling council is spread out in the capitals of the regions across the nation."

Tolemek thought the "system" had lost some of its effectiveness when Angulus had been kidnapped, but he agreed that an assassination wouldn't be enough to let some foreign woman step in and take over. As powerful as she was, the Iskandians could probably turn their entire military might upon her and wear down her defenses sooner or later.

"So, why was she out here and trying to level your mountain?" Tolemek waved in the direction of the Ice Blades.

"That's what I'm wondering. She obviously knows about the dragon statues since she was the one to discover them, but we thought she'd finished with them when she tortured Morishtomaric and apparently didn't convince him to join her. It's possible she thinks she didn't blow things up sufficiently last time and came to ensure we'd never get back into that chamber. I'm sure she doesn't want Iskandians to have dragon allies."

Tolemek agreed that was likely, but couldn't help but wonder if more was going on. It wasn't as if Angulus had announced that he wanted those dragons freed for negotiations.

"Any chance she died when the airship crashed?" Tolemek asked. That would certainly solve some problems.

"I suppose there's a chance, but I wouldn't count on it." Ort thumped his fist against his thigh. "I would have liked to search the area more thoroughly, but when Duck's communication arrived—well, we can't let the dragon attack our people up there again."

"I won't disagree with that." Especially if Tylie and the others were in danger. Tolemek had thought she would be safe going off with Sardelle, safer than she would have been here with him, but that might not have been the case.

A knock sounded at the door.

"General Ort?" A corporal stuck his head inside. "Lieutenant Duck is back, sir. The dragon is attacking the outpost again."

Tolemek clenched his fist. Again? With Tylie there? He couldn't believe the airship had flown through the night and still wasn't there.

"Can't this slug boat move any faster?" he growled, following Ort into the passageway.

He didn't expect an answer, but Ort glanced back as he headed for the ship's ladder. "We're about three hours out, but I can send you ahead in the fliers with Ahn and Captain Kaika, especially if you have a formula capable of hurting the dragon."

"I've been working all night. I have something I can try if I can come up with a delivery method." Tolemek wished he could say he had something guaranteed to work, but until he actually tried it on a dragon, he couldn't. "I don't suppose you have a dragon scale around that I can test it on first?"

"We didn't stock any when we supplied the ship."

"Shortsighted."

"Yes. Get what you need and meet at the fliers."

"Yes, sir," Tolemek said before he caught himself. Sir? Even if he had been a soldier once and yes-sirred many people, he wasn't in Ort's army. Oh, well. If Ort was letting Tolemek go to help his sister, he would sir the man up and down.

Chapter 12

Ridge clenched his fist in frustration as another cannonball sailed into the air, missing the dragon by twenty feet. These weapons had been installed to stave off attacks from slow-moving dirigibles, not agile, fire-breathing dragons. Even when the cannonballs and shells would have struck the creature, Morishtomaric either lazily flapped his wings in time to avoid them or simply raised a magical shield, and they bounced off. Ridge didn't know if a cannonball would do damage to that scaled hide, even if the dragon didn't shield himself. His bullets certainly hadn't done anything during their last fight.

The only good thing thus far was that Morishtomaric hadn't breathed any more fire. The bad thing was that he seemed to be focused on Galmok Mountain. Aside from occasionally dodging a cannonball, he was ignoring the soldiers firing upon him. He kept sailing low along the rugged terrain near the outpost walls, and in his wake came more earthquakes. The tremors did not last long, but they shook the ground vigorously, causing the mountainside to buck and heave, almost as if someone were hurling explosives.

After the third pass, Ridge realized with a sickening feeling that the dragon was doing exactly that, hurling *mental* explosives. That could only mean that he wanted to do more damage, to further collapse the mines. Did he know Sardelle was down there? No, this probably wasn't about her, or Tylie, either.

"He knows Phelistoth is down there," Ridge said as the dragon soared low for another pass. Morishtomaric had attacked Phelistoth twice now. For whatever reason, he seemed to want the silver dragon dead.

"Sir?" the private manning the cannon beside him asked.

"Keep trying to hit the dragon," Ridge said, though he knew it was useless. Nobody had touched him yet. The other guns and cannons along the fortress walls kept firing, coloring the air gray with smoke, but nothing came of it.

Dragon, Ridge yelled in his mind, staring at the golden figure swooping down for another attack. *What do you want?*

Was killing Phelistoth his sole reason for being here, or had something else attracted him to the outpost? His first attack had come *before* Ridge and the others, Phelistoth included, had arrived.

If Morishtomaric was monitoring the thoughts of the humans under him and heard the question, he did not bother responding. He didn't look toward Ridge, or toward the outpost at all. He kept throwing his mental attacks at the mountain. Ridge dug his fingers into his hair, barely noticing when his cap fell off. If Sardelle was alive down there, the last thing she needed was *more* rock falling on top of her. But how could he stop a dragon that wasn't even aware of his existence?

His gaze shifted toward the single flier parked atop the headquarters building. He'd sent Duck off again to warn the others about this new development, but his own craft remained.

"Keep firing, private," Ridge ordered, already halfway down the stairs of the tower. He would *make* the dragon aware of his existence.

He did not run straight for the headquarters building. First, he sprinted for the armory, a stone structure that had withstood the first attack. Half of the building held rifles, bullets, and artillery ammunition. The other half held explosives for the mines. He grabbed matches and an armful of dynamite, then raced back out across the courtyard. Soldiers scattered out of his way, their eyes bulging when they saw his full arms, especially when a couple of the sticks fell from his grasp. He did not slow to pick them up.

Only one man ran toward him instead of away from him. Therrik, his lips curled into his usual sneer, looked like he meant to intercept Ridge.

"Out of my way," Ridge barked, not slowing as he angled for the steps leading up the outside of the headquarters building. He had no intention of stopping to explain himself.

Instead of intercepting him, Therrik fell in behind him. "If you're blowing up the dragon, I'm helping."

"You're the fort commander. You don't get to go on suicidal missions." At a more rational and less desperate moment, Ridge would have laughed at his hypocritical words, but he was too busy sprinting up the stairs and across the rooftop.

"You need someone to throw those," Therrik said, dogging his steps. "Otherwise, they'll all fall out as soon as you flip upside down. I've been up there with you, and I know how incapable you are of flying without doing that."

He had a point.

"Then send a private with me," Ridge said. "You need to stay here."

"Doing what? Nothing we've got hits that bastard."

Ridge flung dynamite into the cockpit, scarcely aware that he was dropping sticks left and right in his haste.

"Damn it, Zirkander. Those aren't that stable." Therrik bent to pick up his mess.

Ridge hauled himself into the cockpit and slapped the ignition. The power crystal flared to life. Therrik scrambled into the back, a stick of dynamite in his mouth and a dozen more clutched in his hands. Ridge glared over his shoulder in exasperation as he buckled himself in, but there wasn't time to argue further. He powered up the thrusters, and Therrik, not settled yet, lurched and nearly fell out.

"Strap yourself in or get out," Ridge said. "We're leaving this roof in three seconds."

"Shut up and get me up to that dragon." A clack sounded as Therrik buckled his harness.

Ridge took off so quickly, he probably left scorch marks on the roof. Dynamite sticks shifted and rolled around his feet. He wasn't planning to fly upside down, but even he had to admit this was dangerous. He fished them up and handed all but a few of them back to Therrik as they accelerated into the blue sky.

Ridge inhaled and exhaled slowly, telling his nerves to settle, his heart to stop thudding so rapidly in his chest. Surprisingly, his body obeyed his wishes. Nothing had changed, but he already felt less rattled. He was in the air now, where he was meant to be. As the wind scraped through his hair, he took his goggles from their holder and tugged them over his head. This was his milieu. Maybe he could even do something effective.

"You got somewhere back here to store these things?" Therrik asked.

"Maybe you can sit on them."

"I'll give you something to sit on," Therrik growled. Apparently, his nerves hadn't settled.

"I'm not interested in your something."

"You actually interested in that witch's something?"

"Is *that* why you ran after me? To ask that?" Ridge spotted Morishtomaric, but kept climbing. He wanted to come at the dragon from above.

"No, I want to blow up that cowardly bastard. He attacked us for an hour last night, never coming down to engage us like a man. The whole time, he was flying around like a damned, damned *you*." Therrik's frustration came through with every word.

"Yes, it's so irritating when things that aren't human refuse to fight like humans." Ridge probably shouldn't goad him, but that comment about Sardelle had him wanting to throw dynamite at more than the dragon.

Fortunately, Therrik stopped talking. When the silence extended, Ridge glanced back. Therrik's skin had paled, and he pursed his lips together like a man trying not to throw up.

"Wonderful," Ridge muttered. His artilleryman was going to puke all over their ammo. He was glad the king had agreed to give the dragon sword back to Cas, even if her decision to request it again made his heart ache. He shuddered to imagine Therrik behind him with it.

As they cruised into a few clouds near the top of Galmok Mountain, Ridge leaned over the side, gauging the distance to the dragon and how close he would have to get to hit it with an explosive.

Just throw it, Jaxi's voice sounded in his head. *I'll help guide it down. We would very much like for that dragon to stop battering the mountain.*

Jaxi! Where have you been?

In precisely the same spot for the last thirty minutes.

Is Sardelle all right? Tylie? Ridge tilted his wings and took them downward. The dragon had turned around and was heading in their direction, though it stayed lower, clearly intending to target the mountainside again. This was his chance to catch it.

For now. Our magical barrier is the only thing keeping us from being crushed. I'm helping Sardelle maintain it, but eventually we'll run out of energy. Phelistoth was trying to burn us a route out of here, but then the mountain started shaking again. Rocks are coming down, even in the levels that hadn't previously collapsed. The levels above our heads.

Are you close to the tram shaft?

Jaxi hesitated. *No.*

Ridge flexed his grip on the flight stick. He *had* to get through to the dragon, convince it to leave somehow. Then he needed to round up everyone in the outpost, miners and soldiers alike, to dig them out.

"Therrik? You ready with the first stick?" Ridge slipped a match out of his pocket. Lighting a fuse up here, with the wind whistling through the cockpit, would be a challenge, but he intended to drop explosives of his own. He wagered Therrik could manage precision on the ground, but there were a lot more variables up here. Like how much one's puke threw off one's aim.

"Ready." Therrik still sounded sick.

The dragon had yet to look up or acknowledge them. Ridge leaned out, timed his approach and the height difference, then held the stick in his mouth while he bent forward to shield the match and light the fuse.

"Captain Kaika should have educated you on the proper—erp."

Ridge lit and dropped his stick. "Maybe you should write down your sarcastic comments and give them to me later. When you're not on the verge of vomiting."

"Writing." Therrik made a gagging noise. Maybe writing would be worse than talking.

At least he did his job, and a second stick of dynamite sailed downward.

Ridge circled so he could track the descent of the explosives. They seemed to spiral down with painful slowness and indirectness, like falling autumn leaves fluttering in the breeze. Therrik's tumbled past the dragon before blowing up harmlessly forty meters away. Ridge's exploded much closer, the edge of the fiery orange explosion catching Morishtomaric's wing.

Whether it did any damage, Ridge couldn't tell, but the dragon *did* wheel in the air and fly toward them.

"You wanted his attention, Ridge," he muttered to himself before raising his voice to call back, "Get another stick ready, Therrik."

He would need both hands and all of his focus to avoid the dragon.

"We want to talk to you, Morishtomaric," Ridge called. He doubted his words would carry over the wind and the distance, but he definitely had the dragon's attention now. Maybe it would listen to his thoughts.

What do you want, human? the creature demanded.

"Don't you already know?" Ridge caught himself asking before something more diplomatic could form in his mind.

To kill my kind.

Technically, Ridge only wanted to kill this one specific dragon, but he doubted that was going to happen today, not unless Duck had found the others, and they were on their way as fast as that doddering airship could fly.

Actually, I just want to know why you're trying to flatten that mountain. We have miners and soldiers in there. Along with the love of his life, the woman who had asked him if he wanted to have children with her. His mother would never forgive him if he lost her. He would never forgive *himself.*

Morishtomaric sailed closer, his fang-filled maw stretching open.

Ridge directed the flier to dip, spinning as he dropped away, hoping to make a more difficult target. It was a good thing, because a stream of orange fire shot out, barely missing the tail of his craft.

Therrik groaned. It might have been because they had almost been incinerated, but it probably had more to do with airsickness.

"Throw it," Ridge ordered.

He glanced back. Despite his wan complexion, Therrik lit a new stick and hurled it over the tail of the flier. The man had a spry arm—the stick spiraled through the air, nearly hitting the dragon in the face. The fuse shouldn't have burned down quickly enough to explode then, but it did, and Morishtomaric's head disappeared in flames.

You're welcome, Jaxi thought.

Did that hurt him?

He's sneezing.

Is that a no?

Yes, sorry.

Dragon, Ridge called out again, trying to direct his thoughts toward Morishtomaric, who was flying out of the fire of the explosion, his nostrils smoking. *Let's work together. If you want something down there, tell me. I command this fort.* No need to mention that where Therrik could hear it. *I can direct all of our resources toward finding what you want if you let me get my people out first. You're just going to make it harder to get what you want if you keep shaking the earth.*

Assuming Morishtomaric actually wanted something down there. What if all he cared about was burying Phelistoth forever?

The dragon flew alongside his flier, matching its pace with two hundred meters separating them. Ridge looked over at him. Had Morishtomaric heard him?

"It's looking at me, Zirkander," Therrik said. "Fly closer so I can shove one of these sticks up its nose."

"Sounds like a good way to get killed by an inferno."

"Might be able to kill it first. Not even a dragon can withstand being blown up from the inside out."

"Unless you're quoting an ancient text from a book written

by a world-renowned dragon slayer, I'm not ready to trust that assertion."

Besides, the dragon wasn't attacking them or the mountain right now. Could it have heard him? Did it want to bargain? The way Morishtomaric kept looking over at them was disconcerting, and Ridge had no idea what was on his mind. Nor did he know how the creature flew straight with his head turned like that.

One day, human.

Pardon?

You have one day to retrieve the artifact, or I will raze your insignificant fort and this mountain to get it myself.

Morishtomaric blasted Ridge with a barrage of images of him doing exactly that. Ridge gasped, the experience so vivid, that for a moment, it felt as if he was himself being swallowed by an inferno as it devoured the outpost. He managed to shake away the feeling, forcing himself to focus on the sky ahead, the fact that he was here in the cockpit and not on the ground.

Trying to sound less rattled than he was, Ridge responded with, *You'll have to actually tell me what this artifact is, so we can find it. There's a lot of old stuff down there. Also, we'll need more than a day to dig it out.*

Another image slammed into Ridge's mind, this time of a pyramid-shaped purple crystal with multiple points. It glowed softly against a dark background. With nothing to compare it with, he couldn't tell how large it was in the vision. A few inches? Twenty feet? He supposed he would recognize it if he saw it—it wasn't as if anything like it had been in Therrik's fork room.

We need at least a week, Ridge thought. Given how many years these mines had been here and how long it took the men to find and pull out power crystals, even that time frame seemed ludicrous, but he trusted Sardelle and Jaxi and Phelistoth could help locate it.

You have one day, the dragon growled into Ridge's head. *One day, or I find it myself. And if your people are in my way, so be it.*

If we find it and give it to you, will you leave Iskandia forever? If he couldn't kill the dragon, Ridge would settle for getting it out of his country.

We shall see, human. If you get it to me before the others arrive, I may feel lenient toward you.

Others? Ridge thought of the cavern where Kaika and the king had discovered those statues. Morishtomaric hadn't managed to go back and free the rest of his kind, had he? *What others?*

The dragon increased his speed, outpacing the flier as he turned and headed away from Galmok Mountain.

Therrik thumped Ridge on the shoulder. "You're letting it get away."

"I think the more accurate statement is that he's letting us live. For the moment." Ridge slumped back in his seat, oddly exhausted from the brief battle. Maybe having to deal with that dragon's power blasting him in the brain was the reason for his weariness. "I made a deal with it. We need to find an artifact."

"What do you mean you made a deal with it? I didn't hear anything."

"It spoke in my head."

Therrik thumped him on the shoulder again, this time harder. "You made a *deal* with it? You don't deal with the enemy, Zirkander. Even you cloud humpers should know that. It's in the regs."

"I was just buying time. Assuming Duck found the others, General Ort's airship should be on the way. Along with Ahn and your sword." Remembering that he was the ranking officer and that he didn't have to explain himself to Therrik, he ended with, "And that's General Cloud Humper, to you. You forget it, and next time I *will* take you close enough to try to shove dynamite up the dragon's nose. Just don't expect me and my flier to stick around while you do it."

When Therrik did not respond with the expected grumpy comeback, Ridge glanced over his shoulder. He promptly wished he hadn't. The colonel's breakfast was finding its way onto his back seat.

"I wasn't even flying upside down," Ridge grumbled, turning back toward the outpost.

The dragon was just visible in the distance, following the spine of the Ice Blades. He swooped down behind a distant peak and disappeared from sight. Ridge had a feeling he wasn't going far and that he would be keeping an eye on his progress here. Twenty-four hours to find a little crystal in a giant mountain. As Ridge glided toward the outpost, he wished the vomit in his back seat was the worst of his problems.

* * *

As the two fliers followed the mountains, leaving the airship behind, Tolemek cast forlorn looks at the craft cruising beside the one he shared with Lieutenant Pimples. He had assumed he would fly with Cas, but she had come up on deck with that sword in its box once again, and he had realized it might not be a good idea. Ort had ordered her to pilot Captain Kaika, and after a glance at Tolemek, Cas had not objected.

Since she was not casting forlorn looks back at him, Tolemek made himself focus on the route ahead. He had never been to Galmok Mountain, or to many places in Iskandia besides the capital. The Ice Blades were majestic, but daunting, too, especially now. The day had started out sunny, what little he had seen of it through his porthole, but it was growing progressively cloudier as they turned deeper into the mountains. In the distance, darker clouds promised a storm.

"Coordinates say we should be getting close," Pimples announced to the communication crystal.

"I'll take your word for it," came Cas's response. "I've never been to the mines."

"None of us have. It wouldn't be much of a secret outpost if we all took training trips there every month."

Tolemek wondered if Cas would appreciate it if he smacked Pimples for being lippy. Probably not. Lippiness seemed to be a requirement among the Wolf Squadron pilots.

The fliers curved to follow the contours of one of the highest peaks in the range, one blanketed in ice and snow, the lower half invisible beneath clouds wreathing the mountain. They were almost upon the outpost before it came into view, a stone-walled fort hunkering at one end of a valley surrounded by mountains on all sides. Evergreen trees grew in much of the valley, surviving despite the altitude, but the area around the outpost had been cleared. It looked desolate. If Tolemek hadn't seen people moving about inside the walls, he might have judged the outpost an abandoned ruin, based on the damage it had taken. As the fliers descended, that damage grew more apparent, with wooden buildings destroyed and everything else charred black.

His stomach sank as he thought about how he had sent Tylie here. A soulblade wasn't worth being fried by a dragon. He should have kept her with him on the airship. No, the airship hadn't been any safer. He should have left her with Zirkander's *mother*. Except that Zirkander's mother did not believe in magic and might not be such a friendly host if she realized what Tylie was. Damn it, why didn't he know more people that could watch after her? Did she ever wish she were back home, still living with their parents and doing normal things with her friends? She ought to be finishing school and ogling cute boys, not flying around on the back of a dragon and being a target for whatever person—or sword—took a dislike to sorceresses.

Another feeling of unease nibbled at him at that thought. For the first time, Cas—and Kasandral—would be in the same space as Tylie. The idea of that sword making Cas attack Tylie twisted his gut into knots.

He touched the ceramic jars in his pocket, wondering if the contents truly had any chance of hurting the dragon. He wanted so much to make it so Cas would never need to take the blade out of its box again. That was the only way to keep Sardelle and Tylie safe. Maybe he could get Phelistoth to give him a dragon scale for a final test. Of course, even if his formula worked, he still needed to come up with a delivery mechanism. A sling with a grenade on the end wouldn't likely catch a dragon. He needed a way past the creature's shields too.

"No sign of the dragon yet," Pimples said. "That's good. Maybe it got bored and left."

"Land in the courtyard," Cas said. "There's not room on that roof."

Roof? Tolemek squinted and saw what she was talking about,

a flat roof on a stone building that appeared relatively free of damage and that held two other fliers. Duck's and Zirkander's? Tolemek hoped it boded well that both craft were there.

"A lot of people down there," Pimples said.

"They're all clustered around those doors," Cas said. "Switch to thrusters before you cross over the wall, and you'll be fine."

Tolemek studied the doors Cas had mentioned. There were four different sets of them sunken into the earth itself, all of them accessible from the courtyard but from different parts of it. Piles of dirt rested to the sides of them, and small towers rose up at the entrances with cables extending through holes in the doors and disappearing under them. One of the towers had been knocked over, its metal supports torn from a cement foundation. All of the men were gathered around a tower that still stood, with the doors next to it yawning open, revealing a dark shaft that descended diagonally into the mountain. As the fliers approached, a train of ore carts rose out of the shaft, and men with shovels jumped to unload them. Tolemek couldn't imagine that the soldiers were worried about ore or power crystals as they recovered from the dragon attack. There had to be another reason they were pulling up rock and dirt, and he couldn't think of anything innocuous.

Cas and Pimples landed in a quiet corner of the courtyard.

Scarcely waiting for the flier to stop, Tolemek jumped out. He had spotted Zirkander during the landing—he was one of the men with shovels—and he strode straight toward him.

"Tylie?" he asked, gripping Zirkander's arm and stopping him mid-shovel.

For once, Zirkander's face was devoid of humor. "She's down there with Sardelle and Phelistoth and a lot of trapped soldiers and miners."

Tolemek edged closer to the open shaft, peering into the darkness. Far below, a few torches burned, the lights not illuminating anything at this distance. Clangs and scrapes filtered up from the depths.

"What happened?"

"Cave-in. But Sardelle and Jaxi are keeping a barrier up.

They're protected for the moment, and we're trying to reach them before, uhm."

"Before they get too tired and can't hold it up anymore," Tolemek said grimly.

Zirkander shrugged helplessly.

Tolemek closed his eyes, his regrets rushing back to him. He *should* have kept Tylie with him. "How did this happen?"

"I'm not sure. They were going to find a soulblade and dig it out, but something happened. The cave-in. Then the other dragon showed up, making things worse." Zirkander stepped around Tolemek and scooped another pile of dirt out of the ore cart. "Grab a shovel if you want to help. No, wait." He lowered the tool and spun toward the fliers. "You didn't bring Captain Kaika, by chance, did you?"

"Yes, she flew with Cas." Tolemek pointed—Cas, Kaika, and Pimples were walking toward them.

"Here." Zirkander thrust the shovel at him, then ran across the courtyard toward the group.

Tolemek stared at the implement, then down the tram shaft again, and he realized what Zirkander had to be thinking. Explosives. Would that help free Tylie and Sardelle? Or would it only cause more rock to fall, enough to bury them permanently?

Chapter 13

HEAT TURNED THE ROCKS RED and then into rivers of steaming magma. Under the influence of Phelistoth's magic, the lava flowed away, sometimes against gravity, and melted its way into side alcoves before hardening and leaving a narrow tunnel free. Sardelle couldn't watch for long—the light was too intense—but she checked Phelistoth's progress often as he worked, burrowing his way back toward the main passage. She kept hoping they would encounter other people who had survived the cave-in, and she wanted to make sure to pull them out before the dragon melted them like so much rock.

There's nobody left alive down here, Sardelle, Jaxi said. *Not on these levels. Some men are up higher, stuck because the bottom third of the tram shaft is buried.*

Logically, Sardelle knew that, but she did not want to accept it. Jaxi was maintaining the barrier around them now, so Sardelle had been free to check with her senses several times. She hadn't found any other life on what remained of their level, but she kept hoping that she had been mistaken, that she was too weary from all she had done, and that her senses were simply dulled.

They're not. I'm sorry. There are people three levels above that are still alive. Only some of their tunnels collapsed, those right over where Phelistoth was digging.

Jaxi, Sardelle cried silently. A big part of her wanted to sink to her knees in the middle of the tunnel and cry out loud. It wasn't that those miners had been paragons of humanity with long and fulfilling lives that they could have lived, but they had still been human beings, and now they were dead because of a quest she had agreed to, one she had been leading. And the soldiers stationed on these levels—some of them must have been good men, just doing their duties. Like Ridge. He had been a soldier here once, after all.

It's not your fault, and you weren't *leading. The lout was.*

Sardelle looked toward Phelistoth, who stood only a couple of feet away as he continued to melt a tunnel for them. His face was set with concentration, and sweat gleamed on his human skin.

He regrets that, I think, Sardelle said. *He knows he thought too highly of himself and his skills. He believed he could get those artifacts and* the soulblade. *He's not pleased that his hubris resulted in this.*

Because he was injured or because he actually cares what happens to puny humans? And soulblades.

He cares what happens to Tylie.

So, we're just lucky that we were standing next to her.

Technically, she's lucky that she was standing next to us. I think Phelistoth realizes that and is appreciative of the help we gave her. And him.

Jaxi made a noise in Sardelle's head, a noise somewhere between a snort and a fart. *I don't know where you're getting this. I can't read him at all.*

I can't usually, either, but when I—when Tylie and I were healing him, he let me feel something of his emotions.

Nothing I've seen suggests dragons have emotions other than arrogance and pride.

Sardelle shrugged. She was too tired to defend Phelistoth, and she wasn't certain that she should. Still, she was glad they were down here with him instead of with the gold dragon.

For a moment, Phelistoth looked over at her, and she felt naked beneath that intense gaze, certain he knew all of her thoughts. If this was what it was like for mundane humans when faced with sorcerers, she could understand why magic made them uncomfortable. Unable to shield their minds, they could never know when someone with power was looking into their thoughts.

Phelistoth turned away, and the air heated again, the passage glowing red as more rocks melted.

Move your shield forward, he spoke into their minds. *We can advance farther.*

The tunnel appeared stable where he had melted the way,

the walls and floor smoother now, the rock cooling unnaturally quickly so that they could walk on it. Sardelle kept her barrier up and waved for the soldiers to stay with them. They advanced about thirty feet, reaching the main passage. The lanterns that had been out there had been crushed—or melted. Maybe both. She didn't see any sign of the two soldiers they had left behind, but she was more relieved by that than disturbed. She shuddered at the idea of a pair of smoldering boots on the ground with nothing left above them.

That's not far from the truth, I'm afraid. Most of the people on higher levels have made their way to the tram chambers, but they're blocked in. Some of them are sitting down to wait. Oddly, some of them aren't.

What do you mean? Sardelle asked.

Some of them are making their way through a natural cavern formation behind the tram shaft. It spans a few levels. It doesn't look like they can go up, but about a dozen are coming down here.

Why? Don't they realize the tram shaft would still be blocked and that they won't be able to escape from down here, either?

Maybe they're after you.

What, as revenge for this mess? Sardelle asked. *How could they know we were the ones responsible?* Sardelle looked at Phelistoth.

I only know that the one leading has an image of you fixed firmly in his determined brain.

I suppose nobody told these people that a dragon was coming down and that he *was responsible?*

I don't believe so. The only ones here who know what Phelistoth is are the two soldiers with you, since they saw him in his real form.

Sardelle walked forward a few steps, as Phelistoth waved for them to advance again. She doubted the miners could pose much of a threat to them, though perhaps that was a cocky assumption, given how tired she and Jaxi were. Usually, they maintained a barrier for a few minutes, the duration of a battle, not for hours, and not against intense heat and tons of rocks. Still, she worried more that the miners would put themselves into a position where Phelistoth might kill them, either inadvertently, by melting nearby rocks, or intentionally, because they represented a threat.

There's no way we can stop him if he decides to do that, Jaxi thought. *Unless you're able to give him a very distracting rash on his nether regions.*

I don't think that would work on scales.

He's not scaled now, Jaxi pointed out.

I don't want to risk turning him into an enemy.

Even if he's going to kill a bunch of humans?

Sardelle grimaced. *Let's wait to worry about that later—maybe we can figure out a way to keep the miners out of our path. Or maybe we can ask Tylie to convince Phelistoth to let them live.* Sardelle looked at Tylie. She appeared very young, her face smeared with dirt and streaked with tears, as she tagged along, a couple of steps behind Phelistoth. Sardelle hadn't noticed her crying. She must have been doing so quietly. Because she was afraid? Or tired? Or knew something Sardelle didn't know? *She has a gentle soul,* she added to Jaxi. *She won't want people killed.*

If she's being threatened, she may not be able to convince Phelistoth otherwise. He's been quite protective of her.

I know. Sardelle waved for the soldiers to take a couple of steps forward, as she pushed the barrier farther up the passage. *What's Ridge doing? Is he all right?* Sardelle longed to change topics and also to let him know they were safe. Sort of. She kept trying to push through the blazing energy that radiated from Phelistoth's aura to reach the surface and find him, but she hadn't managed yet.

Making deals with dragons.

What?

I'm not sure on the details yet. Right now, they're working to clear the tram shaft. If Phelistoth can get us close, maybe we can get out of here.

"This is the main tunnel, isn't it?" Sergeant Jenneth asked, staring at the smooth waves of newly hardened rock that had replaced the chiseled boulders from before.

"Yes," Sardelle said.

"We left Chance and Moz back here. Is there any way to tell if they made it out?"

"They didn't," Tylie whispered. She dragged her sleeve across her eyes. "None of them did."

Sergeant Jenneth's shoulders slumped. "Oh."

The private eyed her and circled his heart with two fingers, the traditional gesture for warding off magic.

"What about up above? In the fort? Is the general and everyone up there all right?" Jenneth asked.

"For now," Sardelle said.

"The outpost wasn't affected by our problem," Tylie said, "but the other dragon is up there. He was the one causing those other quakes. He's stopped attacking now. Phel isn't sure why."

Deals with dragons, Jaxi said again.

"Phel?" Jenneth asked, though he was looking at the back of Phelistoth's silver-haired human head, so he must have guessed who they were talking about.

Care to elaborate, Jaxi?

Tylie nodded to Jenneth and touched Phelistoth's back.

The sergeant's gaze lowered to his butt, as if he was imagining the dragon tail sticking out from that backside. He joined his comrade in making gestures to ward off evil magic.

I'm talking to Ridge now, Jaxi said. *If you're done eyeing Phelistoth's butt, I can share the details.*

I wasn't the one eyeing anything.

Too late. I've already informed Ridge that you were considering another man's anatomy.

Because you know he must be worried up there and you're attempting to alleviate his anxiety by joking with him, right?

Actually, I was trying to distract you from your *anxiety. He needs to know... Huh.*

Sardelle squeezed Jaxi's pommel. *Yes?*

Instead of speaking, Jaxi shared a series of images, images from Ridge's thoughts. Sardelle had touched Ridge's mind before and shared experiences with him, but she had never done it with Jaxi as the intermediary. She longed to be more direct with him, but she accepted what was offered, the memory of him taking off and flying up to confront Morishtomaric. She smiled as his humor and a few of his thoughts came through the link, specifically his distress at having Therrik riding along and being sick in his back seat. But the humor faded as he communicated with the dragon.

A purple crystal? Sardelle wondered. *Is that one of the artifacts locked in the vault?*

You'll have to ask Phelistoth about that. For all Ridge knows, it might be a glowing paperweight.

It's nothing you're familiar with?

No. Jaxi paused. *I'm fairly certain it's not a paperweight.*

That's helpful.

I thought so.

Phelistoth lowered his arm, his head drooping. The light from the melting rocks faded, though the sides of the tunnel ahead continued to glow orange.

"I must rest for a moment," he announced.

He usually spoke in their minds instead of aloud. Sardelle wondered how much he was taxing himself, and she thought again of the miners trying to find a way to them.

Perhaps this would be the time to ask him about dragon paperweights, Jaxi suggested.

Maybe. But what if that crystal is the thing that caught his interest and made him deviate from the soulblade and toward the vault?

Then he should definitely know what it is.

Yes, but would he tell us? What if it's something that could be a danger to humanity? If the other dragon wants it so badly, and if Phelistoth wants it...

Then it would be even better *to know what it is,* Jaxi said dryly. *Besides, do you think it would be possible to keep your knowledge from Phelistoth? He seems to surf around in people's thoughts without worrying about Referatu privacy rules.*

Imagine that. Sardelle decided not to point out that Jaxi had been freely poking into people's minds since they had woken in this time period and the threat of being punished had disappeared.

I only poke to help you. And only in surface thoughts. Don't you want to know when strange, grubby miners want you dead?

Not necessarily. I concede your point about Phelistoth though.

"Are you all right?" Tylie rested her hand on Phelistoth's arm.

He was as dust-coated as the rest of them, weariness slumping his shoulders. He appeared more human than he ever had, with all of the frailties and failings that being human entailed.

An illusion, Sardelle told herself.

Phelistoth stood straight, drawing his shoulders back. "Perfectly fine," he said, glancing over his shoulder at the two soldiers. They did not appear belligerent in any way—unless one counted the frequent hand gestures—but he gave them a baleful glower before looking back to Tylie.

Phelistoth? Sardelle asked silently. No need to share information about enemy dragons or glowing crystals with the soldiers. *Ridge spoke to Morishtomaric and—*

A growl in her mind interrupted her.

I'm not pleased about it, either, Sardelle said, assuming the growl reflected his feelings toward the other dragon rather than toward her. *But he gained some information. Morishtomaric seeks an ancient artifact, perhaps something stored in the very vault you sought.* She was careful to keep any judgment out of her words. *He's given us twenty-four hours to find it, or he'll do his best to collapse the mountain on top of us, not worrying if he kills everyone in the outpost and the mines in the process.*

Humans mean nothing to him.

Do they mean anything to you? Sardelle asked curiously, before she could stop herself. She might not like the answer she received.

Some of them.

Sardelle hoped that included her and Ridge. After all, when Phelistoth had been visiting Tylie, he had been staying in their house. Eating Ridge's cheese.

Let me try to share an image of the artifact with you, she continued. Phelistoth hadn't said anything to suggest he already knew about it. Sardelle did her best to form the crystalline structure in her mind. Since she'd only seen it secondhand—make that third-hand—she couldn't promise accuracy.

It has seven points, not six, Jaxi commented.

Would you like to do this?

Yes. I'm a talented artist.

A skill you honed during your three-hundred-year nap?

No, I was too busy pining for company to hone skills during that time. It's a good thing you finally woke up so I could resume my quest toward self-betterment.

Ha ha. Are you sharing it with him?

Yes. All seven points.

Sardelle looked at Tylie, wondering if she was catching any of the conversation. A slight curve to her lips suggested she might have caught the gist through Phelistoth.

Are you sure *you want a soulblade?* Sardelle asked her.

Tylie's smile widened. *I'm used to having another's thoughts in my head.*

Yes, but are they impertinent thoughts?

Sometimes. Dragons have an interesting sense of humor.

Humor? Sardelle looked at Phelistoth. She couldn't remember him saying anything that would hint at a sense of humor. *Do you have to be a dragon to understand it?*

Probably. He is thinking that he might go out of his way to keep Ridge alive, if it were to ensure that the cheese supply continued.

I see. That's an example of humor?

He seemed to think I should be tickled.

Sardelle scratched her head. Her relationship with Jaxi was starting to seem blessedly simple.

You're welcome.

Phelistoth spoke again. *I did grow aware of that artifact, as you call it, when we were digging.*

He looked at Tylie. She touched his arm again and nodded.

It is also what I sought, he admitted.

Do you know what it is? Sardelle asked.

I would not divert from Tylie's sword for some mystery bauble. Phelistoth narrowed his eyes at her.

Tylie's sword. He was assuming that some ancient soulblade would take her on as a new handler. Maybe he thought he could coerce the soul inside.

Not exactly the most important thing now, Jaxi pointed out. *Phelistoth, what* is *the artifact?*

There are no equivalent human words to name it, but it is a repository of knowledge.

You risked crushing all of us to get your hands on a library?

Phelistoth's eyes narrowed further. His gaze was still directed at Sardelle, as if *she* was responsible for Jaxi's impertinence.

There are other artifacts that may be useful to a dragon, Phelistoth explained, *but the repository is one of many that used to exist in my time. It is a library, yes, but an instructor also. It contains the memories of wise dragons from eras past.*

Why do you and Morishtomaric want it? Jaxi asked. *For instruction? Are you two seeking self-betterment too?*

Sardelle cleared her throat. *Jaxi, would you mind not deliberately goading dragons when you're attached to my hip?*

I do not know what that tyrant seeks. Phelistoth's voice had become a dangerous rumble in their heads, a warning for swords—and their handlers. *I only want answers. It is difficult to tell from here, but I believe the repository is only about a thousand years old. It could have information about my kind, what happened and where they went.* The dangerous tone changed, growing more muted. Almost... sad. *I was put into that stasis room long before that. My people were great and many at that time. I do not know... There is much I do not know that I wish to know. I must know.*

I understand. And Sardelle did. For the first time, she saw the similarity between herself and Phelistoth. Until Morishtomaric had shown up, he had been the last of his kind in the world. When she had woken up, she had also learned that she was the last of her kind, the last of the Referatu sorcerers. She understood why Phelistoth might want to research his past, especially when he didn't know what had happened to the rest of the dragons. For good or ill, her people's fate hadn't been a mystery.

Maybe that's why he's so attached to Tylie, Jaxi mused.

What do you mean?

He's lonely. She's the only friend he had when he came out of that pyramid. Much like Ridge was the only one to be kind to you when you came out of your tomb. You got attached to him rather strongly and quickly, and I don't think it's just because he's pretty.

He prefers to be called ruggedly handsome.

We don't all get what we prefer. Hm. Speaking of your soul snozzle, he wants to run something by you.

Yes?

Phelistoth shook his arms and lifted a hand again, going back to work on their escape route. Sardelle strengthened the barrier once more.

I told him what the artifact was and that Phelistoth knows roughly where it's located, Jaxi said, *but that we're trying to get out, not trying to get back in, and there's no way we can do both by the deadline Morishtomaric gave him.*

And?

He has a plan.

Should we be concerned?

Probably. He wants to get us out before the time's up, clear the tunnels, and tell Morishtomaric where he can find the artifact, so he can come down here and get it himself.

While we watch? Sardelle suspected Ridge had more in mind than that.

While Captain Kaika blows up this mountain for the second time in this epoch.

Ah. Maybe it was silly, but her soul cringed at the idea of destroying everything all over again. What remained of her people's culture and the tools—now artifacts—that they had left behind might be lost forever. A feeling of helplessness and frustration came over her. All this to trap a dragon? To hopefully crush it, as the rubble had almost crushed Phelistoth? That dragon should never have been released into this world in the first place. What *was* it with modern Iskandians and their obsession with solving every problem with explosives?

Shall I tell him you object? Jaxi asked. *Tolemek and Cas are up there now, too, and I gather everyone's concerned about the idea of Cas wielding that sword when you and Tylie are in the same part of the world.*

Sardelle rubbed her eyes and realized they were damp. It wasn't fair to blame Ridge for thinking of explosives, especially if he was trying to protect her, but she also didn't think Kasandral would bat an eye at her or Tylie if a dragon was nearby.

Possibly not, but if you're closer than the dragon, it might not matter. Kasandral isn't that bright.

We need to find those command words.

Getting out of here should be the first priority. And taking a nap.

For you or for me? Sardelle *was* tired, with a throbbing headache pulsing behind her eyes.

I don't need naps.

Must be nice.

Maybe if we get out of here, you can nap with Ridge. He's tired and cranky too.

I'm not cranky.

If you say so. In the meantime, we might want to hurry Phelistoth along. The sooner we get out of these tunnels, the sooner we can help with plans to defeat Morishtomaric.

Weariness wasn't the only emotion making Sardelle cranky. A sense of bleakness smothered her, both because her people's past might soon be forever out of her reach and because she was skeptical whether that plan could work. Phelistoth seemed to read their thoughts easily enough. Wouldn't Morishtomaric do the same?

* * *

A muffled boom came up from the tram shaft, along with a flash of white and the smell of burning sulfur. A few rocks flew out of the opening, the double doors laid back against the earth, but the explosion had taken place more than ten levels below. Most of the damage would be down there.

Cas was watching from across the courtyard, her back to the stone headquarters building. There was nothing she could do to help. If the dragon returned, she would have a duty to do, but for now, she could only watch as Captain Kaika directed the team planting the explosives.

General Zirkander seemed to be in a similar position. He stood behind Kaika, alternating between observing the progress and scanning the sky. Thick clouds had gathered up there, rushing twilight in early and threatening rain. Fortunately, no dragons were darkening the sky, not at the moment. Colonel Therrik would probably be the first one to see one if it did show up. He was stalking the ramparts, alternating between barking orders at soldiers working on repairs and grabbing tools to help. Cas hadn't seen Tolemek for the last hour. He had grabbed his bag, said something about making an acid delivery mechanism, and disappeared into the machine shop. Cas wished there was a way she could help someone. She had little experience in building things, or in blowing them up.

Besides, Tolemek had not asked for help. He hadn't said much since that morning, and she worried she had hurt him with her reaction to being touched. That frustrated her beyond words. They had just been getting closer again, and against her own wishes, she had pushed him away.

Zirkander finished a conversation with Kaika and headed toward the headquarters building. His expression had been bleak since Cas had landed, with none of his usual humor in his eyes. Understandable, with Sardelle trapped down there. She'd also heard that a number of miners and soldiers were believed dead.

He was heading for the doorway, but he paused when he saw her. His gaze flicked to the wall next to her, where Kasandral's box leaned. Cas hated toting it around, but it was too valuable to leave in the flier, especially since seven-eighths of the population of this outpost were criminals.

Zirkander met her eyes, and unexpected guilt stung her as her nightmare returned to her thoughts. He hadn't been in it, but Sardelle was another matter. An urge to apologize to him came over her, for killing his love in her dream. It was silly, but a part of her was terrified that her dream would turn out to be a prophecy.

"You doing all right, Ahn?" Zirkander asked.

"Yes, sir." She tried to wipe her emotions from her face. She wasn't going to talk to her commanding officer about dreams. Besides, she didn't want to worry him further when he already had so many problems.

"How's your buddy?" Zirkander nodded toward the box.

Buddy. Right. "Fine, sir."

"Fine? I heard you fought some Cofah, threw the sword out

of your flier, and tried to lose it in a valley."

"That's not exactly how it went." Cas did not mention her fantasy of chucking the blade over the side of the airship to be lost in a forgotten canyon.

"Well, if it gets to be too much, Therrik has expressed an interest in wielding it against the dragon."

Cas looked toward the outpost walls. Not five minutes ago, Therrik had been bellowing at a soldier, telling him to go down and dig dirt if he couldn't hammer a nail without bending it. Cas shuddered as she imagined him taking the blade. He would enjoy wielding it far too much.

"I can handle it, sir."

"Good. I don't want to take him up in my flier again. He gets airsick. Who's ever heard of a mighty swordsman who gets airsick?"

Cas remembered thoughts she'd had, that the sword might make her kill Zirkander if she flew with him, and another wave of distress washed over her. The thought didn't make any sense, because so far, Kasandral had only shown interest in killing those possessing dragon blood, but she couldn't keep the emotion from welling up inside of her.

"Sir," she said, not even sure why she said it, but her voice cracked, betraying her emotions.

Zirkander frowned and walked over. He leaned against the wall beside her, his shoulder to hers. Technically, it was her shoulder to his arm, since he had a foot on her, but she barely noticed. She was busy struggling to get ahold of herself. She was an officer, not some weepy-eyed girl in a play at Saggaki's Theater on Vail Street.

"Tell me," he said. "What's going on?"

"Nothing, sir. I'm just worried. Sorry, I didn't mean to make you come over."

"You didn't *make* me, Cas," he said dryly. "Look, these legs work entirely independently of your wishes."

She might have kept her mouth shut and shook away the notion that she needed to tell him anything, but she made the mistake of looking up and meeting his eyes. Once again, she experienced that fear that her dream would become a reality, that she would take from him the woman he loved. All of the guilt she still felt over Apex filled her at the thought of hurting him. She loved Tolemek, as a woman loved a man, but she loved Zirkander, too, as a mentor and a friend. Even if lieutenants weren't supposed to be friends with generals, she considered him one.

"I dreamed I killed Sardelle," she whispered, the confession tumbling out before she could stop it. "That the sword tricked me, made me think it was the enemy sorceress, but it was Sardelle. I know it's just a dream, and it's stupid to worry about a dream, but with Kasandral, it's more than that. I already tried to kill her once. I—" Her voice broke, her throat too tight to get more words through it. She turned away from Zirkander, looking toward the courtyard but not seeing it. Not seeing anything.

He nudged her with his elbow. "She's under about fifty million tons of rock right now. You'll have a tough time fulfilling that dream."

His tone was light, as it so often was. She knew that didn't mean he didn't worry, and she wished she hadn't confessed. Now, he would have more reason to worry, about her and the sword. What if he thought she wasn't capable of wielding it—or couldn't be *trusted* to wield it—so he gave it to Therrik? She should have been horrified by that thought, but a secret relief came with it instead. If Therrik had it, she wouldn't have to worry about any of this.

Her relief was short-lived. If Therrik had it, she would have to worry about *him* killing Sardelle. There would be nothing to hold him back. He would be gleeful for the excuse to attack her, and she doubted he would feel any remorse at all for taking Zirkander's love from him. The bastard might even appreciate getting the chance to hurt him.

"Tolemek said he's working on a dragon-slaying weapon," Zirkander said. "Maybe you won't have to take the sword out of its box again."

Cas nodded. "I know he is, and yes, I'm very much hoping that is the case." She used her thoughts of Therrik as a way to steel herself, to remind herself that she *had* to do this. And Zirkander was right. At the moment, Sardelle was inaccessible. Cas was worrying about nothing. The dragon would be here tomorrow, and one way or another, she would be able to put the sword away at the end of the day. "If Tolemek doesn't come up with something in time, are you still going to fly with me, sir? To take me up to fight the dragon?"

"Of course I am. Who else would you want to go up with? Pimples? Duck?"

"No, sir. And definitely not General Ort. He wouldn't let me climb up on the wings so I could reach anything with the sword. That's why I had to throw it."

"He wouldn't let you trot back and forth on the wings? Not even if you tied a rope to your ankle?"

"We didn't have a rope."

"Well, that was shortsighted. I'll make sure we have one."

"Yes, sir. Good."

Zirkander pointed toward the door. "I'm going to make coffee for Kaika. You want one? I hear you all have been keeping odd hours up on that airship."

Cas snorted. Zirkander didn't look like *he* had slept in a while, either. "Are generals supposed to make coffee for captains and ex-lieutenants?"

"Absolutely not, but Therrik is keeping all of the privates busy fixing things. It's terribly inconvenient. Being a general is not quite the reward you'd think. Never let your bosses promote you too far." His expression grew a touch wistful, but he waved in dismissal and started for the door.

"No chance of that," Cas muttered.

She hadn't meant the words for him, but he turned around again. "No? I thought you might come back after this. After being up there in the sky again. Wearing the uniform again. No chance of that?"

"I hadn't thought about it yet, sir." She had only donned the uniform because it had made sense, and she was only here because the king had asked her to that meeting. Still, she had to admit that even with worry knotting her gut all the time, she had enjoyed being in the air again, and she'd even liked joking with Pimples, especially after he'd made it clear he wasn't going to try to kiss her again. It had made her miss Solk, Blazer, Beeline, and the others even more, and want to be a part of the squadron again. "But even if I came back, the odds of me getting promoted, after everything that's happened, have to be close to nil." She smiled, not wanting him to think she was bitter, or even that she had been thinking about promotions. Hells, just a few days ago, she had been trying to start a new career with her father.

"Hah. You're not under the delusion that promotions are merit based, are you?" His mouth twisted into an expression that she couldn't quite read. Wryness? Bitterness? Anguish?

"I... yes. I mean, you've deserved yours, sir. Nobody can doubt that."

Zirkander returned to her side, this time crouching in the dirt, his back to the wall. He waved for her to squat down beside him. "I was just talking about some of this with Sardelle. Look, the army promotes people based on its needs, not yours. I've seen plenty of people passed over for promotions who deserved them, because there wasn't a slot open for a captain or a major in their unit, and I've seen others... well, let's just say that I've failed upward at least three times." There was that twist to his mouth again, something too dark to be considered wry. "Of course, opportunities for promotion come up a lot in our line of work. No need to explain why. If you come back—" he raised his eyebrows expectantly, "—you'll get yours when you've got a couple more years under your belt. And you'll deserve it too. Marksmanship aside, you're steady and calm up there, and the others respect you. You'll get awards too. More of them. Invitations to the castle for celebratory dinners." He gave her an arch look, one that was probably meant to remind her that she had failed to show up for the *last* celebratory dinner invitation to the castle. As if she could have gone, could have accepted some medal, after she had killed Apex.

She shook her head. "That's not—Sir, Apex is... That was unforgivable."

"You'd be amazed at how much can be forgiven if you're

indispensable to your unit." He looked straight into her eyes. "You might even get awards and promotions you feel you don't deserve."

Her breath caught. He knew. He knew how she felt, that she didn't deserve accolades or sympathy, and that getting all that was far worse than if people would just condemn her, the way they did Tolemek. That would have made sense. Seeing him blamed for something he hadn't truly done, while she *wasn't* blamed for something she *had* done... It was devastating. She hadn't thought anyone else understood, but Zirkander did.

"What do you do when that happens, sir? When you're wrongfully praised? Or wrongfully *unaccused*?" She looked away from him, toward the ground between her boots. "How do you live with yourself?"

"You just go on, try to become the person they think you are."

Just go on? She'd been doing that but felt so hollow inside, so empty. How could she have a future when she had denied it of someone else, of someone who hadn't been an enemy trying to invade her homeland, but who had been a friend?

"Seems like there should be more of a punishment," Cas said.

"Coming back to work and being with your colleagues isn't punishment enough?" He smiled, but his eyes were serious.

That *would* be a punishment, in a manner of speaking, dealing with the condolences, the hugs. She'd been hiding from that, not wanting to see those she had betrayed.

"If you want another punishment, there's nothing like the weight of obligation," Zirkander said. "As I've been told, in one general's lecture or another, if you're fortunate enough to have been born with a gift, you owe it to the world to use it in such a way that it benefits the greater good."

"Even if your gift is shooting people?"

"*Especially* if your gift is shooting people." He turned his palm upward. "Look, Cas. It's up to you, but if you want to punish yourself, I hope you'll do it in a way that doesn't deprive your team of your skills and take *you* out of the skies. We need you up there." He thumped her on the knee and stood up. "Coffee?"

"I—yes, sir. Thank you, sir."

"Don't thank me until you've tasted it," he called as he walked away.

She snorted softly. She hadn't been talking about the coffee.

CHAPTER 14

FROM UP ON THE AIRSHIP, the explosions in the tram shaft sounded as faint booms. Ridge paused at the railing to look over the edge and down into the well-lit courtyard. Heavy raindrops spattered onto his cap, and lightning flashed above the peaks, promising a big storm. General Ort and Major Cildark had arrived an hour earlier, anchoring the big craft above the west wall. Ridge had climbed up, via a rope ladder dangling down from the deck, for a meeting with them, and was now heading to the other end of the ship, where Tolemek had returned to his laboratory.

Down below, smoke wafted out of the dark shaft, and men with shovels stepped back. A few meters from the hole, Colonel Therrik stood beside Captain Kaika, pointing and saying something. He looked gruff—as usual—but she appeared unconcerned. Maybe he was just being gruff about his lost breakfast. He had sent a private to clean the mess out of the back of Ridge's flier rather than doing it himself. Soldiers must love working for him.

Ridge pulled back from the railing and continued on. He trusted Kaika to clear the tram shaft effectively. For her, that should be an easy task. Blowing up the mountain and trapping a dragon inside? He was more concerned about that. Surprisingly, General Ort hadn't objected to his plan. Maybe it wasn't that surprising. Ort preferred plans that were conservative and safe, and the original plan that involved Cas chasing after a dragon in the sky with a sword wasn't conservative or safe. Ridge just hoped they could trick Morishtomaric into going down there. He hadn't shared the plan with many people, but now that he had made a pest of himself, the dragon knew him personally. His brain might be the first one Morishtomaric rifled through.

Maybe he could arrange to be asleep or unconscious when he arrived. Would that stop a dragon from gleaning information? Maybe they could *all* be unconscious, at least those in the know, and Phelistoth could relay the message. Ridge slowed down as he descended the ship's ladder and entered the interior passageway. He had been joking with himself, but now he wondered if that might actually work. Tolemek *did* have those knockout grenades. Since Colonel Therrik didn't know anything about what had become Plan A yet, he could oversee the defenses of the fort, if the dragon wasn't fooled.

Ridge knocked before entering the laboratory, in case Tolemek had something toxic or explosive balanced precariously. He took the grunt that came from within for an invitation to enter. He found Tolemek with his hands pressed against a countertop as he frowned down at three ceramic pots. A greenish smoke came from one, and the air had a dubious tang that left Ridge looking for portholes.

Tolemek glanced at him, then turned fully, standing up straight and almost clunking his head on the low ceiling. "What's wrong?"

"Nothing."

"Have they gotten Tylie out yet?"

"Not yet." Ridge lifted a hand. "So yes, something is still wrong, but nothing is more wrong than it was before."

"Comforting. Why are you here?" Judging by Tolemek's continuing frown, he did not believe it could be for a good reason.

"Aside from missing your cheerful company, I came to ask about a couple of things. First off, do you have any idea if a telepath can read your thoughts if you are knocked out? Or would he just find it that much easier to saunter through your brain?"

Tolemek's frown of disapproval turned to a frown of puzzlement. He had quite the repertoire when it came to frowns. "I don't know, but if you're unconscious, you presumably wouldn't be thinking thoughts to be read. He—are we talking about the dragon?—might just have access to your dreams."

"So, he'd get an eyeful of some lurid fantasies rather than, say, secret plans to annihilate him?"

"Lurid fantasies, Zirkander? Really? Doesn't your brain ever take a break from thinking about sex? You're forty years old. That can't be natural."

"I turned forty-one a couple of weeks ago, for your information, and that's *not* that old. Also, I sleep with a woman who inspires such thoughts." Now it was Ridge's turn to scowl. How had they ended up talking about *this*? "To bring us back to the subject, if someone were to take a whiff of your knockout potion, how long would they be out? Fifteen? Twenty minutes?"

"It depends on the dose. A small dose might only make you lose consciousness for ten minutes. A bigger one could last an hour. I can do the calculation based on your bodyweight." Tolemek's frown briefly turned to a grin, albeit a wolfish one. "I'd be happy to knock you out."

"I'm sure you would. If we do this, you and Therrik can play Fangs and Swords to see who wins the honor. Granted, your way would be less painful."

"What is this about?"

"Just a thought for now," Ridge said, "but if you could give me a couple of those grenades or doses of the formula, that might be useful. Is there an antidote, by chance? In case someone needs to be woken earlier?"

"No."

"Ah. All right, next question. Can you make me some special bullets that might actually pierce a dragon's thick hide?"

Tolemek snorted. "If I could do that—" That was as far as he got. He spun back toward his vats of potions, gripped his chin, and stared down at them. "Could that work?"

"I assume that question isn't for me."

Tolemek ignored him. "I had been thinking of a harpoon or a cannonball, but your bullets might actually have a chance of hitting him, *if* we figure out a way to lower his magical shields. I'm afraid... Cas might have to *be* that way, as originally planned."

Ridge almost mentioned that he had another plan in effect,

but the fewer people who knew about the new Plan A, the better. He would already have to drug Sardelle, Ort, Cildark, and himself. Ridge didn't even know if the knockout tactic would work. He needed to talk to Sardelle first. He hoped Kaika was making good progress down there.

"I don't know if your bullets would penetrate the dragon's scales, even if he was distracted and didn't have a magical defense up," Tolemek said, facing Ridge again.

"Yes, that's why I'm here. To see if you can fancy them up. They don't penetrate anything on a dragon right now."

"I can't do anything to increase the ballistics power of your guns, but if the bullets passed through the dragon's defenses and hit it, maybe the acid would be able to start eating at the scales." Tolemek thumped a fist on the counter. "I need a scale to experiment on. Why did those idiots get themselves trapped down there?"

Those idiots? Sardelle and Tylie? Or Phelistoth and the rest of them? Ridge decided not to share the information he'd received from Jaxi, that Phelistoth had been responsible for the massive cave-in. It wouldn't do any good, and it would probably frustrate Tolemek further.

"Well, think about the bullets, will you?" Ridge asked. "I'm useless in the sky without a way to hurt that dragon."

"I'm sure that galls you. No chance to be the national hero this time."

Ridge did not know how to deflect the snide comment without responding with one of his own, so he simply spread his hands in a helpless gesture. He didn't want to fight with Tolemek. He preferred to save his snide comments for Therrik. It would be a shame to run out when one was most needed.

"Let me know if you come up with anything." Ridge turned toward the door, pausing before heading out. "And also let me know if you want me to send Tylie home when we get her out. I can have Duck take her back to the capital and drop her off at my mom's house." There truly was no reason for her to be out there, other than her link to Phelistoth. From what Jaxi had said, the soulblade wasn't anything that could be retrieved quickly enough to matter against Morishtomaric. They could retrieve it for Tylie once they had dealt with the dragon.

"I'll ask her," Tolemek said.

Ridge nodded.

"Zirkander?" Tolemek said.

Ridge turned back warily. "Yes?"

"I... Damn it, Zirkander. I don't know why I always want to clobber you, but I do. I wasn't even that attached to the career you and your wolf cubs ruined for me. I *did* lose good men on that ship." He rubbed his face with both hands with enough ferocity that he was in danger of knocking his lips off. "But that's war. I understand. I can even understand why your people wouldn't want to be annexed into the empire, even if I think it would be easier all around if you simply let it happen. I can look at other Iskandians without having these feelings of irritation—they're just people, and people are the same everywhere. But you—you're special." Tolemek lowered his hands and pinned Ridge with an exasperated stare.

"So my mother tells me," Ridge said carefully. He wasn't sure what to do in the face of all this honesty. Tolemek was probably tired and needed to vent.

"I think that smug, self-contented look you always have on your face has something to do with it."

"Most likely." Agreeing seemed better than arguing. Ridge was starting to feel uncomfortable, and he wondered if he could flee without appearing cowardly. "Was there something else?" He tilted his head toward the passageway.

Tolemek propped a fist on his hip. "I'm trying to apologize to you, Zirkander."

"Ohhh. Was that what that was?"

"You couldn't tell?"

"Sorry, no." Ridge risked a smile, half expecting Tolemek to blow up and call it smug. "You don't apologize to Ahn like that, do you?"

"*No*," Tolemek said with feeling. "I don't want to punch her every time she shows up. I want to... never mind."

"Save those dreams for the dragon."

"Seven gods, you're not planning to knock *me* out, too, are you?"

"Probably not. Unless you figure out what we're up to and can give us away."

"I'll do my best not to muse on your guileful plots."

"Just make me some bullets."

"I'll see what I can do." Tolemek lowered his fist and leaned against the counter. "I hope you had a good birthday."

Ridge blushed slightly at the memory of a very enthusiastic night he'd spent with Sardelle. It had been the last one they had managed—he'd actually found a way to leave work on time that day—and it had inspired some of the lurid dreams he had mentioned. Figuring Tolemek would call him smug if he confessed to it, all he said was, "Nah. I got home late, and a dragon had eaten my cheese."

"Sorry to hear that." Actually, Tolemek looked faintly pleased.

Ridge decided the lie had been the right choice. Maybe later, Tolemek would figure things out with Ahn, and they would find enough happiness that Tolemek need not begrudge someone else his. In the meantime, Ridge could work on keeping his smug self-contentedness to himself.

It's a challenge to dim that light when you're a superior being, came Jaxi's words as Ridge stepped out into the passageway, closing the door to leave Tolemek to work.

I assume you're talking about yourself, rather than considering me superior.

Naturally. That pleased expression you saw on Tolemek's face—he was thinking about your nickname.

Soul snozzle? Ridge grimaced. It was bad enough Jaxi had shared that with the king. Tolemek didn't need to hear it.

No, Puddles. General Ort told Pimples about your past, and Tolemek was eavesdropping. Puddles. She snickered into his mind.

Ridge rubbed his forehead. It didn't seem fair that he had Jaxi's company while being deprived of Sardelle's. *Is everyone all right down there?*

Jaxi's tone sobered. *Sardelle, Tylie, and Phelistoth are fine. The miners that were on this level didn't make it, and some other ones climbed down here and may be planning trouble in the chamber around the tram.*

Trouble for you?

I can't read the leader that well for some reason, but I think he blames the cave-in on Sardelle. They can't know there's a dragon down here. We're getting close to them and will have to deal with them soon.

Can you wait? Kaika should be through with the explosives soon. Then I can deal with them. Ridge's fingers curled into a fist. He was sorry about the loss of lives, but he'd had enough of Iskandians persecuting Sardelle for no reason. He knew she could defend herself without killing people, but Phelistoth's presence would make the encounter questionable. Apparently, the dragon couldn't even drill a hole without killing people.

We'll wait. We can hear the noise of the explosives, so Kaika shouldn't be far. You would think these people would be more interested in escaping than exacting revenge.

Ridge trotted up the steps. *I'll try to hurry things along.*

* * *

"Phelistoth, can you stop, please?" Sardelle asked, shielding her eyes from the intense orange light, even as she continued to shield their small group from the heat. Hours had passed since the cave-in, and it was starting to feel like days. Her headache had intensified to stabbing pain, and her eyes were so gritty and sore that it felt like someone had punched them. The request had been hard to get out, since she wanted Phelistoth to continue, to free them from this prison, so she could lower her magical defenses and walk again in fresh air.

We are very close, the dragon responded.

"I know, but there are people waiting in what remains of the chamber around the tram. We don't want to incinerate them."

Then they should move.

They should, but not all people are as wise as dragons.

Jaxi made a rude noise in Sardelle's mind. *Flattery?*

I prefer to think of it as diplomacy.

Does it make you feel less obsequious when you do that?

Slightly.

The light disappeared. Sardelle leaned against a wall still warm from Phelistoth's earlier attentions. A layer of hardened lava lay under her feet, all that remained of the boulders he had melted.

A distant, muffled boom reverberated through the mountain, and the ground shivered.

Your noisy humans will be more likely to kill them than I, Phelistoth said.

A lot of rocks and debris are falling on them, Jaxi noted. *Captain Kaika is clearing the tram shaft.*

"Why don't they go back up to the higher levels? Do they want to kill me that badly?" Sardelle pressed a hand against her throbbing temple. "That they'd risk their own lives for the mere chance?"

Perhaps you should have flattered them on your way in.

These aren't even the ones we walked past, are they?

I don't believe so, no.

Sardelle wished Ridge were down here. She wanted someone to lean on. "Captain Kaika should break through soon," she said, assuming that was correct. Her brain hurt too much for her to reach out with her senses. "We'll wait here and let the soldiers deal with the miners."

Clinks and scrapes started up ahead of them.

"What is that?" she groaned, even though she knew without checking.

They're eagerly trying to get to us.

How can they possibly know we're here? Close enough for them to get to? Sardelle frowned at the half-melted rocks ahead of them. She didn't think Phelistoth's method of clearing the passage had caused much noise. Now and then, rocks had shifted and thudded to the ground, but that hadn't happened for a while. He had grown quite efficient at melting the rubble ahead of them.

That's a good question, actually. They came down from upper levels. As far as they should know, we could be anywhere. We could even be dead. I wonder why they aren't assuming we're dead?

A thump sounded, then a clank and a clack. Faint light seeped through a tiny hole that had appeared in the end of their tunnel. They were closer to the chamber and the tram than Sardelle had realized. She should have stopped Phelistoth sooner.

You will continue to shield us, Phelistoth thought, *and I will melt the way through the remaining blockage. There is no need to fear these puny humans.*

Just don't hurt anyone, please. Sardelle didn't know how to explain that she feared *for* them more than she feared them.

Phelistoth gave her a disdainful look and raised his arm. Tylie, who had been shambling along half asleep, stepped forward and clasped his hand.

"We understand," she said, smiling at Phelistoth.

Another rock tumbled free, and more light seeped inside, the soft orange from a lantern. Then the light dimmed as a shadow moved in front of the opening—someone's head. Belatedly, Sardelle thought to dim Jaxi's glow, so her group wouldn't be visible, but it was too late.

"They're in here," a man yelled. "We found her!"

Sergeant Jenneth and the private drew their pistols. Would they defend her from the miners or take advantage of her distraction to attack? They hadn't been thrilled to escort her around down here, and they had seen things they might wish they had not.

"Brace yourselves," Sardelle murmured, feeding more of her flagging energy into the shield. "But don't try to shoot anyone. The bullets won't go through my barrier." She could easily imagine the soldiers shooting her by accident, as one of their bullets ricocheted.

This is interesting, Jaxi thought.

What?

With a noisy clatter, more rocks tumbled away from the opening. Several sets of hands gripped a boulder and rolled it out of view. Two miners in coarse wool clothing jumped into sight.

Phelistoth shifted to face them, his body alert. Tylie stood at his side, looking surprisingly calm.

Sardelle attempted calmness, as well, or at least she tried to appear unthreatening. It probably wouldn't matter.

"There she is!" the man blurted. "She's alive."

"Did we do it?" a second man shouted, pushing through the hole. "Did we save her?"

"Save her?" Sardelle mouthed.

"Yes, it's her, the general's woman. She's standing up in there, and so are some other people."

"Will we get a reward? A day off?"

"I'm hoping for a whole week. Here, move the rest of these boulders."

Sardelle gaped numbly at them, her mind slow to process what was happening. They had come all the way down here, risking themselves, not to kill her but to *rescue* her? Even if their motives weren't selfless, this was far better than what she had expected.

Ah, interesting. Yes, now that they're closer, I can get a better sense for their thoughts. Lord Dragon and his giant aura have really been dampening my abilities. Also, you're looking remarkably well for a woman who needed rescuing.

They knew we were down here and came to help? That's not what I expected, given the hate that other group of miners was radiating.

Maybe there's a reason the other group was stuck down here in the deepest, darkest level.

Tylie smiled over at Sardelle, as if she had known all along that these people did not pose a threat.

No, but another explosive is about to be lit in the shaft, Jaxi said. *We may need to figure out a way to protect your new admirers.*

"Everyone," Sardelle called. "Come this way, please. The team from above is about to set another bomb." She could see the rocks that had fallen in the chamber behind the miners and wouldn't be surprised if part of it was also caved in.

Several of the men were already approaching. Sardelle waved, inviting them closer and lowering her shield. A few rocks trickled down from above, one bouncing off her shoulder, but Phelistoth had been clearing the tunnels effectively. If not for the heat from his magic, they might not have needed the protection.

It's lit, Jaxi warned.

What? Already? Help me shield them.

Jaxi offered a mental groan, but some of her power flowed into Sardelle's limbs. She summoned the dregs of her own power and created a new shield, trying to encompass the miners. Some she managed to cover, those who had already entered their small tunnel, but she was still trying to find a way to extend her energy to protect the ones in the chamber when the explosion sounded.

Before, those booms had been muffled, but with their tunnel now open, there weren't walls of rock to insulate them. Sardelle heard the roar distinctly. Flying rocks slammed into her barrier, the edges weak because she had tried to stretch it so far. Their tunnel shuddered, and dust flooded in. Several people dove into the passage, trying to escape what turned into a maelstrom of rocks and boulders tumbling away from the tram shaft entrance.

More power flowed into Sardelle, but it wasn't enough. Neither she nor Jaxi could hold back the entire barrage, and she was forced to draw back, to rebuild the shield across the tunnel entrance. She couldn't stop the rocks falling in the chamber, and frustration welled inside of her because of it. There were people out there.

The crashes and clatters of flying rocks seemed to last for minutes, but it was only a few long seconds. The dirt settled, and their tunnel grew still. Miners hunkered on their hands and knees, protecting their heads. Sardelle realized she had fallen to her knees, too, her legs too weak to support her. Once she saw that the danger had ended, she let her shields drop. She didn't think she could have kept a barrier up any longer if her life had depended on it. She knew Jaxi was as exhausted, based on how little energy she had been able to contribute.

I'm sorry.

I know. It's not your fault.

There are three in the chamber who didn't make it into our tunnel. One is injured, one is huddled by the wall, and one is dead.

Sardelle lowered her head. A few minutes ago, she wouldn't have blamed herself over the loss of more of the miners, but that had been before this pack had come to rescue her. These people hadn't even been in danger from Phelistoth's original cave-in.

They had come down here, specifically for her.

Because you're Ridge's "woman," Jaxi said, *not because they adore you.*

It's better than what they considered me before. They didn't even know me, and they ended up dying for me. Even if they were dying for Ridge, he's... we're the same now. The loss hurts. Sardelle pushed herself to her feet, her knees wobbling and threatening to dump her back onto the ground.

"She saved us!" a miner blurted. He had risen to his knees and was gaping back at a boulder that had slammed into her shield, a boulder that would have traveled down the tunnel if she hadn't stopped it.

"Two-forty-one was right," a miner said. "We *can* trust her. Even though she's a witch."

Before Sardelle quite knew what was happening, men raced forward, some offering to help her stand, others reaching out to touch her sleeve. Phelistoth backed up, keeping Tylie behind him with his arm. His eyes closed to slits as the people swarmed past him. Jenneth and the private fingered their pistols and traded glances with each other, but neither said anything.

"Who's Two-forty-one?" Sardelle remembered that the miners were given numbers, their names taken from them when they were processed here. Ridge had insisted on calling the ones he had met by name. She would, too, if she could learn them.

"He's..." The speaker turned, looking at the faces around him, then frowning toward the boulder. "I don't know if he made it in here." He waved at a couple of his comrades. "Come on, men. Let's move that rock and check on the others."

Her heart heavy with dread, Sardelle followed them.

A cool breeze whispered into the chamber through the now-open tram shaft, and voices drifted down from above, shouts of congratulations that they had done it, that they'd broken through.

Yes, but at what cost?

Sardelle stopped when the miner she was following stopped. He looked down at a man, one who appeared little different from the others, but whose eyes were locked open as they stared at the ceiling without seeing it. The side of his head was a bloody, caved-in mess, and Sardelle knew without extending her senses that it was too late for him.

"Two-forty-one," the miner sighed.

He walked away to help the other two people who had been caught out here. Sardelle knew she should go over and check on the injured one, even if she lacked the strength to heal him right now, but she couldn't help but gaze down at the dead man and wonder why he had stood up for her.

I may know why, Jaxi said. *And I think he may have been the one who knew we were alive down here and who led the way.*

Why? How?

He has—had—dragon blood.

Sardelle's senses were so burned out that she doubted she could have told if the man had been a *dragon*, but she did not doubt Jaxi. Her first feeling was one of shock, but she chastised herself over that. People with the ability to learn to wield magic could be criminals, the same as anyone else. There were also enough distant descendants of dragons out there in the general population that finding them wasn't all that uncommon. The shock would be if there weren't more of them here.

What if he wasn't a criminal? Jaxi asked. *What if he was condemned because of his witchy ways?*

Those suspected of using magic seem to be killed outright in this society, not imprisoned.

This prison is a death sentence, though, isn't it? People are sent here as an alternative to being killed, and they're not expected to last long.

Aware of clanks and scrapes coming from the tram shaft—people with ropes coming down to check on them—Sardelle didn't continue the conversation. She did vow to look up the record of Prisoner 241. And if she had a chance, she would peruse the other records and look for mentions of magic. It would be bad enough if a criminal had given his life to try and save hers. But if someone who had been wrongfully accused had died down here for her, that would hurt even more.

Maybe you don't want to look.

Do you know something I don't know?

Jaxi sighed. *Just that you'll make yourself miserable, no matter what you find.*

Probably so. But she would look, anyway.

Chapter 15

Cas closed the door quietly and stepped into the room full of artifacts, keeping her lantern low so the light would not be visible from the courtyard outside. It was late, with wind and rain hammering at the window, so people should not be out there. She did not have permission to be in the storage room, and she didn't want to be noticed.

She doubted Zirkander would mind, but she didn't want to explain to Colonel Therrik that she was looking for ancient words of power to activate Kasandral. He was still circling his heart whenever he crossed paths with Sardelle. With luck, his day of yelling had made him tired and he had passed out by now. Zirkander had pulled an exhausted Sardelle, Tylie, and Phelistoth out of the mine a couple of hours earlier, and Cas suspected they were all asleep in the rooms downstairs. Duck and Pimples probably were, too, though she hadn't seen much of either of them that day. They had been helping clear the tram shaft, while she had been sucked into assisting the outpost engineer with aligning the sights on the artillery weapons. She had no experience with such things, beyond zeroing a rifle on the range, but Zirkander had either thought it a good task for her, or her reputation for marksmanship had preceded her.

Cas leaned the sword box against the wall by the door. She felt silly dragging it around the fort, but she hadn't wanted to take it up to her cabin on the airship. When the dragon came, she would need to be ready quickly.

She moved past silverware and other oddly mundane household items and headed for the bookcase. All of the old tomes had been tagged and entered into a logbook that lay open on a table, but from the dust covering their spines, she doubted anyone had done more than glance at the titles. A pair of thick gloves rested on the table next to a pencil and the logbook. For handling the centuries-old texts without damaging them? More likely, as some kind of protection to keep magic evils from oozing all over the skin of the person touching the artifacts. She supposed she shouldn't snort with derision since, until a few months ago, she hadn't believed magic existed, but she had always found it asinine to believe in superstitions. Some of her father's prejudices that she had grown up with, maybe. It was ironic that, in a way, those who had believed in and feared magic had been closer to the truth all along.

"One hundred and fifty books," she murmured after a quick count. "What are the odds that information about Kasandral happens to be in one of them? And that I'll be able to read it if it's there." She frowned at the flowery titles, some containing letters that had since changed to other forms or disappeared from the language.

Apex would have known right away which titles might be useful, and he would have been able to read them all too. For a moment, all Cas could do was stand and stare at the books—and miss him. She hadn't been as close with him as with the lieutenants who were closer in age to her, but he'd been a memorable part of the squadron, with his penchant for sharing historical tales in the middle of missions. And he'd had so much knowledge. She felt his loss keenly, especially now.

"Twenty-four hours," she mumbled, shaking herself out of her numb stillness.

She had heard about the ultimatum from the dragon, and knew that half of those hours were already gone. From what she had observed, nobody was down in the mines digging for the artifact that Morishtomaric sought, so she assumed the original plan was still in effect, that she would be expected to go up with Zirkander tomorrow to attack the dragon in the sky. Since Sardelle had spent the day trapped, Cas doubted she had been able to do any research on Kasandral. Cas didn't know how much having phrases to speak to the sword would help with controlling it, but she wanted to put every advantage on her side that she could.

She skimmed through the titles in the logbook, flagging three that promised to share histories of magic, then hunted them down on the shelves. The first two came out easily, but when she touched the third, a tingle of electricity zapped her.

Startled, she backed away, staring at her finger, half expecting the pad to be blackened. She glanced at the gloves on the table. Maybe they were there for more than reasons of superstition.

That one's only for those with dragon blood. You should have brought your scruffy pirate to read it to you.

Irritation arose in Cas's mind with such ferocity that it left her gripping the shelf for support. She glared back at the sword box, knowing it was responsible.

"Jaxi?" Cas asked, forcing her voice to remain calm though that feeling of irritation continued to bubble within her.

She wondered what Sardelle's soulblade wanted. Jaxi had included her in group communications before, but she did not make a habit of telepathically conversing with Cas.

Everyone else is asleep. And I sensed that small discharge of magic. I'm right downstairs in a room with Ridge and Sardelle. They're curled up on a bunk together, snoring and being extremely boring.

Cas wished she and Tolemek were curled up boringly. He was up on the airship, working on his dragon-blood-eating acid. Cas still hoped that something might come of that and she wouldn't be forced to wield the sword, but with so little time remaining, she feared Tolemek wouldn't be able to finish the project. Even if he did, it might be an ancillary tactic, rather than one that could spare her from the fight.

"He's not scruffy," Cas said. "He's handsome."

I'll think him more handsome if he succeeds in making dragon-slaying bullets. That would be a historic first, I believe.

"Jaxi, can you help me research these books?" Cas eyed the one that had zapped her.

I'm way ahead of you. I already skimmed most of these earlier in the day, before Phelistoth's disaster forced me to turn my attention to keeping us alive.

One of the books to Cas's right shifted, the spine pushing out from the shelf. She jumped back, gaping. Yes, she was talking to a magical sword, so she shouldn't be alarmed by the unexpected, but there was something creepy about things moving about in a room where she was all alone.

Creepy. A sniffing noise sounded in Cas's head. *Really.*

The book floated away from the shelf, opened itself with a soft groan from the ancient spine, and came to rest on the table. Kasandral continued to flood Cas with feelings of anger and discontent. She tried to wall herself off from it, to ignore the box and focus on the book. Despite the yellowed pages, the black ink was still dark and surprisingly easy to see, the letters well formed and clear. Too bad the words didn't make much sense.

It's old. Old things often don't make sense.

"Can you read this?"

I can read anything written in the last nine hundred years or so. There was a major shift in written Iskandian when Cofahre invaded and forced us to switch to their louse-covered language, so don't ask me to read anything from before that time period. But Sardelle understands a lot of the old stuff, so I can wake her to ask her to translate if we find something promising.

Cas hated the idea of waking her up when she must be exhausted after being buried alive for most of the day.

She won't mind, not for research questions. She loves research. She only gets crabby when I interrupt her during her lovemaking. She also doesn't care for commentary or critique on techniques. Apparently, she's not on the same quest for self-betterment that I'm on.

"Uh." Cas had no idea what to say to that, but she wondered if Jaxi might be a distant relative of Captain Kaika's. She tapped the open book to see if she would get zapped. "Tools from the First Dragon Era?" she guessed at the title. Numbers did not seem to have changed, and the word for dragon was the same, aside from extra marks over vowels that weren't a part of the written language now.

That's right. I saw a chapter on swords when I was skimming earlier. Also, I can read this book, as it's only eight hundred years old, so it might be a place to start. Kasandral is much older than this book, though, so I can't promise that he'll be mentioned. It depends on how thorough the author was on researching items from the past.

The pages flipped past before Cas could touch them, opening to a chapter near the back.

"Was there ever a Second Dragon Era?" Cas wondered, eyeing the title in the logbook, wondering if there might be any useful notes on it. There weren't. She doubted whoever had cataloged these artifacts had spent any time looking at them, especially the insides of them.

Interestingly, no. It is a little strange that there's an entire block of two thousand years called that, isn't it? Why call it the first unless there were others? I actually never wondered about that before. Several pages flipped. *Here's something about anti-magic swords.*

Cas pulled a chair over and sat in front of the book, though she wasn't sure what the point was, since she couldn't read much of it. Maybe the sword would like it if she appeared a studious pupil.

Jaxi made a snorting noise. *You're thinking of Sardelle. She taught students in the summers. Since she'd always been a studious pupil, she expected everyone else to be the same and was disheartened and distressed when they weren't. Hm.* Jaxi was silent for a moment, then went on with, *All right, listen up. You've probably already figured this out, but here's a disclaimer that would have been nice if it had come glued to that sword.*

Cas nodded. "I'm listening."

Anti-magic tools were made with magic, using a type of enchantment that has been forgotten in recent centuries, since dragons dwindled from the skies and the need for weapons that could harm them died out. Even though the tools were crafted with magic, they were specifically designed to combat all things magical, including dragons and their riders, usually people possessing dragon blood. Some tools were imbued with personalities, similar to that of a guard dog, so they could act as seekers of dragon blood as well as weapons to be used against it.

"Seekers?" Cas recalled that while Zirkander's group had been gone, the flier squadrons had been sent out to hunt down witches and kill them, and that they had supposedly had some tool that allowed them to do so. Kasandral had been with her at the time, so did that mean there was some other tool like it out there? A tool that also made the person who carried it want to attack those with dragon blood?

Possibly so. Sardelle wasn't told much about that, and therefore I wasn't, either, though Ridge may have some details in his fancy new general's office, if not yet in his brain. That won't be important for tomorrow's battle, so let me continue.

"Sorry, go ahead."

You are *a good student. No lippiness or anything. Are you sure you're one of Ridge's people?*

Cas almost said that she wasn't anymore, but she thought of their conversation earlier. Zirkander's suggestion that staying and serving could be her penance. She knew he wanted her to stay for the good of the squadron, and that motivated his words somewhat, but she had definitely sensed that he had spoken from experience, too, and that he truly did understand. And maybe he was right. Running away was the easier route, and staying was the uncomfortable one, the one that she could only choose if she had the courage to do so.

"Yes," Cas said. "I am."

What? I was reading on.

"Never mind. What else do I need to know?" Cas itched to ask about the words of power, but made herself wait. This other information could prove useful too.

Much, I'm certain. But I assume you mean specifically about your guard dog. Another page flipped. *The tools were made to fight dragons and sorcerers from enemy nations, but it does state in here, several times in fact, that they are a danger to allies as well, and that they must be kept on short leashes.*

"Yes." Cas leaned forward, skimming the words for herself, even though she could only understand every other one. "How do I leash Kasandral?"

A surly grumpiness poked at her, and she glanced back at the box. Yes, that sword definitely needed a leash.

The makers of these tools instilled them with command words and phrases, again, much like would be taught to a dog, so they would act in an appropriate manner and so their wielders could control them. Their wielders had to be people without magic themselves, because the tools would fight against their handlers if they sensed dragon blood. Two more pages turned. Ah ha. Here's a list. Several lists. That one is for shields, that one for spears, that one for bows—goodness, I wonder what ever happened to all of these weapons. There's the entry for swords. There's nothing about Kasandral specifically, but you might want to write down that list.

Cas stared blankly at the pages open before her. Aside from the headings, the words in the list were completely incomprehensible. The alphabet wasn't even familiar. She remembered that the words the queen had uttered had sounded like nonsense to her. Would she even be able to pronounce these?

Make a copy for yourself. I'll wake up Sardelle, assuming she and Ridge haven't shifted from snoring to rutting. They're quite randy.

Cas did her best not to blush. Jaxi might even be *worse* than Kaika. At least Kaika divulged details of her own adventures, rather than gossiping about those of others. "Do you share information on their sex lives with everyone you talk to?"

Well, I don't talk to that many people. Start copying. I'll be right back.

A stiff gale hammered the window, rattling the glass in its frame. Rain slashed past, drops thick enough to see even from her seat in the middle of the room. Cas hoped the weather cleared by morning. Battling a dragon in the rain did not sound enjoyable. Of course, if it rained hard enough, maybe Morishtomaric would stay in a cave somewhere.

The doorknob rattled, and Cas turned. Had Jaxi instructed Sardelle to come up here in person? She glanced at Kasandral's box, fear pouring into her. What would the sword do? What might it make *her* do?

"Nothing," she whispered to herself firmly. From the box, Kasandral had no control over her. She willed that to be the truth.

When the door opened, the big uniformed figure that stepped inside was definitely not Sardelle.

Cas lurched to her feet and saluted. "Sir," she said, forgetting that she wasn't technically an officer at the moment. Still, she was wearing the uniform and she had been contemplating

Zirkander's suggestion that she return.

Colonel Therrik, his hard face a mix of shadow and light from the lantern he carried at his waist, frowned at her. He looked around the room, then at the lantern on her table, then at the book, and his frown deepened into a scowl. His cap and the shoulders of his uniform jacket were wet, and water dripped down the sides of his thick neck. He must have spotted her light from the courtyard. So much for her thought that everyone would be asleep and avoiding the storm.

"What are you doing in here, soldier?" Therrik didn't look like he recognized her in the poor lighting. Not that they had ever spoken to each other or spent time together. "With that—*that*?" He pointed at the open book.

"Research, sir."

"About *magic*?" He had already been radiating displeasure, and his scowl turned to a look of incredulity. Incredulity and anger. "Researching magic is forbidden."

Apparently, nobody had mentioned that the army was working with a sorceress now and that some of the old rules were being bent or outright ignored these days.

"Who gave you permission to be in here?" Therrik went on. "This isn't a damned museum."

"No, sir, but with the dragon coming tomorrow…"

"What? You're going to learn magic to use on it?" His gaze dipped to her chest.

Cas tensed. She told herself he was just looking at her nametag, but she couldn't help but think of the diplomat who had pawed her and tried to force her into a sexual encounter last fall. As a young lieutenant, she hadn't had a clue as to how to deal with someone in such a high position, and this would be the same type of situation if Therrik had that in mind. Aside from Kasandral, she hadn't brought any weapons with her, and she knew she couldn't best Therrik in a fight—she remembered him easily pinning Zirkander up against his flier before the mission to Cofahre, and Zirkander was better at hand-to-hand combat than she was.

Fortunately, Therrik's gaze didn't linger long. His scowl

returned to her face, taking on an element of a sneer. "Ahn. You're the one they gave my sword to."

"It was the king's decision, sir." Sort of. Zirkander had been the one who hadn't wanted Therrik behind him in his flier.

Therrik shook his head. "You're just a wisp of a girl. If he had to pick a woman, he could have at least chosen someone like Kaika."

"Ah, yes, sir." Cas wanted to make that *Stick it up your ass, sir*, but saying such things to colonels rarely went well. "You don't by chance know the commands of power for the sword, do you? That's what I was trying to find in the book."

She wished she hadn't asked, because he walked into the room. Even if he didn't have anything inimical in mind for her, she wasn't comfortable being alone with him. She doubted many of his soldiers were. Animosity wafted from his pores, and he seemed quick to jump to irrational dislikes of people, at least when magic was involved.

She backed up as he closed on the table. He only looked at the book long enough to slam it shut.

"You don't need any magic words. Just put the pointy end in the dragon." He curled his lip at her. "If you're big enough to pick *up* the sword, that is."

"I can handle it fine, sir." Some of the lower-ranking meekness disappeared from her tone, but she didn't care. She was more worried that she hadn't gotten a chance to copy the lines in the book.

"Out." He jerked his chin toward the door and dipped a hand into his pocket. Keys jangled.

"Sir, it could make a big difference tomorrow if I—"

"Out," he barked, taking a step toward her.

Cas was debating if there was any way she could reach in, grab the book, and sprint out before he could catch her when a soft knock came at the door. Kasandral growled into her mind.

"Good evening." Sardelle stood in the open doorway. "Is this a private meeting?"

"Yes," Therrik snarled at the same time as Cas said, "No."

She sent a significant look toward the box, to let Sardelle know that Kasandral was in here. Sardelle followed her gaze, nodded once, but did not appear overly alarmed. Because the sword was in the box? Cas wondered if Therrik had noticed it. She hoped not. Maybe she shouldn't have looked in that direction.

"We're fine," Cas said. As much as she wanted Sardelle to come in and for that to cause Therrik to leave, she worried what he might do if he realized his sword was right there, a sword that wanted to kill Sardelle.

Indeed, he was sending the look of purest loathing across the room to Sardelle. Her hair was down, and she wore untied boots and a nightgown, looking like she had left bed and hurried up here. Jaxi must have told her what was going on. Even straight out of bed, Sardelle had an appealing beauty, and Cas couldn't imagine how any man could look at her and see an enemy, but Therrik seemed as single-minded as Kasandral. Maybe they were perfect for each other. If only an enemy stood in the room instead of Sardelle. If Therrik made a move for the box, Cas would do whatever it took to beat him to it.

"Ah, there's the book I was looking for." Sardelle smiled and walked in, appearing oblivious to the hatred etched on Therrik's face, though Cas knew she wasn't.

Surprisingly, he stepped back when she approached the table, making room so she could pick up the book. Or maybe he just didn't want to risk being touched by her. Those gloves looked large enough to fit his hands. Was he the superstitious one who had cataloged these items? It was hard to imagine him not handing the job off to some private.

"You and your kind are the reason that dragon got let out of his prison," Therrik said, his fingers curled into fists. He looked like he wanted to knock her across the room, but he didn't lift a hand.

For the first time, Cas realized that he feared her as much as he hated her. Maybe his fear was *why* he hated her.

She struggled to grasp that. Oh, she could understand fearing magic and what it could do—she distinctly remembered that Cofah sorceress killing her comrades with those fireballs—but she couldn't understand fearing *Sardelle*.

"If people like you hadn't killed *my kind*," Sardelle said, "they would be here now to protect you from dragons. Also, I'm fairly certain Angulus let Morishtomaric go, though the dragon used his power to coerce him to do so."

"He did *not*." Therrik's nostrils flared with his indignation.

For the first time, he peered into the shadows beside the door, straight at Kasandral's box. He jerked slightly. He must have just noticed it. Or maybe the sword was calling to him, filling him with extra irritation the way Kasandral had been doing to Cas. And Therrik would have no reason to ignore that feeling. He might invite it in.

"Were you there? Perhaps you should ask Captain Kaika." Sardelle turned her back on Therrik and faced Cas. Having him behind her *had* to make her shoulder blades itch, but none of her discomfort showed. "I could use an assistant for these translations, Cas. Will you join me?" Sardelle nodded toward the chairs on the other side of the table.

Cas eyed Therrik, remembering that he had ordered her from the room and wondering if he would object—and what she would do if he did. Sardelle might be sleeping with Therrik's superior officer, but that didn't give her any rank over him.

He fumed in silence, glaring at the back of Sardelle's head. He did not acknowledge Cas. Lightning flashed outside, and rain slammed against the window, as if someone had hurled a bucket of water at it.

"Yes, ma'am." Cas did not usually call Sardelle ma'am, but it seemed a good idea to be circumspect all around tonight.

Therrik took a step toward the door. Cas had no way of knowing if he was leaving, or if that step would take him to Kasandral. Before she had time to consider her actions, she sprinted around a table and toward the box, trying to cut off Therrik.

When she was two steps from it, a vise-like grip clamped down on her shoulder. She was yanked backward with such force that she couldn't do anything to counter the attack. As she went down, instead of worrying about landing so that she wouldn't hurt herself, she threw her legs out, trying to stop Therrik, or at least get in his way. He jumped over her as easily as if she were a root in a trail. He lunged, not for the door, but for the box.

Cas rolled to her feet, intending to leap on his back to stop him.

Before Therrik's hands wrapped around the box, it flew straight up. His knuckles bashed against the wall as he flinched in surprise. The wooden box sailed across the room, half an inch from the ceiling, then hovered there above the logbook.

"That item hasn't been properly cataloged," Sardelle said. "Let's leave it in its box for now, shall we?"

Therrik glared at Sardelle, but not for long. He was well over six feet tall and could jump and touch the ceiling. The box floated over the table, making it harder to reach, but he leaped onto a chair and stretched for it again. The box zipped away from him, this time stopping over the window behind Sardelle. Lightning flashed outside again, highlighting her from behind. Her face was grim but calm.

Therrik, with one foot on the table and one on the chair, alternated between staring at her and staring at the sword. Cas had found her feet but hesitated, not certain what to do.

"Should I get the general?" she mouthed to Sardelle.

Cas didn't know if Zirkander's presence would do anything, not if Kasandral was feeding extra fury into Therrik, but if Therrik was going to listen to anyone here on the outpost, it would be a superior officer, whether he liked Zirkander or not.

Before Sardelle could respond, Therrik leaped at her. She didn't flinch as he sailed toward her, arms outward, his fingers curled like talons. Cas sprinted toward them, not sure how she could pull him off. Why in all the hells hadn't she brought a pistol down with her?

Therrik struck an invisible field and flew backward, almost crashing into Cas. She scrambled to the side. He slammed into the table as he landed, and it pitched over, books flying and wood squealing as chairs were shoved away.

The box floated across the ceiling, passing over Therrik's head as he leaped to his feet, then coasting through the doorway.

Cas might have laughed at the exasperated expression

Therrik wore, but his icy glare snapped onto Sardelle *and* on her.

"I am not your enemy, Colonel," Sardelle said.

"You're a witch," he snarled, as if the idiotic statement refuted her claim.

"I don't know what's going on in here," a voice came from the hallway, "but it doesn't sound like the proper use for a room full of priceless artifacts."

Zirkander stepped through the doorway, his eyes hard as he looked past the overturned table and chairs and pinned Therrik with his gaze. He was wearing socks, and his hair was rumpled, but he had thrown on his uniform jacket and cap, the gold general's rank gleaming at his collar and on the cap, above the fancy gold braids.

Therrik growled, but some of the fight went out of his stance. If nothing else, he seemed to realize he had missed his opportunity to hurt Sardelle. To *kill* Sardelle, Cas amended with a shudder. That sword wanted her dead, and Therrik would be pleased to let Kasandral use him for the purpose.

"Can't you keep your people out of my storage room, Zirkander?" Therrik snapped. "It isn't for *tourists*."

"Sardelle has more right to those items than anyone else alive," Zirkander said. "She's hardly a tourist here."

Therrik's brow furrowed, more with confusion than anger this time. He must have never learned her story.

"We have a meeting in the morning," Zirkander continued. "Early. I suggest you get some sleep, Colonel."

His gaze flicked toward the upturned table, and Cas almost expected him to order Therrik to fix the furniture before leaving, but he kept his mouth shut. Maybe he questioned if Therrik would actually obey. Cas hadn't missed that he hadn't called Zirkander "sir."

After a glare at Cas, as if she was responsible for all of his problems, Therrik stomped toward the doorway. Zirkander did not step out of his way to make it easy for him to pass. Cas half expected Therrik to bowl him over, but he merely glowered and stepped around Zirkander. He looked toward the ceiling as he entered the hallway, maybe hoping for another chance to grab Kasandral, but he must not have seen the box, because he stomped off without another word.

"Everyone all right?" Zirkander looked at Cas, but his gaze lingered on Sardelle.

"Yes," Sardelle said.

"Yes, sir." Cas's shoulder would have a bruise from Therrik's grip, but it wasn't worth mentioning. The dragon would surely do much worse to her.

Though Sardelle did not appeared rattled, Zirkander crossed the room and hugged her. The sword box floated through the doorway, back from wherever it had gone, tilted, and settled against the wall again.

"Is it strange that things like that have stopped seeming weird to me?" Zirkander asked.

They hadn't stopped seeming weird to Cas. She wondered how many books and swords floated around their house.

"I don't think so." Sardelle slipped an arm around Zirkander's waist and returned the hug.

They weren't kissing or doing anything overly snuggly and amorous, but Cas thought about making an excuse to leave. Watching other people share affection had always made her uncomfortable. Maybe because she hadn't been around much of that growing up.

"Do I blame Kasandral for Therrik's attack?" Zirkander asked. "Or do I instate disciplinary action?"

Sardelle considered the box.

"It definitely has a pull on people, even through its case," Cas said. "But I don't think he tried to resist it."

"He was probably tickled for the excuse," Zirkander grumbled.

"I wasn't hurt," Sardelle said. "Am I right in that there would be a lot of paperwork involved in this disciplinary action?"

"*Piles*. We'd also be without a fort commander if I relieved him from duty, which could be inconvenient tomorrow."

"Then I have no objection to leaving him be, if Cas doesn't." Sardelle extended a hand toward her.

Cas arched her eyebrows. She hadn't expected to be asked. "I'm fine, sir."

"All right." Zirkander released Sardelle and righted a couple of chairs. "I'll leave you two to your studies then."

"You're welcome to stay if you wish," Sardelle said.

"To translate old words in an old book?" Zirkander flipped the table back into place. "No, thanks. I have to be alert and perky for that meeting in the morning, since I'll be attempting to get Phelistoth to go along with my plan."

Cas waited, curious to see if this plan would be explained. It sounded like something different from their original one.

But Zirkander only waved to the two of them and headed out, frowning briefly at the box before leaving. The last glimpse Cas had of him as he shut the door was of his socks. It was strange seeing her commanding officer half dressed, but she was glad he had come up. She couldn't guess what else Therrik might have tried if he hadn't.

Sardelle picked up the books and sat down, opening the tool one to the page Jaxi had been studying. Cas still felt Kasandral's irritation rubbing at her skin like bristles, but she forced herself to sit down next to Sardelle. She needed to know these commands. Then nobody should be able to use the sword against her—or against Sardelle.

"The new plan doesn't involve having you anywhere near me when I have to take out the sword, does it?" Cas asked. She doubted it would, but she was curious as to what had changed and what could possibly involve Phelistoth. She'd heard his last encounter with the other dragon hadn't gone well.

"No. Are you ready to write down the translations?" Sardelle asked, touching the first line on the list. "You'll need to memorize these words, rather than the modern ones, but it will be helpful to know what you're saying—what you're commanding the sword to do."

So much for getting details about the plan. She ought to be used to being in the dark. After all, she was the lowly lieutenant. Not even that until she officially accepted a commission again. She remembered Zirkander's promise that she would be promoted in a couple of years if she returned and continued to be a good officer. Only days ago, she'd been certain she would never return, but now she wondered if it might be nice to gain more rank, enough to be privy to plans.

Aware of Sardelle watching her, Cas nodded and picked up a pen. "I'm ready."

CHAPTER 16

THE STORM HAD NOT ABATED during the night, and as dawn approached, the wind blew so hard that it batted Tolemek around on the rope ladder, as if he didn't weigh anything. His stomach protested the erratic swaying as he lowered himself from the airship to the dim courtyard below. The courtyard was empty, nobody yet braving the wind and rain. He doubted many were awake yet. The cloud-choked sky wasn't much lighter than it had been in the middle of the night. He knew this, since he had been up then. If not for the cold air beating at him and the rain splattering his face, he would have been yawning and nodding off. He ought to get some sleep, but he wanted to check on Tylie and Cas, and he had sedation formulas to deliver. He also wouldn't mind sneaking into Zirkander's meeting if he could. General Ort had gone down for it a few minutes earlier. It irked Tolemek that he hadn't been invited, but he suspected it had something to do with Zirkander's request for knockout potions.

To his surprise, lights burned around one of the tram shafts. It was the one leading to the tunnels where Tylie and the others had been trapped the day before. A flywheel turned within the tower, moving the cable that raised and lowered the cars. He couldn't imagine that anyone would be mining now, but maybe they were trying to clear more rubble to free more trapped people.

A branch of lightning lit up the sky over Galmok Mountain, the tip streaking down and striking something on the slope. A tree or a bush? He couldn't see, but he wondered how safe the airship was hovering over the courtyard. It had lightning rods and had weathered the storm thus far, but his laboratory had shaken and swayed a lot during the night. He kept expecting the storm to pass, but if anything, the winds were blowing harder now.

At least his delivery errand gave him an excuse to miss out on helping with the work he had made for the airship crew. He had created a couple of buckets of a fire-retardant sealant. He doubted they could apply it effectively while the decks and hull were wet, but they could try to get a first layer down if they wished. He had designed the concoction while waiting for a gunsmith to manufacture the bullets Tolemek had designed for Zirkander and his pilots. That task had been nearly impossible, creating projectiles suitable for the fliers' machine guns, with hollow ceramic tips containing small amounts of the dragon-blood-eating acid. Since that acid also ate metal, the bullets had to be fragile enough to break open upon impact, but strong enough not to crack before or during the firing process. It would do no good if the acid ate through the bullet tips and into the gun barrel before they could even be fired. He just hoped it could eat through dragon scales. Phelistoth had not been around, so Tolemek hadn't been able to ask for a scale on which to experiment. On the chance the projectiles would be effective, he had also designed a small batch for Cas's sniper rifle. She would much prefer using that weapon to Kasandral.

His boots splashed down in the mud, and he jogged for the headquarters building, the vials he had tucked into his pockets clanking slightly, despite the kerchiefs he had used to pad them. Why he hurried, he didn't know, since his clothes were already soaked. What did more rain matter?

As he ran, the tram car rose into view, wobbling as it left the shaft and entered the wind's influence. The gusts were almost as bad in the courtyard as they had been on the rope ladder. A tall, lean soldier hopped out, not as bundled as one should be for this weather. As the person crossed near one of the lanterns, he glimpsed her face. Captain Kaika. She didn't seem to see him as she ran toward one of the stone buildings.

Was she still setting charges? If there were other people trapped down there, wouldn't more soldiers be about, working on clearing rubble? Especially if the dragon was expected to return later in the day?

Don't think about it too much, genius, or you might have be in the room when your gas grenades are set off, Jaxi informed him.

Tolemek decided to obey. He was already concerned that so many people at the top of the command structure were supposedly going to be knocked out as soon as the dragon was sighted. Still, he couldn't help but want to argue with Jaxi. Her tone always made him itch to respond and get the last word in.

Aren't you too busy at your special meeting to monitor me? He assumed Sardelle had been invited, military matter or not, and that Jaxi would be with her.

I'm never too busy to monitor retired Cofah pirates. Also, Ridge is making coffee while we wait for something to be finished, so there's not much discussion happening yet.

Tolemek was standing in the doorway, and he glanced back toward the lit tram shaft, wondering if Kaika had anything to do with that something.

I told you to stop thinking about it.

Tolemek cracked a yawn and stepped inside, closing the door on the wind and rain—and the mystery in the courtyard. *What are the odds that I could get some of that coffee when I'm delivering my goods?*

You'll have to take that up with these officers.

If Zirkander is making it, I suppose they'll be lucky if it's drinkable. I can't imagine he has to do it for himself often. Tolemek imagined privates bringing generals steaming cups in the morning. That was how it had worked in his army. And at home, Sardelle could probably wave a hand and instantly produce a beverage.

Not quite, Jaxi said. *Besides, she's not an early riser, so Ridge has to wave his own hands around the coffeepot. How was the rain? Everyone up here is hoping our dragon friend doesn't show up early. Or at all. But I don't know how likely that is. Morishtomaric sounded awfully impatient. A twenty-four-hour ultimatum for an artifact that's a thousand years old and that has been buried for centuries. As if it's going somewhere.*

Didn't Phelistoth try to make it go somewhere? Tolemek had stopped working long enough the day before to check on Tylie after she had escaped the mines, and she had shared the story with him.

Yes, but he wasn't very good at it.

The aroma of brewing coffee drifted down from the second floor, but Tolemek detoured toward the rooms on the first floor. If he waited until after the meeting started to deliver his goods, he would have a better chance of overhearing interesting details.

And to think Sardelle calls me nosy.

Imagine that.

The offices on the first floor had been turned into sleeping quarters, a necessity since the wooden military barracks had gone up in smoke. Tolemek knocked softly on a door at the end. Most of the rooms held numerous people, as evinced from the multitude of snores floating through the doors. Tylie shared her room with Captain Kaika, though whether Kaika had found any time to sleep since arriving was questionable.

"Come in, Tolie," Tylie called.

Given the early hour, he expected her to be in her cot and snoozing. Instead, a ball of light floated in the air, and she knelt on the floor, painting a mural on the tiles.

"Couldn't sleep?" Tolemek sat on the edge of her cot.

"Phelistoth is concerned."

Tolemek glanced around the room, almost expecting him to be there, but Tylie was alone, her hair brushing the floor as she concentrated. Paint had found its way onto the tips of numerous strands.

"And that keeps you awake?" he asked.

"Sometimes."

"Are you supposed to be doing that?" Tolemek doubted anyone had requested murals on the floor in this room. Judging by the cabinets and desks pushed against one wall, it wasn't used for anything other than filing papers.

Tylie sat up and smiled. She'd managed to get a smear of orange across one cheek. "General Ridge found paints for me."

"He's your enabler, eh?"

"Not very many colors, though. I'm having to mix them on

my own. Look, I'm painting what's going to happen. Phel and Cas and Sardelle and General Ridge are going to slay the mean dragon in an epic battle. You're going to help them with your inventions."

"You'll probably need more than one tile to depict all that."

"I just got started, silly." Tylie set her brush down, one that looked more appropriate for painting a barn than a mural, and flopped onto the cot next to him. "Are you all right? You look tired."

"I am, but you're the one I'm worried about."

"I'm fine." She did seem surprisingly energized for the hour.

"General Zirkander offered to have Lieutenant Duck fly you home before the dragon comes, and I'd like you to go." Assuming the rain and wind ever let up, he did.

Tylie frowned. "It's going to get worse."

"What is?" Tolemek looked at the tile, thinking of the battle.

Tylie waved toward the wall, where shutters protected a small window. "The storm."

"How do you know?"

"Phel knows. He's like a dog," she said brightly.

"Yes." Tolemek managed to keep his tone from sounding too dry.

"He senses things, the way animals do. Even more so, because of his magic. He said it wouldn't be safe for me to ride in a little winged box right now."

Tolemek hated the idea of Tylie being stuck here during a battle. What if the dragon started flinging fire around again? What if more Cofah airships showed up? What if that sorceress found a way to get the other airship fixed and bring it up here? Once again, he wished she was back with Zirkander's mother. Why had he agreed to her coming out here? Sardelle and Phelistoth could have searched for a sword for her without her being present.

Tylie laid a hand on his forearm. "She won't come. She and the mean dragon aren't allies."

"Who? The sorceress? Are you reading my thoughts?" Tolemek wasn't surprised when Jaxi did that, but he hadn't realized Tylie's skills had progressed so much in the last few weeks.

"I'm not *supposed* to, I know. But you're my *brother*."

Such logic. "Then you know I want to keep you safe."

"I know."

He wondered if Phelistoth would consider flying her back home, if a "winged box" wouldn't do. "Will the storm be bad enough that a dragon wouldn't consider flying?"

Maybe if the weather stayed poor, Morishtomaric wouldn't be able to make an appearance, either. If they had a couple more days to prepare, that would be ideal. Then Major Cildark would have a chance to get his airship coated in the fire-retardant sealant, and Tolemek could test his acid on a dragon scale.

"Maybe?" Tylie did not sound confident in her judgment.

"Are you in communication with Phelistoth now?"

"He's at the meeting, sniffing General Ridge's coffee."

"Dragons don't *drink* coffee, do they?" Tolemek's mind boggled at the notion.

"Not yet, but he's tired, too, and General Ridge said it would make him peppy."

Tolemek's mind boggled even more at the idea of a peppy dragon.

"When he's in human form, he's just like us," Tylie said. "Mostly."

"Right." He hugged her and stood up. "I guess you better keep painting until we can find a way to send you home."

Tylie smiled agreeably.

"Do you know where Cas is? She didn't come back to her cabin on the ship last night." He'd checked four times. Neither she nor the sword had been there.

"She was doing something with Sardelle last night in the artifact room."

"Artifact room?" He had been hoping she had been resting, so she had all her wits and energy about her today if she needed them.

"Upstairs, by Colonel Therrik's office."

"Thank you."

Tylie dropped back to the floor and picked up her paintbrush again. By the time Tolemek stepped into the hallway, she was already at work.

When he got to the top of the stairs, he paused at a room with a closed door and familiar voices speaking behind it. He knocked, deciding he might as well drop off the formulas.

"Tolemek," Zirkander said, his face far too bright and cheerful for the hour. "Do you have bullets for me?"

"Not yet, but they're coming. In the meantime, here. Knock yourself out." He smirked as he pulled out the vials he'd created. He also tried to see who else was in the room behind Zirkander. He glimpsed Ort and Sardelle and Phelistoth, but couldn't tell if there was anyone else. He tried not to let it gall him that a *dragon* had been invited to a secret meeting instead of him.

A sword too, Jaxi said brightly. *Just remember. Everyone who comes to the meeting gets knocked out, so you don't really want to be in here.*

Phelistoth too?

Almost everyone.

It must be nice to be special.

It is.

Zirkander accepted the vials. "No grenades?"

"I didn't think you needed it to be that dramatic. Just lie on a cot and inhale the contents."

"Thank you. Bullets next, please. I'd like to get my flier ready as soon as possible. With bullets to eat through dragon hides."

There he went, once again thinking Tolemek was a pharmacy—or in this case, an armory—that could deliver the impossible, as if he was filling a simple order. "You crash in this storm, and those bullets could break open and eat through *you*."

"We're not assuming anything, but we're hoping the dragon won't come until tomorrow. Or next week. Or never."

"Right." Tolemek let himself be waved away.

The door thunked shut, and he continued down the hallway, searching for the artifact room. All of the doors were closed, so he started poking his nose into the ones near the office at the end. Snores came from most of the dark rooms, soldiers sacked out on blankets and on cots. The last room to the left was quiet, but not dark.

At a large table near a window, a familiar form with short, tousled hair slumped across a book, her arm stretched out and her head pillowed on it. Warmth spread through him, pleasure at finding her, but why hadn't she gone to bed? If not to his, as he would wish, then at least to her own?

He didn't think he made any noise, but Cas jerked awake as soon as he stepped into the room. She looked at him, but also looked to his side. Tolemek grimaced. Kasandral's box leaned against the wall there. Of course it made sense that she was keeping the sword close, but he worried its presence meant she would be grumpy with him.

"Morning." He stopped a few feet into the room. "I wanted to check on you."

She groaned, glancing at the window. "Is it morning already?" She stared bleakly at a paper in front of her. "I'm not sure I have these memorized yet."

"What are they?" He resisted the urge to come closer and to sit beside her.

"Command phrases for Kasandral. Like the one the queen used to make me... that let the sword take over."

"I hope you're not memorizing that one." He smiled.

"No. Well, yes, in case I need it against the dragon. I wouldn't use it with you around. Or Sardelle or Tylie." She bit her lip and eyed him up and down. "You look like a lion that fell in the river."

A lion? At least she had chosen a mighty animal for the comparison. He felt like a drowned rat.

"There's enough rain falling out there to fill a few rivers." He nodded toward the water streaming down the window.

"You can come over if you want. I won't... I mean, I'll try not to be... snippy." Cas touched the lines on her page. "There's one I can use to tell Kasandral to back down. Jaxi said he's like an attack dog. Sardelle translated all of the commands listed in this book, and I'm trying to memorize the ones most likely to be useful."

"Sounds like a good idea." Despite the invitation, he walked across the room and around the table slowly.

Cas pushed out the chair next to hers. "I've got the backdown command memorized well. I'm working on one that tells it to guard me but not initiate any attacks. It's hard because the words are gobbledygook to me, and I have to pronounce them correctly. Sardelle wrote down the phonetic spellings, but I'm afraid I'll forget how to say them when I need them."

"You won't." Tolemek slid into the chair she'd offered. "But I can help you practice if you want. Maybe we can come up with some mnemonic memory devices."

"Devices?" Her nose crinkled, making her face even cuter than usual. Not that she would appreciate being called cute, he was sure.

"Tricks to help with memorizing things." He thought about reaching out to brush his fingers through her hair. After her awkward sleeping position, several tufts stuck up.

"What?" She touched her head. "Is it a mess?"

"No worse than mine."

Her eyes widened. "*That* bad?"

Pleased by her humor, he smirked and ruffled her hair.

"*That's* not going to help it." She swatted at his hands, but didn't try hard to stop him.

He switched to smoothing it, and she lowered her arms and let him. Her eyes twinkled, and an ache of longing filled his heart. It had been a long time since that twinkle had been there. Maybe learning the commands gave her more courage, less reason to fear the sword—and her past.

Cas closed her eyes and leaned into his hand. He switched from stroking her hair to rubbing the back of her neck.

"I've missed you," he whispered.

"I know." She sounded sad.

He didn't want her to feel sad around him. He wanted her to enjoy being with him, not to feel guilty about it. But he didn't know how to say that, so he kept massaging the back of her neck, hoping she would understand.

"That feels good," she whispered.

"Good," Tolemek said and wished it didn't sound so inane.

He ought to say something clever and charming, something to make her realize how much she had missed him, something to convince her she should be with him, always.

"I don't know if it's right for me to feel good anymore," Cas said, "but I'm tired of being alone and punishing myself."

"I understand. Do you know that humans are the only animals that do that? Punish themselves?" He sifted his fingers through her fine hair, scraping his nails across her scalp.

A contented sigh escaped from her lips. "What do your snakes and lizards do when they've made a massive mistake?"

"They learn from it, don't do it again, and then move on. Animals live in the present; they don't dwell in the past."

"Must be nice to be an animal."

"If you don't mind spending your life in a terrarium and having a mad scientist milk you for your venom."

Cas lifted her head to look in his eyes. "You're not mad. You're one of the sanest people I've met."

"That's because you spend so much time with those crazy pilots."

"Possibly so." Cas reached out and tugged at the flap of his jacket. "You must be cold. You should get out of those wet clothes."

He blinked a few times, not certain if she was suggesting what he thought, though hope rose within him that she was. "Here?" he whispered.

The twinkle in her eyes had changed to something else, something less playful and more intense. "It's early. We're alone."

"Except for your sword."

Thanks to her description, he was now imagining a dog standing in the corner with its hackles up, staring at them and growling.

"I'll make him be good." Her fingers tightened on his jacket, and she pulled him closer.

It didn't take him more than a second to warm up to the idea of shucking his clothing, sword observer or not, and he was the one to lean down, pressing his mouth to hers. She kissed him back, eagerly, hungrily, as if she had wanted this for weeks.

He let himself hope that she had simply been punishing herself because she felt the situation demanded it. As they kissed, he threaded his fingers through her short, soft hair, tugging gently at the ends, remembering that she liked that. He wanted to make her feel human, to enjoy experiencing pleasure again.

She eased off her chair and slid her leg over his, sitting on his lap and facing him. He slid his hands from her hair to her back, slipping them under her jacket to run his fingers over her warm skin.

"You're wet," Cas whispered against his lips. She tugged at the buttons on his sodden shirt.

"Yeah, it's supposed to be the other way around, isn't it?"

She snorted. "And you're naughty."

"Not that naughty. I didn't bring sponges." Though he would have preferred to see her topless, he helped with his own shirt, agreeing that this would be much more pleasurable if his damp clothes didn't lie between them.

"We can try them next time."

Neither of them mentioned that if the battle did not go well, there might not be a next time.

She pushed his shirt off his shoulders, and he shrugged it the rest of the way off, then grasped her hips and lifted her onto the edge of the table. He pushed his chair back so he could tug the rest of his clothing off. As much as he enjoyed having her in his lap, he would like it much more once they were naked and sharing the... He frowned, his gaze going to the table. Someone had neglected to put any cots or blankets in this room.

"Is this going to be all right?" he asked. "Or do you want to find someplace more comfortable?"

Cas unbuttoned her uniform jacket, her gaze locked onto his bare chest as she did so, her lips parted. His heart swelled at the realization that she was admiring him and enjoying the view. He stepped closer, sliding his arms around her again, helping her remove the jacket.

"Where would that be?" she asked, tugging off her shirt and bra.

He gazed at her naked form and almost forgot the question.

"Uhm, the airship? My lab?"

"So far away." She gripped the back of his head and kissed him hard.

"True," he mumbled against her mouth, returning the kiss eagerly. He pushed down his trousers and struggled to get his boots off without taking his hands from her. He might have fallen over if not for her support, the appeal of her kisses drawing him like a magnet.

"Besides," she murmured, leaning back on the table and pulling him down with her. "You're helping me memorize things."

"Yes. I am. Did you know it's easier to remember things when you're relaxed and enjoying yourself?"

"Is it? That's useful."

"Very."

They smiled, papers crinkling under them as they stopped talking and focused on enjoying themselves.

* * *

"This *plan* is abysmal," Phelistoth said. "I will not go along with it."

Ridge leaned back in his chair, wishing the coffee could somehow invigorate him enough to make dealing with uptight dragons easier. He couldn't see a clock, but knew this meeting had been going on for hours. Part of that was because they were waiting for Kaika to finish up, but part of the problem was their recalcitrant ally. Ridge looked at Sardelle, who sat opposite him and beside General Ort. She merely shrugged back at him.

"Why?" General Ort asked.

"You would give *him* the repository that *I* seek."

"The plan isn't to give it to him, but to turn it into bait, to lure him into the mountain, which we'll collapse with explosives as soon as he's down there. It's my understanding that you barely survived the cave-in down there, and that was only a couple of levels of rock coming down. If we can drop even more…"

"Then the repository will be buried down there forever,"

Phelistoth said.

"We can dig down and get it later. Along with that soulblade you were eyeing for Tylie."

Phelistoth paused, looking abashed that he had forgotten about that.

Maybe we can even find a different soulblade that's closer to the surface, Sardelle murmured into Ridge's thoughts. *An Iskandian one.*

Phelistoth turned a baleful stare onto her. Ridge shuddered inwardly, reminded that he probably knew all of their thoughts and that Morishtomaric would too.

Your plan could work, Sardelle reassured him. *If he doesn't notice Kaika and sift through her thoughts.*

She has to stay awake to detonate the bombs.

I know. He shouldn't be aware of her. Jaxi and Phelistoth would be too hard for him to read, and if we're unconscious, you're right in that the information would be inaccessible, so long as we're not dreaming about it.

Ridge hadn't considered that, and a feeling of bleakness burned in his stomach like acid. Would his *dreams* betray him?

You'll be fine. Think of something else before falling asleep.

Ridge held her gaze across the table, trying not to worry, since she was monitoring him and then *she* might worry. He wriggled his eyebrows and feigned nonchalance. *Such as a sexy woman who can survive even impossible situations?*

That's not what I was going to think about, but whatever you want to tantalize the dragon with. Sardelle smiled though it did not reach her eyes. She had been more reserved than usual since being pulled from the mines.

Once this is resolved, Ridge thought, guessing at part of what bothered her, *I'll have someone dig into the records to see if any more of the inmates were accused of witchcraft before they were brought here.*

She had shared what had happened down in the mine, telling him about the men who had tried to save her and the one who had died doing it. He could understand why she would be disturbed, and it saddened him, too, to know that someone who had wanted to help her had been punished for it. There were precious few people around who wanted to help a sorceress.

I know you will, Sardelle responded. *Thank you.*

General Ort cleared his throat, and Ridge realized some time had passed since he had spoken out loud.

"All we need you to do," Ridge said, trying to draw Phelistoth's attention back, "is to tell him its location when he shows up. Sardelle said—well, she believes that you can keep Morishtomaric from knowing your thoughts."

"Of *course* I can."

"So if you tell him about the crystal, he won't be able to look into your mind and see that there are explosives down there. We'll put ourselves to sleep, so he can't pry into our minds and find out through us." Ridge was particularly worried that the dragon would poke into *his* mind, since he was the one who had made the deal.

"He will not be so foolish," Phelistoth said. "He will sense the trap."

"How?"

"Why else would I give him this information when I covet the same thing that he does?"

"Perhaps," Sardelle said, "you've changed your mind. After he's beaten you twice in battle, you've decided it's best to join forces with him."

"He did *not* beat me twice," Phelistoth growled.

"We're including the time he chased you out of our yard, leaving a flaming couch in your wake," Ridge said.

Ort sighed. Whether it was because they had to argue with a dragon or out of lament for the lost couch, Ridge did not ask.

"I led him away intentionally so Tylie would not be harmed," Phelistoth said stiffly.

"All right, but listen. If you assist us by fibbing to him, we'll help you retrieve whatever you want from the mountain. It may take us a while, but we'll do it." Ridge imagined how happy Therrik would feel about such an assignment, but after attacking Sardelle, he deserved it.

"I don't need your help."

"Are you certain of that?" Sardelle asked mildly.

Phelistoth sighed with far more dramatic flair than Ort had. He stared down at his feet, or maybe he was staring toward Tylie's room and communicating with her.

When seconds drifted into minutes without a change in pose, Ridge got up to pour himself another cup of coffee. He wondered if Cas and Kasandral had ever left the artifact room—Sardelle had left her studying there the night before, which hadn't been all that many hours ago. Maybe Ridge could find the sword and use it to prod Phelistoth into motion.

I wouldn't go in there, Jaxi thought.

Oh? Why?

Last I checked, Cas and her pirate were doing untoward things to a table in there. They weren't even concerned that there was a priceless, thousand-year-old book under them.

Ridge set down his coffee mug. *What?*

It's true. They deserve itchy ink on their naked butts.

I meant—er. Ridge had no objections to any untoward things, especially when they would be going into battle, possibly this very day, but he hadn't thought the sword would allow it. *Was Kasandral there, uhm, watching?*

Yes.

And they—she wasn't *bothered by that?* Ridge didn't know quite how the sword worked, just that it made Ahn—and Therrik—eager to kill anyone with dragon blood. That should include Tolemek.

She learned some commands to keep it from trying to coerce her into killing him. Why should she care if he watched? You don't mind if I'm in the room watching.

Sardelle said you look the other way. Ridge raised his eyebrows at her, wondering if she was hearing any of this conversation.

Sardelle thinks I'm more of a lady than I am.

The door opened before Ridge could decide if he needed to choke over that comment. A dripping Captain Kaika walked in, her cap pulled low over her eyes and the flaps of her jacket turned up.

"It's done," she said wearily. "I can detonate everything from the tram tower."

"Thank you, Captain." Ridge wished he could tell her to take a rest, since she had been up planning her strategy and then planting the explosives all night. "Get whatever you need ready for an air battle. Don't load a flier yet—" he waved toward the window to indicate the rain that would be pouring into those seats right now, "—but have a pack ready to go if the dragon shows up and this doesn't work. Plan B." Or was it Plan C?

"Are there any bombs *left* for her to pack?" Ort asked. "She raided Cildark's stores thoroughly."

"Always got a few more, sir." Kaika managed a tired wink.

"As soon as you're done, you can dry off and get some rest," Ridge said.

"Yes, sir." She gave them more of a wave than a salute and closed the door.

"Very well," Phelistoth said, lifting his head, his first movement for several minutes. Ridge had almost forgotten what he was debating. "I will assist you, but I insist that the repository be retrieved as soon as Morishtomaric is eliminated. I also insist that all effort be made to get Tylie a soulblade." His eyes narrowed to slits. "An *appropriate* soulblade."

A Cofah one, he means, Sardelle told Ridge with a mental sigh.

Ridge shrugged. Tylie's sword wasn't his priority right now.

"We agree," Ridge said and stuck out his hand. Did dragons clasp wrists? This one had been sipping from a coffee cup and seemed almost human when he was in this form.

Phelistoth did not see the offered hand. His head had swiveled toward the window.

Lightning flashed in a sky that hadn't brightened much with the approach of dawn.

"He's coming," Phelistoth said.

"What?" Ridge was afraid he knew exactly *what*, but he didn't want it to be true. Not now. They weren't ready. It hadn't been twenty-four hours yet. Besides, what kind of intelligent being would be out flying in this?

"Morishtomaric is coming," Phelistoth repeated. "And he wants the repository."

Chapter 17

An alarm wailed, and Cas awoke with a start. An arm tightened around her waist, Tolemek's arm. They were curled up on a rug they had dragged into a corner of the artifact room, with nothing but her clothes pulled over them for a blanket—his had been too wet. At the time, this arrangement had seemed more logical than trying to find a room with a cot. Not that cots were made for the vigorous bedroom activities of two people. Of course, tables weren't, either, and that hadn't stopped them.

She grinned, but the insistent wailing of the alarm drove aside any thoughts she might have had of continued snuggling. She swatted his arm and twisted her head to look at his closed eyes.

"Wake up. There could be a dragon bearing down on us right now."

Tolemek's eyes were still closed, his ropes of hair tickling her bare shoulder. "Mmzzt, jus' wind."

The wind *was* still railing at the building, but she knew an alarm when she heard one. As she extracted herself from his grip and grabbed her clothes, she hoped nobody had been looking for her.

Tolemek finally opened his eyes, his hand grasping too late for the jacket that had covered their torsos. "What is it?" he asked, his words more coherent this time.

"I don't know." Cas stuffed her legs into her trousers, wishing she had time to find the lavatory and wash up, but she had better see if they were under attack first. She didn't hear any guns firing outside, but the alarm could mean the dragon had been sighted and wasn't yet in range. "You're the fledgling sorcerer. You tell me."

"I don't have a formula that can see through walls and ceilings." Tolemek climbed to his feet, wincing when he stepped off the rug and onto the cold wood floor. He walked over to the window and peered outside. "There are men running on the parapet that I can see. And it's hailing."

"What kind of dragon comes for a visit in the hail?" Cas growled, tugging her undershirt over her head. "It's still early, isn't it?" The thick storm clouds made it hard to guess. Thuds and shouts came from the hallway, soldiers racing outside.

"I haven't noticed that dragons are particularly considerate in the timing of their visits. Or with anything." Tolemek plucked his wet trousers off his pile of clothes on the floor. "It's occurring to me that I should have hung these to dry."

"Yes." Cas had found both boots, though one had managed to end up behind a chair on the far side of the table. She jammed her feet into them.

"You were distracting me."

"Sorry."

He grinned at her. "I'm not."

She would have loved to stay and banter with him—and tease him mercilessly for leaving his clothes on the floor to molder—but the alarm called to her, making her keenly aware of her duty. She ran across the room as she buttoned her uniform jacket, stopping only long enough to grab Kasandral's box.

"Maybe you can ask Sardelle to teach you how to dry clothes. Sounds like that would be useful. I'm going to find the general and see what's going on." Cas waved, figuring she could find him later and update him once she knew, but with a lurch, she realized she might be on her way into battle.

She had the door open already, the shouts from the first floor floating up the stairs at the end of the hallway, but she dropped Kasandral's box and ran back to him. He was still naked, standing with his soggy shirt in one hand and his trousers in the other. She stood on her tiptoes, gripped his shoulders, and kissed him soundly. He seemed surprised, but then pleased as he dropped his clothes and pulled her tight for a fierce hug. Maybe he realized what she might be running off to do too.

"I love you," he whispered when she pulled away.

Hearing that he still felt that way warmed Cas's soul, but with the alarm blaring, she couldn't linger, no matter how much she wanted to.

"I love you too." She swatted his bare butt. "Now get dressed and get out there before Colonel Therrik comes in to ask what obscene thing you were doing naked in his storage room."

Tolemek grinned, his gaze shifting toward the table.

Cas released him and sprinted out the door, grabbing the box on the way. She wished she had her Mark 500 slung over her shoulder, too, but if a dragon *was* the reason for the alarm, her sniper rifle wouldn't do any good against it.

Colonel Therrik's office door was closed, so she ran straight for the stairs. She wouldn't have wanted to get her updates from him, anyway, not after what he'd tried to do to Sardelle. If she'd had her rifle with her last night, she might have sniped *him* in the ass, rank notwithstanding.

Cas followed the flow of soldiers out of their rooms and into the courtyard. The hail Tolemek had promised splatted into the mud and bounced off people's shoulders. A stiff wind shoved her sideways, and she nearly stumbled off the walkway and into a slushy mud puddle.

The soldiers all had duty stations and knew exactly where to go, most sprinting for stone staircases that led up to the fort walls and towers. Cas got out of the way and slowed down, searching for General Zirkander. Colonel Therrik's shouts came from the center of the courtyard, orders to get to battle stations, but she did not see Zirkander anywhere. She jogged far enough from the headquarters building to look toward the roof. Duck's and Zirkander's fliers were still up there, but neither man was in sight. With the wind and hail, she couldn't imagine flying. The airship was still anchored over one of the outpost walls, and even with its massive size, the wind knocked it around as if it were a child's balloon.

She turned a full circle, looking for Sardelle or anyone else from the squadron. Was General Ort down here? Or had he stayed up to command from the airship? Had the higher-ranking officers already had their meeting? The people flowing past all belonged to the fort, and she didn't recognize any faces. She was on the verge of heading up to stand beside the fliers when she spotted a golden figure soaring under the dark gray clouds. The dragon.

"Raptor," Pimples called, coming out of the headquarters building, attempting to button his jacket while juggling his gear bag in his arms. Duck, already dressed and with his pack slung over his shoulder, came out behind him.

"Did you—" Pimples followed Cas's gaze toward the sky. "Uh. I thought he wasn't supposed to be back until later."

If the wind, rain, hail, or lightning flashing over the mountains bothered Morishtomaric, it wasn't apparent. He had to flap his wings more to maintain his altitude and position as he circled the outpost, but he did not appear alarmed. Cas hoped lightning would strike him. Aside from the mountaintops themselves, he was the highest point in the sky.

"Do you know what's going on, Pimples? Duck?" Cas asked. "Where's Zirkander?"

"He just said to be ready to take to the air at any moment." Duck glanced toward the fliers on the rooftop, then at the clouds shooting hail down at them. "I can't imagine doing so in this."

Cas would have preferred to wait somewhere more protected than the rooftop, but she took a step in that direction, figuring Zirkander would expect them to be there when he came looking.

"You cloud humpers, get over here," came a bellow from across the courtyard. Therrik.

"Is that us?" Pimples asked.

"I'm not sure," Duck said. "That's one of the more flattering terms for pilots that I've heard come out of his mouth. He's more crotchety than a bear that got his fish stolen."

Cas did not want to go talk to Therrik, but a couple of local soldiers scattered from around him, and she could see him waving, clearly talking to her, Pimples, and Duck.

She jogged over, keeping her expression flat, though she couldn't help but wonder if he would blame her for keeping him from throttling Sardelle—or whatever he'd had in mind. Even with rain and hail pounding him, he was an imposing figure as he shouted orders, a rifle in one hand and a truncheon and short sword hanging from his weapons belt. What if he ordered her to hand over Kasandral? General Zirkander wasn't around to stop him.

Therrik's eyes tracked Cas as they approached, but he didn't mention the night before, other than to point at her box. "You might as well take that thing out, Lieutenant. Looks like you'll need it soon, and the wood doesn't seem to do nearly as much to dull its attributes as your witch friend suggested." He scowled.

Cas tried to decide if that meant he believed it had coerced him to attack. She was sure Kasandral had helped that along, but she also wondered if he might have used the sword as an excuse.

"Join Captain Kaika in the tram tower," Therrik said, this time talking to all three of them. "She'll keep an eye on you until your dauntless leader wakes up from his nap."

Nap?

"General Zirkander, sir?" Cas asked.

"Yes. Go." Therrik shooed them away, then cursed as the dragon soared down from the sky, his talons outstretched. Men on top of one of the artillery towers scattered—one flinging himself over the outer wall. "Where is that silver-butted freak?"

Er, was that Phelistoth? Fortunately, the question was not directed to her. Without another word for them, Therrik grabbed his sword and raced toward the tower.

The dragon did not attack anyone. He merely alighted on the big shell gun, making it appear like a toy as his massive talons curled around the barrel.

Kasandral's wooden box hummed, almost vibrating in Cas's grip. The sword's agitation beat at her mind, containing a mix of eagerness, fury, and a desire to kill.

"*Meyusha*," she whispered, "*Meyusha*." It was the word Sardelle had translated that meant *stand down*. Relax. At least for now. She'd spoken it in her mind last night to get the sword to stop harassing her about Tolemek.

It didn't work as well this time. Maybe asking Kasandral to calm down when there was a dragon thirty meters away was too much.

"Hiding in the tram tower, or better yet, down in the mines, doesn't sound half bad," Pimples said, his gaze locked on the dragon.

"I'm not hiding anywhere," Duck said. "I want another chance at that oversized canary. Tolemek was supposed to be making some bullets that could hit him. Cas, you know if that happened yet?"

"Uh." Probably not, since Tolemek had been busy with her this morning, unless he'd gotten them done before coming down. "Let's see if Kaika has something for us."

She took a step in that direction, but Tolemek jogged out of the headquarters building, and she paused to see if he would come over. The courtyard had cleared somewhat, with most of the soldiers at their posts now, and he spotted her. He waved, but he headed for the airship instead of in her direction. He glanced around the outpost and nearly tripped when he spotted the dragon on the tower. He ran several steps with his head craned all the way around before picking up his pace and racing to the ladder.

"Maybe he's going to get those bullets now," she said.

But Pimples and Duck had left her, already heading for the tram tower. She ran to catch up.

Captain Kaika stood alone in there, looking bored as she leaned against a big piece of machinery and gazed through the open sides of the tower toward the dragon's perch. A wooden box rested at her feet, a plunger in the upright position. Cas recognized the detonator for what it was and halted well away from it. Between the machinery, giant cable spool, and a tram car half hiding Kaika from view, it was crowded in the small tower even without four people inside. At least it provided some shelter from the hail and wind.

Kaika's eyebrows arched. "Can I help you?"

"Therrik said you were in charge of us," Cas said, "that General Zirkander is busy doing something." Napping, supposedly, but that sounded extremely unlikely.

"Lucky me."

"Are we supposed to help you with—uhm." Duck bit his lip

and looked down at the detonator.

"Nope. Therrik probably wanted you out of the way."

"Do you know what's going on?" Cas asked.

"Yup, but I'm not supposed to talk about it," Kaika said. "Or think about it. Everyone's hoping the dragon won't notice me, since someone had to stay awake who knew what was going on."

"Uh, what?"

Kaika held a finger to her lips and nodded toward the artillery tower.

Therrik was below it, waving his rifle and pointing up at the dragon. Morishtomaric wasn't looking at him. Instead, he was studying the silver-scaled dragon standing on all fours in the courtyard behind Therrik. Phelistoth was not glaring defiantly up at Morishtomaric, as Cas would have expected. His neck was bent low, his head near the ground, his eyes turned toward the mud.

"Why does he look like a dog about to roll over and give up his belly?" Duck asked.

Cas shook her head. She had no idea what was going on. Were the dragons communicating?

The soldiers stationed on the walls all had their rifles trained on the dragons—both of them. From the way those men shifted about, glancing at each other and muttering imprecations, they had to be nervous. A bullet wouldn't likely hurt Phelistoth, but he had proven himself an ally, at least nominally. What would he think if Iskandians started shooting him?

Morishtomaric leaped into the air.

"Get back," Kaika whispered. "Hide behind the car." She crouched behind the machinery, so she wouldn't be visible to the dragon.

Cas did as instructed, though she hated not being able to see what Morishtomaric was doing. She crouched down, the sword box in her lap, and she curled her fingers around the lid, resting them on the latches. Therrik had said to take it out, but wouldn't the dragon be more likely to sense Kasandral then? Back in the castle, the others had spoken of keeping the blade in the case until she was ready to strike. She would need surprise on her side to have a chance of cutting down a dragon in a sword fight. Surprise and a lot of luck.

"Look out," someone shouted in the courtyard.

"It's going in the mines?" came a questioning shout from the wall.

Cas wanted to get up and look. The box buzzed in her hand, and even though Kasandral did not speak, she could imagine his words if he could: *Take me out. I'm ready. Must fight!*

Kaika made a patting "stay down" motion with her hand. She appeared calm, almost bored. She must have known that wherever the dragon was going, it wasn't aiming for them. The detonator rested on the ground an inch from her knee.

Cas caught a flash of gold between the tower's support post and the dangling tram car, then the dragon disappeared. Only as Kaika stood up and gazed toward the tram shaft did Cas realize he must have gone down there. She was surprised the massive creature had fit through the open double doors. They were large, with room for tram cars and ore carts, but that dragon was so big. Then she thought of Phelistoth and the way he could shift to human form and presumably other shapes. Maybe Morishtomaric had made himself thin enough to fit.

"He go all the way to the bottom?" came Therrik's voice from outside the tower. Thuds and splashes sounded, as he ran closer.

Cas eased out from behind the tram car, so she could see the open shaft. Pimples and Duck crowded behind her, as if they had been waiting for her to move so they could too. Therrik charged up to the shaft's edge and peered down, both his rifle and his sword now in hand.

"Yes," Phelistoth said. He had changed back to human form and walked up behind Therrik. He glanced into the shaft, sniffed derisively, and strode toward Cas.

He was looking past her, so she skittered out of the way, stepping on Duck's foot in her haste. Starting to get the gist of what was going on, she did not want to delay anything.

"Ouch, Raptor," Duck said. "Your heels are as sharp as your sights."

"You shouldn't stand so close to her," Pimples said. "She only cozies up with Deathmaker."

With her eyes locked onto Captain Kaika's face, Cas did not respond to them.

"Is it time?" Kaika asked Phelistoth.

"Soon." Phelistoth closed his eyes. "He is navigating the passages on the lower level." His mouth twisted. "Passages that *I* cleared."

"I'm sure he'll appreciate your good work."

"Doubtful. He is arrogant."

Cas kept herself from snorting, though she wondered if dragons thought all other dragons were arrogant, except for themselves.

That is an essential truth, Jaxi spoke into her mind.

Cas twitched. She didn't know if she would ever get used to having another entity randomly speaking into her mind.

Sardelle and Ridge are sleeping, so I have few people to talk to. Besides, I thought I should warn you that if this doesn't work, you'll need to be ready to use that sword soon. Might want to unbox him.

I don't understand why they're sleeping. Cas frowned down at the box. Therrik had said the same thing. Maybe everybody else was right.

So Morishtomaric couldn't read their thoughts and see this plan. I expect everyone will run when the explosives go off, even though Kaika was supposed to plant them so that the outpost itself wouldn't be in danger. If I were you, I would stay right there, next to the tram shaft. Try to get first blood if he comes out that way.

Cas pushed open the tram car door and laid the box inside. *Sardelle, Tylie, and Tolemek aren't around, right?* She knew Tolemek had gone up to the airship, but if Tylie and Sardelle were in the courtyard or nearby when she drew Kasandral...

They're in the headquarters building. Just remember those commands so you can make Kasandral work for you instead of the other way around. And remember which phrase you don't want to say.

Cas shuddered as she unlatched the box. She had recognized the phrase as soon as Sardelle had translated it, the one the queen had used, the one that translated to "take over."

As Cas took the hilt into her hands, the sword thrummed

contentedly. Up in the flier, there hadn't been time to remember what that blade had done in her grip back in the castle, but as soon as she lifted it, her forearms flexing with the unaccustomed weight, she started sweating. Sardelle and Tylie weren't nearly as far away as she had hoped they would be when she drew Kasandral from the box. She wished they were up on the airship, far out of reach.

"Now," Phelistoth said, the single word stirring Cas from her dark thoughts.

"Now it is." Kaika depressed the plunger on the detonator.

Cas stepped around the corner of the tram car, so that she was only a few feet from the shaft entrance. The hail had grown heavier, the icy balls bouncing to the ground larger. A white film coated the muddy courtyard.

"Get back, girl," Therrik growled and reached for her shoulder.

The signal Kaika had sent arrived at its destination before he could touch her. The distant boom was muffled, but the ground shook enough to make Cas sink into a crouch for stability. A second boom followed before the first had died out, and then a third. She soon lost track of how many explosions sounded from the depths of the mountain. Dust and the scent of something burning arose from the shaft, and she fought the urge to step back.

Wood snapped down below—supports that had survived the previous day's cave-in finally snapping. A roar drifted up through the shaft, along with more dust. Rain was already dripping into Cas's eyes, and now the dust assailed them too. She kept them open to a squint, certain that if the dragon came out this way, she wouldn't have more than a split second to attack before he shot into the sky.

We're hoping he's crushed to death down there, Jaxi informed her.

The last of the booms faded, rocks settling far below. Cas risked creeping closer to the shaft and stared into the depths. The weak daylight did not filter down far, and she could only see the ore tracks, the iron gleaming with dampness, for the first ten or twenty feet. Beyond that, it was too dark to tell what exactly had collapsed.

The half-frozen ground crunched beside her, making her realize how quiet it had grown. Therrik stepped up beside her, eyed the sword, then also stared into the shaft. Did he want to take Kasandral from her, to use it himself? A part of her wouldn't have minded giving him the responsibility, but handing it to someone so dangerous and so full of hate and fear was too cowardly to contemplate.

Phelistoth also came close to the shaft on Cas's other side, and Kasandral thrummed angrily in her hand. She whispered the relax command to it several times, but her skin crawled with the urge to swing the blade at him. She stepped around to the other side of the shaft, putting some space between them.

Oblivious—or indifferent—Phelistoth squinted thoughtfully into the dark passage.

"Well?" Therrik asked. "Is it alive?"

It wasn't clear whether he was speaking to Phelistoth or simply asking the world in general. He didn't look at the silver-haired man. From the way he clenched his sword, his knuckles tight on the grip, he wasn't nearly as calm as he sounded.

"He lives," Phelistoth said. "He may be trapped."

"Trapped is good," Cas said.

Kasandral's constant thrumming somehow conveyed displeasure at her statement. Maybe Jaxi and Sardelle were wrong, and the blade *was* intelligent.

Phelistoth and Therrik glowered down at her.

"*Dead* is good," Therrik said.

"I concur," Phelistoth said.

A buzz made Cas's palm tingle. Was that a warning?

Phelistoth's shoulders slumped. "He's coming."

Therrik said something, but the ground shuddered, and rocks cracked far below, the noise loud enough to reach up through the layers of earth to them. Phelistoth backed up, moving out of Cas's peripheral vision. Therrik scooted back too.

Cas remained, the sword in her hands, her knees bent to jump if she needed to. Rain dripped down the sides of her face, or maybe that was sweat. She wished the blade felt more comfortable in her hands, but she was aware of her inexperience, of the fact that the handful of katas the sword had guided her through the first time she'd carried it did not make up for the fact that she had never learned swordsmanship.

"Pimples," came a distant call. Was that Tolemek? She glanced toward the airship and caught him leaning over the railing with a megaphone. He hefted a small wood crate with a rope tied around it. Pimples and Duck sprinted away from the tower, crossing the courtyard toward him. Kaika, a pack slung over her shoulder, trotted after them.

Cas tried not to feel all alone as her comrades departed. They were getting ready to fly, and she would join them if this didn't work, but Jaxi was right. This might be her only chance to ambush the dragon.

The rain and hail picked up, beating onto the top of her cap, pounding her bare hands and bouncing off the blade. The earth shuddered one more time, a heave that made her feel like she was riding atop a wave.

Three seconds, Jaxi warned.

Cas tore her gaze from her comrades and focused on the shaft again.

Two.

She licked her lips and prepared to jump.

One.

The dragon streaked out so quickly all she saw was a blur of gold. Cas leaped, thrusting forward and up with the blade. She glimpsed something glowing purple clutched in the creature's talons. As ready as she'd been, she almost missed hitting the dragon at all—that was how fast he was. But Kasandral, guided by its power as much as her swing, bit into a golden-scaled leg, just above the talons.

A roar of pleasure sounded in her mind, Kasandral's satisfied cry.

The dragon screeched, dropping the purple object to the ground. It pulsed, shedding lavender rays onto the hail and mud. Cas had no idea whether it was a weapon or not, but she dared not look at it. Morishtomaric wheeled in the air, spinning toward her.

Cas jumped, trying to reach him for another swipe, but he was more than ten feet above the ground now. Even with the sword's reach, it wasn't enough. The blade swiped through the air a foot below those flexing talons. A flash of chagrin filled her as she realized Therrik would have been tall enough to land that blow.

Move! Jaxi cried, and an image of flames filled Cas's mind.

Morishtomaric opened his mouth. Cas sprinted for the tram tower, nearly crashing into the car hanging there. The metal supports of the tower wouldn't keep the flames from roasting her. She leaped into the car, sending Kasandral's box skittering.

Orange light and heat engulfed the tower. Cas rolled to the side of the car entrance, the sword clattering on the metal flooring. Sweltering air blasted her skin. The glass windows cracked, then blistered and started to melt. Cas tried to close the door, but already, it was too hot to touch. She yanked her burned fingers away. All she could do was roll to the side wall, hoping the metal car wouldn't melt around her.

The cable snapped, and the car fell to the ground with a jolt. The air scorched Cas's lungs, and she covered her mouth with her sleeve. She couldn't take much more of this.

Jaxi, she yelled in her mind. *Kasandral.* Couldn't any of these swords help her?

The flames stopped. With the air and the metal flooring under her still so hot, she might not have noticed right away, had the light level not dimmed a thousand times.

Cas wanted to stay in a tiny ball until the dragon went away forever, but she made herself rise to her knees. She'd dropped Kasandral, and she reached for it as she tried to see through the half-melted windows. Metal had melted, too, and splatted to the floor all around her like candle wax.

Another screech came from outside, similar to the earlier one. Who was attacking Morishtomaric now? Hope rose in her chest that some weapon had gotten through.

Kasandral's hilt burned her hand, and she hissed in pain. Though she wanted to leave it, she dragged her jacket sleeve over her palm, grabbed the weapon, and scrambled out of the car.

The purple thing, some sort of crystalline structure about a foot and a half tall, pulsed in the hail-covered mud in front of the tram shaft. The dragon was gone. Cas ran over and kicked the crystal back into the shaft. At the least, she could make it harder for Morishtomaric to retrieve it when he came back from wherever he had gone.

Another screech sounded from the sky above her, and she realized he wasn't gone. He was under attack.

Phelistoth had changed into his natural form again, and he and Morishtomaric were writhing in the air, biting and clawing at each other. Dread filled her stomach as she saw how much smaller their dragon was than the golden one. Gunshots rang from the walls of the outpost, but Cas knew they would not do any good. She didn't even know if the soldiers were targeting the right dragon.

He won't last long, Jaxi said. *Hurry to the fliers. I'm trying to wake the others. Plan B.*

Chapter 18

WAKE UP, JAXI ORDERED. JUDGING by the exasperated tone of the words, it wasn't her first time saying them.

Sardelle sat up. She was on the floor in the office where she and the others had discussed strategy that morning, the office where they had inhaled Tolemek's concoctions in order to knock themselves out. Ridge still lay unconscious beside her. General Ort was slumped in a chair at the table.

Wake up your soul snozzle too. He needs to get in his flier. It didn't work, and there's not much time.

Saving the questions for later, Sardelle rested her hand on Ridge's shoulder. She pushed aside the fog in her mind and the headache Tolemek's potion had left her with to clear the drug out of Ridge's system. Though she was focusing on the work, she couldn't help but hear the thunder of cannons and the hail of rifle fire outside.

Some of that hail is actual hail, and some of that thunder is real too. It's a mess out there.

Ridge's eyes popped open. He winced, probably having a headache too. When his gaze locked onto hers, it was cogent, the question in his eyes clear.

"Plan B," she said.

Cursing, he rolled to his feet. He staggered, caught himself on the table, and raced out the door. Sardelle looked toward General Ort, wondering if she should stay behind to wake him, but he wasn't part of the flight contingent for Plan B. He should wake soon enough on his own. Judging by the commotion outside, Sardelle might be needed right away.

She ran through the empty hallway to the stairs, taking the

steps four at a time. Even with her haste, she was well behind Ridge. He'd already climbed to the rooftop by the time she stepped outside. A hail pellet the size of a coin smacked her shoulder, and she faltered. Seven gods, he couldn't fly in this. The cockpits were open, and the wings were made from cloth. They had a waterproof sealant, but could that protect the material from hail like this?

No choice, Jaxi said, and Sardelle looked up.

Phelistoth and Morishtomaric fought in the air above the fort. Sardelle's first worry was that Tylie was around and in danger, but when she checked, she sensed the young woman in her room with her nose pressed to the window. Surprised Phelistoth had intervened and was helping them, Sardelle ran up the stairs to the rooftop.

Don't be so surprised. Morishtomaric came up with the crystal our dragon wants for himself.

Ah.

Down in the courtyard, Pimples was already in his cockpit. On the rooftop, Duck was helping Kaika load a pack full of explosives into the back seat of his flier. Ridge was hefting a crate into his own craft. He jumped up and pulled himself in after it. Therrik stood on the rooftop, too, though he was yelling at someone in the closest artillery tower rather than having anything to do with the aircraft.

Sardelle spotted Cas standing next to Ridge's flier and froze. She carried Kasandral, the sword out of his box and glowing that familiar sickly green.

His complexion hasn't improved, has it? Jaxi asked.

Cas met her eyes, concern blossoming on her face. But she firmed her chin and nodded once, as if to say she had full control of the sword. Sardelle hoped so. Either way, Cas would be in the sky with Ridge soon and not close enough to reach her. It would be fine.

A pained screech came from the sky above and stirred Sardelle into motion. Fat blood drops spattered the frosty roof as the dragons fought overhead. How they clawed and bit and lashed out with their tails without falling from the air, she couldn't tell.

"Pimples has room in his flier, Sardelle," Ridge called to her without looking up. He was loading bands of bullets into his machine guns. "Are you coming up with us?"

Was she? She looked at the fighting dragons, then toward the soldiers on the walls, and toward miners watching from the barracks buildings that hadn't been destroyed, men and women who were staying out of the way but who couldn't tear their gazes from the battle. She thought of the miner with the dragon blood, a man who may or may not have deserved to be here and who had died for nothing. As much as she wanted to stay close to Ridge, there were hundreds of lives at stake down here. Besides, if the battle stayed as close as it was now—she glanced at the blood drops on the roof—she could help him *and* protect the fort.

"I'll stay here and do my best to shield these people," Sardelle said, "but I'll keep an eye on you too."

Therrik had stopped bellowing at his men, and he must have heard her statement, because he looked over at her. She couldn't tell if he intended to say something sarcastic, but it didn't matter. Ridge was hopping down from his flier and running toward her.

He hugged her fiercely. "I know you will. Even if I don't deserve it."

She returned the embrace, burying her face in his shoulder. "You deserve everything you have and more."

"I love delusional women." He kissed her, then raced back to his flier as another ear-splitting screech sounded from above. Before pulling himself into the cockpit, he glared over at Therrik. "You try to stab Sardelle in the back while I'm up there, and I'll hunt you down in my flier and fill you full of bullets."

Therrik snorted. "Save your bluster for the dragon, Zirkander."

Ridge swung up into the cockpit. "Ahn, you coming?"

"Yes, sir."

Cas reached up to toss Kasandral into the seat behind him, but she froze as words sounded in Sardelle's mind.

Antyonla masahrati!

It was Morishtomaric's voice.

Sardelle yanked Jaxi from her scabbard. She might not have remembered those words if she hadn't been translating them the night before, but they were the same ones the queen had shouted right before Kasandral possessed Cas in the castle.

Cas responded right away, her eyes growing round for a second, then narrowing with determination. She lowered Kasandral and assumed a fighting stance. At first, her gaze locked onto the fighting dragons, and Sardelle thought the sword might focus on them as the greater threats—the greater sources of dragon blood.

Then Cas spun toward her.

Not again, Jaxi groaned into her mind. She flared with bluish silver energy, and power flowed into Sardelle's limbs, but she knew Jaxi didn't want this fight, not now. Sardelle didn't want it, either. Not with the dragons trying to kill each other right over their heads. Phelistoth was buying them time, time they needed to use wisely.

Cas advanced toward her, that horrified expression on her face again.

"*Meriyash keeno,*" Sardelle yelled, making sure Kasandral heard her over the gunfire and dragon screeches. They were the words that should order the sword to stand down. If Cas couldn't manage to utter them in her present state of mind, Sardelle would do it for her.

Cas hesitated. Ridge jumped down from the flier and grabbed her from behind.

"Stand down, Ahn," he ordered. "Wrong target."

Antyonla masahrati! Morishtomaric repeated, power lacing the command.

Cas jabbed backward with her elbow with more force than she could have mustered on her own. Ridge stumbled away from her, clutching his solar plexus. Sardelle lifted a hand and created an invisible barrier in the air between her and Cas. Off to the side, Therrik advanced toward them, but she had no idea if he meant to help stop Cas… or to help Cas kill her. Kaika and Duck jumped down from the other flier, but they were on the other side of the roof.

Cas's lips moved. She seemed to be uttering the stand-down words, but Kasandral only flared more brightly. The blade swiped sideways, cutting into Sardelle's barrier. It disappeared, like a popped soap bubble. Sardelle struggled to remake it, but Cas was already lunging for her.

Damn it, how had the dragon known the blade's command words?

Ridge drew his pistol and aimed at the back of Cas's leg, but he hesitated to shoot. Sardelle couldn't blame him. Not only was she a friend, but they needed her to fight the dragon. She needed to figure out how to break Morishtomaric's influence on Kasandral before drastic measures were required.

Meriyash keeno, Sardelle repeated, this time using telepathy and focusing the words right at the blade.

Cas was close enough to strike. Her movements were jerky, her face flushing red with the effort of trying to stop Kasandral.

Silver scales flashed, and the roof trembled. Phelistoth landed on his back, flung down by Morishtomaric, who flapped his wings in the sky twenty feet above them. Blood streamed from those silver scales, and Phelistoth lay stunned for a moment, his legs in the air like those of an upturned turtle. Hail bounced off his exposed belly.

Sardelle raised Jaxi, intending to help shield him if she could. Surely Morishtomaric would attack, pressing the advantage and not worrying about the humans on the roof. Instead, he swept toward the courtyard, toward the shaft where he had dropped his crystal.

Cas roared, the sword flaring such a bright green that it hurt to look at it. Instead of lunging at Sardelle again, she ran toward Phelistoth, Kasandral leading the way.

"No," Sardelle yelled, then shouted the command words again. "Not him."

Ridge charged in from the side and dove. Cas swung at Phelistoth's defenseless side. Ridge slammed into her legs before the blade bit in. They tumbled to the ground, and the sword flew from Cas's grip. It skidded across the roof, bits of hail flying in its wake, and landed at Therrik's feet. The green glow flashed, beckoning him to pick it up.

"Don't even think about it," Sardelle yelled and tried to use her power to fling it away from him.

When Kasandral had been in his box, that had worked, but now the gust of wind she created blew right across the blade without doing anything. Therrik bent down and picked up the sword.

Ridge jumped to his feet, his pistol out again. He aimed it at Therrik's chest.

"Drop it."

A boom sounded from above. The airship was firing at Morishtomaric. Phelistoth rolled over, the corner of the roof crumbling underneath him. He caught himself on the edge and pulled himself back up, his legs underneath him now. For a moment, he looked at Ridge and Therrik, who were so busy staring at each other, the glow of Kasandral between them, that they did not notice the dragon's movement.

Sardelle had no idea if a bullet would stop Therrik when Kasandral was in his hand. Jaxi could block gunfire. She brushed Therrik's mind and tried to convince him to drop the sword, but it was like grasping at dandelion seeds in the wind. She couldn't get a grip.

Cas climbed to her feet and pulled out her own pistol. She gave Sardelle a look of anguish, but she didn't say anything. She added her weapon to the one already trained on Therrik.

Therrik turned away from both of them and strode toward Phelistoth. The dragon had recovered enough to spring into the air. Before Therrik got close, he was twenty feet above them. He flapped his wings a few times, looking around, then arrowed toward the courtyard. Morishtomaric had disappeared into the shaft again. Looking for the crystal?

With the dragon no longer close, Therrik did not hesitate. He spun toward Sardelle, his lips rearing back into a snarl. He sprinted at her.

Sardelle yelled the stand-down command words at the same time as Cas did. Kasandral's glow dimmed just as Ridge fired.

The bullet lodged into the side of Therrik's thigh. He faltered for a second, but then he continued on, his face a rictus of rage and pain. Sardelle braced herself, Jaxi glowing in front of her, the confrontation inevitable. Even if Kasandral was lessening his grip on his handler, Therrik wanted this too much.

Or so she thought. She leaped to the side, Jaxi ready to defend, but when he drew even with her, he didn't swing. He ran down the stairs, his gait lopsided but determined. Sardelle raced to the edge of the roof.

Therrik gained speed and reached the shaft as Morishtomaric flew out with the purple crystal structure clasped in his talons. Phelistoth dove down from the sky and bowled into him. The dragons struck the ground, mud and frost spattering everywhere. They rolled head over tail, like fighting cats. Therrik leaped into the fray, chopping down with Kasandral as if it were an axe.

"Damn it," Ridge growled from Sardelle's side. "Does he even care which one he hits?"

She shrugged helplessly. Those dragons were twisting and writhing so quickly, it was all a blur.

He just nicked Morishtomaric, Jaxi said, *but I think Ridge is right. He's aiming at both of them.*

The crystal flew free, landing in a puddle.

"I'm going to try to get that," Sardelle said. She wasn't doing anything else and had a notion that it might be used as a bargaining chip.

More likely, it'll make you a target.

I'm getting used to that.

Ridge started after her, but she stopped him with a hand to his chest. "Plan B, right?" She nodded toward the fliers. "If you have bullets in there that could hurt him..."

A mix of emotions flashed across Ridge's face, but he nodded curtly and ran to the flier.

"You coming, Ahn?" he barked.

Cas stood in the middle of the rooftop, her shoulders slumped, her face full of self-loathing. "I don't have a weapon that will do anything, sir."

"Yeah, you do. Your Mark 500 is in your seat."

"But—"

"And Tolemek sent down a bag of bullets with your name on it."

Sardelle was running down the stairs and did not hear Cas's response. She raced across the courtyard, wincing as hail struck her head. *Shield me, will you, Jaxi?* She could deal with the hail, but she remembered the last time she'd been in a battle in this courtyard, with the soldiers just as happy to shoot at her as at the enemy shaman.

Humans are so fragile. The pummeling stopped.

I know. She could have done it herself, but she feared she would need her power to protect herself from Therrik or the dragons—or both.

For the moment, the dragons weren't paying attention to him. He kept having to jump over a tail or leap back from the fray before diving back in, but even Kasandral could not drive them apart. Morishtomaric and Phelistoth were so engrossed in their own battle for that crystal that the rest of the fort might as well not have been there. At least the soldiers had stopped firing, probably because their fort commander was in the middle of the fray. She wondered if he was doing more harm than good by being down here.

So long as he's not attacking us.

Sardelle agreed. She spotted the crystal in the mud behind them. *I'm starting to think that thing is more than a library.*

One does wonder.

She took a circuitous route around the writhing combatants, giving them a wide berth. Even so, a tail shot out, going rigid, and she had to jump to avoid being struck. When she reached it, she touched the crystal before picking it up, worried it might have a defense against humans. Surprisingly, it hummed with a gentle warmth that she found inviting.

One of the dragons roared, and Morishtomaric's golden body stiffened.

Therrik got a good hit, Jaxi said. *He—*

The next cry was human. Therrik.

Sardelle lifted the crystal and backed away in time to glimpse him flying high through the air. He landed thirty feet away from the dragons with bone-crunching finality.

Morishtomaric did not like it, Jaxi said.

The gold dragon had put some space between himself and Phelistoth, who seemed to be catching his breath. Either that, or he was too injured to continue. Morishtomaric had his share of bloody gashes, but they were nothing compared to Phelistoth's injuries. Blood poured from the side of his neck, and broken silver scales littered the ground around the battle scene.

Might want to get out of here with your new paperweight, Jaxi suggested.

Sardelle was trying to creep around the dragons, so that she could check on Therrik. Anything that had made him cry out had to have been a grievous injury, and landing after that flight across the courtyard couldn't have felt good, either. And then there was the fact that Ridge had shot him...

Before Sardelle could get close, Morishtomaric flexed his wings and faced her.

Told you, Jaxi said.

Sardelle halted, the crystal clutched to her chest. A part of her wanted to fling the artifact at him, in the hope that he would take it and go away forever, but the fact that he wanted it so badly made her nervous. Whatever secrets lay within, could they be anything good for humanity? Besides, Morishtomaric had already proven that he was a menace if left to fly around on his own. He'd killed countless people and burned entire villages. He had to be stopped here.

Yes, and how are we going to do that?

I'll let you know as soon as I figure it out.

The dragon's eyes narrowed, and he stepped toward her. His maw stretched open, and Sardelle threw her strength into the shield Jaxi was already maintaining. She turned to run, knowing the dragon's fire would only drain their reserves, but the hammering of a machine gun broke across the courtyard. A couple of bullets struck Morishtomaric's hide, and he turned his attention from her.

Ridge's flier was in the air. He arrowed toward the dragon, his twin guns firing. In the seat behind him, Cas leaned over the side, her sniper rifle in hand. Unfortunately, the next round of bullets was deflected before touching the dragon. Sardelle hoped the ones that had reached his scales would do some damage, but she couldn't tell.

"Zirkander," Therrik yelled as the flier swooped low, his voice weaker than usual. He was on one knee in the mud, one hand pressed to his chest while the other gripped Kasandral, its tip also resting in the mud. Its glow had left, as if the sword knew his handler had no fight left in him. Blood dripped from the corner of Therrik's mouth, and he was gasping for air.

Sardelle did not know if Ridge heard him over the buzz of his propeller and the sound of his own guns, but Therrik drew back his arm. As the flier reached its lowest point before it had to steer upward again, he hurled Kasandral into the air with all of his strength.

"Sir," Cas blurted and stuffed her rifle between her legs.

Ridge tilted the wings. Sardelle didn't think the sword would make it to them, and she tried to give it a nudge, to take it higher so they could reach it. To her surprise, this time Kasandral allowed her touch. The sword sailed upward, and Cas leaned out to grasp it.

The flier curved up into the sky, the wheels just missing the top of the outpost wall nearest the mountain. With Ridge flying away, at least until he could gain altitude to swoop down for another attack, Sardelle thought Morishtomaric might target her again. She still clutched the crystal to her chest. Instead, the dragon leaped into the air and flew after Ridge. Maybe a couple of Tolemek's special bullets had slipped through and were doing damage, so Morishtomaric had to deal with the threat.

Relieved for herself but terrified for Ridge, Sardelle ran to Therrik's side. Throwing the sword must have taken the last of his strength. He had collapsed onto his back, and hail battered his exposed face. He was conscious, but his eyes were starting to glaze, his gasps for air weakening.

"Phel!" came a nearby cry. Tylie raced across the courtyard, running past Sardelle.

Phelistoth lay on his belly in the mud, his legs folded beneath him, his head on the ground and his eyes closed. He wasn't dead, but he didn't look like he had any more fight in him.

Watch her, please, Jaxi. Sardelle dropped to her knees beside Therrik and rested a hand on his chest. Morishtomaric had struck his chest with enough force to break ribs and force the splintered bones into his organs. Among other injuries, one of his lungs had collapsed and the other was damaged. He would die soon if she didn't help him.

I was going to watch you, Jaxi said, *because I know you'll heal someone even if he's a huge pest who nobody would miss.*

You know me well. See if you can convince Tylie to take shelter, please. Sardelle eyed the ramparts warily. Most of the soldiers were looking upward, toward the gold dragon and the two fliers tangling in the skies. Duck and Kaika had joined Ridge and Cas up there, and Pimples was taking off to join them. The airship had pulled in its anchor and flew overhead. Sardelle hoped their forces would be enough to take down their enemy.

I don't think Tylie is any more likely to take shelter than you are. She's hugging up to Phelistoth and crying on him.

Sardelle did not respond. Therrik needed a lot of help, and she didn't know how much time she would have, especially when she was the one holding the artifact Morishtomaric had come to get.

CHAPTER 19

"SHOOT THE *DRAGON*," TOLEMEK GROWLED, "not the fliers."

He knelt behind the railing on the airship, half watching the battle and half trying to adjust the fuses on his smoke grenades. He had no idea if they would bother Morishtomaric, but he had mixed a tiny bit of the acid into the formula inside. If Cas and Kasandral managed to take away the dragon's ability to defend himself with magic, maybe some smoke would get through and burn his eyes. Tolemek lamented that he couldn't think of more that he could do—he wasn't even sure he should do this, since their own people were out there.

After battling Phelistoth in the courtyard, Morishtomaric had taken off after Zirkander and Cas, and Tolemek had a hard time tearing his gaze from that. Duck and Kaika were out there, too, but they were not the dragon's primary target.

Tolemek held his breath every time the creature drew close to Cas, certain he would bathe the flier in a stream of fire. Morishtomaric was faster, stronger, and more agile than the manmade aircraft, but Zirkander had an uncanny knack for anticipating attacks. So far, they hadn't been hit, at least not by the dragon. Hail rained from the sky, giving Tolemek another reason to worry. Fierce wind batted at the fliers, especially now that the battle had risen higher, away from the protection of the valley walls.

A cannon boomed a few feet away. Tolemek glowered at the artilleryman, not certain anyone should be shooting with the fliers so close to the dragon. It wasn't as if the cannonballs and bullets could harm the dragon—Tolemek had given all of his modified ammunition to the pilots. They *could*, however, hit the fliers.

Major Cildark paced the deck, watching the battle and giving orders to the artillerymen. He seemed to think that the airship needed to look useful, whether it was or not. Hail slanted in under the balloon and bounced off the deck. Now and then, rips sounded above, just audible over the gales tearing down from the mountaintops. So far, the holes were too small to affect the ship's ability to stay aloft. So far.

"Here." Tolemek waved aside a private about to load a new cannonball. He wiggled his grenade, having to shout to be heard above the wind. "We're shooting this instead."

"Uh." The soldier glanced toward Cildark, who must have been watching, because he waved a go-ahead. "Yes, sir."

"Let me know when it's ready to fire." Tolemek nodded at the soldier holding the rammer. "Be gentle packing it in, and don't take long. The fuse will be lit. Got it?"

"Yes, sir."

"And aim this at the *dragon*," Tolemek told the man responsible for targeting. "Understood?"

"We're trying to hit the dragon, sir. It moves a lot, and when we do hit it, the balls bounce off."

"I know. I'm hoping Cas will be able to do something about that." Hail the size of a bullet slammed into Tolemek's temple. He growled, tempted to throw his grenade at the sky. If only that would help.

Lightning flashed overhead, branching down toward the airship. A crack and snap came from above. Tolemek gripped the railing. The lightning hadn't cut into the balloon, had it? The material shouldn't attract it, but the lightweight frame inside might be another story. Was there metal in that?

A charred rod tumbled from above, quickly dropping below the railing and out of sight.

"That was one of our lightning rods," Major Cildark said, coming to the rail beside Tolemek. "They had better finish this fight quickly."

"The cannon is ready, sir." The artilleryman nodded to Tolemek.

Tolemek rested his grenade against the lip of the barrel,

but he did not light it yet. He studied the fight, looking for an opportunity. A third flier had joined the others in the sky. From here, Tolemek couldn't tell if it was Pimples or General Ort. All of the pilots had their caps pulled low and their scarves wrapped around their necks and heads, with only their goggles exposed on their faces.

A stream of fire lit up the sky as the dragon twisted back on itself, performing gravity-defying acrobatics to target the flier behind him. Zirkander's. Caps and scarves couldn't keep Tolemek from identifying Cas's slight form in the back. Even as he watched, she lifted that sword. The flier jerked to the left, narrowly avoiding the flames. It *should* have avoided the flames, but the wind gusted hard, hammering it in the side. The wings wobbled, and the craft was pushed back toward the fire. Zirkander took them down, but not before the tip of one wing burst into flames.

Tolemek's heart lurched. "Now, now," he barked and lit the grenade.

Zirkander was diving, but the dragon hadn't yet turned to follow. "Got him in my sights," the artilleryman said.

Tolemek dropped the grenade into the barrel. There was no time to tamp it down the way a cannonball would have been. He waved away the man with the rammer. "Go, go, fire now."

All he could do was hope that the igniting powder would fling it far enough—and that it might actually distract the dragon.

To his horror, Cas leaped out of her seat. Zirkander had straightened their flight so she could crawl along the wing toward the fire at one tip.

"Seven gods," Cildark breathed. "She'll fall off for sure."

Tolemek couldn't take his eyes away, not even to shoot the major a well-deserved glare.

The cannon boomed, and his grenade shot away. The dragon was already on the move, dipping down to chase Zirkander's flier. Cas had reached the end of the wing and was batting at the flames with a cloth. The grenade arched through the sky, dropping near the dragon.

"Any time now," Tolemek whispered, then realized the fuse

might have gone out. Between the wind and rain, that seemed so likely that he groaned. A cannonball would have done more good.

Just as he'd given up, the grenade exploded. It wasn't a huge explosion, not like one of Captain Kaika's bombs, but smoke flooded the heavy air. The dragon was close, but not close enough to take the brunt of it in the eyes, as Tolemek had hoped. Would it bother him at all?

Morishtomaric pulled his wings in, diving for the flier. With Cas out on the wing, Zirkander couldn't buck and gyrate the way he usually did. Cas looked up, then scrambled back for the seat well. She traded the cloth for the sword and stood in her seat, the blade raised, its green glow visible even through the hail.

"Sit *down*, Ahn," Cildark growled.

But Cas remained on her feet, staring defiantly up at the dragon as it streaked toward them. Zirkander shouted something back to her, then turned, the flier tilting. She bent her knees and kept her balance, but the dragon looked like he would tear off the tail of their craft without ever getting close enough for her to hit.

Then Morishtomaric shook his head, his neck bending oddly. He had flown out of range of the smoke, smoke that was already dissipating in the wind, but maybe he had gotten some in his eyes, after all. His head shook again, and a strange noise reached Tolemek's ears.

"Is that dragon sneezing?" Cildark asked.

In another situation, Tolemek would have laughed. All he could manage now was to be relieved that Morishtomaric's inevitable descent was disrupted. Zirkander's craft climbed back into the air as the dragon passed fifty meters behind it, sneezing. Duck's flier swooped down, giving chase. Machine gun fire pounded the dragon—or more likely his magical shield. Tolemek kept hoping some of his bullets would slip through, but even while sneezing, Morishtomaric could protect himself. Soon, his wings flapped, and he was climbing again.

"Throw more grenades, Deathmaker," the major said.

Tolemek snorted. "Is it easier to hit a sneezing dragon?"

"It might be."

Tolemek did pull out a second grenade, but he had a hard time focusing on the fuse. Instead of chasing after Zirkander again, this time the dragon flew straight toward the airship.

* * *

"He's focusing on the airship," Ridge called back to Cas, hoping she heard him. The wind was screaming in his ears, the hail turning to snow. The snow made it harder to see, but it hurt less as it pummeled his head and shoulders, so he wouldn't complain. "This might be our chance to get on his ass."

He had been trying to circle around, to get behind the dragon so Cas could attack him, but Morishtomaric had taken the shots Ridge had fired in the courtyard personally. He had been too busy trying to get behind *Ridge* and shoot fire up *his* ass for them to do anything but evade and run.

"You have to get me close enough, sir," Cas yelled back. Her mouth was only a foot behind his ear, but he could barely make out her words.

"You have the rope tied around your ankle, right?" He had been terrified he would lose her when she had scampered out on the wing to put out that fire.

"For the fifth time, *yes*."

Morishtomaric shot a writhing orange stream of flames out of his mouth, his target the airship envelope. Ridge accelerated, trying to get there in time to stop him. Thus far, the dragon had ignored the airship, but he must not have liked whatever Tolemek had fired at him. Now, his talons stretched out, and they sank into the balloon, ripping and shredding.

Ridge pressed down on the triggers, firing relentlessly. He thought a couple of his bullets had struck the dragon down in the courtyard, before Morishtomaric had realized he was coming, but since then, they had all bounced away before reaching his scales. These did the same.

"Anyone got any ideas how to get it to stop clawing up Major

Cildark's balloon?" Ridge asked as he swept past. He eased off the machine guns, both because they had flown out of targeting range and because he did not want to waste any more of the special bullets. They needed to get the dragon's shield down first.

"Kaika and I are coming in with a bomb," came Duck's voice over the crystal.

"I'm on Duck's tail," Pimples said, "for all the good it's doing. I'll try to shoot after the bomb goes off. Maybe it'll distract him."

"Do it," Ridge said, wishing he could offer more. "Ahn," he called over his shoulder, "I'm going to get you close enough to use that letter opener of yours."

"Looking forward to it, sir."

Duck reached the dragon, sailing past above him, his flier's wings wobbling noticeably in the wind. Kaika leaned over the side and dropped one of her bombs. Ridge had circled around to face the dragon again, but he did not want to run into their explosion, so he weaved back and forth, waiting for his chance and cursing as Morishtomaric continued to rip into the balloon. The cannons and shell guns on the ship fired, but as usual, the projectiles bounced off. Ridge watched the bomb's descent, hoping the explosive would do more damage.

It almost fell too far, tumbling past the dragon on the side farthest from the airship. But it exploded as it dipped below his legs, and for a moment, flames melted the snow from the air. Morishtomaric jerked away, his wings tucking into his body. He bumped the side of the airship, breaking a large portion of the railing.

Ridge lined himself up to shoot again, hoping that impenetrable shield might have disappeared. Pimples came in from another angle, doing the same. The orange light from the explosion had already died out, but smoke remained, and Ridge couldn't tell if they struck anything. He banked so that he could circle around and come in again, this time to get Cas in close.

The dragon fell below the body of the airship, and Ridge allowed himself to hope Kaika might have done some real damage, but by the time he completed his circle so he could head back in, Morishtomaric was even with the envelope again, ripping into it with angry talons. He exhaled a great cloud of fire, the breadth even greater than before. Had they done nothing more than incense him?

On the airship, the cannons and big artillery guns roared, but the deck tilted sideways. That balloon could take a lot of bullets and hail, but if the side was completely torn open...

Ridge glanced down, hoping they were still near the fort, that the airship could land someplace safe if necessary. The wind had carried them out over the side of Goat Mountain, with glacier-scoured slopes, craggy canyons, and tall pines waiting below.

"Wonderful," he muttered. At least the airship was sinking slowly. If it crashed, those on board had a good chance of walking away from it. Pilots rarely walked away from flier crashes. "Back off, Duck and Pimples. I'm taking Cas in for a poke."

"Poke him good, Raptor," Pimples yelled.

"Sir?" Duck said. "I know this isn't the time to bother you, but we just took a hit. Lightning. I can't—" His words broke off with curses.

Ridge craned his neck, trying to spot Duck's flier. He was on the other side of the dragon, losing altitude fast as smoke billowed from his cockpit. The entire nose of his flier had been scorched and turned black. Kaika leaned forward, batting at the air in front of Duck with a scarf. Fire in the cockpit? That was all Ridge could guess before the dragon blocked his view.

"Get back to the outpost, Duck," Ridge said. "While you still can. We're on the dragon."

He made himself focus on their enemy instead of worrying about his people. He flicked the ready sign over his shoulder for Cas.

"Going up on the wing, sir," she yelled.

They had almost reached the dragon. Morishtomaric was taking his time, bathing the side of the airship in flames. Ridge fired again, though he was reluctant to waste more bullets when they weren't piercing his enemy's defenses.

Behind him, Cas stood in the seat, one hand on the wing and one holding the sword. A tether wrapped around her ankle would keep her from tumbling hundreds of feet to the ground if she fell, but he worried it wouldn't protect her from other danger. Ridge flew straight at Morishtomaric, trying to make the ride as smooth as the wind and snow would allow.

Lightning flashed again overhead. Only in this forsaken place would snow and lightning go hand in hand.

Ridge took them right below the dragon's belly. Morishtomaric wasn't hovering—he didn't know if that was possible—but the creature was swooping back and forth along the airship's length, sticking close. Flames leaped from the balloon and from the side of the craft now too. Despite the best efforts from the soldiers on the deck, they weren't able to keep the dragon away. Knowing Tolemek was on there, Ridge hoped for Cas's sake that the craft found a safe landing spot.

As he came in under the dragon, Ridge took them up, trying to get close enough for Cas to reach the creature. As he did so, he watched those talons, aware that they could tear the wings off his flier with one swipe. Just getting hit by the tail could knock him out of the sky.

He didn't have the right angle to shoot as he flew past under the dragon, so all he did was hold his breath and glance back at Cas. She had climbed onto the top wing. He gulped when she jumped upward, trying to strike Morishtomaric's leg with the sword. The flier continued forward while she was in the air, and she came down somewhere behind the wing. Ridge couldn't tell if she had struck the dragon or not; he was too busy wrenching his neck around, making sure she hadn't fallen completely off the flier.

She straddled the fuselage, between the back of the wing and the tail. Her face was red, her expression furious, but she still held the sword. She yelled something, but he couldn't hear it. He touched his ear, then focused forward again, guiding the flier away so he could swing around and they could try again.

It took Cas time to untangle herself and climb over the wing and back into the seat. Ridge banked, turning them for another run at the dragon, only to see the airship sinking toward the mountainside. Huge plumes of black smoke wafted upward, mingling with the ominous clouds above.

"Sir," Cas yelled, "I couldn't reach him. We have to get *closer*."

"*Closer*? I was practically shaving that dragon's belly with our propeller."

Morishtomaric flapped his wings idly, watching the airship's descent. Ridge was starting to wonder if all of their plans would come to naught, if the only way to defeat a gold dragon was with *another* gold dragon. As he flew back toward their seemingly indestructible foe, he looked toward the outpost, wondering if Sardelle had any advice.

She's trying to save your colonel's life, Jaxi said.

My colonel?

The one you shot.

Ah.

My advice would be—actually, let me give this to Cas, Jaxi said. *Take her back in close. Closer.*

Everybody wanted closer. Ridge sped toward the dragon, determined to do his best.

The snow was turning to sleet, and it beat at his goggles, needling his skin through his scarf. Even with gloves on, his hands felt so numb that he worried he would lose his touch when he needed it most.

He thought Morishtomaric might fly after the sinking airship, to help send it on its way, but the dragon must have decided the craft did not offer a further threat. Instead, he wheeled slowly, coming about to face Ridge and Cas.

"We're going in," Ridge yelled over his shoulder.

The dragon's powerful wings beat the air, scattering snow as he sailed toward them.

"Ready, sir," Cas called back.

Ridged wished he was.

* * *

Cas crouched on the wing, her hand curled around the edge, as Zirkander flew them toward the dragon. Anyone heavier would have punched right through the cloth, but she hunkered there like a statue, ignoring the wind, the sleet, and the terror that rode her as the inevitable clash approached. She glanced at the tether tied around her ankle, wondering if she should take it off, if she *had* to take it off to do as Jaxi suggested.

I didn't suggest you turn suicidal, Jaxi spoke into her head again. *Especially not now. Sardelle is fighting to keep the big brute alive down here, and we're too far away for even me to levitate you if you fall.*

Cas believed that. It had been a long time since she had glimpsed the outpost. The wind had blown them out over the mountains, and the sleet made it impossible to see more than a hundred meters.

She thought about responding to Jaxi, but the dragon was almost upon them, fury burning in its eyes. Fury and pain. Whatever Morishtomaric had come for, he seemed to have forgotten. They had hurt him, and he was enraged. She was sure a few of Tolemek's bullets had made it through when Kaika had dropped that bomb, so they should be eating away at the creature's hide even now. This was her chance to open him up to further damage, to lower his defenses permanently. Then she could make up for her shameful moment on the rooftop when, once again, she had failed to control Kasandral.

"Hang on," Zirkander yelled back to her.

Not easy while gripping a sword. She risked sheathing it for a moment, so she could grip the edge of the wing with both hands and anchor one boot on the other side. She kept one foot beneath her, ready to spring.

Zirkander made it look like he was going to fly around the dragon, to avoid the beast's deadly fire, but at the last moment, as Morishtomaric turned to track them, he went into a dive. Cas gulped, muscles straining as she struggled to hold on.

He leveled out quickly, surprising the dragon as he twisted to dip down and follow them. Zirkander came up again, and for a moment, Morishtomaric was heading straight down while their flier was heading straight up. They passed in parallel, with no more than ten feet between them. A small distance in an aerial battle, but a canyon for someone in a precarious perch. Cas did the only thing she could do if she wanted to hit her target. She sprang free from the wing, tearing the sword from its sheath.

The wind beat at her as if she were a leaf, but her powerful spring sent her toward the dragon's belly as they were passing each other. Even so, she might have missed him if gravity hadn't been on her side. Almost immediately, she fell downward as well as outward.

With the snow lashing sideways, she couldn't see the ground and had no idea how high she was, but that might have been for the best. Already, such panic clutched her that she almost forgot what she was supposed to be doing.

Fearing she might reach the end of her tether before she touched the dragon, Cas slashed over her head, her movements more wild than calculating. She had no idea how far out the dragon's invisible shield extended from his body. All she could do was hope it was like that of the sorceress's around the Cofah airship and that she could lower it by striking it.

Even though she wanted to connect with it, when she actually did, the surprise and power of the moment struck her like a bolt of lightning. At first, she thought she *had* been struck by lightning. Power crackled around her, jolting her to the spine, and a flash nearly blinded her. If not for a bubbling hum of pleasure that coursed up her arm from Kasandral, she wouldn't have been certain she had encountered the dragon's shield.

A second jolt racked her body, and she almost dropped Kasandral. This jolt came from her ankle, and fiery pain burst up her entire leg. The tether, she realized numbly, as she was dragged into the sky with such speed that it stole her breath. She forced herself to yell cogent words, though she only wanted to scream in pain.

"I got it," she yelled, hoping Zirkander could hear her. "It's down! Get him!"

She had no idea how long it would take before Morishtomaric could reestablish his shield, and she hoped he had been zapped even more fiercely than she. As she was dragged behind Zirkander's flier, her shirt flew up around her armpits, and she lost her cap and goggles. Sleet beat at her face and her bare stomach. She could scarcely see, and only her senses told her they were turning, the centrifugal force tearing at her as the tether pulled her in the flier's wake.

When she had envisioned herself doing this, she had imagined climbing back up the tether to the seat again as easily as a monkey, but between the wind and the speed and the force from the flier's turns, it was all she could do not to let go of Kasandral. She feared she was going to be stuck back there until Zirkander landed—or this ended some other way. Could she even survive a landing?

"Worry about that later," she muttered, the wind stealing her words from her lips. They had a dragon to defeat before she could think about her own safety.

Gunshots rang out, both from ahead of her and from behind. Confused, she twisted her neck in time to see a second flier streaking toward the dragon. Pimples, of course. He gaped at her as his machine guns cracked. She had a ludicrous thought that he might be gaping at her exposed torso and laughed. Was this what going mad felt like?

A roar came from the dragon. It was almost a scream. Part rage and part agony?

"Did we hit it?" she yelled, as if anyone could hear her or she could have heard Zirkander if he replied.

The guns halted. She twisted, trying to spot the dragon, but she couldn't even see Pimples anymore. Her shirt whipped at her face, and though she struggled one-handed to push it down, it was in vain. She flapped about at the end of her tether, as helpless as a flag to do anything.

A tug at her ankle surprised her. Something had snapped in her knee earlier, and a fresh jolt of fiery agony raced up her leg. She gasped, blackness encroaching on her vision. She blinked rapidly as if she could drive the darkness away.

It took her a moment to realize she was being pulled in. By Zirkander? It couldn't be anyone else, but how was he managing that while flying? Her rope was secured to the frame of the back seat.

"Ahn!" came his cry, sounding a mile away instead of twenty feet. "If you're conscious, I need your help. The dragon is after Pimples at this second, but we haven't got much time."

They were still flying at full speed. What help could she give? She waved her sword, if only to let him know she was, indeed, conscious. She tried to twist and grab the tether with her free hand, but she wasn't strong enough to best the force generated by their speed. With another slightly insane laugh, she decided she should have run this idea past Pimples and had him calculate just how impossible climbing back into the flier would be.

Despite her uselessness, she was pulled inexorably closer until her foot bumped something hard. Zirkander, twisted halfway out of his seat and flying with his *boot*, hauled her into the flier. The expression contorting his face was impossible to read. Maybe that was for the best.

As she clawed her way into her seat, he yelled, "You're crazier than I am, Ahn."

"That's why we tied me to the tether, wasn't it?" she yelled back, halfway between elation and disbelief that she was still alive. Kasandral kept smacking the rim of her seat well, and she realized it was because her hands were shaking so much. "Did we get him?"

"We hurt him before he got his defenses back up, but he's still flying." Zirkander lowered himself into his seat, taking the stick in hand again.

"Little help, sir?" Pimples asked over the crystal. "He's—"

A crack like a rifle firing sounded from Pimples' cockpit. Cas's stomach sank. She was certain he didn't *have* a rifle with him.

Zirkander turned their flier around, and Cas caught sight of Pimples' craft as it sailed downward, streaming smoke, the tail on fire. Distress and fear brought tears to her eyes. Pimples might or might not survive his landing. Either way, she and the general were all alone now.

Chapter 20

I HATE TO INTERRUPT YOU, BUT I'm sensing more trouble on the horizon.

Sardelle was using her mental powers to rebuild Therrik's collapsed right lung, and the concentration required was intense enough that she had lost all track of the outpost. She had already knitted the gash in his left lung, as well as the broken rib that had been responsible for it. He had other wounds, but those could wait until they weren't in the middle of the courtyard with a battle raging overhead.

That battle is over the back side of Goat Mountain right now, but that's not the trouble on the horizon. Also, there's so much sleet and snow falling that I'm only guessing there's a horizon out there somewhere.

When Sardelle reached a point where she could stop working on Therrik and he wouldn't die, she knelt back, opening her eyes and blinking around her. As Jaxi had promised, Ridge and the others weren't in sight. That didn't mean much since clouds hung thick around the mountains and sleet continued to slash from the sky, reducing the visibility. Jaxi was still protecting Sardelle and her patient from the elements, but she could hear the wind roaring through the valley. She also heard General Ort issuing orders from one of the towers, but she could only make out the outpost wall closest to them. She tried to sense Ridge, to check on the battle, but he was out of her range.

He's alive, Jaxi said, *probably just beyond the edge of your senses. The wind has driven them away from the valley. The airship was attacked—mutilated—and went down. Duck and Kaika's flier was hit by lightning, and they were forced to land in the valley. Ridge and Cas are still out there. Pimples' craft was damaged, and he's trying to find a spot to land.*

Is the dragon wounded at all? Sardelle couldn't keep the frustration and despair from her words at this devastating report.

Yes, they've hurt him, but all that has done is enrage him. He's either forgotten about the pretty crystal, or he's decided to annihilate everyone before coming back for it.

The artifact lay on its side in the mud where Sardelle had left it. She and Therrik were alone in the courtyard, aside from Phelistoth and Tylie. When last Sardelle had looked, Tylie had been leaning against her wounded dragon and crying on him. Now she lay atop his back, arms wrapped around his neck. It was the position she rode him in. After a long look to the south, Phelistoth rose slowly to his feet. Blood stained the frosty earth under him, and weariness and pain made his movements slow and stiff. Despite his injuries, he crouched and sprang skyward. His wings beat with enough power to take them into the air. Tylie's tear-streaked faced turned toward Sardelle.

He's too hurt to fight more, Tylie whispered into her mind. *He says to leave the crystal, that it's not worth dying for.*

Is he taking you somewhere safe?

Yes. Do you want me to ask him if he'll come get you too?

Phelistoth had already disappeared from Sardelle's view, flying into the clouds hanging low in the valley.

I can't leave while Ridge and everyone else is still in danger, Sardelle said, *but I agree with his thought to take you somewhere safe.*

I don't. But I'm too puny to be any help. Tylie's sad sigh came through the mental link.

Someday, you won't be.

If we live that long, Jaxi interrupted. *Phelistoth's tragic departure isn't what I was warning you about.*

I was afraid of that.

At first, I thought I sensed the sorceress.

Here in the outpost? Sardelle dropped a hand to Jaxi's pommel. She was still on her knees beside Therrik, but she would get up to fight if she had to.

No, at a lower elevation. On foot or maybe on horseback and heading this way, but another problem showed up, and now I can't sense her. I'm not even positive it was her that I felt.

What problem? Sardelle could only think of one thing that would overwhelm Jaxi's senses.

More dragons.

Dragons? Plural?

Yes, and they're flying this way.

From where? The cavern?

Unless you know of a place where more dragons have been hiding, that would be my guess.

Sardelle stared down at the purple crystal. Who had released them? And was the crystal what they were coming for? She could feel its power, but she couldn't imagine that power acting as a beacon across hundreds of miles. Phelistoth hadn't sensed it, as far as she knew, until they had been down in the mountain and close to it.

First off, I'm not positive that's true. Second, it was in a vault before, and I think that vault insulated the artifacts inside. I certainly was never aware of the existence of the fancy paperweight or anything else dragon-kissed, and I came in and out of the mountain thousands of times over the years with my handlers. What you need to decide now is whether we're going to try to hide it from the new dragons or stand back and let them have it. Judging by how much trouble we're having with one *dragon, I suggest the latter.*

While Sardelle was staring bleakly at the crystal, which glowed softly but otherwise offered no advice, Therrik opened his eyes.

He still lay flat on his back in the ice and mud, and she felt guilty that she hadn't taken him into the machine shop where there were blankets and cots for the injured.

He should be tickled that you didn't throttle him while he was unconscious. I might have.

"What's... status?" Therrik rasped, a hand going to his abdomen. He should be able to breathe normally now, but he still had damage that would hurt.

"The airship is down, General Ort is on the wall, and Ridge and Cas are fighting the dragon." Oh, how Sardelle wished she could monitor that fight. When she had decided to stay behind, she'd assumed the air battle would be nearby and that she could help Ridge if necessary. She hadn't factored in the wind. Now she wished she was up there. Even if Cas had to fly with Ridge, she could have ridden behind Pimples. Maybe she could have kept him in the air. And Duck and Kaika too.

If you'd left, your biggest fan would be dead. Stop berating yourself, and then decide what we're going to do. I can shield you from hail all day, but not from a pack of dragons.

A pack? Did they all get released from that cavern? And if so, how? According to General Ort's report, the Cofah had been *bombing* the cavern, not rescuing dragons from it.

There are three coming, and I didn't ask them. Maybe the bombing is what broke their magical prisons and freed them.

"Dragon?" Therrik asked. "Are they hurting it?" He had been craning his neck, probably wondering if there was anyone else besides Sardelle that he could appeal to for information.

Maybe he's afraid he'll have to be civil to you now that you've saved his life.

Ignoring Jaxi, Sardelle offered Therrik an arm. "My understanding is that they've hurt him, yes, but that they're having trouble getting their bullets through his shield to finish him off, and Cas isn't able to get close enough to hit him with the sword. Do you want to stand? If you're careful, you should be able to." Sardelle looked toward the southern sky, as if she could see the threat coming through the snow. "I'll need to see you again later, but your lungs are in working order. They'll be tender. Don't overdo anything."

Instead of accepting her offer of a hand up, Therrik touched his chest, staring down at his blood-spattered jacket. He touched his mouth. The blood he had been spitting up earlier had dried, but she didn't know if he could feel it or even if that was what he was trying to feel. He seemed dazed.

I'm sure he's never been healed before. Sardelle? Jaxi rarely showed signs of anxiousness, but her agitation came through now, along with her insistence that they do something.

I know. I just don't know what we can do. Would it be possible to get back down into the mountain and hide the crystal in the vault again? So they can't sense it?

You mean the vault that Morishtomaric melted with his mind?

Ah, possibly.

Therrik pushed himself slowly to his feet. Sardelle's knees were cold from kneeling in the mud, and she stood too. She picked up the crystal, more because she felt she had been anointed its keeper rather than out of a desire to hold it. She worried that Phelistoth hadn't told them enough and that giving it to the dragons could be a bad thing, especially if these dragons were coming from that cavern. The plaque on the wall there had promised they were imprisoned because they were criminals.

I'm asking Phelistoth—he hasn't quite flown out of my range yet. He says it's only a repository of knowledge, nothing more. Definitely not a weapon.

Knowledge can be a weapon, Jaxi.

He thinks they want to know what he wants to know—what happened to their kind. Maybe they'll find out and then leave this world to join them.

What if the dragons all died? I doubt these ones will make a suicide pact to join them. If the others went somewhere else, what if... what if there's a way for them to come back? What if they're able to communicate with other dragons and invite them to return to our world?

You're speculating wildly. Whatever's in that rock, it's not worth dying for, not when nothing could be gained from your death. Just leave it in the mud and let them fight among themselves for it.

Is that what they would do? Can you get a sense of them? Sardelle doubted Jaxi could read any of the dragons' thoughts, since neither of them had gotten the gist of Phelistoth's or Morishtomaric's minds.

I can see that they're not flying in a happy V like ducks. They seem to be racing each other.

"I'm going to report to General Ort," Therrik said.

Sardelle almost waved goodbye to him, with the notion that clearing the courtyard would be a good idea, but she had to warn the soldiers that more company was coming, even if their artillery weapons could do nothing to stop them.

"Therrik?" Sardelle asked.

He had taken a few steps, but he paused, a wary expression on his face.

"Please tell General Ort that there are three more dragons

coming. Jaxi—" She paused, debating if he already knew about Jaxi or if she would have to explain the sentient soulblade to him. In that moment, the first dragon came close enough for her to sense it. *Her.* A female.

Two are male and one is female, the one in the lead, Jaxi informed her.

"If you're trying to make me piss myself in fear," Therrik said, "that's not going to happen. Your cloud-humping boyfriend is the only one who's ever managed to get me to lose control of bodily functions."

A second dragon came within her range, and she barely heard his comment. The pressure that came with a dragon's presence started to build in Sardelle's head again.

"I'm not," she said, realizing Therrik was staring at her. Waiting to see if she was joking? As if she would joke about such a thing. "I'm the one who got stuck cleaning your lost control up the first time."

Therrik grunted, then waved to her. Whether it was in acknowledgment or dismissal, she did not know. He turned his back and strode toward the nearest set of stairs leading up to the wall. At the moment, the guns weren't firing, not with Morishtomaric behind the mountain and out of the soldiers' sight, but she could hear the men's voices as they wondered what was going on. More than a few of them were gazing down at her and Therrik, and the miners were still watching the courtyard and the skies from the doors and windows of their barracks. She reminded herself that she had stayed behind to help those people.

Sardelle hefted the crystal.

Jaxi's pommel flashed red in irritation.

Don't be crabby. I'm just going to try something. Sardelle peered in the direction that the dragons were coming from. She couldn't see anything, but they were flying faster than Ridge's best flier, so it wouldn't be long before they descended upon the outpost. *Any idea as to which one seems the most likely to make a deal with a human?*

They haven't introduced themselves to me.

The third dragon came within Sardelle's range. *Perhaps the one losing the race?*

Whatever you're planning to do, try it soon. Ridge and Cas are having trouble. The dragon has stopped trying to catch them with fire and is hurling his magic around.

Sardelle closed her eyes, fresh worry eating at her. Fresh guilt too. There was one more flier in the fort, wasn't there? The one Cas had piloted from the airship the day before. Yes, it was in the corner behind the headquarters building. Now that Therrik was on his feet, could General Ort take the flier up to join the others? She didn't know what he could do, but maybe being up there and harrying the dragon would help Ridge and Cas stay alive.

I'll ask him while you toss the crystal on the ground and forget any plans you have involving dragons.

Jaxi... Sardelle didn't think Jaxi had communicated with Ort before, and this wasn't the time to alarm him with her existence. *I'll go up there myself. In a minute.* She prayed that Ridge *had* a minute, and tears sprang to her eyes at the thought of losing him because of a foolish decision. But he wouldn't want her to abandon the fort and all of these people to help him.

It doesn't matter *what he would want. He's more worth keeping alive than these clods.*

Jaxi sounded more emotional than rational, something Sardelle had no problem understanding. *I didn't realize you were so attached*, she thought sadly, little humor in the comment. *I'm going to—* She halted, an idea popping into her head. *Wait, Jaxi. I take it back. Talk to Ort. Tell him to get his flier ready. We need to get into the sky right away.*

Understood. Jaxi must have seen Sardelle's intentions in her mind, because she didn't argue.

That might or might not mean approval, but there was no time to ask. Sardelle closed her eyes and envisioned the dragons—three golds—fighting the wind as they approached the front of Galmok Mountain. They were angling to fly around it, in the direction of the outpost rather than toward Goat Mountain and the battle. Alarming, but a relief all the same. If they had been going to join Morishtomaric, there would not have been any way she could join Ridge before it was too late. As it was, Morishtomaric might have started flinging magic about instead of fire because he sensed them coming and knew he was out of time.

Dragon, Sardelle called out to the gold losing the race, falling farther behind the two leaders. She wished she knew the creature's name. She would recognize it if he introduced himself, since she had studied all of the names on that plaque, but she had no way to know which three dragons were coming.

Rude of them not to wear nametags.

Ha ha. Did you talk to Ort?

Yes. He's worried about the others too. He's willing to go up if you can keep the flier aloft in the weather.

I can promise to help with the weather, yes. Keeping it aloft against everything else... that was tougher to promise.

He's on his way down.

Dragon? Sardelle called again, wondering if he hadn't heard her or if he was simply ignoring her. She jogged toward the flier in the corner of the courtyard while hoping she wasn't wasting her time. If this one was too self-important to talk to her, she would try the second-place dragon.

Dragon? came a response that made her stumble with its power. *I am the god! Bhrava Saruth! You may worship me when I arrive.*

Oh, no. He's not self-important at all, Jaxi said.

I am looking forward to doing so, Sardelle responded, ignoring the incredulous noise Jaxi made in her mind. *I have something for you.* She sent an image of the crystal in her arms as she rounded the headquarters building and the flier came into sight.

"Sardelle?" General Ort was in the cockpit and had already started the flier. Good man.

"Coming." She tossed the crystal into the seat behind him, assuming a thousand-year-old dragon artifact wouldn't break easily.

Maybe if you crack it, they'll all lose interest in it.

Yes, Bhrava Saruth said, almost purring into Sardelle's mind. *You must keep it for me. Do not let those lesser dragons have it. They are not gods.*

Even though they can fly faster than he can? Jaxi asked.

Ssh.

I will make you my first high priestess in this era if you bring it to me, Bhrava Saruth added.

An appealing offer, Sardelle responded, once again ignoring noises Jaxi shouldn't have been able to make since she didn't have lips.

We've discussed my talents before, Jaxi said.

If I bring the crystal to you, Bhrava Saruth, will you take it and leave this continent?

You wish me to leave?

Was that genuine distress in the dragon's tone? She hoped she wasn't starting something that would have unforeseen consequences.

Oh, I think that's a given, Jaxi said.

Well, you would be welcome to stay, Sardelle amended. *But these other dragons are troublesome. Especially that Morishtomaric.*

Morishtomaric, the dragon replied with a derisive snort. *He has always been trouble. And ill-tempered. Nobody would listen to him if he weren't so strong.*

Yes.

Sardelle wondered if she should find it encouraging that another gold dragon thought Morishtomaric powerful. Maybe that meant that other encounters with dragons would not be quite so impossible, if they had to deal with more in the future. Still, three medium-powered gold dragons didn't sound much better than one extra-powered one.

He ruts with horses, you know, Bhrava Saruth added.

I—uh. What did one say to that? Sardelle decided to ignore it. *Is there any chance you can convince him and these other two to leave? Then you can claim this territory for yourself.* Sardelle grimaced, not sure how one dragon would manage what she was asking or why he would. Also, what would King Angulus say about her granting part of his nation to a strange dragon? As Ort fiddled with the controls in the cockpit and the flier lifted into the air, inspiration struck. *I seek to protect the humans who live here because they are your future worshippers. Morishtomaric has been killing your worshippers.* She sent an image of Ridge rubbing his lucky dragon figurine before lifting off into the air, then showed him in the air shooting at Morishtomaric.

That figurine—is that me? Bhrava Saruth asked, his tone impressively full of glee considering he was sprinting around the mountain after the other two dragons and had to be doing the dragon equivalent of panting, sweating, and cramping.

Ridge is a devoted dragon worshipper, Sardelle said, hoping he would forgive her later. He would probably be amused. So long as they didn't have to build a temple devoted to Bhrava Saruth together. Generals definitely did not have time for that.

I will protect him! Bhrava Saruth promised. *Just bring me the repository.*

We're on our way in the mechanical aircraft. She hoped Bhrava Saruth wasn't tricking her even more than she was trying to trick him. She was well aware that Morishtomaric had originally been released from the cavern because he had deceived King Angulus.

"Which way, Sardelle?" Ort called back over the wind as they gained altitude. Jaxi had extended her shield to protect the flier from the elements as much as possible without interfering with the propeller's draw, but that mostly meant covering them from above and not from the sides.

"Southwest," she called back. "Around Galmok."

You know he thinks we're going to help Ridge, right? Jaxi asked. *I didn't mention the dragons.*

Didn't Therrik tell him?

That they're there, yes. That we're going to visit them, no.

As they finished their conversation, the lead dragon came into view. Ort stiffened and glanced back at her, his eyes wide behind his water-spattered goggles.

The second dragon came into view right after the first, flying just behind the female. Even as they watched, he caught up with the leader enough to lash out with a claw, slipping through whatever defenses she had around her and raking the back of her thigh. The lead dragon hurled wind or some mental energy at the offender, flinging him through the air like a salt shaker knocked off a table.

Sardelle thought of Jaxi's suggestion to leave the crystal in the mud and let the dragons fight over it. Maybe that hadn't been a bad idea. But as large and powerful as they were, the dragons could flatten the outpost and everyone in it with their battle.

Now you know why I let them lead, Bhrava Saruth said smugly into her mind.

Sardelle had no idea if he truly was letting the others lead and fight to his advantage, or if he was trying to save face in the eyes of his new "high priestess." Either way, he had come into view, too, a distant golden blob against the dark clouds hugging the mountain.

"Sardelle, what do we do?" Ort called. "Can we avoid them?"

"We have to. Avoid the first two and take us close to the third one so I can deliver this to him." She held up the crystal.

General Ort gave her such a long, hard, incredulous look that she was certain his next words would be an order for her to get out of his flier.

"Care to explain why?" he asked, his tone calmer than the expression on his face implied it should have been. Maybe he was used to keeping his calm—at least outwardly—when confronted with crazy plans from subordinates.

He's Ridge's boss. Isn't that a given?

Sardelle had no idea how to "explain" in such a short time. The lead dragons had stopped squabbling and were racing straight toward their flier. Ort was going to have to do some fancy flying to avoid them.

"He's willing to help us if we do," Sardelle said. "The other ones aren't."

Ort's lips thinned. He faced forward again, banking hard to take them out of the dragons' path, but nothing in the tense set of his shoulders implied he would follow her directions and head for the third gold. He probably meant to take them back to the fort—or to find Ridge.

"He's willing to help Ridge and the others too," Sardelle added. "And they're desperately in need of that help." She hoped Jaxi would update her and tell her she was exaggerating, that the others were doing well.

She didn't.

Ort's shoulders lowered. In defeat? Acceptance?

He's positive you're going to get him killed.

"I'll keep you alive." Sardelle gripped his shoulder, hoping she wasn't being too familiar and also hoping she wasn't making far too many promises, promises that she wouldn't be able to keep.

Whether he believed her or not, Ort nodded once and took them down toward the mountainside, looking for a route that would let them bypass those dragons. Sardelle put all of her strength into shielding them, remembering the powerful blow the lead dragon had inflicted upon her nearest competitor. That could easily wreck them.

As they flew, Sardelle couldn't help but look toward Goat Mountain. Not only did she hope they could reach their chosen dragon savior, but she hoped that it wouldn't cause them to be too late to help Ridge.

Chapter 21

"Are you sure you're ready?" Zirkander asked.

Cas sat on the edge of her seat, Kasandral in one hand and the tether in the other. She was staring down at the latter, her stomach churning as she considered what she planned to do—what she *had* to do. Zirkander didn't know. If she told him, he would try to stop her. He would call her suicidal. She wasn't, not anymore. This was just the only thing she could do, the only thing that might rid them of the dragon and ensure that at least *somebody* survived this fight. She blinked away tears that were trying to form again, tears at the acceptance that the "somebody" could not be her.

"Ready, sir." As if they had a choice. With Pimples gone, Morishtomaric was bearing down upon them, the last obstacle in the sky. "Sir, promise me you'll tell Tolemek I love him? Please?" Her voice cracked, and she hissed at herself. She wasn't going to cry. She was going to do her cursed duty. That was it.

Zirkander looked back, frowning. She lowered the tether so he wouldn't see it, wouldn't see that she meant to cut it. Had he already guessed?

"That'll sound a lot better coming from you," he said.

"If I don't make it," she said. "Promise." It came out sounding more like an order than a request, but there wasn't time to phrase it more respectfully. The dragon was only ten seconds away, and she needed Tolemek to know she had been thinking of him, in case this was the end.

"I promise," Zirkander said, holding her gaze for a long second, then thrusting his arm back toward her. For a startled instant, she thought he meant to grab her or to make sure her tether was tied, but he was holding something out. His wooden dragon figurine. "Better rub it for luck."

Cas felt ludicrous rubbing a little fake dragon with a *real* dragon trying to kill them, but it was easier to obey than to argue. She patted it awkwardly with her gloved hand.

Zirkander withdrew his arm and turned back toward the oncoming dragon.

Cas took a deep breath and sliced through the tether. She wasn't harnessed, so she braced her legs and gripped the edge of the seat well hard. If she didn't hang on, she would fall out prematurely. Zirkander was going to have to do some creative flying to get her into a position where she could leap out again and cut through the dragon's shield. Only, she intended to do more than poke his shield this time. She would do more... or die trying.

"Try to come at him from above," Cas ordered, hoping he would do it without questioning her. She wouldn't have a chance of landing on the dragon if they crossed paths vertically, as they had last time.

Zirkander didn't look back or acknowledge the order. Morishtomaric opened his maw, and fire streamed out. Fire and *power*. Zirkander had already been dodging, cutting to the side as those teeth flashed and smoke thickened in the back of the dragon's throat, but even as they evaded the flames, a blast of air struck them.

It should have hurled them wingtip over wingtip—and it might have hurled Cas from her seat—but somehow, Zirkander rode the power, like a surfer on a wave. The flier bucked and shuddered, but he guided it around, curving back toward the dragon and increasing their altitude as he did so.

Her moment was coming. As their craft cut to the side so that they could fly over the dragon, Cas squeezed the sword so hard, it hurt. She realized she wasn't breathing and forced herself to inhale and exhale deeply. Then there wasn't time for anything else. She stood, one foot on the body of the flier, one hand gripping the craft. The wind railed at her, threatening to hurl her over the side too early. Using all of her strength, she maintained her position, and she counted down. Three. Two.

One. As Zirkander took them over the dragon's back, Cas dropped over the edge, utter terror almost choking her as she imagined what would happen if she miscalculated. What a waste her death would be.

She tucked her legs and led with the sword pointing below her. If it didn't break his shield quickly enough, she might bounce off and miss getting her chance to truly hurt him.

Kasandral flashed green as it cut through the invisible barrier. As before, an electrifying jolt seared her nerves. Then Cas landed square on the dragon's back, the sword point leading. It dove in, sinking more than two feet, as if cutting through butter instead of muscle and scales.

Morishtomaric screeched, not only out loud but into Cas's mind. His pain crashed into her like a battering ram. It made her forget the pain in her knee and her plan to take him down, everything but holding onto Kasandral, lest she be thrown from the dragon's back. He bucked like a horse, and her feet slipped off the sleek scales. She found herself dangling from nothing but the sword's hilt. With her weight hanging from it, or perhaps only because of Kasandral's sheer hunger, the blade sank lower.

As she scrambled to get her feet back under her, to throw a leg over the ridge of Morishtomaric's spine, Cas watched the back of the dragon's head, hoping to see it dip in defeat, hoping that this blow would be enough to kill him.

But Morishtomaric was still flapping his wings. They were furious, erratic flaps, and his head and neck thrashed about, but he wasn't in danger of falling out of the sky, not yet. A wall of air, something roiling, dark and ominous like the storm clouds, rushed over her. She could feel it brush against her cheeks, but it did not budge her. Kasandral was flaring more brightly than ever, the green glow washing over the golden scales below her. Golden scales and blood. If she could reach a more vital target, maybe she could stop those wings from beating permanently. But dare she pull out the sword to move to another spot? It was her only anchor, her only handhold. With the dragon bucking and twisting and doing his best to knock her from his back, how could she possibly stay on?

Morishtomaric's head whipped around on his long neck. They started to lose altitude, but he didn't look like he cared as his fierce, furious eyes and giant fangs came into view. He snapped at her, and Cas fell to the side of his spine, using the dragon's body for protection as she hung onto the sword's hilt. He tried to bite the blade free, but Kasandral flared green and somehow deterred him. Morishtomaric flung some new magical attack at her, something that battered at the edges of her mind. Once again, she felt the sword protect her, power that should have destroyed her failing to harm her.

Morishtomaric must have realized he was falling, because his head turned forward again, and his wings flapped hard, regaining altitude. Cas struggled to get back astride him, trusting he would try to unseat her again.

The buzz of Zirkander's propeller reached her ears. She dared not take her eyes from the dragon to look toward him, but she didn't have to. She knew he would have realized what had happened by now. Whether he would forgive her or not, he was too practical not to take advantage. She had to put herself into a position that he could do so. Right now, she was in the middle of the dragon's back. He might be able to shoot if she got to one end or the other. Perhaps Tolemek's bullets could do what she hadn't yet managed.

With that thought in mind, Cas found the best grip she could, her knees digging in as if she rode a horse bareback, and she pulled Kasandral free. The dragon immediately threw another wall of air at her. Once again, Kasandral protected her through a power she did not understand. She simply accepted it and inched her way up the dragon's spine, staying low so the natural wind wouldn't tear her free. Sleet beat at her, and lightning flashed, but she pressed on, squinting her eyes and never taking her focus from her target. The dragon's neck.

If she could reach it and land a killing blow, Morishtomaric would finally go down. Inevitably, she would go down with him, but it would be worth it to get rid of him. A fitting fate for the person and the sword who had killed Apex. And to save Zirkander and perhaps other lives... it was a fair trade.

With that thought in mind, she crawled closer to the dragon's neck. The wind had knocked the blood off Kasandral's gleaming blade, but the sword called out to her, urging her to give it more. One way or another, she would obey.

* * *

Ridge swooped back and forth, shooting at the dragon's tail and backside with careful, precise shots. As precise as he could make them with his target bucking and writhing in the air like a fish fighting the hook reeling it in. How the creature remained airborne while he was doing all that, Ridge couldn't guess. He could only shoot. He dared not unleash the machine guns fully with Ahn crawling along Morishtomaric's back. He shook his head with horror every time he glimpsed her, but he understood why she'd made the choice she had. He just hoped they could shoot down the dragon—or she could cut the bastard's head off—and he could somehow get her off before she crashed right along with their downed foe.

Since she had dropped, the dragon's protective barrier had been down, and Ridge riddled Morishtomaric's backside with bullets. As he sailed close, he saw that some of them had burrowed through the scales, smoking as they ate into dragon flesh. He did not know if they would be enough, but if Ahn could stay on and land the killing blow that she clearly intended to make, the ancient sword might do what the army's technology and Tolemek's science could not.

As Ridge came in for another pass, barely missing the thrashing tail, Morishtomaric opened his fang-filled mouth and breathed fire once more. Instead of streaming out of his maw in a straight line as it usually did, it curled around his head, the flames stretching toward Ahn.

Her eyes bulged, and she buried Kasandral in the dragon's back, hanging onto it and hiding behind the sword. She must have been too far up his spine for Morishtomaric to snap at her again, but this was just as bad. Ridge's stomach dropped when the flames wrapped around her. They didn't burn her to a crisp instantly—Kasandral must be offering some protection—but from the way she bared her clenched teeth, she wasn't entirely immune.

Ridge diverted his path. Instead of heading for the back of the dragon again, he wheeled around so he could angle his guns toward Morishtomaric's face. Not certain he could get into position quickly enough, he formed words of desperation in his mind.

Sardelle or Jaxi, if you're able to help, now would be a very good time.

He didn't expect an answer and kept on his path, as the dragon's smoking snout came into his gun sights, the flames still streaming from the open jaw.

We're doing our best to get to you, Jaxi said, the words coming quickly, as if she was in the middle of a battle too. *We're on the other side of Galmok—too far to reach you and help. Once we get past these other dragons, we'll try to get there. Stay alive!*

Other dragons? What in all the hells?

Jaxi did not respond.

Ridge was close enough now. Being careful with his shots, he fired in short bursts. The bullets smacked into the snout, and he imagined he could hear the satisfying thuds over the wind. Morishtomaric's head jerked up, and the fire ceased. As soon as it did, Ahn lifted her head. She pulled Kasandral free and crawled closer to his neck.

Ridge allowed himself a tight smile, feeling the first sense that they could do this, that the dragon would finally die. Smoke wafted from the bullet holes in his snout, a fitting punishment for one who lit human beings on fire.

As he flew past, Morishtomaric's eyes locked onto Ridge, hatred scorching him as sure as fire. *You have no sword to protect you, mosquito*, the dragon snarled into his mind.

"You weren't supposed to notice," Ridge muttered, gripping the flight stick tightly and bracing himself for another wind attack. He couldn't let his craft be damaged; he couldn't leave Ahn up here alone.

A boom and a flash came from the engine compartment,

blinding him momentarily. Smoke assailed his nostrils, and he batted at the air with one hand. For a moment, the flier continued running smoothly, and he couldn't guess what had happened—had lightning struck his control panel? But as his eyes cleared, sight returning, he found himself focusing on the white energy crystal that powered his craft. It lay dark, lifeless.

With growing horror, he looked at the dashboard, saw the speedometer, and confirmed what he already knew by instinct. He was slowing down, the power to the propeller dead. And there was nothing he could do about it. It hadn't blown up—that would have killed him instantly—but the end result would be the same.

Ridge banked back toward the dragon, hoping he might get a few more shots in before he dropped out of the sky. He ought to land as soon as he could, in the hopes that he could glide down in a semblance of a controlled landing. But he couldn't leave Ahn, not if there was any chance of helping her.

He steered toward the dragon, knowing it would be for the last time. As he fired a few final shots, grazing the belly of the beast since he was already losing altitude, he experienced some satisfaction in seeing that Ahn had reached the base of the dragon's neck. He prayed that she would be able to land the killing blow, though he lamented that there was now no way that he could rescue her once she did.

His flier dropped, falling faster now. He couldn't see through the snow and sleet to gauge the terrain below. All he could do was try to keep the nose level, to hope he had some momentum to carry him forward as well as down, and to further hope for a flat stretch of land to welcome him, since the thrusters would also be inoperable without the power crystal. He doubted he would find any of what he needed.

As he fell faster, his stomach dropping along with the flier, he thought of Sardelle, wishing he'd had a chance to say goodbye. He also wished he had been more enthusiastic when she had brought up children, because now he felt a deep sadness that he would leave her with nothing of himself, nothing to remember him by.

The clouds parted, revealing rocks and a steep slope below, nowhere fit for a landing even if he'd had power.

I love you, Sardelle, he thought, hoping that she would hear him, or at least that Jaxi would, and that she would know his last thoughts had been of her.

* * *

Sardelle never thought she would be urging her pilot to twist, turn, and flip upside down, not after the terror of flying with Ridge, but as the two gold dragons swooped down to follow their craft, she was tempted to throttle General Ort and make him go faster. To zigzag more. Perhaps fly upside down. Whatever it took to shake the dragons as their craft streaked through the sleet, following the terrain of the back of Galmok Mountain, but not following it as closely as Ridge would have. He would have flown scant inches from the craggy ground, hugging the bumps and rises like a lover in an attempt to lure his pursuers into tracking too close and losing control, or losing him in a maze somewhere. Ort kept things safe.

For her part, Sardelle tried to distract the dragons, asking them what one would do if the other grabbed the crystal first. Unlike her delusional dragon, Bhrava Saruth, the other two golds would not deign to talk to her. They were probably too busy racing each other, seeing which one could bring Ort's flier down first.

Fire coming, Jaxi warned.

"Dodge," Sardelle yelled to Ort, not certain if Jaxi had shared the warning with him.

Oh, I did, Jaxi said as the flier turned and dipped into a valley that a glacier had long ago scraped into the mountainside. *He's getting to know me right now, whether he wants to or not.*

Ort's turn wasn't sharp enough or unpredictable enough to fool the dragon taking a bead on them. Or maybe it was that *both* dragons had opened their mouths and exhaled flames. Even Ridge couldn't have dodged all of that.

Sardelle shielded them, aware of Jaxi throwing her power in

with hers, adding to the barrier's strength. Ort cursed as flames danced in the air around them, and he zigzagged, trying to escape them. Sardelle was thankful he didn't have to be told. Defending against a dragon's power drained her strength rapidly, but he might not know that.

"How do we escape them?" he yelled. "They're faster than we are."

They're not even going full speed yet, Jaxi informed them. *I think they were curious as to what this contraption is.*

"So curious they're trying to burn it to ashes?" Ort asked.

I believe they got over their curiosity.

The dragons followed them through the glacial valley, spreading apart to flank the flier. Teaming up to hunt. So much for them being competitors for the crystal. They seemed willing to work together now.

"Fly up," Sardelle yelled and pointed. "There's our third dragon up there."

"He's against the wind," Ort yelled back. "The others will catch us easily if I try to take us over there."

"Try now."

As she had done before with Ridge, Sardelle channeled some of the air blowing around the mountain. She pushed them from behind, creating a draft for them to glide through. The flier surged forward as another burst of dragon fire seared the air behind them. They picked up speed, angling upward, toward where Bhrava Saruth circled like a vulture waiting for the wolves to finish bringing down their prey so it might slip in for a bite.

A vulture? That is an unappealing comparison, especially for a god. I should think I'm at least as noble as an eagle. Or an osprey. I do so love seabirds. I grew up on an island, you know.

I'll think of you however you like if you do something to help us, Bhrava Saruth.

Hm, yes, I am considering my options. Why don't you fly into that canyon down there? Stay low and see if you can lure them in behind you. I shall attempt to do something with my cunningness.

"Ort, fly into that canyon, please," Sardelle yelled. "Our ally promises to be cunning."

This should prove interesting, Jaxi thought.

The two dragons had caught up and were right on the flier's tail again, so Sardelle did not have a chance to reply. This time, instead of fire, a wave of power slammed into them. It knocked away the wind she had been channeling, leaving her stunned, as if she had been personally attacked. Worse, it flipped the tail of their flier over their nose, and the world spun as Ort lost all control. He kept his calm, struggling to stop their spin, but it was Jaxi who settled the craft, slowing its rotation. A snowy glacier skimmed past below them, scant meters away. Trying not to think about how close they had come to crashing into it, Sardelle struck the surface of the hardened ice and snow with her mind, flinging a cloud of white slivers into the air.

"Turn," she barked, hoping the dragons would miss seeing them cut into the canyon through the cloud she had made. She knew their magical senses were more powerful than their eyesight, but maybe they wouldn't check for a few seconds. At the least, maybe they would inhale some ice crystals and suffer a moment of discomfort.

The deadly frost nostril attack, Jaxi said.

Something inside of the flier rattled as Ort took them into the canyon, but the craft responded once again to his guidance. He hugged the bottom, the lighting dim as they flew between high walls lined with ledges of ice and snow. One side towered above the other, several meters of a glacier poised at the edge. Some of it had broken off and tumbled to the bottom, leaving a jumble of ice boulders for them to fly over and around.

"When is this cunning attack going to happen?" Ort yelled as they neared the end.

Both dragons have entered the canyon, Jaxi reported. *Their nostrils appear unharmed.*

That's disappointing.

Before answering Ort, Sardelle stretched out with her senses, hoping she would find Bhrava Saruth waiting ahead, poised to spring a trap. He hovered hundreds of feet over the canyon, as if he was a spectator at a horse race.

"Wonderful." Sardelle *did* spot something ahead. "I'm not sure about the attack, but there's a dead end coming up soon."

"I see it." Ort waited until they got close before pulling up. Maybe he hoped the dragons wouldn't see the cliff and would crash into it.

That might work against an inexperienced flier pilot, but Sardelle doubted a dragon would crash into a canyon wall any more than a bird would.

As they rose, a rumble sounded behind them, then booming cracks. Stone falling? No, she realized. It was more than that. The glacier above the canyon was *moving*. Instead of the couple of feet it might usually traverse in a day, the miles-long thick sheet of ice surged over the edge. It broke and tumbled into the canyon, pouring in as rapidly as water from one of the great northern falls. Their flier just missed being caught by the snapping and cracking ice.

Gleeful laughter sounded in Sardelle's mind as Ort took them into the air, alternating looking ahead and glancing back, his mouth gaping open.

That will hurt, Bhrava Saruth announced smugly.

Will it kill them? Sardelle doubted it, especially when Morishtomaric had survived having a mountain dropped onto his head.

No, but they will have to dig out. That will take a while since someone is melting and freezing the top of the glacier so the ice fits in the canyon like a plug in a human bathtub. After a pause, the dragon asked, *Do humans still have bathtubs? Your kind always felt great pleasure in using the tubs at the dragon rider station near the hot springs at the fjords.*

Even though Sardelle couldn't think of anything she was less interested in discussing at the moment, she latched onto his mention of what she hoped were the Taroth Fjords. Maybe that meant he had served Iskandia once, before he'd done whatever had resulted in him being imprisoned in that cavern.

"Take us to Goat Mountain to help the others," Sardelle told General Ort. "When last Jaxi checked, the battle had been blown toward the back side."

Yes, we still have bathtubs, she answered the dragon. *We need to help Ridge and Cas now. Are you coming to get your crystal?*

A part of her wanted to keep hold of the crystal until they had reached Ridge, so she might use it again as a bargaining chip to enlist Bhrava Saruth's help with Morishtomaric, but that hadn't been the deal, and he had already helped with the other dragons.

Yes, I'm right behind you, Bhrava Saruth said cheerfully.

Sardelle glanced back, and her gut lurched with instinctual fear when she saw how close he was, flapping his wings easily to keep up with the flier, his fanged snout scant feet behind their tail. She should have sensed his approach, but maybe she was too tired, or her senses were too dulled from being in proximity to so many dragons. Either way, finding him so close was alarming. Despite his light tone, his face was no less fearsome than that of the other dragons, and his massive, muscular form dwarfed their craft.

Your contraption is quite interesting, he said. *I have never known humans to fly on their own. But you still need dragons, yes? You do not worship that metal object, do you?*

Uhm, no. We don't worship the fliers. If I toss the crystal in the air, will you be able to catch it?

Of course!

Though it felt strange to carelessly relinquish the very thing she had been guarding assiduously for the last hour, Sardelle tossed it into the air. As promised, Bhrava Saruth caught it easily, then performed the dragon equivalent of a pirouette.

Sardelle expected him to leave as soon as he had it, but he continued to fly after them as Ort left the relative shelter of Galmok and took them through the windier air between the mountains. Sardelle turned her focus forward, trying to get a feel for what was happening, if the fight between Ridge and Cas and Morishtomaric still raged on, or if they were too late. Jaxi was strangely silent on the matter. Sardelle wanted to ask her for an update, but that silence worried her and made her afraid to inquire.

Ort flew low, using Goat Mountain for protection from the elements as they rounded its craggy terrain. Unexpectedly, Sardelle caught sight of the airship crashed on a hillside below, the hull caved in and most of the balloon burned away. Feeling guilty that she hadn't had many thoughts about them, she checked for survivors and was relieved to find that many people were alive, maybe all of them. There were definitely injuries, but the balloon must have held together for long enough that the landing hadn't been too fast. She picked up Tolemek's aura, shining slightly more brightly than that of those without dragon blood, and sensed his fear and worry. He had to be as concerned about Cas as she was about Ridge.

We're checking on them, she sent to him, though Ort had already flown past, and she didn't know if she had been close enough for him to hear her.

"We'll come back to help them," Ort yelled back.

Sardelle nodded. She would have strangled him if he had diverted from his route now.

They reached the back side of the mountain, and her stomach sank when she sensed Morishtomaric's presence. He was still in the air. She tried to locate Ridge, but they were at the edge of her range, and of course Morishtomaric's aura overshadowed every other living creature around him.

Sardelle...

What is it? She gripped the edge of her seat, certain from Jaxi's hesitant tone that she didn't want to know the answer.

Morishtomaric is injured, Bhrava Saruth announced, sounding pleased. *He won't be harassing the hindquarters of any more mares.*

Sardelle barely kept herself from telling him to shut up. *Jaxi?* she prompted.

Cas needs our help, Jaxi said at the same time as Ort pointed and blurted, "I see him!"

"Ridge?" Sardelle leaned forward.

No, he was pointing at a gold dragon feebly flapping his wings as he descended toward the side of Goat Mountain. Morishtomaric was, indeed, injured. Very injured.

"Where are our people?" Sardelle asked, the question as much for Jaxi as for Ort. Where was *Ridge?*

Cas saw him get hit—his power crystal was destroyed. He went down.

What do you mean down? Sardelle's mind did not want to—

could not—work through the meaning of the word.

Cas is clinging to the neck of that dragon, Jaxi said, her tone subdued. *Ask your new god to help her, please.*

Sardelle mulishly wanted to sink down in her seat and tell Jaxi to ask him herself, but she forced herself to focus on Morishtomaric and Cas. She couldn't see her yet, not with the sleet still falling, but she could sense her now, clinging to the dragon. She was injured and exhausted, only hanging on because Kasandral had been driven into the back of Morishtomaric's neck and she gripped the sword hilt. The wind battered her relentlessly, even as the dragon's uneven flight threatened to hurl her free. Morishtomaric kept snapping back at her, trying to rip her off his back.

"Going in," Ort said with determination, trying to adjust his flight and speed to intercept the dragon.

Sardelle doubted he would be able to get close enough for them to grab Cas without crashing into the dragon. She would have to levitate Cas free, if she even could with that sword in her hand. Kasandral had accepted her last attempt to use magic on him. Maybe he would do so again.

Bhrava Saruth? she asked. *Can you rescue that human? She's our friend.*

Another worshipper?

I—maybe she could become one if you saved her. Continuing the ruse made her feel sick, *sicker*. Her stomach was already queasy with worry. But she didn't want to risk angering the only dragon around who was helping them.

She has a slayer blade!

Yes, but I'll tell her not to attack you.

Hmmrph.

From that response, Sardelle couldn't tell if Bhrava Saruth was concerned or not, but she tried to communicate with Cas as the dragon passed over their flier and flew ahead of them. There wasn't much time. Ort might not be able to see it in the storm, but they were only about five hundred feet above the ground.

Cas? A new dragon is coming to help you. Don't attack him. Do you understand?

Cas did not respond. She barely seemed conscious. Had she lost blood? Or just been battered nearly senseless?

Bhrava Saruth swooped down toward Morishtomaric, whose wings had stopped flapping. He was picking up speed, heading straight for the mountain.

Cas, don't fight, Sardelle urged one more time as Bhrava Saruth, pumping his wings hard to catch up, closed in. His talons extended, but they jerked back a few feet from touching her.

The sword fights me, high priestess!

Cas, let go, Sardelle yelled, willing her to hear and understand.

"Why doesn't he grab her?" Ort demanded.

The ground was visible now, to eyes as well as senses. The rocky mountainside waited less than a hundred feet below the plummeting Morishtomaric.

"He's trying," Sardelle said, as the dragon reached in again, attempting to pluck Cas away, only to be halted before he reached her.

Jaxi, can't you do something?

Cas slumped off to the side, letting go of the sword and tumbling away from Morishtomaric's back.

Sardelle would have risen out of her seat if she hadn't been strapped down. She started to stretch out, thinking she might be close enough to use her power to levitate Cas so she didn't hit the ground. Bhrava Saruth caught her first.

He flapped away like an eagle with a fish as Morishtomaric smashed into the mountainside with a puff of snow. He did not move.

Like an osprey, Bhrava Saruth corrected.

What? Oh, yes. Sorry, I forgot. Jaxi, did she lose consciousness or did you do something?

Perhaps you should start writing down my preferences, Bhrava Saruth said, *so you will easily be able to guide my followers.*

She lost consciousness. I couldn't do anything to her with her hand wrapped around a fully unleashed Kasandral.

Sardelle sank down in her seat. She cast about with her senses again, hoping in vain to catch Ridge's aura out there somewhere.

Your god is awaiting a response, Jaxi said.

About writing things down? Sardelle grimaced. *I didn't think that required a response.*

He asked you where to put his new worshipper. A high priestess should pay more attention to her god.

Jaxi, I'm not in the mood.

I know. I'm sorry.

Bhrava Saruth? Sardelle asked. *Can you take her back to the outpost, please?*

Yes, high priestess.

Sardelle closed her eyes, not in the mood to explain that she had no interest in being a priestess, high or otherwise. *Watch out for friendly fire.*

Understood.

Ort says there's not any point in searching in this weather, and he's heading back to the airship to see if they need help, Jaxi said.

What? We can search. We aren't limited by eyesight.

We don't have a flier.

Sardelle huffed. Would Ort listen to her if she asked him to search for Ridge first? Hadn't she done enough to help the army and the outpost? Didn't she deserve a favor?

We'll come back out when the storm stops and see if we can find him, Jaxi promised. *The people in the airship will need your healing, and maybe Pimples and Duck and Kaika too.*

Sardelle could not deny the logic, but that didn't mean she wanted to accept it. She did refrain from asking Ort to stay out. She had known Jaxi for so long that she suspected there was a reason she didn't want Sardelle to stay out and look for Ridge, that she knew something Sardelle didn't.

Just that I don't sense him anywhere, and if he was alive, I would. He couldn't have been knocked so far off course as he crashed that he would be out of my range.

There have been times before when we thought he was dead because we couldn't sense him. Sardelle thought of the Cofah volcano lab, where Ridge had fallen through a trapdoor into an incinerator room with metal walls. Neither she nor Jaxi had been able to sense him through the iron.

I'm sure he didn't fall into an iron box as he crashed.

Damn it, Jaxi. Stop being so logical.
I'm sorry.
I know. Sardelle wiped at the tears trickling down her cheeks.

Epilogue

THE SKY WAS STARK AND clear, the sun gleaming off the glaciers draped across the back side of Goat Mountain. They could see for miles, but nobody had yet seen the one thing they were looking for. General Ridgewalker Zirkander. At the least, they sought his crash site. Then they would know if...

Cas closed her eyes. They would know.

"Doing all right?" Tolemek asked from the back seat of their flier.

"Fine."

He touched the back of her head, then laid his hand on her shoulder. The gentle gesture said he knew she wasn't fine, and he was right. She was glad to have him back there today to support her. If she had lost both men, it would have been intolerable. Maybe it was a good thing that she had been unconscious for most of the time the rescue team had been retrieving survivors from the downed airship. Otherwise, she would have spent hours worrying about him. Instead, she had woken with Tolemek sitting in a chair next to her cot, smiling down at her, with only scrapes and bruises to prove he had been in a crash.

Cas looked toward the other two fliers in the distance, each working with her to fly a search pattern along the mountain. Pimples' back seat was empty, in case they found Zirkander, while Duck flew with Sardelle behind him. Sardelle had said very little that morning. She leaned over the side of the craft, watching the icy terrain below, hoping against the odds. Cas knew how she felt. Sardelle and Zirkander were closer, but Cas had known him longer, and he had changed her life. He'd stood up to her father and taught her to be more than she thought she could be.

As much as Cas hoped they would find Zirkander, standing down there and waving for a pickup, she knew in her heart that he was gone. They had been too high when his crystal died, and there hadn't been anywhere he could have landed safely out here, not without any power. Once again, she couldn't help but feel guilty that she had survived when someone else who had as much right to life had not.

"Those are the two we don't need to worry about, right?" Pimples pointed ahead, where a large gold dragon soared on the air currents. Phelistoth, his form silver and noticeably smaller, maintained his distance from the gold. Tylie rode atop his back, also watching the rugged terrain below.

"Sardelle says yes," Duck said. "They're not a threat. The two who might have been a threat were talked into leaving after some politicking and clashing of antlers last night."

Cas doubted Sardelle's explanation had included moose analogies. Cas did wonder what had gone on between the dragons. She'd heard some of the story the evening before, though Sardelle had been extremely reserved and spoken little. Only General Ort's firm tone had elicited answers from her about this new dragon, one who apparently believed himself a god and was collecting worshippers. Since Cas had barely been conscious as she hung from Morishtomaric's back, certain she would die with him, she had been surprised to learn she was beholden to the new dragon. Fortunately, he hadn't asked for anything. Yet.

Tolemek leaned back and started to remove his hand, but she laid hers on his, wanting him to know she was glad he had come along.

"I know you'll miss him," he said. "It's all right. I mean, of course it's all right, but you can talk about it—about him—with me if you want."

"I know. Thank you." Cas released his hand and turned to follow the contours of the mountain. She appreciated the offer but probably wouldn't take him up on it. Tolemek had never liked Zirkander. Death had a way of resolving grudges, but she would probably go to Sardelle to talk. Later.

I may have found what you seek, human followers, a chipper voice said in her head.

"Human followers?" Tolemek asked. "That's not Phelistoth."

"The new one, I assume." Cas couldn't remember his name. She hadn't been in the mood to learn new things when she had woken up.

"What we seek?" Pimples asked. "It's not Cas's evil sword, is it?"

"Raptor's sword saved us in the end," Duck said.

"General Ort and Colonel Therrik already retrieved it this morning." Cas steered the flier toward a saddle between two ridges where the gold dragon circled. "It was still stuck in Morishtomaric's body. Therrik pulled it out."

"He has it?" Pimples asked. "It's not—he's not a danger to Sardelle again, is he?"

"I think he just cleaned the sword and put it back in its now-rather-charred box."

"Sardelle says Therrik has made his peace with her," Duck said. "Or at least isn't being as much of an ass since she saved his life."

"He's probably decided Sardelle and I are nothing to worry about," Tolemek said, "when compared to all these dragons flying around."

Cas, focused on the ground under the gold dragon, did not respond. She had glimpsed something dark halfway up a steep, rockslide-covered hill that sloped downward, then turned vertical and dropped hundreds of feet to a river.

She swooped low, though she already knew what she was looking at, the remains of Zirkander's flier. The fuselage was torn open, the thrusters smashed, and one wing mangled. The other wing had been ripped off and lay fifty feet higher up the slope. The tail of the craft had disappeared altogether. Into the river, perhaps.

"I don't see a body," Tolemek said quietly.

No, and there was no place to land and look for it. The ground was too steep. Cas flew low over the area. She hated the idea of finding his battered remains, the humor gone forever from his eyes, but if they could take his body home to his mother to bury, they owed him that.

No humans live down there, Phelistoth announced, coasting nearby, not coming as close as the gold dragon.

"Is it possible he fell into the river?" Duck asked.

"If he did, nobody would survive that fall," Pimples said sadly.

"You're not going to talk math formulas, are you?"

"No."

No. He didn't have to. They all knew. Even Sardelle must know. She had a hand over her face, her head down.

"What now, Raptor?" Duck asked.

They still treated her as if she were the highest-ranking lieutenant.

"Let's go home," Cas said, the ache in her heart almost too much to handle. She hadn't realized that she, her father's cold and detached daughter, could care so much.

She reached behind her with one hand, wanting—needing—Tolemek's touch. Maybe she would talk to him about it later, after all. He twined his fingers through hers.

"What will you do when we get there?" he asked.

"Rejoin Wolf Squadron, if they'll have me. I have… obligations."

THE END

Printed in Great Britain
by Amazon